THE LOTTERY

RICHARD L. MONTGOMERY

PublishAmerica
Baltimore

Softcover 9781630008338
PUBLISHED BY PUBLISHAMERICA, LLLP
www.publishamerica.com
Baltimore

Printed in the United States of America

For my beautiful wife
Cheryl

ACKNOWLEDGEMENTS

I want to thank my daughter, Casey Bushey, for her untiring support and ability to keep me on track with the plot, twists and complex characters portrayed in this book. She has an uncanny ability to remember what she has read and where a particular phrase is located in the book. Her talent in providing constructive criticism complemented with her adeptness in re-writing and adding in the necessary amplifying rhetoric is only surpassed by her willingness to read and re-read my manuscripts.

I also want to thank my friend, Oliver Dimalanta, for his imagination and superb artistic talent in designing the cover for *The Lottery*.

The Lottery is the latest in a series of thrillers coming from this hardcase new writer, and this guy just keeps getting better and better. Some guys are natural talents, other guys learn the rules over time. Montgomery is a born natural, with a fast-paced but laconic style, mean and lean as hickory, but darkly funny in a way that only ex-military guys or cops can pull off. I'm told Montgomery was a U.S. Navy pilot. I don't know the guy but from the way he writes he had to have been a carrier pilot. His books come off the deck like a Super Hornet riding the thunderbolt into a forty-knot headwind. If you're going to ride with him, strap yourself in and kiss your ass goodbye. First-rate work from a brand new talent. As if I needed the damned competition. I love this guy. Read him or weep.— *CARSTEN STROUD*
   New York Times Best-Selling Author

PROLOGUE

NORFOLK, VIRGINIA
OCTOBER 15, 2012
MONDAY
2030 HOURS

Lynn Morgan glanced at her watch as she exited Nordstrom's second level south entrance into the parking garage. That section of the garage was nearly empty as usual. Several of the overhead lights were out. Lynn didn't remember it being that dark when she drove in. A small car with one of those glasspack mufflers started up a couple of rows to her right. It was close enough to startle her. Her heart began to race as she hesitated momentarily, but she purposely took no notice. The sound echoed throughout the garage.

There was a slight chill in the air. A strong breeze entered carrying the unmistakable odor of dead fish, seaweed and diesel fuel. The combination was not pleasing to the senses. The Norfolk shipyard was a few blocks south of MacArthur Center. Lynn wrinkled her nose in response to the pungent odor. She glanced around and then daintily shifted her shoulders to help reposition her scarf in hopes of somehow masking the smell.

Lynn wasted no time making her way to the far end of the garage where her silver Mercedes 500SL was safely parked in an end space. She parked on the end out of habit, even in an empty garage. The two shopping bags she carried hung at her side like large trophies. It was a successful night of shopping. The only sound remaining was the hollow tapping made by her heels. Her heartbeat had returned to normal.

Lynn didn't hear the driver-side door open on the black Chevrolet SUV that was parked six rows from her car. The interior lights didn't come on, and there was no sound to alert anyone that the keys were still in the ignition. The driver slid out and gently pushed the door closed, making only a slight clicking sound. Lynn didn't hear that either. The driver was in full black, including the silk balaclava that covered his entire face exposing nothing but his eyes. He looked around and moved deftly among the shadows of the sparsely parked vehicles. He was careful not to touch any. He didn't want to inadvertently set off an alarm. The planned lack of overhead lighting helped to conceal his movement. He didn't make a sound as he wove his way toward Lynn. He was behind her within seconds.

Lynn pressed the bottom button on her key fob. The trunk of her 500SL popped open. She was about to put the bags into the trunk when the masked man grabbed her from behind. He twisted her left arm up behind her back holding her wrist firmly with his right hand. He simultaneously slapped his gloved left hand over her mouth. She could taste the worn leather as he pinched her lips together between his second and third fingers. He pulled her head back sharply. She couldn't move. Her heart was now pounding. She dropped both bags to the floor of the garage. Something broke in one of the bags. The man leaned forward, his head close to hers, and spoke very clearly into her right ear. She could smell his breath. It smelled of stale cigar smoke and garlic.

"Tell your husband to back off...*or else*! Do you understand?" he barked.

Lynn was frightened. She tried to say something, but before she could, the masked man pulled her arm higher and squeezed her face with his left hand. Her body tightened and she let out a muffled groaning sound.

"DO YOU UNDERSTAND?" he growled impatiently as he pulled up on her left arm.

She could feel a slight popping as a tendon in her shoulder tore away from the muscle. Lynn rose up on her toes in defense, trying to lessen the pain. She almost passed out but mustered enough energy to nod that she understood. The driver released her arm and moved away quickly. Lynn nearly fell to the pavement but regained the strength in her legs. She steadied herself with her right arm, leaned forward, and then threw up next to one of the Nordstrom bags. She rose up, took a couple of deep breaths and turned just in time to see the black SUV exit the garage. The windows were heavily tinted. There were no running lights visible. The SUV was out of sight within seconds.

The aroma of her Issey Miyake perfume was not strong enough to mask the smell of dead fish, seaweed, diesel oil…and Lynn's Chinese Chicken Salad.

CHAPTER ONE

Seventeen Days Prior

The rain was unrelenting. It had been raining all day, and only in the last few minutes was there a slight hint that it was beginning to let up. The rain was typical of northwest Florida in the afternoon. However, it didn't seem to matter to John Kilday. He stood on the porch leaning forward, both hands gripped the railing as he stared out at the water. The veins in his arms were pronounced from lack of movement. Raindrops magnified the numerous age spots on the back of his hands. There was no discernible expression on his face. The Old Fashioned he had mixed nearly an hour earlier was sitting on the railing. It was thoroughly diluted and running over with rainwater. The ice had long since melted.

The rain had come in waves. Sometimes it rained so hard that he shut his eyes, but he never let go of the railing. He was soaking wet and cold. His khaki pants were nearly transparent. They hugged his legs like a wet sheet. He hadn't moved for nearly twenty minutes. He just stood there staring out at the bayou wondering how he could have been so stupid, how he could have lost so much money. He was a smart man who had always been conservative. How did he fall for such an obvious scam?

A large great blue heron stood motionless two feet from shore looking down into the water. The heron took one step forward and again went motionless. It seemed to be pointing. The heron's legs probably looked liked small trees to the unsuspecting fish. Suddenly, its head lurched forward. Its beak penetrated the water, and in an instant, dinner was served. John Kilday saw nothing. He just stared at the bayou, oblivious to the rain, oblivious to the heron and oblivious to the symbolism of the heron and its prey.

It had been a little over a year since Marti Kilday had passed away. She had died so suddenly that her husband of fifty-three years didn't even get a chance to say goodbye. One minute she was there smiling, happy and talking about their recent Alaskan cruise. The next minute she was gone. It was so sudden. He had just gone into the kitchen to get her a hot tea and a couple of wafers. He remembered standing there frozen. He looked at her in disbelief. There was a slight smile on her face. John Kilday had never known another woman. Marti was his love, his best friend, and his soul mate. They had known each other since the third grade. No, life hadn't worked out the way he thought it would, the way he had planned.

He had been a very good provider. As a career naval officer, he and Marti had made seventeen moves in his twenty-six years of naval service. Although they lived from paycheck to paycheck, they kept every house they had bought except the first one. As a result, they didn't live as high on the hog as his peers, but they lived well. They lived within their means. He and Marti had always bought houses they could afford. His navy buddies kidded him and would ceremoniously refer any real estate questions to the resident expert, "John the Slumlord." It didn't bother him. He knew it would pay off someday. He wouldn't need a part time job to make ends meet when he retired, and he certainly wouldn't be standing at the entrance of Walmart greeting people and handing out grocery baskets.

No, he and Marti were frugal. His planning paid off. When he retired, "John the Slumlord" sold eleven houses. After all real estate fees, federal and state taxes and remaining mortgages were satisfied, John and Marti put one million two hundred and fifty-seven thousand dollars into thirteen different savings accounts. He had also taken the

Survivor Benefit Plan that would guarantee his wife fifty-five percent of his captain's retirement pay.

He had guaranteed a good future for Marti as well as a nice inheritance for their only grandchild, Nancy, who they had raised as their own daughter. Nancy came to live with them when she was just three years old after her parents were tragically killed in a freak car accident. Nancy's mother was John and Marti's only child. At least they were able to preserve a piece of their beloved daughter through Nancy. She was their saving grace, and they were hers. John and Marti were the only parents Nancy had ever really known. They were a very close and loving family. Nancy was their pride and joy.

While he had no control over the fate of his loved ones, John Kilday was able to control his financial future, and he had planned well… up until now. He had an overwhelming feeling of desperation, like helpless prey captured in an intricate web.

The rain was just about to stop when a lightening bolt struck one of the small Florida pines that was clustered in a haphazard pattern near the bayou. The thunder was immediate. The strike couldn't have been more than one hundred yards from where he was standing. It was close enough to startle the great blue heron. The heron made a deep guttural sound as it flapped its wings and slowly headed out over the bayou. It made a sweeping turn and then flew over the top of John Kilday's house, leaving a large white milky deposit on the wooden walkway between the house and pier. The lightening and accompanying thunder jolted John Kilday from his semi-conscious state. It had jolted him back to reality. The light had come on in his head. He looked around the backyard and then down at his clothes. He realized that he was drenched to the bone. He had a confused look on his face, one that said, "What am I doing out here? Why am I all wet?" He reached over and picked up his Old Fashioned. He looked at it suspiciously. The glass was full of rainwater. He flipped the contents of the glass onto the lawn and then turned and walked toward the sliding glass doors. The milky residue from the heron was running through the cracks and off into the grass.

He started to go in but knew that if Marti were alive, she would get all over him for messing up the den. He kicked off his deck shoes and stripped off his wet clothes. He stood there, buck naked, for several seconds before going into the house. It didn't matter. There was no one on the bayou. No one to see him. The nearest house was hidden by a thick row of bushes and scrub oaks. He really didn't care anyway. He was focused on the fact that he had just lost a great portion of his life savings. He left his shoes and clothes on the deck and went into the den. The air conditioning hit him like a blast of artic air. He was suddenly very cold, and now very much aware of what he wanted to do. No, he would not go down without a fight. He refused to be diminished to helpless prey. In that moment, John Kilday knew exactly what he was going to do.

CHAPTER TWO

Carl Peterson sat back in one of his Italian glove-leather recliners. He would rotate sitting in the chairs so that they would wear evenly. It had been a long day, a long week for that matter. The Napoleon brandy helped relieve the week's tension and take away the chill he was feeling from the den. A slight smile crossed Carl's lips as he thought about how cold it was. Where was all this global warming? Where the hell was Al Gore when he needed him? "Climate change" was certainly a more accurate term. It was innocuous enough to be safe, yet still appease the environmentalists. Global warming meant that the scientists actually knew what was causing the earth to heat up. Climate change meant that they had no idea what was going on, but at least the funding would put food on their tables. Whatever the term, the liberal scientists had the "Great Hairy Unwashed" believing that man was the cause. Carl took another sip of brandy as he held the snifter in both hands. No matter what the term was, it was very cool for an October evening.

As he was musing to himself, the phone rang. There were only a few people who would call him this late on a Friday night and fewer still that he would even consider answering. There was only one individual who was still at The Peterson Group office when he had left at 1900 hours. That was Roland Carpenter. When Carl left, Roland was in the process of packing his things into his black leather soft-sided briefcase. So Carl decided to let the answering machine pick it up. He leaned back and shut his eyes. The warm brandy felt good in his hands. Brandy was relaxing. The answering machine made a beeping sound to signal that the person on the other end was about to leave a voice message. Carl immediately recognized the voice; it was a voice he hadn't heard in several months.

"Uncle Carl, this is Mike. Please give me a call." Carl was already at the phone before his nephew had a chance to hang up.

"Mike don't hang up…are you there?"

"Yes, I'm here Uncle Carl," he answered, sounding somewhat relieved.

"I'm sorry. I must admit that I was screening my calls. How are you doing? How's the navy treating you?" asked Carl, a bit surprised to hear from his nephew on a Friday night. Relatives always seemed to call on Sunday afternoon during the Redskins game.

"I'm doing well," responded Mike, "and the navy is fine," he added.

Carl caught the tone of something else in his nephew's voice, although he didn't want to ask him directly.

"How's Nancy?" asked Carl hesitantly.

"She's fine. In fact, that is the reason I am calling."

"She's okay?" asked Carl interrupting, his voice signaling concern.

"She's fine Uncle Carl. It's her dad we are worried about. We haven't heard from him in several days. She's very concerned, and quite frankly, so am I," responded Mike.

Carl took a sip of the brandy. Although he only talked with his nephew on special occasions, he always liked the boy and had followed his career from a distance. Mike Holloway was Carl's only nephew. He was a lieutenant commander in the navy and presently assigned to the USS Nimitz as the Assistant Air Operations Officer. The kid was on the fast track. He had a good name. His great uncle was Admiral Holloway, the former Chief of Naval Operations. The kid had good genes.

"If I remember correctly, isn't he a little older?" asked Carl.

"Yes, he is technically Nancy's grandfather. I'm not sure if you remember, but Nancy's parents died when she was three. Her grandparents raised her. They are simply Mom and Dad to her," explained Mike.

"That's right, now I remember," said Carl. "Has he ever...*disappeared* before?" he asked, being careful with the word disappeared.

"Never," responded Mike firmly. "Since my mother-in-law died, Nancy talks to him at least once every other day and sometimes more than that. He has stayed with us on several occasions. This is not like him to just drop off the face of the earth."

"Maybe he met somebody? If I remember correctly, since he retired, he and his wife were always taking a yearly cruise. Maybe he went on a cruise by himself?"

"We thought about that, but there is no way he would have scheduled a trip without telling us. No, that's not like him. Something is wrong Uncle Carl."

Carl took another sip of brandy. It was still warm.

"Mike, are they...," Carl corrected himself, "is *he* still living in Panama City?"

"Yes, although he has considered moving out here closer to us and the grandkids. He was here about three weeks ago and had found a patio home that he liked on the golf course. He is scheduled to come back in November to meet with a real estate agent."

"I would guess by now he has accepted his wife's passing. How long has it been?" asked Carl.

"Just over a year. It has been very difficult for him. He's coping, but he will never get over her. They had known each other since grade school."

"Has he been sick or depressed lately?" asked Carl.

"I wouldn't say that he was depressed, but he has been acting strangely. Disengaged may be a better description," responded Mike.

"Disengaged?" asked Carl as he put his brandy on the coffee table.

"Something has been bothering him, but he wouldn't tell us what it was," responded Mike. "I guess Nancy and I thought that whatever it was, it would just go away."

"Give me his address," said Carl, "and also his email address if he has one."

"I will email it to you as soon as I hang up. I didn't want to bother you with this, but both Nancy and I are really concerned."

"That's no problem; I'm glad to help. I assume you have notified the police," said Carl. It wasn't a question.

"We have, but they said it was too early to file a missing person's report. They said they would go by the house, but we haven't heard a thing from them. It's difficult for us being so far away."

"All right, don't worry. I'll have one of my guys go over there first thing in the morning. Let's see what he can find out before we put out an all-points bulletin," said Carl. "How's your mom doing?"

"She's doing great. You should give her a call," responded Mike. "I think she would really like to have a closer relationship with you."

"I'll do that. Say 'hi' to her for me, and try not to worry about your father-in-law. I'm sure he's okay. You know Mike, us old guys get a little forgetful at times. Don't worry about him. He's a tough old bird. I'm sure there is a logical explanation."

"Thanks Uncle Carl. Next time it will be a social call. I promise."

Carl hung up the phone and finished what was left of his brandy. He sat there for a few minutes thinking about Mike. Mike was a good kid. Hell he wasn't a kid anymore; he was at least thirty-four or thirty-five. Being a senior lieutenant commander, he would most likely screen for a department head tour. The only thing wrong with the kid, as far as Carl was concerned, was that he was a fighter pilot. Carl would overlook that slight character flaw. Carl was partial to the attack community.

Since the telephone conversation had interrupted his brandy, he decided that it wouldn't go against his three-drink limit if he made himself another one. As he was warming the snifter, he couldn't help but think about his baby sister. Amy was a surprise to everyone, including her mother and father. Carl was ten years old when Amy was born. She was still playing with her Barbie dolls when he was running on Tahiti Beach in full combat gear with his newfound buddy, Rick Morgan. He really never knew her. She was more like a niece than a sister. As a result, Carl always felt like he was an only child...with a slight imperfection. He had purposed in his heart that he would become closer to her, but it hadn't happened yet. She had her world, and he had his.

He looked at his watch. It was an hour earlier in Destin. It certainly wasn't too late to give Tony Ramos a call. Tony had made a full recovery from the stab wounds he had received during his last assignment from Carl Peterson. Carl figured he was probably out having a few drinks. Carl grabbed his cell phone and dialed Tony. Surprisingly, Tony was at home and picked up the phone on the second ring.

"Ramos," he answered in a strong baritone voice. He did sound quite healthy.

"Tony, Carl Peterson here."

"Good evening Mr. Peterson. How may I help you?" responded Tony very respectfully.

"Tony it's Friday night. Please, call me Carl. You have certainly earned it."

"Okay Mr. uh…sorry…Carl. What's going on?"

"I just got off the phone with my nephew. Seems his father-in-law is missing. I would like you to do a little investigating. Are you free tomorrow?" asked Carl.

"Of course. For you I am always free…uh, that is from a time standpoint," said Tony with a slight hint of a laugh. "Only kidding Mr…uh…Carl," he added.

"Actually, keep track of your hours," responded Carl. "My company can use the write-off."

"So where does this guy live?" asked Tony.

"He lives in Panama City," responded Carl. "His name is John Kilday. Address is 515 Blue Heron Drive. I'll email you all the particulars."

"How long has he been missing?" asked Tony.

"Apparently not long enough to get the attention of the local police, but long enough that my nephew is worried," responded Carl. "A couple of days at least," he added.

"No problem Carl. I'll head out first thing in the morning. I'll call you as soon as I get there. How old is this guy?"

"You know, I'm not sure exactly. I assume he's in his mid-seventies…he's a great grandpa…but still too young to just go wander off," responded Carl.

"Is there a wife, lady friend?" asked Tony.

"His wife died over a year ago. As far as my nephew knows, there is no lady friend," said Carl. "He likes to cruise, but my nephew said he wouldn't have taken a cruise, or any trip for that matter, without telling them."

"Okay Carl. I'll be in touch."

"Talk with you later," said Carl as he hung up the phone.

Carl went back and sat in the other leather recliner. The glove leather felt cool to his back and arms. He nursed the brandy as he thought about Tony Ramos and their *search for Snake*. Carlos Garcia had brought Tony into the operation. Carlos had known him from the Special Ops Command at Hurlbert Field in Florida where Tony was a member of Delta Force prior to his retirement. Tony had almost died during his encounter with Kevin Macavoy. Macavoy had been with MI6 but went rogue and was hired by a Russian security officer to hijack a naval weapon system called *Snake*. Macavoy had attempted to get information from Tony Ramos but found him to be a lot tougher than he had expected. Tony ended up in the hospital. Macavoy ended up on a cold slab in the Okaloosa County Morgue. It all ended well, and Carl Peterson put Tony Ramos on the payroll as a contract employee.

When Carl finished his drink, he went to his laptop and opened his email. There were several new emails. The only one he opened was the one from his nephew. It contained all the information he and Mike had discussed. Carl hit the forward button, addressed the email to Tony Ramos, added some additional instructions and then hit send. The email was gone in a flash. As he looked at the information, he decided to forward the email to Roland Carpenter. He provided a brief overview and asked Roland to see if he could access John Kilday's computer. In particular, Carl wanted to get into Kilday's email. Also, he wanted to find out what websites he was visiting. He asked Roland to look for anything that might give them a clue to John Kilday's whereabouts.

He closed his laptop, perused his recliners and then sat in the one that looked less disturbed. He took a sip of brandy, leaned back, and continued to think about global warming…or was it climate change. A slight smile crossed his face. No matter what they called it, it was always about the money!

CHAPTER THREE

Rick Morgan passed the FedEx truck for the third time. He looked in the rearview mirror and then at the dashboard clock. It was nearly two p.m. He had gotten off to an early start. The weather was really nice for traveling. The sky was mostly clear with only a few clouds visible in the western sky. The weather guessers were correct; it probably wouldn't rain for the next several days. As a former navy pilot, Rick was convinced that the meteorologists couldn't tell you what the weather was *yesterday* with any real certainty. It was a little cold for early October. However, that was good since there were still three more weeks left in the hurricane season. Hurricanes liked warm water, so the colder the better. He looked into the rearview mirror. He was finally putting some distance between himself and the FedEx truck. They had been playing leapfrog for the past hour. It had turned into a game. Rick was tired of playing the game.

He finished what was left of his coffee from the large thermos Lynn had packed for his trip. He had also raided the tempting goodie bag she sent with him. She most definitely knew how to take care of Rick. He looked in the rearview mirror, the FedEx truck was nowhere in sight. Maybe he pulled off. It didn't matter. Rick had won the leapfrog race. He turned north on US Route 1 just south of Dover. It wouldn't be long before he would be crossing the Delaware Memorial Bridge.

There was a Cracker Barrel at the first exit just on the other side of the bridge. He would stop there for a late lunch.

Rick's thoughts shifted to Lynn. He really missed having her on the trip. She was great company and had the uncanny ability to talk for at least a hundred miles without taking a breath. She would pass out, sleep for an hour or two, then wake up and talk for another hundred miles. With Lynn along, Rick didn't need an audio book to keep him company during the ten and a half hour trip to upstate New York.

However, Lynn needed to stay behind and help their daughter, Brooke, prepare for a trip to Bolivia. Brooke was doing research for another story about the CIA's role in the death of Che Guevara. It was her third short story since *The Last Witness*. Rick had planned to accompany her, but the unexpected death of one of his first cousins caused him to change plans. He hadn't been to Bolivia in a very long time. Rick wasn't too happy about letting Brooke go by herself. He tried to talk her out of going, but being Rick's daughter, she inherited many of his traits. She was strong-willed and stubborn just like him. No amount of talking was going to dissuade her from going.

At a little after 1400 hours, Rick pulled into the Cracker Barrel. There was no wait. Rick was seated at a table in the center section next to the window. He could see his Escalade parked on the end of a half-filled row of cars. He liked to keep his car in sight, since he always carried a loaded weapon in the glove compartment. Old habits were hard to break. The server approached with coffee in hand. He put in his order and thought about Brooke.

Brooke had become an accomplished writer. Her articles on the Witness Protection Program and the ATF were widely acclaimed. Her first novel was with a publisher in New York City. She used Rick as a sounding board and editor and genuinely welcomed his input. She was particularly excited about her upcoming trip. Rick's thoughts drifted to Bolivia. Brooke had known that her dad was somehow involved with the events that led to the capture and jungle execution of Che Guevara, but he had never told her the whole story, or the part he had played. Most of it was classified. Just then, the waitress came with Rick's order, and in an instant, Rick was back in America.

As Rick exited the Cracker Barrel, his cell phone rang. He glanced at the caller ID. It was Carlos Garcia. He was looking forward to hearing from Carlos.

"Carlos, you're still alive. How was the wedding?" asked Rick, knowing that Carlos sometimes overindulged during the reception phase.

"Yes I'm still alive, and the wedding was great," responded Carlos. "Gonzaga married well…and well above his station. She's a gem."

"Yes, he did get a sweetheart. How's it going to work out with him in the navy and her in the air force?" asked Rick.

"Young love has no bounds," responded Carlos.

"Young love has no bounds?" repeated Rick slowly in a questioning voice. "I see that Ann has introduced you to something other than *Soldier of Fortune*," said Rick. "Young love has no bounds," he repeated again.

Carlos could hear a muffled laugh.

"I read!" responded Carlos, his voice sounding like a wounded teenager.

"You?" said Rick, his tone signaling disbelief. "When do you get time to read?"

"Trust me, I get time. But to answer your question, Gonz could get orders to the Special Ops Command…with a little help. However, I understand that Elena is thinking about transferring over to the navy," added Carlos.

"At this point, neither of them is thinking about the service," responded Rick. "However, I'm sure with Carl's contacts he could call in a favor and get these two, at the very least, in the same city."

"That would be nice," responded Carlos, adding, "are you at home?"

"No, actually I'm on my way to upstate New York," responded Rick.

"Upstate New York? I thought you and Brooke were going to Bolivia," said Carlos.

"Brooke is still going. I had a first cousin pass away unexpectedly. She and I grew up together as kids; we were very close. She has been helping take care of my mother," responded Rick. "Her father is the last of my uncles, and a guy that I really like. I needed to make this trip," added Rick.

Carlos didn't respond right away. He understood and could tell by Rick's voice that it bothered him.

"Sorry to hear that Rick. How long will you be gone?" asked Carlos changing the subject.

"About a week. I plan to do a little work on my mom's house while I'm there," said Rick.

"Do you want me to go to Bolivia with Brooke?" Carlos asked. He was sincere.

"Her boss is going to provide contractor support. But thanks for asking," said Rick as he started the car. "I'll keep in touch."

"Talk with you later," said Carlos. "Sorry to hear about your cousin," he added as he hung up.

Rick put the phone in one of the cup holders in the console and headed for the New Jersey Turnpike. He looked at his watch and confirmed that he would hit the Parkway at a good time, if there ever was a good time to travel through New Jersey. Unfortunately, he would hit Albany during the rush hour. He turned on the CD player and began to listen to *Niceville*.

Just prior to reaching Exit 11 on the Turnpike, his cell phone rang again. It was Carl Peterson.

"Hey Carl," he answered.

"Rick. How's the drive going?"

"Good. Not a whole lot of traffic and I'm listening to a good book," responded Rick.

"Listen Rick, I'm not trying to rush you, but when will you be back in town?" asked Carl, his voice signaling that there was business to be done.

"A week to ten days. Why, do you need me sooner?" asked Rick.

"No, I didn't mean to imply that. Well, maybe I did. I've got Tony Ramos doing some investigative work. If it turns into anything, I would like you to look into it," responded Carl.

"I need to attend a memorial service on Monday night. If you need me, I can certainly head out on Tuesday morning. What is Tony looking into?"

"My nephew's father-in-law hasn't been in touch with him for several days. I had Roland access his computer and it appears he has won a large amount of money in one of those international lotteries. Then he turns up missing," said Carl.

"Hell, I'd probably go into hiding myself if I won. Can you imagine the unwanted attention?" responded Rick. It was a rhetorical question.

"I agree with you, but he's a little older and not quite like us, and he *always* maintains near-daily contact with his daughter. Might not be anything but just wanted to give you a heads-up," said Carl.

"Let me know if you need me. I can head back anytime after Monday," responded Rick.

"Thanks pal. Talk with you later," said Carl as he hung up.

Rick paid the toll and headed north on the Garden State Parkway. The traffic wasn't too heavy. Rick thought about the lottery. He had personally known a couple of people who had won significant amounts of money. Their life was never the same.

CHAPTER FOUR

Bolton Landing, New York
October 6, 2012
Saturday
1500 Hours

When the call came in, Sheriff Wade Hollister was sitting in his patrol car just inside the entrance to The Sagamore Resort in Bolton Landing. He had a clear view of Lake George and was sipping on a fresh cup of coffee that he had poured less than two minutes earlier. It had been a good summer in the Lake George area despite all the negative news about the economy. By mid-July nobody seemed to care one way or the other. The stock market was showing signs of a slight recovery, the older folks were enjoying their retirement, the restaurants were almost full, and the young…well, the young really didn't have a clue.

As he sipped his coffee, he thought about entitlement programs and their effect on the economy. He was convinced that the retirement age for social security would eventually be raised to seventy, and there would be no early retirement. Maybe by then the young would figure it out, become more informed and consequently more involved. Hopefully it wouldn't be too late. He took a healthy swallow of coffee just as his phone rang.

"Hollister here," he answered in his official I'm-on-duty voice.

"Sheriff, I just got a call from Fred Duffy. He thinks that there is something wrong over at Wayne Abshier's house," said Deputy Luke Monroe, his voice sounding as though he were itching to get out of dispatcher duty. None of the deputies liked being on the desk, but this year's budget didn't allow for a full time dispatcher. They all had to do their time.

"Wrong? What the hell does he mean by *wrong*?" asked Sheriff Hollister. He never liked words that were not clearly descriptive.

"He said that there were several days of mail in the box and several newspapers on the ground. He drove up the driveway and could see Abshier's car," responded Deputy Monroe. "Said it was all covered in leaves."

"Covered, huh? Did he knock on the door?" asked the sheriff as he took another drink of semi-hot coffee.

"No he didn't," responded Deputy Monroe.

"Okay Luke, I'll check it out," said Hollister. "What's the address?"

"Hold on Sheriff, I've got it right here."

Sheriff Hollister could hear Deputy Monroe shuffling through some papers. He finished his coffee and screwed the chrome cup back on top of his large green Aladdin thermos, the one that he had since his college days.

"The address is 1478 Bolton Landing Road," reported Monroe.

"Okay, I got it. Why don't you give Abshier a call. If he answers, call me right back so I don't waste my time," said Hollister.

"Will do," responded Monroe.

Sheriff Hollister pulled out from The Sagamore and turned south on Route 9N. He didn't turn on his lights or siren. If the mail was piling up, and Abshier's car was in the driveway covered with leaves, chances were that Wayne Abshier was past the point of needing somebody's help in a real hurry.

The trip through Bolton Landing only took a couple of minutes. This time of year was family time in the Adirondacks. There were quite a few couples walking hand-in-hand while window shopping. Several kids were running, weaving in and out among the pedestrians. Sheriff Hollister kept the speedometer on twenty-five.

Within fifteen minutes of the call, Hollister was turning up Abshier's driveway. As he turned in, he could see that the mailbox was overstuffed with mail and that several newspapers were strewn around the entrance of the driveway. A couple of newspapers were nearly twenty feet south of the driveway and clearly victims of fast moving traffic. The driveway was fairly steep and opened into a small clearing. Hollister parked next to Abshier's 2009 silver Lexus. As described, it was covered with leaves. Obviously the car hadn't been driven in several days. Before getting out, Sheriff Hollister called Deputy Monroe to let him know that he had arrived.

"Luke, I take it no one answered at the Abshier residence," said Sheriff Hollister. It wasn't a question. "Run this license plate number, LG295A, just to make sure it belongs to Abshier," he added.

"Will do Sheriff," responded the deputy.

Hollister got out of the car and placed his hand on the hood of the Lexus. It was a habit, and as expected, the hood was cold. The leaf pattern confirmed that the car hadn't been driven in several days. He looked back toward the lake but couldn't see the water through the trees. He thought to himself that if he owned the property, those trees would have been cut down a long time ago. He walked up on the porch and knocked on the door.

"Mr. Abshier, Sheriff Hollister here," he said in a loud clear voice.

He tried to look through the glass in the door, but the curtains blocked his view. Again he announced his presence.

"Mr. Abshier, Sheriff Hollister here. Are you in there?" he asked as he knocked with authority on the door. There was no answer or any sounds that he could discern coming from inside the house.

Hollister moved off the porch and walked around the house. He tried to look in the windows but all the blinds were pulled shut. He tried the back door, but it was locked. He went back around the front of the house and got back into the patrol car and called Deputy Monroe.

"Yes Sheriff," answered Monroe, unable to hide the anticipation in his voice.

"The house is shut up tighter than a drum. Did you run the plate?"

"Yes sir. The car is registered to Wayne F. Abshier," responded Monroe. "He's a retired army colonel. His wife passed away several months ago. He's eighty-three years old," he added.

"Any relatives in the area?" asked the sheriff.

"I'm still working on that," responded Monroe.

Sheriff Hollister went back to his car. He really didn't want to break into the house, especially if Colonel Abshier went on a trip with a friend and forgot to tell anyone. People usually notify the post office or have a friend pick up the mail. He had some experience with picking a lock and decided to try that before breaking in.

"I'm going to try to pick the lock. In the meantime, see if you can find out who the Colonel hangs around with…maybe a lady friend," said Hollister.

"Okay Sheriff," responded Monroe.

Hollister opened the glove compartment and took out a small locksmith kit. He went back to the porch announcing his arrival one more time.

"Colonel Abshier," he yelled as he knocked on the door. "Colonel, I'm going to try and open your door," he added. There was no sense getting shot by a startled colonel who probably had several weapons in the house and knew how to use them.

Sheriff Hollister had little trouble unlocking the door. However, the door had a chain lock that prevented him from opening the door all the way. It didn't matter, the unmistakable smell of death made him wince. He closed the door quickly and went back to the patrol car and called Deputy Monroe.

"Yes Sheriff," answered Monroe, knowing by now that the Sheriff probably had some information.

"Call the coroner," directed Hollister, "and have Deputy James meet us up here at the Abshier residence. Make sure he brings the crime kit just in case," he added.

"What is the scene?"

"I'm not sure," responded Hollister. "The door was chained from the inside, but there's no doubt that whoever is inside has been dead for several days. Make sure the coroner brings some extra masks with him. I'm not going into the house until he arrives."

"I'm on it Sheriff," responded an excited Deputy Monroe.

Hollister sat back in his patrol car and took the top off his thermos. He poured another cup of coffee. It was still very hot. He took a drink, but the smell of death was still in his nostrils. As a result, the coffee didn't taste very well. He looked at the cup, made a face, rolled down the window and emptied the coffee into the grass. Eating or drinking at a death scene or while performing an autopsy provided Hollywood with an interesting backdrop, but it was rarely done in real life…if ever. Most of the time, even experienced deputies couldn't keep from throwing up.

Within ten minutes, Deputy Monroe called to say that the county coroner was on the way. He'd be there within a half hour. As they were talking, Deputy Ronny James drove in and parked alongside Sheriff Hollister's patrol car.

"What do we have here Sheriff?" asked Deputy James as both men exited their vehicles.

"Probably nothing more than a routine death from old age, but you never know. The corner is on the way. From the smell coming from inside the house, I'm fairly certain this guy has been dead for several days," responded Hollister. "Do you have a couple of extra masks with you?" he added.

"Let me check. I'm pretty sure that I do."

As the deputy looked in the trunk, Coroner Fred Williams drove into the small clearing and parked the county station wagon in front of the two story Tudor-style house. Being a rather large man, it took him a couple of swings forward to get out of the car. He couldn't seem to move all of his body in one motion.

"Good morning Fred," said Sheriff Hollister as he extended his right hand.

"Morning gentlemen," responded Fred Williams as he shook hands with both men. "What do we have here?" he asked.

"Not sure Fred. The door is locked from the inside, and the smell is pretty strong," responded the sheriff.

Deputy James was standing there with two facemasks in his left hand. They were the cheap ones that were purchased at Home Depot. Coroner Williams looked at them, smiled and opened the back of his vehicle.

"You might want to wear these instead," he said as he produced two high-quality breathing masks. "This could be bad," he added as he also handed each man a pair of white surgical gloves.

Hollister opened the trunk of his patrol vehicle, reached in and came out with a very large pair of bolt cutters.

"Let's do it," he said as all three men put on their masks and approached the front door.

Hollister easily cut the chain and pushed the door open. It opened into a large foyer with a spiral staircase sweeping up to the second floor. There was a crystal chandelier that was on, but the dimmer was turned quite low. At first glance, the house appeared to be neat and clean. Sheriff Hollister called out to Colonel Abshier.

"Colonel Abshier. Are you here Colonel?" he yelled. "Sheriff Hollister here."

There was no answer. The three men proceeded to enter the den where they found Colonel Abshier hanging from a rope that was tied to an overhead railing.

"Stay here," said the coroner as he proceeded to look up at the body of Colonel Wayne F. Abshier.

Unfortunately, this wasn't the first time Sheriff Hollister had come upon a suicide by hanging. All the typical signs were there. There was the overturned chair along with a urine stain on the floor and on the front of Abshier's pants. It was certainly a bad ending to a long life. This was the first hanging for Deputy James. Sheriff Hollister noticed that James hadn't moved. He appeared to be turning a bit pale.

"Why don't you go outside and get some fresh air," encouraged the sheriff.

James didn't say anything. He was happy to leave. Fred Williams smiled at the sheriff as they heard the deputy throwing up. They had all been there.

CHAPTER FIVE

The report sounded like a car backfiring in the distance. Several people turned and looked around. A couple of them gained eye contact, shrugged their shoulders and returned their attention to the lacrosse game. It was probably nothing. There were never loud noises in Coronado. It was the perfect little community. Anyone living on the island could walk almost everywhere and anywhere they needed to go. There were a lot of retirees. Most were those fortunate enough to have bought on the island when it was *almost* affordable.

Although it was a scrimmage game, the girls were giving their all. But they were getting tired and it was beginning to show. Almost all of the attendees were parents. Most fit the description of soccer mom. However, since it was Saturday, several dads had also made the practice game. While their enthusiasm didn't quite rival that of the soccer moms, they certainly made their presence known. About two minutes after the suspected backfire, sirens could be heard. They were still some distance away, but the Doppler effect indicated that they were getting closer. There seemed to be a geometric correlation between the approaching sirens and the attention to the game. The closer the sirens got, the less interested the spectators became.

Everyone's attention was finally diverted as two police cars came racing down F Avenue, their sirens announcing that something was happening, or had happened, close to the field. Both cars stopped along the curb in front of a condo complex on F Avenue. It was directly across the street from the field. Four officers exited the vehicles and were met by an attractive older lady in tan slacks and a black sweater with tan and green stripes. She was quite anxious. Her hand shook as she pointed to the entryway that led to the individual condo units. She was clearly quite upset and spoke with a slight accent. The officer did his best to calm her. None of the people at the game could hear what she was saying.

As she and the officer were talking, another siren could be heard as it turned onto F Avenue. The other three officers, two males and a female, listened intently to the older lady as a rescue vehicle pulled up and two people exited, medical bags in hand. The lacrosse game continued, but most of the attention was now directed across the street toward the condo complex. By now, several more people had come out of their units. Most of the game spectators had even migrated close to the fence. They weren't paying any attention to the game. The girls were still running and making funny little noises as they ran up and down the field, but it was evident they had lost their intensity with the excitement growing across the street.

Sergeant Hector Delgado held his people back as he continued to question the older lady.

"What is your name ma'am?" he asked.

"Ann Delsignore," she responded. She was acting very nervous.

"Are you the one who made the call?" he asked.

"Yes, I made the call," she responded, claiming responsibility. A look of ownership briefly crossed her face.

"What did you hear?"

"I heard a gunshot coming from Mr. Nathan's unit," she said, her lower lip now quivering uncontrollably.

"How many shots did you hear?" asked Delgado.

"One. I heard only one shot," she responded. Her eyes were beginning to tear up.

"Are you absolutely sure that it was a gunshot?" asked the sergeant. He made a few notes in a small black notebook.

"I'm sure. My husband had a gun, and I would go with him to the range. I'm certain that it was a gunshot that I heard," she responded.

"Where is your husband?" he asked.

"He died three years ago," she responded solemnly, hers eyes looking downward.

"Do you know this…Mr. Nathan?" asked Delgado. "And, is that his first or last name?" he added before she had time to answer.

"It's Charles Nathan. We are *close* friends," she added with emphasis on the word close. She began to cry.

Sergeant Delgado suspected that they were indeed close friends. He turned and brought his team of officers around him in a semi-circle.

"I think we may have a suicide here, but let's make sure we don't run into some nut with a gun. Mike, you and Sylvia look around back. Carl and I will take the courtyard. Listen, be alert."

The three officers acknowledged. Officer Mike Namanski and Sylvia Cunningham removed their weapons, flipped the safety off with their thumbs and proceeded around the eastern side of the complex. Many of the residents were standing outside their units. Sergeant Delgado asked them to go back inside and lock their doors. They all complied willingly.

Sergeant Delgado and Officer Carl Winslow proceeded to check out the courtyard. The courtyard was very small and well maintained. There were no obvious places where anyone could hide without being seen. There were only two units on the upper level. Both were at the rear of the complex. Delgado asked Ms. Delsignore which unit belonged to Charles Nathan. She told him that Charles's unit was the one on the top right. He and Carl started to move into the courtyard. They had a clear view of the upper level.

"Ms. Delsignore," summoned Delgado.

"Yes," she responded. She had regained most of her composure.

"What is the layout of Mr. Nathan's unit?"

She paused for a few seconds and then responded.

"There is a very small foyer that opens into a large den. The kitchen is on the right and there is one bedroom on the left. The bathroom is on the left side of the bedroom as you enter," she said.

"So basically, there are just four rooms?"

"That's correct," responded Ms. Delsignore.

"I assume you live here also?" asked Delgado.

"I do," responded Ms. Delsignore pointing to one of the units near the end of the courtyard on the left hand side.

"I need you to stay here. I'll let you know what we find," said Delgado.

Ms. Delsignore knew exactly what he meant. She was expecting the worst. Sergeant Delgado thought about the layout. He looked back at the entrance to the condo complex and signaled with a closed fist for the two rescue squad people to hold their position.

"Carl, stay here. I'll go up the stairs," said Delgado as he drew his weapon.

"I got you covered," responded Carl as he un-holstered his weapon and moved the safety into the firing position.

With his right hand, Delgado grabbed the two-way radio that was attached to the top of his left shoulder. He turned his head just enough to talk into the unit. He kept his eyes on the upper deck.

"Mike, Sylvia, anything at your end?" he asked as he slowly proceeded up the stairs.

"Everything is clear back here Sarge," responded Namanski.

"Stay there just in case someone jumps out the back window," said Delgado.

The two rescue squad people remained at the entrance to the complex. They knew to stay away from officers who had drawn their weapons. The spectators across the street were oblivious to any danger and held on to the chain link fence like monkeys waiting for someone to start tossing peanuts. Sergeant Delgado reached the top of the stairs and rapidly looked in both directions. The small walkway was clear. There was no place to hide. He crossed to the back wall and moved slowly toward the door of Charles Nathan's unit. When he got to the door, he crouched down and moved to the far right side of the passageway. The door was now to his left. With his left hand he reached down and tried the doorknob. It was unlocked.

He didn't open the door all the way. He signaled Officer Winslow to come up. Winslow took a position on the far left side of the door. Delgado put up a hand and mouthed the words, "In five, four, three, two, one." He also counted the numbers with his left hand. When he reached "one," he swung the door open and both officers entered the unit. Delgado went in high and Winslow went in low.

The unit was not very large and appeared to be laid out just as Ms. Delsignore had described. It was probably only fifteen hundred square feet at most. Delgado yelled out.

"Mr. Nathan. Charles Nathan. This is Sergeant Delgado from the Coronado Police Department. Are you here?"

He and Officer Winslow waited for a response. There was no answer. Delgado signaled for Winslow to hold his position. Delgado then moved rapidly into the bedroom looking in all directions. He yelled out "CLEAR!" Winslow came in behind him as Delgado went into the bathroom. He came out shaking his head as he holstered his weapon. Winslow knew the look. Sergeant Delgado talked into his two-way radio.

"Mike, call the ME and the forensics team. Have the rescue people come up. It's just as I suspected...a probable suicide."

"Will do," responded Officer Namanski.

Delgado motioned to Winslow and they both entered the master bath. Charles Nathan was sitting in his bathtub. His head was thrust back and resting against the wall. The entire room was covered in plastic. Nathan had also taped plastic to the walls and ceiling. He had obviously taken a lot of time to cover everything. He had used painter's blue tape to secure the plastic to the walls and fixtures. He had also put a plastic bag over his head. It appeared that he had put the barrel of a Thirty-Eight Special into his mouth and pulled the trigger. The weapon was still in his right hand being held only by his trigger finger.

The bag was a bloody mess. His face was barley visible through the plastic. It wasn't a pretty sight. Delgado made the sign of the cross as he looked at the remains of Charles Nathan. He looked around the room still shaking his head. Mr. Nathan didn't want to leave his mess for someone else to clean up. He had obviously never seen anyone who had decided to eat the end of a Thirty-Eight Special. The bullet had blown part of the back of his head into the bag. The bullet had continued through the bag and had lodged near the top of the wall just below the ceiling. Sergeant Delgado continued to shake his head almost involuntarily as he looked over at Officer Winslow. Winslow seemed to be fixated on the bathtub scene. Charles Nathan had decided on a permanent solution to what was probably a temporary problem. Problems are always temporary.

"Mike, Sylvia doesn't have to see this…unless she wants to," said Sergeant Delgado.

Sylvia Cunningham had only been on the job for two and a half weeks. This would be her first encounter with a *real* body. Suicides weren't pretty. They were never pretty. Delgado remembered his first. Took him several months to get over the scene. Every once in a while he would see it in his sleep. It would now be replaced with the image of the late Charles Nathan.

"Says she needs to start somewhere Sarge. I'll send her up," said Namanski.

"Better get her a barf bag," replied Sergeant Delgado, "it ain't pretty. Send up the rescue squad people while you're at it," he added.

Sylvia Cunningham was the youngest officer on the Coronado staff. She was fresh out of the Academy and eager to do well. Everyone liked her. When she entered the foyer, Sergeant Delgado looked her straight in the eye.

"You know you don't have to do this," he said in a fatherly manner.

She was a very attractive young lady with big brown eyes and an innocence that was about to be lost forever.

"It's part of the job," she responded.

Delgado and Winslow waited at the door as she entered the bathroom. She threw up almost immediately. They hoped she had remembered to use the barf bag. Delgado had seen many experienced officers lose their lunch. No one would ever say a word.

The medical examiner arrived within the hour. Officer Winslow stayed on scene as Sergeant Delgado went back outside to let Ms. Delsignore know what they had found. She began to cry as he approached, before he said anything. The look on his face had said it all.

"I'm sorry Ms. Delsignore. It appears that Mr. Nathan took his own life. Do you know if he has any relatives close by?"

She didn't say anything for several seconds. She wiped her tears with a worn Kleenex and then looked at Sergeant Delgado.

"His wife died several years ago. He has a son in Kansas, but they haven't talked in years from what I understand," she responded.

"Have you known him very long?"

"A little over two years. We are…were…very close friends. I just can't believe he did this. It was that damn lottery!"

CHAPTER SIX

As Carl Peterson entered his outer office, he was greeted by his secretary, Elaine Drew. The smell of coffee indicated that she had been there for a while. She always showed up well ahead of everyone else with the possible exception of Roland Carpenter. Elaine had been with The Peterson Group since its inception. She had known Carl Peterson from his days in the CIA. She had been a secretary at Langley for nearly twenty-two years when she decided to retire and go with The Peterson Group. Elaine Drew was the consummate secretary—smart, personable, efficient, resourceful, and most importantly, she was happily married.

She greeted Carl with her usual good morning smile, and without asking, immediately got up and prepared a cup of coffee just as he liked it with two sugars and a smidge of half and half. She had a smile on her face as she re-entered the room. Steam was rising from the coffee cup.

"Roland wanted me to let him know when you arrived," she said as she gently placed the coffee mug on a Scrimshaw coaster. It was one from a set of four coasters that Carl had bought when he was a guest lecturer at the Naval War College in Rhode Island. At the time, Rick Morgan was in the audience as a young lieutenant commander. It was their first encounter since their CIA days in the field.

"Thanks Elaine," responded Carl as he took a drink of the coffee. It was perfect as usual.

Coffee was one of Elaine's specialties. She kept the pot exceptionally clean, used only bottled water and picked up freshly roasted coffee beans on a weekly basis from a coffee house on Prince Street.

"Also, there was a message from Mr. Savage. He asked if you would give him a call at your earliest convenience."

"Did he say why he was calling?" asked Carl.

"No sir he didn't, and unfortunately he hung up before I had a chance to ask him. Do you want me to call and find out?" she asked.

"No, it is probably nothing. Everything is always a crisis with him. He probably needs an upgrade to his Mac. I'll give him a call," said Carl, "and Elaine, let Roland know I'm here and to come to my office."

"Yes sir," she responded.

Carl sat back in his chair. The usual newspapers were arranged neatly on the left side of his desk. His favorite, the *Wall Street Journal*, was on top, followed by the *Financial Times, Washington Times, Chicago Tribune, New York Times* and *USA Today*. Carl never read them all. He would scan them, compare important articles and then draw his own conclusions based upon the known political leanings of the paper. In order to make a valid argument, it was imperative to know both sides of the political issue.

The closer he got to retirement, the more he became interested in his own personal financial matters. He particularly liked reading the *Financial Times*. It was rapidly becoming his favorite. However, the news always seemed to lag the ups and downs of the market. No paper or magazine was a good predictor. The *Financial Times* did the best job and was extremely good at explaining why things happened… after the fact. To do well in the market required a lot of homework. As he began looking at the front page of The *Wall Street Journal*, Elaine Drew announced that Roland Carpenter was in the outer office.

"Please send him in," said Carl as he folded the *Journal* and placed it neatly back at the beginning of the pile of newspapers.

"Good morning Mr. Peterson," said Roland as he entered Carl's office.

Roland had been with The Peterson Group for over five years. He was young, talented, loyal and extremely dedicated. Carl wished he had a dozen guys like Roland Carpenter.

"Good morning Roland. I hear you have finally started drinking coffee. Would you like a cup?" asked Carl as he motioned for Roland to take one of the large straight back leather chairs positioned in front of the desk. Roland sat down. He had a small spiral notepad in his left hand.

"No thank you sir. I've already had my one cup for the day," he responded. "Some water would be nice," he added.

Carl got up from the desk and opened the small refrigerator that was centered under a painting of Admiral Farragut's ships passing Fort Morgan during the Battle of Mobile Bay. He took out a bottle of Fiji water and handed it to Roland.

"So, what do you have for me Roland?" asked Carl, knowing by the confident look on Roland's face that he had completed his initial assignment. Roland was a brilliant young man and a computer whiz. The only thing that drove Carl crazy was that Roland rarely wore socks. Carl didn't understand not wearing socks. It reminded him of a scientist who did contract work for the Pentagon. The guy was a Ph.D. who never trimmed his eyebrows. Carl had never seen anyone with longer eyebrows than this guy. They almost reached his hairline. Leonid Brezhnev would have been envious. The problem was that Carl was so fixated on his eyebrows that he never did listen to a word the guy had to say. It was a real distraction. In retrospect, he wondered if the guy grew them that way on purpose, because in reality, he had nothing important to say after all. Carl purposely chose not to focus on Roland's ankles.

"I was able to log into Mr. Kilday's computer. It appears that he made reservations to Nassau on Friday, September twenty-eighth. I also checked the manifest, and he did board the aircraft," said Roland.

"Maybe he just decided to take a short vacation," said Carl. "Was there anything else that was interesting?"

"Yes there was. His email and written correspondence indicates that he was *one* of the winners of an international lottery. He also transferred a quarter of a million dollars to secure those winnings."

Carl got a sardonic expression on his face as Roland continued.

"From what I can gather from his emails, after he made the transfer of funds, he was unable to reach the lottery people again. His emails were returned as undeliverable."

What a surprise, Carl thought to himself. He didn't say anything for a minute or so. Carl was familiar with lottery scams and deposed dictators who wanted to transfer very large sums of money. In fact, less than a month ago, he had received a request from someone in Nigeria who wanted to transfer over fifty-two million dollars in order to preserve their funds. For his consideration The Peterson Group would receive a nice commission. Of course, The Peterson Group would have to put up some "good faith" money in an offshore account to confirm their commitment. It was the third request of that type he had received in the past year. All of those requests were scams. He would always forward the email request to the State Department. As expected, he never heard anything back. They never seemed to do anything constructive about the requests. If they did take any action, it was done in secret and obviously ineffective.

"Sounds like Mr. Kilday was the victim of a scam," said Carl as he sipped his coffee. It was still quite warm.

"It certainly looks that way. I checked with his bank, and he did transfer a large sum of money. They wouldn't give me any details. I could hack into his account but don't want to push my luck. I'm sure that you could easily find out the particulars with your Homeland Security hat on," said Roland supporting a little smile.

Roland was correct. Carl could easily get any information that he needed with his Homeland Security clearance. He would just need to get permission from the program manager to use his company's credentials for that purpose. Regardless, he would be doing the investigation on The Peterson Group's nickel. He didn't mind spending a little of his own money.

"Thanks Roland," said Carl. "By the way, how long did it take you to access Kilday's computer?"

"A couple of minutes. He used a typical password. In his case, it was his wife's birthday," Roland responded as he got up from the chair and headed for the door.

"Thanks Roland," said Carl as he thought about his own password selection. How prosaic. He would change it.

As Carl contemplated the whereabouts of John Kilday and Roland's findings, he remembered that John Savage had called. Savage was a director with Homeland Security and The Peterson Group point of contact for the Omnibus Contract that was awarded to The Peterson Group in 2007. The contract was up for renewal. There was certainly no reason why Homeland Security wouldn't exercise the first option period, which would carry the contract forward for another five years. That was probably the reason John Savage had called. Carl picked up the phone and dialed John's direct number.

"Savage, how may I help you?" he answered in a firm voice.

"John, Carl Peterson here. I understand that you called this morning."

"Morning Carl. I did. I just wanted to personally let you know that we will be exercising the first option of your contract. Your people will need to submit the paperwork, and if you want to add some changes, now is the time to do it."

"Well that's good news, especially in this budget environment. I believe my people already have the paperwork completed. By the way, there are no changes. We plan to stay within the normal rate escalation, and we are not adding any new labor categories."

"That's fine. Seems like many of our other contractors are trying to squeeze every dollar out of us they can. By the way, how *is* business?" asked Savage.

"We are doing quite well. Business increased by over eighteen percent this last year. I am also picking up quite a bit of work in the private sector. A lot of security-related work. So business is good and getting better," responded Carl.

"That's good to hear. Our experience has shown that so many companies rely solely upon government contracts. They lose funding and then can't survive. The 8(a) firms are the worst for not planning ahead."

John paused and then added, "Will you be coming over for the next program review?"

"I am planning on it," Carl responded as he took a drink of coffee. "John, before I forget, we have been tasked in the private sector to look into the disappearance of an individual who may be the victim of a lottery scam. May I have your permission to use our Homeland Security credentials to do some investigating? As you know, these things can lead to individuals wanting, and planning, to do harm to the United States."

"I see no problem. Use me as a point of contact. Carl, I'm getting another call. I need to take it. Talk with you later," said John Savage as he hung up the phone.

Carl hung up and took a drink of coffee. He had been sure that his Omnibus Contract would be renewed, but it was always good to get verbal confirmation from the program director. He drank the rest of the coffee and cupped the mug in both hands as he thought about John Kilday and the lottery. Older people were ripe for the taking. He had personally known several senior citizens who had lost their entire savings on get-rich-quick scams. This time it was close to home…it was personal. He looked at the calendar and then at his watch. This was a good project for Rick Morgan and his team. He picked up the phone and called Rick.

"Good morning Carl."

"Hey Rick, how's it going?"

"Slow. I have been going through a bunch of old papers in my mom's basement. I'm just having some eggs at the Old Fort Diner," responded Rick, knowing that Carl had something for him.

"Rick, I certainly don't want to push you, but that issue we discussed on Saturday has taken a turn, and I could really use your help," responded Carl.

"I could leave here first thing in the morning. Probably make it to D.C. by thirteen hundred hours," responded Rick.

"I appreciate your willingness. I just needed to know for planning purposes."

"Have you located the father-in-law?" asked Rick.

"Yes. We found out that he transferred a quarter of a million dollars to an account in the Bahamas. Appears he has gone there to try and get his money back," responded Carl.

"Get his money back?" asked Rick.

"Yes. Remember that lottery money I told you he won? Well, it appears to be a scam," said Carl. "So many…"

Before Carl could complete his thought, Rick interrupted.

"Hold on a second Carl," said Rick as he reached for the local newspaper. "I just saw an article about an apparent suicide. Yes, here it is. Give me a second."

Rick quickly scanned the article.

"Seems that a retired military officer who lived just north of Lake George village committed suicide. He was a widower, and Carl, apparently he had just won a large amount of money in an international lottery. It may just be a coincidence, but I suggest you have Roland look into it. It would be interesting to see if there are others who have recently won an international lottery and met a similar fate."

"I'll get Roland on it. You can actually start the team process from up there," added Carl.

"Tell you what. I will touch base with the Warren County Sheriff and see what I can find out," responded Rick.

CHAPTER SEVEN

Carl Peterson's call caught Tony Ramos just as he turned into John Kilday's neighborhood. Tony had made the trip from Destin in one hour and fifteen minutes. He picked up his phone from the console and saw that it was a call from The Peterson Group. He correctly assumed that it was Carl Peterson.

"Good morning Mr. Peterson," he answered confidently.

"Good morning Tony, are you still in Destin?" asked Carl, hoping that he had caught Tony before he left for Panama City.

"Actually, I'm just down the road from John Kilday's house," responded Tony.

Carl was silent for a few seconds and then responded.

"I'm sorry. I should have called you earlier. The trip may have been unnecessary. It appears that Kilday has taken a flight to the Bahamas."

"Have you made contact with him? Is he okay?" asked Tony.

"I don't know. We haven't made contact, but we are sure that he's in the Bahamas," responded Carl. "We are in the process of trying to locate him as we speak," he added.

"I could still take a look around his place. Maybe talk with a neighbor or two and see what I can dig up if you want."

Carl thought about it and then decided that there was no sense in totally wasting Tony's time.

"That sounds like a good idea. Sorry I didn't get to you earlier," said Carl.

"No problem. I needed to get out of the house anyway. Besides, I have a lady friend over here who I called last night. I haven't seen her in a couple of months, so I would have made the trip anyway. I need to get back into circulation if you know what I mean," said Tony.

"I do know what you mean," said Carl. Carl had never found the right one since his high school sweetheart married his best friend Charlie. He had given up looking a long time ago. It had bothered him for years until he ran into her at his fortieth high school reunion. She was still pretty…all two hundred and eighty pounds of her. Thank God for Charlie. Charlie didn't look very happy.

"Do you have the specs on his car?" asked Tony. "I would assume he flew out of Panama City. I will check to see if his car is there," he added.

"Good idea. Hold on a second," said Carl as he buzzed Elaine Drew and asked her to have Roland find out the particulars on Kilday's vehicle.

As he was waiting to hear from Carl, Tony pulled into John Kilday's driveway. There were many small leaves covering the driveway and sidewalk. Tony got out of the car and looked around. From the driveway, no other houses were visible. Kilday had a nice piece of property that was isolated just enough. The house and property were well maintained. Tony was sure that if Kilday was at home, the leaves would have been raked up and bagged.

Tony knocked on the front door as a matter of courtesy, knowing that there would be no response, unless there was a house sitter. From the looks of everything, nobody would be there. He waited a minute or so and then proceeded to walk around the left side of the house. He was peering through one of the two garage windows when Carl came back on the line.

"Tony, are you there?"

"I'm here Mr. Peterson," responded Tony. Tony had forgotten all about calling him Carl.

"He drives a 2008 white X3 BMW. Florida plate number JFK-GLK. Should be real easy to spot."

"I will take a ride out to the airport. If the car is there, I will find it. I will call you later this afternoon," said Tony.

"Thanks," responded Carl. "Hope you have a nice time with your lady friend," he added as he said goodbye and hung up.

Tony looked into the garage again. There was no BMW or any other car for that matter. There was a riding lawn mower and a significant number of yard implements. Kilday must have spent a lot of time in the yard. The garage was neat and clean. Everything appeared to have an assigned place on the wall. Nothing seemed to be missing. Tony walked out back. The view was very nice. There were several great blue herons and a couple of white egrets standing still in the water looking for breakfast. As he was in the process of mentally counting the birds, several small fish broke the top of the water. Something else was also looking for breakfast.

Tony looked in through the sliding glass door. The blinds were pulled just enough to keep out the sun but opened enough to allow him to see the entire room. There was an open newspaper on the coffee table and a half-full glass of water. Tony imagined that John Kilday was sitting there when he made the decision to go to the Bahamas.

He continued looking around the perimeter of the house. Everything seemed to be in order. He looked at his watch. It was probably a little too early to call his lady friend. He decided that he would try a couple of the neighbors and then head out to the airport.

FORT EDWARD, NEW YORK

0910 HOURS

Rick Morgan finished his third cup of coffee. He had always enjoyed trips to his hometown, seeing friends and having breakfast with several of his old school buddies. As he walked outside, he heard a car horn. He didn't recognize the car or the person driving, but they must have recognized him. Small towns were like that. People truly cared for one another, and they were genuinely interested in the success or failures of those who, for whatever reason, had left the area.

Rick got into his car, and as he started it up, he looked back at the small diner. It reminded him of his cousin's restaurant and the many times he would sit there with his dad listening to the conversations of the old timers. They weren't formally educated, but they were street smart. There was nothing to compare with a local diner. They weren't franchises, they were personal, they had character. They were places where you could sit down with people of all ages and have meaningful conversations with a real exchange of ideas based upon years of experience. They were places where the younger generations would learn from their elders. There was a genuine admiration and respect for those who were older and wiser. Unfortunately, that diner culture has been lost in today's society.

Rick stopped by his mom's house and looked up the number to the Warren County Sheriff's Department. He had driven by there for years, but he had only been inside on a couple of occasions back when he worked as a policeman for the village of Lake George during his summer break from college. He dialed the number.

"Deputy James here. How may I help you?" said a clear voice on the other end of the line.

"Good morning," said Rick. "Is the sheriff in?"

"Sheriff Hollister will be in by ten. May I be of assistance?" Deputy James asked.

"I wanted to talk with the sheriff concerning Colonel Wayne Abshier."

"Are you a friend of the family?" asked James.

"No, I'm not. I work with Homeland Security and am interested in the reason behind his apparent suicide," responded Rick.

"*Apparent* suicide?" questioned the deputy. "Do you have reason to believe his death may not have been a suicide?" he added.

Rick realized that his choice of the word *apparent* triggered the wrong response and a whole lot of questions he didn't want to address. He didn't want to be interrogated.

"I didn't mean to imply that his death was not a suicide. I am more interested in the reason why he decided to take his own life," Rick responded, trying to distance himself from the unintended implication.

Deputy James didn't say anything for several seconds.

"And you're with Homeland Security?"

Rick wasn't sure if the deputy's response was a statement or a question.

"I am actually under contract with the Department of Homeland Security. I believe I may have information that would be of interest to your investigation," Rick said in an attempt to stimulate James's interest.

"What investigation?" he asked.

Rick realized rapidly that his conversation was going nowhere. For a second, he visualized Barney Fife looking for his bullet.

"There may be a connection between Colonel Abshier and a case we are working on in Florida," said Rick.

Deputy James was obviously mulling over the additional information. Neither of them said anything for what seemed like a very long time.

"I'll pencil you in for a meeting with the sheriff at ten fifteen," said James.

"Thank you. I will be there," responded Rick.

Rick hung up before Deputy James could say anything else. The deputy was either very clever or dumb as dirt. Rick decided to go with clever. He looked at his watch and realized that he needed to hurry a bit to make it to the sheriff's department by ten fifteen. He made sure that he had his Homeland Security ID with him and then headed out the door.

Rick took Quaker Road around Glens Falls and then turned north on Route 9. Not a whole lot had changed over the years. However, there was a lot more traffic than he had remembered. He wondered where all these people came from. Where did they work? The job outlook in upstate New York wasn't good. Rick entered the Warren County

Sheriff's Department at ten minutes after ten. A young deputy sat behind the desk. He reminded Rick somewhat of Roland Carpenter.

"Deputy James?" said Rick.

"Yes, you must be Mr. Morgan. Would you please sign in? And I need to see your ID," said James with his best official voice.

Rick took his ID from his wallet and handed it to the deputy. He then signed in as requested and watched Deputy James as he seemed to read every word on the ID. Rick wondered if this was the first Homeland Security ID the young deputy had ever seen. He didn't want to embarrass him by asking.

"May I also see your driver's license?" asked James.

"Of course," said Rick as he took it and his military ID from his wallet.

"Thank you," said James as he rapidly scanned both the Virginia driver's license and Rick's military ID.

"Thank you Commander. My brother is a lieutenant stationed aboard the Roosevelt," he said proudly as he buzzed the sheriff.

"Sheriff, Mr. Morgan is here to see you," he said into the small intercom.

"Send him in," came an immediate response. It seemed rehearsed.

Rick entered the sheriff's office. Sheriff Wade Hollister sat behind a large wooden desk that was well maintained. Nothing was out of place. As Rick walked in, Sheriff Hollister rose from his chair and walked around the desk. He was a tall man, probably somewhere in his late fifties. His hair was thick and nearly all gray. He obviously worked out as evidenced by his posture and firm handshake. He had the wrists and forearms of a lumberjack.

"Mr. Morgan. I seem to remember you from a long time ago. Fort Edward High School, right?" he asked.

Either the sheriff did remember Rick's name, or he had done his homework. Rick wasn't sure which it was. He knew that the name Hollister wasn't familiar to him.

"You have me somewhat at a disadvantage. I am afraid I don't recall *your* name," said Rick trying to place Sheriff Hollister.

"You wouldn't remember me. I was a couple of years behind you. I went to Saint Mary's for a couple of years, and then our family moved to the western part of the state. My dad got a pretty nice job with Kodak. If I remember correctly, you went to college on a track scholarship."

"That was a long time ago Sheriff," said Rick, surprised that the sheriff remembered. "And where did you go to college?"

"I started out at Syracuse on a football scholarship then had the misfortune of cracking a couple of vertebrae in my neck. That ended my football career...and scholarship. Ended up at Adirondack Community College and got an associate degree. Met and married a girl from Luzerne, and here I am many years later."

"Well Sheriff, you can't beat the area," responded Rick. "And it looks like you have done well."

"So why is Homeland Security interested in Colonel Abshier's suicide? And we have concluded that it was indeed a suicide," responded Hollister, leaving no question that his investigation was thorough and over.

Again, Rick regretted using the word *apparent.*

"We are more interested in the reason behind the suicide. I understand that he was a lottery winner," said Rick.

"That's correct," responded Hollister.

"Do you know if he had received his winnings?" asked Rick.

"We know that he *didn't.* It appears that he was the victim of some sort of lottery scam."

"Do you know if he had to send money to secure his winnings?" asked Rick.

"We understand that he transferred two hundred and fifty thousand dollars to an offshore account," responded Sheriff Hollister.

"Do you know where?"

"The Bahamas," responded Hollister.

CHAPTER EIGHT

Rick Morgan drove into his mom's driveway. He pulled all the way forward so another car could park behind him and not block the sidewalk. He wasn't expecting anybody; he just pulled all the way forward out of habit. The meeting with Sheriff Hollister had gone well. Rick was convinced that both Wayne Abshier and John Kilday were not only victims of a lottery scam, but also they were victims of the same lottery scam. He was also convinced that there were probably many more individuals who had suffered similar fates. What he wasn't sure of was exactly how the two were connected. There were certainly striking similarities. Both men were retired military officers, both were elderly, both were widowers, both were living alone and both were quite well to do. At this point, any pursuit beyond finding John Kilday would be at the discretion of Carl Peterson. He would be the one to determine whether or not the team would try to identify the mechanism used to select these potential marks.

Being a former company owner, Rick knew the importance of marketing, and especially marketing one's self to stay employed. He certainly didn't need the work, but the whole idea of the chase as well as creating business opportunities, was still very exciting. Besides, Rick had a whole team dependent upon him to provide those opportunities. However, the more he thought about the lottery scam, the more it upset him that someone would prey upon senior citizens, taking advantage of their circumstances and their frailty. And if they were specifically targeting retired military officers, that really pissed him off.

He knew that in order to employ The Peterson Group's time and resources, he would need Carl's permission. He also knew that it would be relatively easy to convince Carl. Carl was always looking for opportunities. Rick picked up his cell phone and dialed The Peterson Group office. Elaine Drew answered the call almost immediately. The caller ID indicated that it was Rick Morgan. It brought a smile to her face.

"Good afternoon Rick," she said in a cheerful manner, indicating that she genuinely enjoyed her job.

"Good morning Elaine. How are you doing?" asked Rick.

"I'm doing well. How is Lake George?" she asked. "I haven't been in that part of the country in years. I assume it's still just as beautiful."

"The lake is still pristine," responded Rick. "You should plan a trip. This is a great time of year to be in this area. Last week was the hot air balloon festival, and this week there are antique cars everywhere," he added.

"Bill would love the cars," she responded.

Bill was Elaine's husband of thirty-two years. He was a retired air force colonel and was now flying for Southwest Airlines. He was the perfect complement to Elaine Drew. Elaine didn't say anything for several seconds. She must have been thinking about a vacation. She came back on the line. The tone of her voice suggested that her focus had shifted momentarily.

"I assume you want to speak with Carl?" she asked as if she just remembered that Rick was on the other end of the line.

"Yes I would. Is he in?"

"He is indeed. Hold on a second Rick."

Elaine put Rick on hold. Mozart's "Minuet in D" was playing. Rick smiled to himself. He was certain that Carl Peterson had hand-selected Mozart as background music. Carl did have a touch of class, which was occasionally interrupted by forays into the world of the classic rube. Carl was definitely a study in contrasts. He really was a great guy and a lifelong friend of Rick's.

"Rick, how's it going?" asked Carl as he came on the line.

"It's going well. By the way, I talked with Sheriff Hollister this morning concerning the Abshier suicide. He wasn't just a winner in any lottery. I am convinced he was a winner in John Kilday's lottery," said Rick.

"How can you be sure about that?" asked Carl.

"After I spoke to the sheriff, I stopped by Glens Falls National Bank. Abshier transferred the exact amount of money as did Kilday to an account in the Bahamas. The funds were transferred from his savings account on September twentieth, which fits the timeline."

"Were you able to obtain the offshore account number by chance?" asked Carl doubtingly. He knew that Rick would have tried to get the number, but there was a near impossible chance the bank would have given up that information, even to a representative of Homeland Security, especially one without a court order.

"As you can guess, it's not that easy," responded Rick. "It's going to take more than my credentials and a lot more evidence to obtain a court order to get that information. The good news is that in order to open an offshore account, certified proof of identity is required from the owner of the account, including a passport copy certified by an officer of the bank."

"So, with a little horsepower, we may be able to find out who the account owner is," said Carl.

"You would think so. But we would be dealing with the Bahamas. The whole idea of an offshore account is anonymity. Hell, even the President is getting stonewalled trying to get a list of offshore accounts being used by U.S. companies. *Legally*, it won't be that easy."

Carl completely understood what Rick meant by emphasizing the word legally. If the situation dictated, neither Carl nor Rick would have any trouble using whatever means were necessary to gain the information they needed.

"I understand what you're saying," said Carl. "So I take it you believe this scam goes much further than John Kilday and this fellow, Abshier?"

"I can build any number of scenarios in my mind. Has Roland's search revealed any similar cases?" asked Rick.

"I just put him on it a couple hours ago," responded Carl. "Knowing Roland, it won't take him very long."

"I would bet a year's pay that he will locate at least a dozen more individuals who have been victimized by the same lottery scam. At two hundred and fifty thousand a pop, the money adds up quickly," responded Rick.

Carl was quiet for a few seconds. Numbers were rolling around in his head. All of a sudden, he broke the silence. He must have had an epiphany.

"You know Rick, this could be really big. There may be a considerable amount of money involved. It just dawned on me that whoever is behind this has used both the mail and the Internet, which makes it a federal case. That means there would be a fifteen percent finder's fee, which could be quite significant," said Carl. "Not to mention that we would be doing a good deed," he quickly added.

Rick agreed that the amount could be staggering. He could almost hear the little cha-ching registers going off in Carl's head.

"Have you located the actual whereabouts of Kilday?" asked Rick, slightly shifting gears.

"Yes, I meant to tell you. Roland sent a picture of him to the authorities in the Bahamas. We just got a call from them saying that they have an unidentified individual in the hospital fitting Kilday's description. They are quite sure that it is him. They are supposed to fax me his finger prints."

"Do they have any idea what happened to him?" asked Rick.

"They believe he was mugged. Sounds like he was really worked over. He has amnesia. He doesn't even know his own name or why he is in the Bahamas," responded Carl.

"What's the prognosis?" asked Rick.

"It's too early to tell at this point. They are trying to stabilize his condition right now," said Carl.

"Do you want me or one of my team members to go over and talk with the authorities?"

"I'm going to give my nephew a call first and see how he wants to handle this. I'm worried he will want to head to the Bahamas. I just don't want him to get into any trouble. He can be a little hot headed at times. You know these type-A personalities. I think it would be best if we can get Kilday back into the states as soon as possible. I'm sure it will depend on his condition. If Mike and Nancy do decide to go, I may need to tag along. The last thing Nancy needs is for Mike to be out of control."

"Your going is probably a wise thing to do. Let me know what Roland comes up with. I'm sure he is going to find a few more victims," said Rick.

"If he does, I will approach Homeland Security. I don't think I'll have a problem convincing them to provide some additional funding to investigate. Just in case, will you develop a draft delivery order for John Savage's signature?"

"I can do that," responded Rick. "Carl, I need to go to the memorial service tonight, but I am planning on heading to D.C. early tomorrow. My gut tells me that this lottery scam is much bigger than we think."

"I suspect you are correct. I'll give you a call as soon as Roland has something. Talk with you later Rick."

Rick hung up and thought more about the scam. Money always seemed to be at the root of evil. There were many famous quotes about money. P.T. Barnum said, "A fool and his money will soon part." But the one quote that caught Rick's attention the most, and the one that made the greatest impression, was a quote by Henry Fielding. Fielding said, "Make money your God, and it will plague you like the devil." Money could fund a lot of wonderful things, but it could also provide the fuel for evil. Rick wondered what the money was being used for—life's circus, or evil deeds.

Rick looked at his watch. It was nearly 1400 hours. He would go downtown, grab a late lunch and then start the difficult process of going through the last of the memories stored in his mom's basement. He had already put one box aside that contained pictures of his dad's flight squadron in France during World War I. Rick's father was with the first group of American Army pilots to go over and fly alongside the famed Lafayette Escadrille. His dad flew Spads.

As a young boy, Rick was fascinated by his dad's stories. He would sit and listen to his dad for hours. Sadly, many of his dad's letters were stored in cardboard boxes in the basement, most of which did not survive the occasional flooding that plagued many of the basements that were common in that part of the country. As Rick looked at the pictures, he wished he had taken better care of his father's mementos. It was something he wished he had thought about sooner; unfortunately, it was too late now.

The process of going through a lifetime of treasures was difficult at best. It was impossible to keep everything. One of the pictures caught his eye. His father was standing with three other intrepid aviators. He turned the picture over. There was no writing on the back. He wished he knew their names. As he looked at the photo, he realized how much he resembled his dad. His father was a great influence in his life.

Rick felt his eyes begin to well up as he became painfully aware of how fast time goes by. What he would give to have just one more minute with his dad, to say the things he wished he had said and apologize for some of the things that he actually did say. As he carefully placed the photo in a manila envelope, his cell phone rang. It was Carl Peterson.

"Hi Carl," answered Rick somewhat unenthusiastically.

"Rick, you okay? You sound a little down," responded Carl.

"Sorry buddy. I was just going through my mom and dad's things, and it brought back a lot of good memories. I thought this would be a lot easier, but it isn't."

Carl didn't say anything for a minute or so.

"It's never easy pal," responded Carl. "How's your mom doing?" he asked.

"She is doing okay but certainly needs around-the-clock care. There is no way she can stay here alone," added Rick.

Neither man spoke for several seconds. Carl broke the silence.

"I do have some news from Roland that I thought you would want to hear," offered Carl.

"How many?" asked Rick, knowing the news Carl was about to deliver.

"Seventeen so far in addition to Kilday and Abshier. All were retired military officers, widowers, wealthy and supposedly winners of an international lottery."

"I'll head out in the morning," responded Rick as he placed the picture of his father in the box that he would take with him.

CHAPTER NINE

Marcie Decker looked at the departure board. There was a flight leaving for Tampa, Florida, at 1920 hours. She checked in with the ticket agent who reluctantly informed her that the flight was already full and there was another flight attendant looking to claim the jump seat. He then quickly offered to pencil her in on the morning flight that was scheduled for ten o'clock. The agent, a young man by the name of Orlando, wanted desperately to accommodate her wishes, but it wasn't going to be possible. He had seen her on several occasions. He wanted to strike up a conversation, but the opportunity never presented itself. Besides, she didn't seem at all interested, especially this evening. Marcie had just arrived from her Beirut flight. She was tired, and she really wanted to get to Tampa.

Her flight from Beirut, Lebanon had been fairly routine, until they landed in Germany where two U.S. State Department employees sauntered on board. It was evident they thought very highly of themselves. The younger guy wasn't quite as obnoxious as the older one. Both had on wedding bands that seemed to mean nothing to either of them, and both already had way too much to drink. Marcie was somewhat surprised and disappointed to see that they had first class tickets. She was hoping one of the other flight attendants would have to deal with them. Unfortunately, they were going to be her problem.

The old guy hit on her every chance he got. She could feel his eyes burning a hole in her butt. His contrived laugh was loud and sickening. A couple of times she wanted to stop and address his off-color remarks. It was difficult, but she had maintained her decorum. Neither of them was worth the trouble or the meaningless reprimand she would be subjected to. She thought to herself that if these two mooks were examples of the best the government had to offer, it was no wonder the U.S. was in the state that it was. While she enjoyed her job, Marcie was thankful when the flight was over.

It was her second year as an overseas flight attendant. She had been with the airlines for a little over eight years. Marcie Decker had graduated from Emory University with a degree in communications. After a bit of soul searching, she went on to get her master's degree in political science with a concentration in Middle Eastern politics.

In her final year at Emory, Marcie entertained serious thoughts of becoming a news anchor until she learned about market share and that she wouldn't start at the top. She wasn't impressed with any of the areas of the country that were currently hiring. She went on three interviews and soon decided that being a news anchor wasn't all that it was cracked up to be. She didn't mind having to do research, preparing her own articles and working all hours of the day and night, but putting up with some of the women bosses that she encountered would be too much to bear.

Marcie had always wanted to travel. The airlines certainly offered the best opportunity to see the world. Even though the airlines weren't as particular concerning looks as they used to be, at five foot nine inches, one hundred and thirty-six pounds, dark hair and midnight blue eyes, she would easily make a lasting first impression. Marcie Decker had movie star looks, a wonderful smile, and the posture and grace of a princess. Although there were procedures to be followed, she was basically hired on the spot. So much for the feminist movement.

This particular overseas run was popular with many of the flight attendants. She had filled in for the past six months, but now it was her regular run. Although it was a long working flight, the time off between flights was well worth the inconvenience. She informed the ticket agent she would wait a little longer just in case something opened up. She headed to Starbucks for a refreshment. She ordered a tall skinny caramel macchiato and blueberry muffin. The muffin was still warm and not one bit crumbly, just the way she liked it.

As she sat there, she thought about Lebanon. Beirut was a beautiful city. At one time it was considered the Paris of the Middle East. The people were extremely friendly and the city was actually safer than Washington, D.C., even with Hezbollah in control. Marcie Decker could easily pass as a Middle Easterner as long as she didn't have to carry on a conversation. As she sat in Starbucks enjoying the caramel macchiato, her cell phone rang. She looked at the caller ID. It was Tarek. She hadn't planned on calling him until she knew that she would be on a flight.

"Masaa el kheer," she answered, using one of only several Arabic phrases she had memorized.

"Kaifa haloki, eshtaqto elaiki katheeran," responded Tarek as he laughed, knowing that she had absolutely no idea what he had just said.

"Adrusu allughah al arabia mundu shahr," she responded slowly, pausing as she tried to think of and pronounce each word.

"Hada shay'un Jameel," Tarek responded.

"Okay, you win. I have no idea what you just said."

"I said that I am so happy you are almost home and that I miss you. You told me that you have been learning Arabic for a month and I replied that that was good."

"I'll never learn this language," she interrupted.

"I will teach you French. Most Lebanese speak French anyway. It is easier and certainly more romantic," responded Tarek. "How is my cousin Rasheed? Were you able to see him?" he asked, changing the subject.

"I spent a few hours with him. He is doing well. I think he has a new girlfriend. Her name is Rolla."

"Rolla. Ah yes, Rolla. She is actually an old girlfriend. They grew up together in Zahlé," responded Tarek. "Did you have an opportunity to give him the book?" he added.

"I did, and this time he had one for you. He said it was a collectible. It does look very old. The cover is quite fragile."

"He always loved books and has wanted me to collect them for years. I enjoy them but really have no interest in starting a collection that I couldn't possibly afford to maintain. Did you get a flight?" asked Tarek.

"Not yet. I may not be able to fly out until morning," the disappointment in her voice was evident. "I am looking forward to seeing you habibi," she added, trying to cheer herself up a little.

"I will be there whenever you arrive," responded Tarek.

Marcie smiled as she ended the call. She didn't make the evening flight.

GLENS FALLS, NEW YORK
1900 HOURS

The memorial service for Rick's first cousin, Maria, went very well. The church was full, and the minister said all the right things. There were quite a few relatives and friends of the family that Rick hadn't seen in years. He recognized most of the relatives but only knew a handful of Maria's newer friends. Some of them had aged very well and some hadn't. It made him wonder how he looked to them. Actually, he knew the answer. Rick was in very good shape overall and looked ten years younger than his actual age. Unfortunately, his knees hadn't faired so well. They were a dead giveaway. He was beginning to walk like an old man, and he knew it. He tried to hide his discomfort but to no avail. As he looked around the room, he realized that the ones who hadn't aged very well were the ones who had started smoking and drinking at a very young age. They were the ones who were "more mature" than the rest of the kids. Rick had tried a cigarette once when he was twelve years old. Once was enough.

Maria's father, George, was Rick's only living uncle. Although an uncle by marriage, Rick had always considered him a blood relative and was very close to him. He would always make it a point to see him when he made the trip north. Considering the situation, George was holding up quite well, although they both agreed that parents should never outlive their children

By 2300 hours that evening, Rick had put together the delivery order for Homeland Security. The purpose was to investigate a lottery scam that was potentially providing funding for terrorist activities. It was a wild guess at best, but it didn't matter. Rick was sure it would trigger additional funding.

Homeland Security had more money than it knew what to do with and any viable, well-written, unsolicited proposal would most likely be approved to the benefit of both Homeland Security and The Peterson Group. Rick chose his words carefully and included several fairly generic tasks. After reading it over a couple times for accuracy, he emailed it to Carl Peterson. Carl would send it on to John Savage who would add his signature and send it back to The Peterson Group. The start date would be upon acceptance of the delivery order by the contractor. Rick estimated that the job required a project engineer, three subject matter experts and one senior analyst. Rick made sure the qualifications for the subject matter expert were very specific, and in this case, only Rick's team would be qualified to execute this particular delivery order. He estimated that the project would be completed in two months. There would be no competition. It was important to know how to play the game in the government contracting world.

Rick sat back looking at the screen on his laptop. His desktop background was a picture taken from the balcony outside of the Commander's Palace restaurant in Destin, Florida. He was about to give Lynn a call when his cell phone rang. It was Carl Peterson.

"Carl, what's going on my friend? Isn't this a little late for you?"

"Actually it is. I was just going to turn in when I got your email with the delivery order."

"What do you think?" asked Rick.

"You're the expert. It looks fine to me. You seem to have made the necessary connection to a possible terrorist event quite well. I have already forwarded it to Savage. I'm sure he'll turn it around before noon tomorrow. He was looking to spend more money anyway. He may actually want to increase it to a six-month effort."

"That would be a stretch," Rick responded.

"Well, I wouldn't want to turn it down. I'm sure you could think of something to keep your team occupied. By the way, my nephew is headed to Miami. Kilday has been transferred to a hospital in South Miami, so I won't have to chaperone a visit to the Bahamas after all."

"Well that's good news. How is Kilday doing? Has he regained his memory?" questioned Rick.

"Still no memory improvement, and he's not out of the woods at this point. It's good that he is back in the states and that Mike and Nancy will be with him."

"I'm sorry to hear that he is not doing well," offered Rick.

"Also, I have a meeting tomorrow morning with the ambassador at the Bahamian Embassy on Massachusetts Avenue," said Carl.

"Do you really think the ambassador will be of any help?"

"I'm sure that he won't be. I just wanted to get his view for the record," responded Carl. "Are you still planning on heading this way tomorrow?" he added.

"That I am. I want to get together with Carlos and Ann and start working on a plan to find out who is behind this lottery scam," said Rick. "My gut tells me that it will take more than just a cordial visit to the Bahamas," he added.

CHAPTER TEN

Washington, D.C.
October 9, 2012
Tuesday
0900 Hours

Carl Peterson arrived at the Bahamian Embassy on Massachusetts Avenue at 0900 hours. He was scheduled to meet with the ambassador at 0915. As he walked toward the office, his inner voice was telling him that the meeting would probably be a waste of time. He had met with numerous State Department officials and country representatives over the years. Only the Israelis delivered on their promises.

He was convinced that the Bahamian Ambassador, like most diplomats, would glad-hand him. As he approached the entrance, he found himself mouthing the words, "We'll look into the matter and get back to you." He looked around to see if anyone had heard him. There was no one close by. He slowed his step and considered turning around, but he had made the trip from Old Town in stop and go traffic. Might as well give it a shot old boy, he thought to himself. He smoothed his shirt, adjusted his tie and entered the office building. Who knows, maybe this guy would be different.

The outer office was neat, clean and typical. The decor included a map of the Bahamas, several detailed pictures of the Atlantis Resort, a Bahamian flag and a large overbearing portrait of the Right Honorable Hubert A. Ingraham. There were the usual magazines and brochures that could be found in most offices throughout the D.C. area.

The receptionist looked up as Carl approached. She gave him a momentary glance from head to toe. Her eyes darted back and forth.

He was flattered but knew the eyeball frisk had nothing to do with his physique. He had purposely left his shoulder holster, Beretta and extra fifteen shot clip locked up in the car along with his leg backup. Her smile was genuine, revealing a set of perfectly matched white teeth that had probably paid for her dentist's swimming pool. Before he had a chance to speak, she introduced herself.

"Good morning Mr. Peterson, I'm Ms. Anderson. The ambassador is expecting you. Would you be so kind to sign our guest log?"

Carl was not surprised. They had done their homework and checked him out. She probably had a folder in her desk drawer with his picture, biography and a list of The Peterson Group's current contracts. The obvious holes in his biography would probably draw some attention. His company's history would give some indication of his past and certainly provide a trained eye enough insight to fill in the holes. They would assume he was formerly CIA. That would be a good assumption. He knew from experience that it was always better to err on the high side.

"Thank you Ms. Anderson," Carl responded returning her smile. He was the first to sign the log sheet for the day.

As Carl took one of the chairs facing the entrance to the ambassador's office, Ms. Anderson came around from behind her desk and asked if he would like anything to drink. She was a striking woman. Her perfectly tailored black pinstripe suit accentuated her tall, slender figure. Carl could tell that she worked out. The only jewelry she wore was a small gold chain around her neck. There was something on the chain but it was mostly hidden behind her blouse. Her hair was jet black and pulled back into a stylish knot that was held in place by two large knitting needle sticks. He was all too familiar with the sticks. To an untrained eye they looked to be merely a hair ornament. Carl knew their true purpose.

Carl briefly had a vision of Ms. Anderson fending off two would-be attackers, kicking them in the groin and using the sticks for their designed purpose. It brought a smile to his face. She smiled back waiting for an answer. She suspected that he had other things on his mind. Most men did when they first encountered Ms. Anderson.

She wore little makeup. Her perfume was subtle, semi-sweet and just strong enough to bring him back from his foray into the world of Cynthia Rothrock. He almost forgot that she had asked if he would like something to drink. He recovered from his daydream.

"Napoleon brandy would be nice, but I will settle for a cup of coffee with cream and two sugars," he said, looking for a reaction.

She suppressed what he assumed, or hoped, would be a smile, nodded and walked over to the single cup coffee maker. He couldn't help but continue to notice that she was indeed quite fit. She had well-defined calves and slender hips that added just enough flare to her suit coat that invited a closer look. She certainly seemed to be out of place as a receptionist for the Bahamian Embassy...Russian Embassy maybe, but not the Bahamas. Anderson couldn't possibly be her real name. What was she doing as a receptionist, Carl thought to himself. It was probably the influence of all the James Bond movies. The ambassador probably fancied himself as some kind of secret agent. Hell, they were all spies.

She delivered the coffee, smiled without saying anything and returned to her position behind the desk. She was about to pick up her phone when she noticed that line one was in use.

"Mr. Elliott is on the line. He is normally quite punctual," she said almost apologetically. "If there is anything else I can do or get for you, please let me know," her smile was not forced. "It will be just a minute," she added.

"Thank you. I'm fine," he responded. His head was telling him that he was still in his forties, but his body was telling him otherwise.

Rick Morgan made the trip from Fort Edward, New York, to Washington, D.C., in less than eight hours. Although he had cut his trip short, he managed to pack several boxes. By the New Jersey Turnpike he had become accustomed to their musty smell. The trip had given him enough time to think more about the lottery scam, which had already claimed at least nineteen victims. There were likely more. At two hundred and fifty thousand a pop, the loot was substantial. It certainly provided enough incentive for someone to take the inherent risk. It was hard for him to believe that so many seasoned individuals could, or would, fall for such an obvious scam.

By now, Roland had undoubtedly completed a thorough analysis of the victims. Rick was sure that Roland's findings would be no surprise and most likely reveal a consistent profile of widowers who had lost their spouse within the last year or so. They were certainly vulnerable, would make easy targets and would be too embarrassed to let anyone know that they had been duped.

Rick turned into the parking garage off Prince Street and parked in one of The Peterson Group's visitor spots. Carl's black Escalade was also parked in one of the visitor's spaces. The CEO's space was empty. Rick chuckled to himself and shook his head. Carl was a trip. Whoever he thought he was fooling had to be blind not to notice the personalized plates that clearly spelled out "B1U3SKY" even though the "L" was a "1" and the "E" was a "3."

Only three other people in the world knew the real story behind Carl's nickname, *Blue Sky*. All three were presently working for The Peterson Group and were sworn to absolute secrecy under penalty of death. Regardless, they would never let him live it down. While the teasing certainly had exaggerated the events of the actual story, the fact that Carl had never married only compounded the mystery.

The walk across Prince Street to The Peterson Group office was just long enough to work out the kinks in his lower back and loosen the stiffness in Rick's left knee. He had his right knee replaced the year before, and it made a drastic difference. Unfortunately, it seemed to magnify the pain he had in his other knee. As soon as he entered the office, Elaine Drew spotted him.

"Well good morning Mr. Morgan!" she called out in a playful tone as she turned and walked toward him. She was holding a cup of coffee and a blueberry bagel with honey-walnut cream cheese spread evenly on the pieces.

"And good morning to you, Ms. Drew. How did you know?" he reciprocated her playfulness as he made a hand gesture toward the coffee and bagel that he knew belonged to Carl.

She smiled and offered them. He politely waved her off, but she could tell that he really wanted them.

"Carl wanted me to let him know as soon as you arrived."

"Please," she said as she again offered the coffee and bagel. "I can make another one for Mr. Peterson."

"Thank you Elaine," Rick responded. "The bagel does look inviting, but would you mind making another cup of coffee with just a little half and half? You can save that one for Carl. He never did get away from the two sugars."

As soon as Rick sat down, Roland Carpenter walked up with his laptop tucked under his left arm. He had a couple of cables in his left hand and a newly opened bottle of Fiji water in his right. Rick looked down at Roland's penny loafers. Still no socks. Rick and Carl had a bet as to when it would be cold enough to force Roland to wear socks. The year before, Roland started wearing cowboy boots so the bet carried over into the New Year. Neither of them wanted to ask him if socks were hiding under those boots. It would spoil the bet.

"Good morning Mr. Morgan," said Roland.

It would always be "Mr. Morgan." Rick had given up a long time ago trying to get Roland to call him Rick. Actually, it was refreshing.

"Good morning Roland," responded Rick as he pointed to the computer. "By any chance are you here to brief Carl on the lottery scam?"

"That would be correct Mr. Morgan," replied Roland.

"How many victims so far?" Rick asked as he took a bite of the bagel.

"Twenty-six and counting. Certainly more than needed for a valid analysis," responded Roland just as Elaine Drew returned with Rick's coffee.

"Good, you're both here. I'll let Carl know," she said as she handed the coffee to Rick.

Rick stood up and he and Roland followed Elaine to her desk. She knocked quietly on the door to Carl's inner office and opened it slightly.

"Carl, Rick and Roland are here to see you," she announced in a quiet voice as she walked in with the coffee and bagel.

Rick and Roland could hear Carl tell her to send them right in. Rick held the door and ushered Roland in ahead of him. Roland nodded to Carl and without a word went straight to the conference table and began setting up the laptop. As Rick entered, Carl was already around in front of his desk with an outstretched hand. He and Rick shook hands and then embraced.

"Sorry to hear about your cousin," Carl said with genuine compassion. "I assume that this was unexpected?"

Rick hesitated before answering.

"She was my age. She had diabetes but never took care of herself," responded Rick. "I guess you can say it was a bit of a surprise, but unfortunately, not entirely unexpected."

Both men remained silent for several seconds.

"So what do we have here Carl?" said Rick breaking the silence.

Carl motioned for them to sit at the table. Roland already had the laptop up and running. The cover page on the screen had the Homeland Security logo in the upper left hand corner. The Peterson Group logo was in the upper right hand corner. The project was titled, "LOTTERY SCAM." Mr. Rick Morgan was identified as the project manager. His name was underlined. Carl nodded and Roland commenced the briefing.

"Gentlemen, first of all this analysis is skewed, but not flawed. It is based upon the known suicide victims that had participated in the alleged lottery scam."

This was the first time any of them had used the word alleged when referring to the scam. Carl smiled at Rick and interrupted Roland.

"You're watching too much TV Roland," he said with a laugh. "Alleged?" he said again as he suppressed a smile.

Roland made a surrendering gesture and continued on with the brief.

"So far we have identified twenty-six victims. All of them are between the ages of sixty-one and eighty-seven. All of them have been widowed in the last two years. All were retired military, and all were officers," he continued.

The brief went on for another fifteen minutes. When he was finished, Carl was first to speak. Rick hardly said anything throughout the brief. He had been in his listening mode and making notes.

"So from what you have presented, you believe there are more victims that are alive, and for whatever reason, have not come forward?" said Carl, leaning forward in his chair and placing both elbows on the table. He rested his chin on his thumbs, a gesture that he always did when he was fully engaged.

"There are undoubtedly more victims," responded Roland.

"How do you suppose the scammers identified their marks?" Rick asked as he also leaned forward. He had already formulated a couple of scenarios in his mind.

Roland smiled, knowing full well that Rick could easily figure several ways to identify the marks.

"I looked at how I would have done it. There are several ways. However, I believe the fastest way would be to hack into the Defense Enrollment Eligibility Reporting System known as DEERS. The system includes over twenty million records," Roland responded.

"That makes a lot of sense," offered Rick. "That would require an accomplished hacker…or someone on the inside."

CHAPTER ELEVEN

Flight 1249 departed as scheduled. The flight was almost full. Fortunately for Marcie there were three vacant seats aboard the Airbus 320, which meant that she didn't have to sit in the jump seat. There was one window seat and two aisle seats available. She had taken one of the aisle seats. The army ranger next to her had hardly moved when she sat down. He appeared to be sound asleep. His tan beret was pulled down over his eyes. It was obvious that he really didn't want to be disturbed. That was fine with Marcie Decker.

As the flight reached altitude, the ranger made a little snoring sound, which startled him and caused him to awake momentarily. He made a slight adjustment and seemed to fall right back to sleep. She gave him the once over. He was young. It appeared he hadn't shaved for several days. His uniform was neat, clean and only slightly wrinkled. Unfortunately, his deodorant had failed somewhere over the Atlantic. Marcie smiled. She had almost become immune to the myriad of smells aboard commercial aircraft, especially aircraft traveling to and from the Middle East. Couscous and a curious reluctance to use antiperspirant were two of the major contributing factors. Some things would never change.

Marcie put her head back and slowly closed her eyes. Overseas flights were exhausting. She would never get used to the time zone changes. She had tried melatonin but to no avail. However, she did find the resulting dreams to be interesting to say the least.

She smiled to herself as she thought about Tarek and their chance meeting at an Atlanta Thrashers game. She had been introduced to hockey while she was a student at Emory University. While she was certainly a Thrashers fan, she had also become a die-hard Alex Ovechkin fan. The only problem was that he played for the Washington Capitals. She always routed for the Thrashers unless the Capitals were in town. Then it was Alex all the way. Her friends would, for the most part, ignore her loyalty transgression.

She was at an Atlanta home game when she met Tarek Haddad. It was his very first hockey game, and he just happened to sit on the aisle seat in her row. After two periods and several adjustments as Marcie maneuvered past him, he had become very much aware of her perfectly curved backside. He was able to make eye contact at one point but found himself tongue-tied when she lingered and looked back at him a little longer than he had expected.

She had deep blue eyes that seemed to pierce his soul. In the third period, while trying to reach her seat just before the game continued, she caught the toe of her right foot on the seat in front of Tarek. Instinctively, he caught her as she fell. He got a full handful of Marcie Decker. She was definitely all woman. And that was all the courage Tarek Haddad needed. They have been together ever since.

The flight was uneventful and landed twelve minutes ahead of schedule. As the seat belt sign went off, along with the corresponding bell, the young ranger immediately awakened and unfastened his seat belt. He looked over at Marcie, smiled and looked out of the window as if to evaluate his surroundings and give instructions. He looked back at Marcie who was now standing in the aisle. She looked back at the ranger. He probably was younger than he looked, but his eyes told a different story. In the past year she had seen too many soldiers who were too young to drink a beer but old enough to lose a limb or their life in a war that seemed, to her, to be quite senseless. She knew the Middle East…and more importantly, she knew their politics. Things would never change. What a waste, she thought to herself.

She held her position and let the ranger out as the line began to move. He was a bit shorter than she had imagined and walked with a slight limp. Another causality of war that would soon be forgotten.

As she entered the gate area, she was met by Tarek and a large bouquet of her favorite flowers. He kissed her on both cheeks. She shut her eyes and imagined more than a kiss. On the way out of the gate area, he asked if she had the book.

CHAPTER TWELVE

Carl Peterson pushed himself away from the small conference table, got up and walked slowly to his desk. His right ankle made several popping sounds. His days of sneaking up on someone were long over. Rick and Roland continued to discuss the results of the lottery scam analysis. Carl listened as Rick continued to question Roland and watched as Rick carefully wrote some more notes into the small notebook he carried in his back pocket. Carl picked up the phone and told Elaine that they were about to finish the meeting, and if she didn't have anything pressing, she was free to close up shop. She asked Carl if there was anything else he needed, and if not, she would be leaving in a few minutes.

Elaine Drew knew more about Carl Peterson and his operation than anyone. The only thing she didn't know was the mystery behind his nickname, *Blue Sky*. She tried to trick Rick into telling her the origin, but it didn't work. Rick was a vault. Carl hung up the phone and sat back in his swivel chair. As he put his full weight into the chair, it went back just far enough to startle him. He threw out his arms in a reflexive action to balance himself. He made a slight noise that caused Rick and Roland to look in his direction. They all laughed. He would never get used to that chair, but he would never consider buying a new one.

Although he appeared to be listening to Rick and Roland, his mind had wandered to the meeting he had had earlier that morning with the Bahamian Ambassador. In particular, he thought about Ms. Anderson. He felt a slight twinge in his stomach. The little voice in his head kept telling him there was much more to Ms. Anderson than met the eye. He had a feeling about her.

Over the years he had run into women like her. His gut was always right. She was dangerous…in more ways than one. As Rick and Roland continued to talk, Carl slowly turned his chair as if expecting it to fall off its pedestal. He retrieved two Montecristos from the Gondolier humidor that was positioned on the left side of the Italian credenza behind his desk. The cigars and humidor were a gift from an old friend who was still making trips to Havana…mostly at night. The humidor was next to a five by seven picture of four young intrepid CIA agents. Carl paused and looked fondly at the picture. All wore camouflage, their faces modestly covered with light green and black leaf-shaped patterns. Carl was on the left. Rick Morgan stood next to him. Anya Peters stood next to Rick, and Carlos Garcia was on the right. There were no smiles. The background was typical of the foliage found in Central America. The picture had yellowed with age. The photographer, Maria Sanchez, was raped and killed two hours after taking the picture by a roving band of Sandinistas. Carl's team found them all before sundown. There were no prisoners.

As Rick and Roland were wrapping up their discussion, Carl clipped the end of one of the cigars, sat back slowly in the chair and rolled the cigar back and forth in his mouth. It had a mellow coffee taste. He saluted the picture with the tapered end of the cigar and put it back into his mouth, still unlit. He continued thinking about the early morning meeting with the Bahamian Embassy. Roland closed the laptop, gathered up the cables and turned toward Carl.

"Will that be all Mr. Peterson?" Roland asked, knowing that his presentation had left little doubt but certainly opened the door for further speculation.

"Yes, that will be all Roland. Good work. I will let you know in the morning the direction we have decided to take and how you can help. Drive carefully," Carl responded.

He didn't offer the kid a cigar. Roland didn't appear to have any of the usual vices. He was young yet mature beyond his years. Roland was the most apt information technology expert that Carl had ever known, and he had an uncanny ability to answer questions before they were asked. The kid was not only brilliant but he was also a self-starter. They were hard to find in this day and age. He wished he had several like Roland. Carl couldn't help but take one last look at Roland's feet—still no socks. Roland noticed the subtle glance and perplexing expression on Carl's face, but he didn't acquiesce to the moment. Instead, he smiled and nodded to Rick as he left the room.

"So what do you think Rick? Is there anything more to this than some smart-ass college kid with big balls who knows too much about computers and offshore accounts? Do you really think terrorists are behind this?"

Rick sat down in one of the Italian glove-leather chairs. The chairs were strategically positioned at opposing angles facing Carl's desk. Carl continued to maintain eye contact as he twirled the cigar in his mouth waiting for Rick's take on the situation. Rick focused his attention on a little knot, shaped like a cat's eye, on the front of Carl's desk. Carl didn't interrupt him. He knew that Rick was in scenario-development mode and would shortly provide a straightforward conclusion, which would be followed by a simple course of action. Rick Morgan was very good at getting to the heart of the matter.

"I don't think we're dealing with college kids," said Rick diffidently. "The John Kilday piece is what doesn't fit. Why would some college kid, smart enough to pull this thing off, hire a couple of thugs to beat the hell out of him, nearly kill him. No, my gut tells me this goes a lot deeper than some smart-ass college kids just trying to scam money."

Carl pondered Rick's statement as he leaned forward to reach for his clippers.

"So if there is more to it, what are you thinking?" asked Carl as he clipped the end of the other Montecristo. He offered it to Rick.

They both lit up and seemed to be in competition to see which one of them could blow the largest smoke ring. Carl was winning. Rick probably smoked two cigars in the past year, and both of those were in the office with Carl Peterson. Carl never smoked at home. He would only smoke in the office, and only after hours. His evenings at home were reserved for classical music, reading the remainder of his newspapers and enjoying a couple of Napoleon brandies.

"I need a little more time to go over the information," said Rick as he rolled the cigar between his thumb and first two fingers of his right hand. The cigar had a nice aroma. "How's Kilday doing? Has he regained his memory?"

"He's still in pretty rough shape. He did recognize Nancy and Mike but does not have any recollection of the attack. The doctors are keeping a close eye on him. Even though he's in pretty good condition, he took a significant beating to the head. The extent of his memory damage is still unknown," responded Carl.

"How is your nephew taking all this?" asked Rick.

"He's young, and he's a hot head. You know the type. He's ready to go to Nassau and beat the hell out of everyone in sight," responded Carl as he blew a near perfect smoke ring. "I'll make sure he stays in the states," he added.

"It would be nice to know exactly when the attack occurred. We can certainly retrace Kilday's steps and develop an accurate timeline," said Rick as he took a healthy drag on the cigar.

"What are you thinking?" Carl asked, the lines in his forehead becoming more pronounced as he again leaned forward. He placed his cigar on the edge of the large ashtray that contained the remains of several cigars.

Rick didn't answer right away. He seemed to be pondering the band on his cigar. There were several scenarios going through the sea of thoughts in his mind, but only one kept floating to the surface. He took another puff on the slow burning cigar and blew a fairly large smoke ring that reminded Carl to retrieve his cigar from the ashtray. Carl was about to say something when Rick spoke.

"I think the key to this may actually be the attack. Either it was an incredible coincidence, or John Kilday ruffled somebody's feathers… and ruffled them good," Rick paused as he maintained eye contact. "I would really like to know whose feathers he ruffled," he added as he slid forward in the chair.

"Any idea who that might be?" asked Carl.

"I have my suspicions," responded Rick.

Both men were silent for a few seconds. Smoke rings filled the air like little hollow clouds. Rick slid back into the comfort of the recliner.

"Carl, we're both somewhat familiar with offshore accounts. And as you know, banks do not react very well to unexplained account activity or the unexpected transfer of large sums of money, especially without much warning."

"And?" asked Carl as he flicked the ashes from his cigar into the sterling silver ashtray.

"And if John Kilday was beaten shortly after visiting the bank, I believe there is a strong possibility that the account manager is, shall we say, dirty? That would certainly make a good starting point."

Carl leaned back in the chair; his affirmative nod was hardly discernable.

"Maybe we should get Roland to access that account," said Carl. It was both a statement and a question.

"You can task him. I have no idea how difficult it would be for him to access such an account. I suspect they are using the most current state-of-the-art technology. I have a feeling that the current Administration has tried it."

"I remember the Administration saying they were going after the offshore accounts," Carl responded, "but I haven't heard anything since that initial announcement. They probably ran into a brick wall."

"Or a damn good firewall. Offshore banking is probably as secure as advertised," responded Rick.

Both men were silent for a minute or so as they continued to enjoy the Montecristos. Carl blew a large smoke ring that spiraled toward the ceiling and said, "Roland will certainly know. However, I don't want The Peterson Group to gain any unwanted attention. Offshore banking is a very sensitive issue."

"Carl, why don't we do this, have Roland find out who the account manager is and check out a few of the bank's key personnel. Let's see what he can turn up. Obviously, the bank is our best lead at this point."

"Follow the money," responded Carl as he got up from the desk and looked out toward the King Street metro station. The evening traffic had moved out. The parking lot in front of the station was nearly empty. There was one lone yellow cab parked in front of the bus stop with its parking lights on.

"Since in the case of John Kilday, time is no longer of the essence, what's the next step?" asked Carl.

Without hesitation, Rick responded.

"Depending on who is behind the lottery scam, time may *indeed* be of the essence," responded Rick with strong emphasis on the word indeed. "No matter what course of action we decide upon, I intend to prepare Carlos and Tony for a trip to Nassau. I'll work on their mission assignment tonight. Carlos is very good at getting information. By the way, how did your meeting go with the Bahamian Ambassador?"

"Just as I thought it would," Carl responded. "I will look into the matter," Carl said in his best attempt at a British accent. "However, I cannot promise anything. I do not have the resources to do a full-blown investigation. In this environment, muggings unfortunately have become quite common, especially if one should wander off by themselves after having a few drinks…blah, blah, blah," Carl continued as his accent took on a more mocking tone.

Rick smiled at Carl's lame attempt to speak with an accent while imitating a stiff-necked British-trained diplomat.

"Did he *really* sound like that?" added Rick, suppressing a smile.

Carl didn't say anything for several seconds.

"There was one thing," Carl added. "The receptionist seemed a bit out of place."

"What do you mean, out of place?" asked Rick.

"I don't know, maybe I've been in this game too long, but she reminded me of Anya when we first met her—tall, slender, fit yet very feminine, and quite capable of cutting your balls off and shoving them down your throat if you crossed her. She wasn't your typical golly-gee, big-boobed secretary looking to land a Washington power broker. No, she gave me an eye-scan that wasn't prompted by my good looks, if you know what I mean," responded Carl as he took a deep drag on the cigar and blew the winning smoke ring. "Her hair was held in place by a couple of knitting needle sticks. The kind that aren't used with yarn," he added.

"Well, let's have Roland check her out," said Rick. "I'll give Carlos a call tonight," he added. "The sooner we follow up the better."

Rick got up from the desk. His left knee reminded him why he needed to stay out of the field. Field operations were for the young. Both men walked to the parking garage. It was nearly twenty hundred hours. The drive to McLean would be a piece of cake at this time of night.

"You want to stop by for a drink?" Carl asked.

"Thanks Carl. I'd love to, but I need to come up with a plan and bounce a few things off Carlos. I'll see you in the morning."

Rick drove out of the garage first. Carl was right behind him. Neither man noticed the midnight blue BMW parked a block and a half away. It was just far enough away that they wouldn't have been able to make out the female driver with black hair held neatly in place by two large knitting needle sticks.

There wasn't much traffic on I-495 this late at night. It was always feast or famine in the D.C. area. This was the famine hour on the Beltway. Most commuters were home by now either cleaning the dinner dishes or having a few drinks and relaxing. The bad news was that it would start all over again early the next morning.

The short trip from The Peterson Group office in Old Town to the Ritz Carlton at Tysons Corner gave Rick a little time to think about the lottery scam. There was certainly a chance that Carl could actually be right. The whole thing could be just a couple of smart-ass college kids with too much time on their hands, employing their computer skills to dupe a bunch of old people out of a good chunk of their life savings. Kids were clever, and unfortunately, the old folks were easy targets and willing victims for the most part. Maybe that's all it really was. But Rick's little warning flag was stirring up a tempest in his gut, one that was telling him that there was definitely much more to this lottery scam.

As he approached Braddock Road, and mostly out of habit, he decided to take a slight detour—one designed to determine if he was truly alone on his way back to the hotel. There was certainly no reason to believe he was being followed, but one of the cars behind him had maintained a fairly constant separation. Besides, it was good practice and would give him more time to think.

Rick slowed the car, put on his blinker and took the westbound exit. He glanced in the rearview mirror. Two other cars also exited. Neither of them used their turn signal. He went west on Braddock Road for about a half mile then turned around at the second crossover and proceeded back east on Braddock. He glanced to his left at the other two vehicles that had also exited. One was a light colored Ford Explorer and the other a dark colored BMW. He didn't remember seeing either of them in Old Town. Neither vehicle slowed or gave any indication that they had been following him. He continued to watch them in the rearview mirror. Neither car appeared to be slowing down or giving an indication that they were looking for a place to turn around.

Rick continued east on Braddock and then re-entered I-495 westbound. He continued to check the rearview mirror. Nothing suspicious. From experience, he knew that it was extremely difficult to tail a trained operative at night, especially in light traffic. An experienced tail would not maintain a consistent separation. Less traffic made it very difficult to tail and not be spotted. If he were being followed, his little maneuver would send a signal that he had spotted the tail, or at the very least, given the impression that he had spotted the tail. An experienced tail would have broken it off unless there were two of them. In which case, the partner tail, knowing the maneuver, would have pulled to the shoulder to wait for him to re-enter the Beltway. Rick smiled to himself. Experience works both ways.

At about five minutes from Tysons Corner, Rick decided to give Carlos a call. Carlos answered just before the fourth ring.

"Hey Rick, I thought I heard the phone," said Carlos, sounding a bit out of breath.

"I didn't catch you at a bad time, did I?" asked Rick, trying not to imagine Ann and Carlos in the middle of a romantic moment.

Carlos caught the inference and laughed.

"No, nothing like that. I just came in from a short run. Besides, Ann is in New York City providing a security briefing to several execs that are heading to Dubai on business. She'll be back sometime tomorrow afternoon. You're not back from New York yet, are you?" he asked, sounding a bit surprised.

"Yes, I just left The Peterson Group office and thought I'd give you a call."

"So, what's up Rick?" responded Carlos, his voice signaling that he knew that Rick hadn't planned to leave New York for at least another week.

"Something very important. We've got a project that should keep us employed for the next couple of months, maybe more. Can you meet me at the office tomorrow morning at zero nine hundred? I'll fill you in on all the details then," responded Rick as he glanced in the rearview mirror.

"Sure, I'll be there," responded Carlos. "Frankly, I was afraid that Ann would ask me to accompany the suits to Dubai," added Carlos, sounding somewhat relieved. "You know how much I would have enjoyed that trip," he continued sarcastically.

"I can only imagine," responded Rick, knowing that Dubai offered numerous challenges to security, even under the best of conditions. "Will Ann be available? I have included some funding for her also," added Rick.

"I believe so. She's got a lot on her plate, but nothing that I know of that she couldn't delegate," responded Carlos.

"Good. By the way, Tony Ramos is already onboard. See you in the morning."

Rick put the phone down thoughtfully. Carlos was great. No questions. Just a simple, "I'll be there." He could always count on Carlos. Rick pulled into the parking lot at the Ritz. He turned the lights off and sat in the car for a few minutes thinking about Roland's briefing and waiting to see if any cars pulled in. He hadn't noticed anyone following. Either there was no one, or his little maneuver worked as designed. Truth be told, he really didn't care if he was being followed, but if he were, then his initial gut feeling about the lottery scam was probably very close to being dead on.

He was just about to exit the vehicle when a dark colored BMW drove into the parking lot and backed into a space that provided a good view of his vehicle and the entrance to the Ritz. He sat back in the seat. BMWs were quite common in a Ritz Carlton parking lot, but this one looked very much like the one that went past him on Braddock Road.

Rick waited for a few more seconds. The driver didn't get out. Rick turned on the overhead light and began to look over his notes from the morning meeting. He purposely didn't look in the direction of the BMW. He was quite confident that he would notice if someone exited the vehicle. No one did. He thought about getting out of the car, going over to the Beemer and knocking on the driver's side door...but that was Hollywood. In the real world you could easily get embarrassed, punched in the nose, or worse yet, even shot. No, he was too old to make that mistake.

However, if this was the same BMW that had exited on Braddock Road, then the driver was either damn good at catching up unnoticed, or there was a tracking device somewhere on Rick's vehicle. Hell, it wouldn't be too difficult to track a car by hacking into the onboard GPS system. It would certainly be a clever way to do it. No additional tracking device would be necessary or discovered. There were only a few agencies that possessed that know-how or had the horsepower to get the necessary warrant.

Rick turned the overhead light off and exited the vehicle. He purposely didn't look in the direction of the car. He entered the Ritz and took the elevator to the sixth floor. When he exited the elevator, he looked out into the parking lot. The BMW was gone.

CHAPTER THIRTEEN

OLD TOWN, VIRGINIA
OCTOBER 10, 2012
WEDNESDAY
0915 HOURS

Carlos was already sitting, coffee in hand and talking with Elaine Drew in Carl's outer office, when Rick arrived. They both got up when Rick walked in. Rick and Carlos shook hands. Elaine made an inviting gesture toward her coffee cup. Rick nodded that he would like a cup. He was just about to start filling Carlos in when Roland Carpenter showed up, laptop and cables in hand.

"Good morning Mr. Morgan, Mr. Garcia," greeted Roland with a smile as he put the computer and cables down on the coffee table.

"Good morning Roland," responded Rick. Carlos offered a perfunctory nod in Roland's direction. Carlos was never one for small talk.

"I take it you have some good information for us," added Rick.

"I do," responded Roland just as Elaine returned with a fresh cup of coffee for Rick. She was also carrying an enticing tray of assorted sweet rolls, donuts, bagels and a variety of cream cheeses, all of which were very tempting.

"I don't think we can eat all of that," said Rick with a teasing smile as he eyed one of the blueberry muffins.

Elaine returned the smile as she set the tray on the coffee table.

"Carl had another meeting this morning, so he is running a little behind," announced Elaine. "Please help yourself, we have plenty," she added, pointing to the tray.

"That is a lot of sweet rolls," said Rick as he looked over the assortment.

"Carl has another meeting later this morning," responded Elaine.

Serving donuts and other refreshments was not just a courtesy. Rick and Carl had learned a long time ago that government personnel seemed to take meetings more seriously when there were special treats. And besides, you could tell a lot about a person by what they selected and the way they ate. Eating was somewhat disarming. Both Rick and Carl were well trained in the art of body language. Besides, it was rather difficult for a person to maintain a position of superiority with powdered sugar all over their chin and a big glob of jelly plopped smack-dab in the middle of their tie. Rick took a drink of coffee and turned his attention toward Carlos.

"I will bring you up to speed while Roland sets up. It's a fairly simple scenario, but one that may prove quite interesting. By the way, Carl has a vested interest in this one. One of the victims is his only nephew's father-in-law."

The revelation got a raised eyebrow from Carlos.

"Victim?" responded Carlos as Elaine announced to Carl that everyone was present. They could hear Carl say, "Send them in."

Carl's office was neat as a pin as usual and set up for a much larger meeting. There were fourteen chairs around the large oval conference table and another eight chairs positioned strategically along the wall facing the large video conferencing screen. Pencils and pads were also available and stacked neatly in the center of the table. A coffee station was set up complemented with large blue Peterson Group coffee mugs stacked in a pyramid. The mugs were the kind that the participants were expected, and encouraged, to take with them. Carl came around from behind the desk.

"I have a meeting with Homeland Security at ten thirty. Could lead to some new work and a lot more funding," Carl said supporting a confident smile, indicating that it would most likely lead to a lot more funding.

"Sit here," said Carl, motioning toward the end of the table closest to his desk. "Roland, you can set up anywhere. Good to see you Carlos," he added as he shook Carlos's hand. Carl's eye contact with Carlos was genuine and spoke of many years of mutual respect.

Following the usual pleasantries, and before Rick had an opportunity to brief Carlos, Roland was set up and ready to proceed. Without saying anything, Carl gave Roland a go-ahead nod. Rick leaned over and whispered to Carlos that he would fill in any holes later.

"Good morning gentlemen. As you know, we had identified twenty-six victims of the lottery scam. Currently, I can confirm thirty-three. All of them had transferred money to the same offshore account. We've been watching that account as it continued to build. Two days ago the account was closed. Just prior to closing, there was nine million dollars in the account. That suggests to me that there were at least forty victims."

No one said anything. This was a lot bigger than they had imagined. Rick looked over at Carl. It was really surprising that so many people had fallen for such an obvious scam. Carl was intense. While his personal connection to this case certainly stirred up more emotion, Carl was still a businessman. With that amount of money on the table, The Peterson Group could stand to make a substantial finder's fee in addition to the calculated profit associated with the new project. Roland looked around the room, and with no questions, he continued.

"The offshore account manager is a long-time banker by the name of Ian McAllister. He used to be with the World Bank and lived in the south of France for nearly twenty-two years. He has been with this particular bank in the Bahamas for a little over fourteen years."

Roland paused and took a drink of bottled water. Still, no one asked any questions. Rick was the only one taking notes. Roland was confident that the next point would start the question and answer part of the brief.

"I did some more digging and discovered that when the lottery offshore account was closed, one million of the nine million dollars was transferred from the account to a bank in the Cayman Islands."

Carl raised an eyebrow, leaned slightly forward and was first to speak.

"And I take it the account in the Caymans was in the name of Ian McAllister." It was more of a statement than a question.

"Actually, the account was in the name of a holding company, Island Enterprise," answered Roland, a slight smile crossing his face. He loved the cat and mouse game, especially when Carl was the mouse. Roland was young, but he was learning to be a player.

Carl leaned back slowly, a hint of disappointment was evident, but he was still contemplating the connection as he returned to his position on the perch. Rick leaned forward with his forearms crossed on the conference table and addressed Roland.

"So, I assume you have made the connection between Island Enterprise and Ian McAllister?"

"I believe I did. It may be far reaching, but it's a connection nonetheless. Seems Mr. McAllister is an avid coin collector with a particular interest in early American coins. Lately, he has focused on Walking Liberty half dollars." responded Roland as he looked over at Carl and then back toward the screen. "Also, Island Enterprise basically focuses on the acquisition of old gold coins. Just yesterday the company procured a significant amount of Dutch Guilders. In my opinion, that's just too many coincidences," Roland added.

"So it looks like McAllister could be our guy," said Carl, the intensity on his face became more evident as he leaned further forward.

Roland was about to continue when Elaine Drew interrupted.

"Please excuse the interruption," she said softly. "Carl, you *need* to take this call," she added, emphasizing the word *need*. She had a concerned look on her face.

Carl nodded as Elaine quietly shut the door.

"Let's take five," he said as he picked up the phone and pressed the button that was now flashing.

Rick and Carlos got up from the table and went over to the refreshments. Rick poured two cups of fresh coffee. Roland retrieved a bottle of Fiji water from the small refrigerator. Carl was looking out the window as he continued to talk in a low voice. Rick moved close to Carlos who was about to bite into a large jelly donut.

"I suspect this is not good news," he said as he took a drink of coffee. He continued to look in Carl's direction. He knew Carl Peterson. Carl would only turn his back if it were personal. The call was clearly personal, and it didn't last very long. Carl hung up the phone and continued to look out the window for several seconds before he turned around. Rick took the coffee pot and went over to Carl's desk.

"Refill?" he asked.

"I'll get it," Carl said as he came around from behind the desk.

Carl had a pensive look on his face. No one said anything as Carl prepared his coffee. He took a drink and looked directly at Rick.

"Seems we have a development. John Kilday has slipped into a coma."

"What's the prognosis?" asked Rick solemnly.

"Not good. He is currently on life support. And short of a miracle, he's not expected to make it through the day."

Carl walked slowly back to his desk and stood for a minute or so looking out the window.

Everyone was silent for a couple of minutes as they took their seats at the conference table. Carl took another swallow of coffee, turned around, looked down at his desk and turned the page on his notebook. Without looking up, he asked, "Roland, what about Ms. Anderson from the embassy? What did you find out about her?"

"Ah, she is an interesting one," responded Roland as he skipped ahead with his presentation. He stopped on a picture of a middle-aged woman with matronly looks and glasses that were too small for a face that had seen too many donuts. Carl had a quizzical look on his face as he addressed Roland.

"That's not the woman I met," he said.

"I'm sure that it wasn't," responded Roland. "This is Ms. Lorraine Fisher…the *real* secretary. She has been the secretary for the Bahamian Embassy for the past twenty-three years. Seems she was recently taken ill, and a substitute was hired."

"And the substitute was Ms. Anderson," filled-in Carl.

"I can only assume the substitute was your Ms. Anderson," responded Roland.

"Assume?" questioned Carl.

"It seems that the temp agency used by the embassy doesn't exist," responded Roland.

No one said anything for a few minutes. Could it be that Ms. Anderson was a plant? Rick wrote a couple of notes and then addressed Roland.

"Would I be correct in assuming that she took her position at the embassy this week, right around the time the offshore account was closed?" asked Rick.

"You certainly would," responded Roland. "In fact, Ms Fisher was taken ill the day before the account was closed," he added.

"And what was her illness?" asked Carl.

"Food poisoning," responded Roland. "It was severe enough to put her in the hospital. In fact, she is still there in the ICU."

Carl made eye contact with Rick and then with Carlos and then leaned back in his chair. Slipping something into food was a very easy way to eliminate a target either permanently or temporarily. Fortunately for Ms. Fisher, it appears that it was a temporary gesture.

"So, is there anything you *can* tell us about Ms. Anderson?" asked Carl.

"Not at this time. The only thing I can say with certainty is that someone diverted the request for a secretary to a bogus temp agency," responded Roland.

"And I assume that is easy to accomplish?" asked Carl.

"It is very easy to accomplish. I know how I would do it. And from what I can gather so far, it was done the way I would have done it. However, whoever did it was also good enough to cover their tracks."

"Since Ms. Fisher is still in the hospital, most likely Ms. Anderson is still at the embassy. It would be very easy to get some pictures and fingerprints. We could put Ann on it," said Rick. "Since we don't have a picture of her, will you provide a description for Ann?" asked Rick, looking at Carl.

"I can do better than that. I'll get with Roland and we'll come up with a composite drawing," responded Carl. "Anything else Roland?"

"No, that's it for this morning. I'll get back to you as soon as I locate the IP address that was used to spoof the agency," responded Roland. "However, I suspect that the IP address I find will lead to a dead end," he added.

Carl understood.

"Thanks Roland. Good job. I'll get with you a little later," said Carl. It was obvious from Carl's tone that he had other things on his mind.

Roland nodded and left the room. Carl stood up, empty coffee cup in hand, and looked out the window again. John Kilday was weighing heavily on his mind. Rick and Carlos remained seated at the table knowing what Carl was about to say. Carl turned and put down his coffee cup. He placed both hands firmly on the table and leaned forward.

"I want you to do whatever is necessary to find out who is behind this thing, and I want to take them down…permanently!"

CHAPTER FOURTEEN

Carlos followed Rick back to the Ritz Carlton at Tysons Corner. Both agreed that the restaurant would offer the perfect environment to discuss their next move. The normal luncheon jabber would be loud enough to mask the salient parts of their conversation.

As they approached the entrance, there was a short line of people still waiting to be seated. The restaurant was rapidly filling up with the usual lunch crowd. Most were young women in short dresses who wore too much make-up and who worked in the various shops that comprised the adjoining mall. Others were business people from out of town who were taking advantage of the *view*, fine dining and generous travel expense accounts.

As Rick and Carlos approached the small podium that served as the mandatory checkpoint, a strikingly attractive hostess greeted them. She already had two luncheon menus in hand in anticipation. She looked to be of Asian descent. Her skin was flawless. It gave new meaning to the expression, "China-doll complexion." Her straight dark hair was pulled back neatly and held in place by a lavender ribbon. Her sleek black dress fit like a glove, and her smile was genuine.

Before she spoke, Rick placed a folded twenty-dollar bill into her hand and pointed to a booth at the far end of the dining room. Without looking at the bill, she smiled and led them to the booth. It had a reserved sign sitting prominently on the front edge of the half-round table. She skillfully removed the sign as though it was never there and announced that the server would be with them in just a moment. She would later blame the oversight on one of the newer employees. She smiled and walked away knowing that she had the full attention of nearly every male in the dining room, including many of the females—some envious and others interested.

The booth provided a clear view of both the dining area and the front entrance to the restaurant. However, it only provided a partial view of the bar area. Rick could live with the partial view. There was certainly no reason to believe at this stage of the project that anyone was following them, or even interested in them for that matter. The choice of booth location was made strictly from habit.

As soon as they were seated, a server in black tuxedo trousers, crisp white shirt and black vest made his way toward them. His nametag identified him as Maurice. Rick and Carlos recognized the small blue, white and red flag mounted on the right corner of his nametag. With so many foreign exchange students, the country identification was gaining popularity.

"Good morning," he said, working hard to overcome a thick French accent. "May I get you something from the bar?"

Maurice smelled particularly good for a Frenchman. However, no matter how hard he tried, he would never lose the accent. Rick looked over at Carlos. Carlos was thinking that a nice cold one would really hit the spot. Rick was aware of Carlos's drinking preference, so he closed the wine list and handed it to Maurice.

"I would like a Crown Royal and ginger ale with two ice cubes," responded Rick as he picked up the menu. Carlos was a bit surprised, since Rick hardly ever had a drink before noon.

"Would you happen to have Modelo Especial?" asked Carlos, not expecting the Ritz to carry Mexican beer.

"That we do sir," responded Maurice. "Would you like a frosted mug with that?" he added.

"That would be wonderful," responded Carlos as he closed the wine list. He was relieved that he didn't have to make a choice. His knowledge of wine was limited at best. He normally left the wine selection to Ann.

Even though her favorite was any Pinot Noir from Oregon, she was well versed when it came to red wine in general. Maurice responded with the typical obligatory facial approval and headed toward the bar.

"Do you think Carl is too close to this one?" asked Carlos as he leaned forward placing both elbows on the table. His folded hands provided a resting place for his chin.

"Maybe he is a little too close, but I certainly understand where he is coming from," responded Rick. "Besides, I don't think we are dealing with a couple of wise-ass college kids. The people who did this to Kilday are thugs at best, and I am willing to bet a month's pay that Mr. Ian McAllister was the one who hired them."

"Can we be absolutely sure of that?" asked Carlos.

"We'll have to be. We need to make that connection," answered Rick as he glanced around the room. Maurice was already heading in their direction with a tray balanced on the fingertips of his right hand.

"May I tell you our luncheon specials?" asked Maurice as he deftly maneuvered the tray from over his head in a single sweeping motion and placed the drinks on small circular napkins.

"Actually, I am not that hungry," responded Rick. "Soup and salad would be nice," he added, knowing that neither he nor Carlos had planned on a large meal.

"We have some wonderful Maryland-style she-crab soup, or you may want to try the chef's signature tomato bisque," responded Maurice. "Both are very nice."

"I'll have the tomato bisque and a small house salad with honey mustard dressing on the side," said Rick.

Maurice stood at parade rest. He nodded and looked to Carlos for his choice.

"I would like a bowl of the she-crab soup and another Modelo Especial," responded Carlos as he handed Maurice the empty bottle.

"That is a fine choice," said Maurice as he picked up the menus, smiled and headed for the kitchen.

It was always a fine choice, Rick thought to himself. Lynn would have asked a million questions. Just once he would like for a server to answer her question of whether a dish is good with, "No ma'am, that is an awful dish. I'm not even sure why we have that item on the menu."

"I assume I will be heading to Nassau," said Carlos as he emptied the mug. Carlos had been to Paradise Island on numerous occasions. Only one other time was it for business, and that was at night. Most of the countries he visited were one-night stands, compliments of the U.S. Government.

"Yes. I want you to get right on this and take Tony Ramos. You can head out tomorrow," responded Rick as he swirled the glass in his right hand and took a modest swallow. He was about to continue when a tall woman with jet-black hair entered the restaurant and caught his attention. She seemed to be looking around for someone. She didn't find them. Rick continued to watch as the hostess led her to a small table for two at the front of the dining area. She sat facing the entrance.

The restaurant was now full. A rather large woman, wearing a 1940s-style hat with gaudy pink feathers, was competing with the rest of the conversations in the restaurant. She had a shrill voice and a laugh that rivaled nails on a chalkboard. Unfortunately, she was winning the decibel derby with the other patrons. Hopefully her food would arrive soon and force her to concentrate more on chewing than talking. Rick tried not to stare in her direction but found it difficult. He really wanted to gain eye contact to convey his displeasure.

It reminded him of the time in Monterey, California when he and his friend, Enrique, were dining in one of the finer restaurants. A fat man with slicked back hair, red suspenders and chubby-fingers adorned with several gaudy rings was sitting two tables away and was smoking a fowl smelling cigar. Enrique summoned the server and asked if he would kindly ask the gentleman to put out the cigar so that he and the rest of the patrons could enjoy their dinner. The fat man refused. He looked around and loudly exclaimed that if anyone didn't like it, they could kiss his ass.

That was not the response Enrique had wanted. The server shrugged his shoulders in surrender. Enrique got up and walked over to one of the serving stations. He picked up a large pitcher of water, proceeded to the fat man's table and then dumped it over his rude head. The water baptism put out the cigar. Enrique slammed the pitcher on the table. He never said a word, but the look he gave the fat man needed no interpretation. As Enrique returned to the table, the applause by the other patrons served to mitigate any retaliatory thoughts the fat man may have entertained.

"So what is the plan?" asked Carlos, his question interrupting Rick's quick trip into the past.

"I believe we could employ the same scenario that we used in El Salvador when we uncovered the mole who was providing information to Fidel's people," said Rick.

Carlos looked up.

"If you recall, we lost one of our guys during that operation."

Rick remembered it well. It was the second time he had been to El Salvador. It was always a risk when you had to employ some of the local *talent*. Unfortunately, their loyalty was driven by money, which meant their loyalty waffled based upon who provided the most money. Ideology looked good on paper, but in reality it had nothing to do with loyalty.

"We won't have to use any locals. You and Tony will be the only players."

Before Carlos asked the next question, Maurice, and a skinny associate from the kitchen, arrived with lunch. The soup was piping hot and the salad was crisp.

"Is there anything else I may get you?" asked Maurice. "Perhaps another Crown Royal?"

Rick looked at Carlos. Carlos waved his hand signaling that he was set.

"I believe we are fine for now. Thank you Maurice," responded Rick.

Rick tasted the tomato bisque. The seasoning was very nice as expected. Carlos was already adding pepper to his she-crab soup. Rick smiled to himself. Carlos loved pepper. He would put pepper on just about anything. There were only two people Rick knew who would cover a slice of cantaloupe with pepper. Carlos never did get Rick to try it that way...and neither did Rick's father-in-law.

"Since Tony will fly out of Florida and you will be flying out of D.C., no one will make the connection between the two of you. If we run this like El Salvador, you can flash Kilday's picture around the local bars. Tony can back you up from the shadows."

"So I take it that our first objective will be to find the thugs who beat up Kilday?" asked Carlos. It was a rhetorical question. "How far should we go?"

"All the way. Remember, they had no trouble beating up a helpless old man. You can work out the details with Tony. I'm sure no one will miss them."

"How many do you think there are?" asked Carlos.

"I am assuming there is more than one. Probably no more than three, but you never know. They'll size you up and make that decision. Tony should be prepared to take out at least two. You can question the remaining one. You know the drill. We need to send McAllister a message loud and clear, one that will encourage him to give us the name of the person who opened the account."

Carlos nodded without saying anything and finished the she-crab soup.

"Let me know what tools, if any, you might need. I have a good contact in Miami who is well known in the Bahamas. He is a frequent overnight visitor at the marina and can enter and leave without raising suspicion. He is quite resourceful and can provide any needed items," said Rick.

"What about McAllister? Assuming we make the connection, are you going to contact him, or do you want me to handle it?" asked Carlos.

"I prefer that you handle it. Once you get the information you need, set up a meeting with him. Make him aware of what we know about his participation in the lottery scam, his account number in the Caymans and the fate of his local accomplices. I don't think you'll have a problem with him. Once McAllister is aware of the situation, I believe he'll be more than eager to provide you with the name of the account holder."

"Do you want me to eliminate him?" asked Carlos as he took a drink of the Modelo Especial.

Rick thought for a minute and then responded. "Carl's direction was clear. For someone his age, a heart attack wouldn't raise suspicion. Do you have any questions?"

"No questions," responded Carlos as he polished off the last of his beer. "It is always easy during the planning stage," he added.

Rick chuckled. They always won on paper. Up close and personal wasn't as predictable as a movie script. There was no director to yell cut. There was no best boy to reposition the players. There was never an opportunity for a clean re-take.

"When does Ann get back in town?" asked Rick as he summoned Maurice.

"I'm picking her up at Dulles at fifteen hundred," responded Carlos.

"Good. Fill her in on what's going on and put her onto Ms. Anderson. We need to find out who she is and where she fits into this whole thing. When do you plan on contacting Tony?"

"I'll give Tony a call this afternoon," said Carlos.

"Good. I'm heading back to Virginia Beach later today. I'll call my contact in Miami. Let me know your schedule and what you need."

"Will do boss," responded Carlos.

As Rick requested the bill, he caught another glimpse of the tall woman with jet-black hair who had come in alone. She was on her way out the door. While she was quite far away, Rick did notice something glisten in her hair. He looked more intently. It appeared to be a knitting needle piercing the twist of hair that was stylishly secured at the back of her head, but he couldn't be certain.

CHAPTER FIFTEEN

As soon as Rick entered his room, he called Elaine Drew and asked her to call the Bahamian Embassy to see if Ms. Anderson was there. He told Elaine that he would hold while she made the call. Elaine indicated that she was just about to call him because Carl wanted to speak with him. She let Carl know that Rick was holding on line one. Carl immediately picked up the phone.

"Rick, are you still in town?" asked Carl. He had assumed Rick had planned to leave for Virginia Beach following their morning meeting.

"Yes, but not much longer. Carlos and I just finished lunch. We have decided on a course of action. He and Tony Ramos will be heading to Nassau early tomorrow. He will also brief Ann concerning Ms. Anderson. I'm planning to leave in about an hour or so. Is everything okay?" asked Rick, suspecting that Carl was about to provide a not-so-good update on John Kilday. Rick's gut feeling was right.

"I just got word from Mike that his father-in-law passed away about an hour ago. Kilday never regained consciousness. I will be leaving for Miami later today," responded Carl. His voice was strong, but there was a slight hint of concern for his nephew and Nancy. "I'll fly them up to Panama City," he added.

Rick didn't say anything for a few seconds. Both he and Carl had known that the chances of Kilday recovering from the coma were slim to none. The severity of the beating, compounded by his age, was a fatal combination. They both had expected this outcome but not quite so soon. Rick knew that this turn of events wouldn't set well with Carl. Carl was normally in control of his emotions, especially under fire, but this was family. The event had become family business with the first phone call from his nephew.

"I'm sorry to hear that. How is your nephew taking this?" asked Rick.

"Hell, he's ready to head to Nassau and beat the crap out of every swinging dick in town," responded Carl. "I need to get down there and calm the kid down. Nancy is devastated, although she appears to be handling the loss of her father better than Mike," added Carl.

Rick knew that she was probably in a mild state of shock. Reality would set in very soon. They would both need genuine consoling.

"What about you?" asked Rick. "Are you okay?"

"I'll be alright," responded Carl. His reply was diffident at best. Going to Nassau had also crossed his mind and was still looming as a real possibility.

Rick didn't say anything. He could tell that Carl was about to say something else.

"Rick, this whole thing really pisses me off," the tone of his voice indicated that he wasn't a happy camper. "The kid is my only nephew. I certainly don't want him running around like a loose cannon, making a fool of himself. You know how the navy frowns on stuff like that," offered Carl.

"In spite of the fact that he *is* a fighter pilot?" added Rick, trying to lighten the mood.

"Especially since he's a fighter pilot," chuckled Carl, picking up on Rick's gesture.

Having worked with many pilots over the years, Rick and Carl shared the same opinion of fighter pilots. Most were pretty good guys, but some were thoroughly caught up with the idea that they were the cream of the crop. And unfortunately, they let everyone know it. They never accepted the fact that their assignment to jets was based solely upon the needs of the navy, nor did they understand that the grade cut off was based upon those needs for that particular assignment period.

As far as they were concerned, they got jets because they were the best of the best. They truly believed their shit didn't stink. The only thing bigger than their watch was their ego.

"Listen Carl, we'll take care of this," said Rick confidently.

Rick could hear Carl take a couple of deep breaths.

"Thanks buddy. I'll call you when I get to Panama City. Be sure to let Roland know if you need any technical support. Talk with you later."

When Carl hung up, Elaine Drew came back on the line.

"Rick, you still there?" she asked.

"I'm here," he responded.

"I called the embassy. I got a recording and then the call went directly to voice mail. I assume they must have shut down for the lunch hour. Do you want me to keep trying?" she asked.

"No, that will be fine. Thanks Elaine, see you next time," responded Rick.

Rick hung up and stood there for a moment thinking about the mysterious Ms. Anderson. Could the tall woman with jet-black hair who had slipped in and out of the Ritz be the mysterious Ms. Anderson? The fact that Elaine was unable to contact her was still not enough to convince Rick that she was the lady he saw at lunch. He had looked in her direction several times but had never caught her looking in his direction. While he didn't have a completely clear view of her, she did seem to meet the criteria of Carl's description. Experienced operatives would strategically position themselves to take advantage of a reflecting surface, such as a mirror, to conceal the fact that they were watching. However, there was no mirror that could have been used to provide a clandestine view of Rick and Carlos's booth.

The fact that no one answered the phone at the embassy may be a coincidence. A competent secretary would most likely have forwarded incoming calls to a cell phone, but only if that were the standard operating procedure for the office. Rick couldn't imagine any embassy shutting down for lunch. However, he really didn't know for sure. Maybe they all shut down for lunch. Maybe this Ms. Anderson was merely a temp. Maybe she just happened to shop at Tysons Corner.

Besides, how would she know that he would be at the Ritz? And if so, how did she even know to follow Rick in the first place?

As Rick looked out into the parking lot, he realized that there were too many maybes, too many un-answered questions so early on in the project. There certainly were many tall women fitting Ms. Anderson's description working and living in the D.C. area. But then again, how many of them wore knitting needle sticks in their hair…and were those actually knitting needle sticks that he saw, or were they just some random hair ornament.

DULLES AIRPORT

1520 HOURS

Ann's face broke into a big smile when she saw Carlos standing in the receiving area. She greeted him with a soft kiss and squeezed him ever so gently. He pulled her in closely, both arms wrapped around her securely. He could feel her heart pounding as she rose up on her toes to kiss him again. Her eyes sparkled with sincerity. How things had changed since Sigonella.

"I missed you!" she exclaimed as she kissed him again. Her voice was soft and inviting. "New York is nice this time of year, but it would have been a lot more enjoyable if you were there. We could have taken in a couple of plays," she said smiling, knowing that Carlos would rather be tied face down on a hill of fire ants than go to a Broadway play.

"Yeah right!" he laughed. "I've been meaning to take in *Fiddler on the Roof*," he added sarcastically.

The fact that Carlos even knew the name of a play caught Ann a bit off guard. She smiled back at him, and without saying anything, she threw her arms around him and hugged him again. Carlos decided he would wait until later to tell her that he was headed to Nassau in the morning. There was no sense spoiling her arrival, or the evening for that matter. The short trip from Dulles gave them just enough time to catch up with her latest project.

"So how did your briefing go?" asked Carlos.

"Typical," she responded. "The execs are aware that this is a dangerous time for any American traveling in the Middle East, and it probably will be for many years to come. After the brief they asked if my company would provide on-site security personnel."

"I didn't think that you were planning on providing a security force?" questioned Carlos.

"I wasn't. I reminded them that their request for proposal didn't ask for or specify on-site security."

"So they are going it alone?" asked Carlos.

"No, I gave them a contact who has the resources and will be able to provide the necessary security personnel."

"Even with security there are no guarantees," said Carlos. "Security personnel tend to be too obvious and can be a magnet for every wanna-be martyr."

"I know, but they don't know that. I certainly didn't want to offer your services," she said as she gently squeezed his right thigh.

"So who could provide services on such short notice?" asked Carlos.

"I called Neal. He was to meet with them early this morning. I assume his people will get the job," she responded.

"Neal?" asked Carlos, his mind searching known associates.

"Yeah, Neal. You remember Neal Cummings," said Ann.

"Neal Cummings?" said Carlos surprisingly. "I thought he was killed in Paris a couple of years ago."

"Well, he's obviously still alive. I understand that he was shot several times and underwent quite a long rehab process, but he's still out there kicking ass. He has a fairly large company that provides contract work and worldwide security services," she responded.

Carlos could see Neal Cummings in his mind. Neal was a couple of years older than Carlos. Neal was much taller, had a lighter complexion, was very handsome and was always in outstanding condition. Neal could hold his own with anyone. Carlos had thought that Ann might have had a thing for Neal. He was never sure. Carlos took a long deep breath that came out like a sigh.

"I know what you are thinking Garcia," said Ann. She always referred to him as Garcia when she was upset or making a point. She smiled at Carlos and squeezed his thigh again. "I never, repeat *never*, liked Neal that way. Besides, he probably liked *you* more than he did me," she added as she howled with laughter, knowing that little tidbit probably just blew Carlos's mind.

Ann peaked over at Carlos with a raised eyebrow. He had a puzzled look on his face. Carlos smiled to himself. Women were so perceptive. He knew that Neal wasn't Ann's type, but he had never suspected that Neal might have swung in the other direction.

Following dinner, and while having a glass of wine, Carlos briefed Ann on the lottery scam project along with what little information The Peterson Group had on Ms. Anderson.

"So when are you heading to Nassau?" she asked rather matter-of-factly as she took a sip of wine.

"Early tomorrow morning," he responded with slight hesitation. He looked for her reaction.

"And you were going to tell me this when…*Garcia*?" she asked with emphasis on Garcia. "After you have had your way with me?" she added.

Carlos didn't know what to say, although he knew that she wanted to make a point. Before he could respond, Ann reached over and took the wine glass from his hand and placed it on the coffee table. She put her glass next to his. She then got up from the couch, gently touched his face and gave him that seductive look that only she could give.

"Then we don't need to be wasting any more time sitting here on the couch, now do we?" she said as she slipped off her shoes and led him to the bedroom.

CHAPTER SIXTEEN

The flight to Grand Bahama International Airport gave Carlos more time to go over the entrapment scenario that he and Rick had employed many years ago in El Salvador. Although it was a long time ago, the scenario was still applicable. It was simple, basic and easy to accomplish. No rehearsing was required.

He had called Tony Ramos the night before and filled him in on all the particulars associated with the lottery scam and how they would handle the situation in Nassau. Tony was happy to get back into the game. The wound he had received from Kevin Macavoy had healed well, although it was still sensitive to the touch and had left a dark purple scar. He would be arriving in the Bahamas later that afternoon. As agreed, they would not meet in person. However, they would maintain contact through satellite phone until it was absolutely necessary for them to be together.

As the flight began its approach, Carlos's mind wandered back to the mission in El Salvador. It was a long time ago; however, he would never forget Maria Sanchez. She was only eighteen and so full of life. He and Rick were young and, unfortunately, naive. They tended to believe everything they saw and more than half of what they heard. They soon realized to trust no one.

It was no accident that the Sandinistas were on the trail. It was Maria's cousin who sold them all out for 500 colóns. Rick, Carlos and

Carl Peterson had been airdropped at night from an unmarked C-130 out of Hurlburt Field. Anya Petrov met them. At that time Ann was still considered to be a double agent. She had requested asylum and wanted to defect to the United States. The Russians didn't know it. The Americans were testing her. Their mission was to assassinate Jorge Santiago. Jorge was a devoted follower and protégée of Che Guevara. He was a local hero who continued to rally the peons. The mission was supposed to be a simple in and out. Carlos would be the bait, and once they had determined where Jorge was hiding out, the rest would be a piece of cake. So simple, but the collateral damage left its mark.

As the flight taxied from runway two-four, Carlos took out a picture of John Kilday from his shirt pocket. The picture had been taken from Kilday's passport file, blown up, retouched and made to look like a family photo. Roland had done a good job. Kilday was a pleasant looking man. He looked happy. He certainly didn't deserve this ending.

Roland had also provided a copy of Kilday's hotel reservation. Carlos had all he needed to play the private eye role, including an official-looking badge, ID in the name of Samuel R. Fernandez, a flowery shirt, khaki pants and dirty brown sandals. He would certainly have no problem passing for an aging PI. He purposely dressed a bit sloppy for effect, to give any would-be attacker a fatal dose of overconfidence. His oversized Caribbean Joe shirt was perfect for helping him hide his well-muscled physique.

The scenario was fairly simple. Rick believed that after Kilday checked into the hotel, he probably wasted no time going directly to the bank. The long trek from Panama City would have fueled his anger. He would be itching for a confrontation. However, since the account was an offshore account, Kilday would run into a brick wall. He most likely made a scene and was told there was nothing they could or would do. Bank security would intervene and firmly escort him from the property.

Kilday probably headed back toward the hotel and went into the first bar he saw. He would be reeling from his encounter at the bank. His adrenalin would be pumping, and he would probably be saying things for all to hear. Finding the bar shouldn't take too long. It was most likely one very close to the bank.

From experience, Rick and Carlos knew that there were always one or two local characters who showed up each night, as if on cue, to take up a position on *their* assigned barstool. This was their bar and, as far as they were concerned, the nightly routine didn't start until they were there. They were the pseudo-intellects who would provide unsolicited solutions to the world's problems, which in their case, was confined to a two-block radius. Finding this colorful individual should be no problem. They usually wore some identifying trademark like an out of place cowboy hat that would undoubtedly set them apart from the other regulars. They would remember John Kilday, and they would likely be more than happy to fill in any blanks.

The first bar between the bank and the hotel would be where Carlos would start the investigation. Tony Ramos would stay outside and shadow Carlos from a safe distance to see if anyone followed him when he left the bar, or showed up to follow him. Either way, Carlos and Tony would set the trap. The key would be to select a secluded spot where they would lead and overpower the assailants. Carlos would do a recon of the area and make that determination. Nighttime would be their third partner and provide the necessary cover. Once inside the terminal, Carlos called Rick via the satellite phone.

"Good morning Carlos," answered Rick. "I take it you had a good flight," he added, knowing that as a former naval pilot, any landing you walked away from was a good landing.

"Not bad. Had to get up quite early, but it made the commute to Dulles bearable," responded Carlos.

"Do you have everything you need?" asked Rick.

"We do," responded Carlos, inferring that Tony Ramos was inbound.

"So I take it I don't need to call Miami?" asked Rick, although he meant it more as a statement.

"Tony prefers the knife," responded Carlos. "Besides, he said that a gun with a silencer is illegal," added Carlos. Rick could hear the dry sarcasm in his voice.

"He said that since we will have the element of surprise, a couple of thugs should be no problem. I agree with him," said Carlos.

Rick thought about the scenario and agreed that Tony and Carlos could easily handle a couple of thugs, especially ones who had been drinking and who thought they were going to rough up an over-the-hill private dick.

"What about Ann?" asked Rick.

"She'll pick up Ms. Anderson around lunch time. She knows the drill and to keep you informed," responded Carlos.

"Sounds good Carlos. Be sure to let me know if there is anything you need. And Carlos…you and Tony get out of there as soon as you have the information."

"Okay boss."

Carlos hung up, looked around the terminal and went to pick up his rental car.

BAHAMIAN EMBASSY
WASHINGTON, D.C.
1115 HOURS

Ann Peters took up a position on a bench across from the entrance to the Bahamian Embassy. She had on dark jeans with rips at the knees, a JMU sweatshirt, sunglasses and a ragged backpack that she had dug out of a box in the back of her garage. It smelled musty. She had stuffed the backpack with several crumpled up pages from the previous day's *Wall Street Journal*. The backpack looked full but was light as a feather. She sat on the bench with her head down, looking at what appeared to be a brand new iPad. In fact, she was looking at a composite drawing of Ms. Anderson that Carl had put together with Roland's help.

As she sat there, several people entered and left the embassy. At 1145 hours, a tall dark-haired woman, fitting Ms. Anderson's description, left the embassy and headed in the direction of the L'Enfant Plaza Metro Station. Ann followed at a safe distance, keeping the woman in sight. The metro station was full of people heading in all directions. Many of them wore backpacks. Ann would easily blend in. She watched as

Ms. Anderson got a ticket on the yellow line. Ann could see that she had paid one dollar and ten cents. Ann got a ticket for five dollars and followed Ms. Anderson to the boarding area.

The ramp area was full of people heading to various destinations. A young couple with three impatient kids, one on a leash, looked totally lost. The father was wrestling with a map. The young mother was doing all she could to keep the children close to her. Ann kept her distance. She didn't need anyone flagging her down and asking questions that may attract unwanted attention. If Ms. Anderson was in fact a trained operative, then she would easily remember seeing the backpack, JMU sweatshirt and Ann giving directions.

Ann purposely kept her distance where she could maintain a more youthful appearance. The blue line showed up first. Ms. Anderson didn't move. A couple of minutes later the yellow line pulled in. It was on time. There was a slight stampede as the doors slid open. Ms. Anderson got into the third car. Ann got on the same car, didn't make eye contact and maintained her distance.

The car was full. There were no seats available. The only way to get a seat on the metro was to be about nine months pregnant, anything less and it was every man for himself. Ann looked in Ms. Anderson's direction. A young guy was standing close to her and was obviously eyeing her from head to toe. She turned and said something to him that made him move away without looking back. Ann noticed one knitting needle on a slight angle piercing the bundle of hair that was neatly coffered at the back of her head. From the angle, Ann concluded that Ms. Anderson was right-handed.

As the metro approached the Pentagon Station, Ms. Anderson moved further away from the door. The usual crowd was exiting and entering at the Pentagon. The doors closed and Ann could see Ms. Anderson's reflection in the window. As the metro approached Pentagon City, it was obvious that Ms. Anderson was preparing to exit.

Ann began moving toward the door but needed to stay far enough back in case Ms. Anderson got off to let people out and then got right back into the car. It was a classic move by a trained operative to determine if they were being followed. If it worked, she would be waiving goodbye. Ann had experienced that maneuver firsthand and was determined not to fall into that trap again.

As the doors opened, Ms. Anderson left the car and didn't turn back. At this point, she had no reason to believe she was being followed. Ann exited just before the door was about to close. She remained far enough behind so that she wouldn't have to stop or pretend to be looking at something if Ms. Anderson turned to look back. It was always easy to spot a tail in heavy foot traffic. Inexperienced eyes would stop suddenly or turn to look at something or anything close by. A trained operative would spot them in a New York second. Game over.

Ms. Anderson exited the metro station and moved swiftly across the street. Without hesitation, she got into a black Chevrolet SUV with tinted windows that was parked in a no-parking zone. Ann took out a small camera and took several pictures of the SUV as it pulled away from the curb.

She was unable to get a shot of the license plate without making a move that would have potentially compromised her position. She shook her head, placed the camera in her pocket, continued to cross the street and headed toward Macy's. She sat on a bench in front of the entrance and called Rick. Rick was on his way to Virginia Beach and answered without looking at the caller ID.

"Morgan," he answered, not knowing who was on the line.

"Rick, it's Ann," she said, sounding somewhat frustrated and a bit out of breath.

"Ann, how's it going?" he asked.

"I followed Ms. Anderson to Pentagon City but lost her when she jumped into a waiting SUV. I got some pictures, possibly a partial of the driver but not the license plate."

Rick thought for a few seconds before answering. He knew that losing even an inexperienced *rabbit* was always a strong possibility.

"No problem. You can re-engage back at the embassy."

Rick knew that Ann was upset about losing Ms. Anderson.

"Actually, this will give you time to check the parking garage. Let's see what she is driving," said Rick. In his mind he visualized a dark colored BMW.

CHAPTER SEVENTEEN

Marcie Decker looked at her watch as she walked into the terminal at Tampa International Airport. The airport was already crowded with passengers trying to get a head start on the weekend. Many of them were young. Most wore ragged jeans, t-shirts and flip-flops. They would risk flying standby. Some purposely planned to give up their confirmed ticket to go on a later flight in order to receive a voucher for whatever incentive was offered. Marcie moved quickly through the terminal with a medium-size black leather travel bag designed to fit perfectly in the overhead compartment. It wasn't the standard airline issue, but one she had picked up in Beirut a few weeks earlier. It served her purpose well.

She had tied her long dark hair into a neat ponytail that looked as if it were a part of the black and gray beret that she always wore tilted slightly to the right. Her ponytail swung back and forth in harmony with the ever-present clicking sound of her high heels as she continued to walk briskly through the terminal. Her tailored uniform fit perfectly, outlining a figure sculpted by many years of pilates, weight training, and a very clean diet consisting mostly of fruits and vegetables. Marcie was certainly a head-turner. There were dozens of eyes undressing her as she continued past each gate. Their dreams would never be realized. Her uniform, with gold wings above the left pocket, left little doubt that she was a flight attendant.

She was more than an hour early and should have no problem catching a flight to Atlanta and then on to London's Heathrow Airport. She would meet her crew and pick up her run there, spending the next three days and nights shuttling between London and Beirut. Then she would be home for her long break. The long break was considered one of the perks for a demanding schedule. The glamour of being a flight attendant went out with the day of the "stewardesses."

Marcie had a small flat in London that she shared with two other flight attendants. She hardly ever saw them. On occasion, there would be the tale-tale signs that her roomies enjoyed a wild weekend, evidenced by empty beer and wine bottles strewn about the apartment along with the unmistakable torn end of a condom wrapper that didn't quite find its way to the trash can.

Ever since she met Tarek, she would fly back to Tampa and stay with him whenever possible. Even for a young flight attendant, this routine was exhausting, especially with the time change. The schedule was beginning to take its toll.

The previous three days with Tarek were enjoyable, although he had seemed to be distant…certainly preoccupied. Marcie couldn't put her finger on it. She had asked him several times if anything was wrong, but he shrugged her off with his usual wave of the hand, signaling that he did not want to discuss the issue. After a few seconds he would look at her, acquiesce and add, "Everything is okay. I just need to make a few more calls. It's just business." However, Marcie knew that this time was different.

Tarek had spent more than his usual amount of time on the phone, speaking mostly in English. He would uncharacteristically turn his back to her and speak in a low soft voice, his large hand nearly covering the small cell phone. His body language indicating the conversations were not to his liking. She could tell something wasn't going well. He would pace back and forth, his head movements punctuating strong rhetoric.

She didn't want to appear to be eavesdropping; however, she desperately wanted to know what was going on. During one of his conversations, she picked up an occasional word or two. He had hesitated and used an Arabic word or phrase as if there was no translation for what he really wanted to say. The few words that she was able to hear didn't paint enough of a picture to determine what he was talking about. But whatever it was about, it wasn't good. The one thing that she did understand was the phrase spoken clearly in English, "Take care of *it*." He had said it loud enough for her to hear. He had placed particular emphasis on the word it.

When he finished that call, he didn't move for a few seconds. He stared blankly out the window, not looking at anything in particular. When he turned, Marcie could see the concern in his eyes. Maybe it was anger. It faded rapidly as he caught her gaze. She had never seen this side of Tarek. He put the phone in his pocket and slowly walked toward her. His smile was forced.

Virginia Beach, Virginia
1430 Hours

Rick had been home for only fifteen minutes when his cell phone rang. He had just read a short note from Lynn. She had gone to Harris Teeter to pick up a few things for dinner. Rick looked at the caller ID. It was Ann.

"Yes Ann."

"Rick, are you home?" she asked.

"Just got in a few minutes ago," he said adding, "what's up?"

"I checked out the garage. The embassy has four assigned spaces. There were only two cars there. One was a white Ford and the other was a dark blue BMW sedan, one of the big ones with low profile tires and tinted windows. Had Georgia plates," she added.

Rick didn't answer for a minute or so prompting Ann to ask if he was still there. He had remembered seeing a dark colored BMW on two occasions: one on Braddock Road and the other in the Ritz parking lot. No one had gotten out of the car. The cars were probably one in the same. He was now sure that the BMW belonged to the illusive Ms. Anderson.

"I'm here. Just thinking about the BMW. I'm willing to bet that it belongs to our Ms. Anderson. When you get a chance, lift some prints and we'll have Roland check her out."

"Already have the prints. I have my computer in the car and will send them to Roland. I have already sent the pictures from my cell phone," said Ann.

"You're amazing. I should have known that you would show up with your bag of goodies. Good job."

Before Rick could continue, Ann interrupted, "Rick, if I remember correctly, the agency had a lot of vehicles with Georgia plates. Could be a coincidence. But the car does seem to be a bit overboard for a receptionist."

"Well if she is with the agency, she might be staying in one of the hotels close by. You may need some help following her," added Rick.

"I've got some help on the way. I suspect she will be back any minute. It will be interesting to see if she is dropped off or if she takes the metro. I suspect she will take the metro."

"I would bet on the metro as well. Call me when you find out where she is staying," said Rick.

"Rick, have you heard from Carlos?" she asked.

"Yes, he and Tony are onsite. I'm sure he will give you a call once he is settled in," responded Rick, knowing that Ann wanted to be a part of the Nassau operation. "Ann, please know that I wrestled with sending you with Carlos, but I felt that I needed you here more," he added.

"No. I understand," she responded. "Call you later."

Rick hung up. He knew that Ann was disappointed. She could certainly handle herself in any situation, but he needed her to be the one following Ms. Anderson. Carlos was good, but he just didn't have the patience to sit, wait and follow the *rabbit*. Besides, women were always better following women for a number of reasons, one of which is a woman's penchant on checking out other women.

The BMW was another issue. It raised more questions regarding the identity of this Ms. Anderson. If she does belong to one of the alphabet agencies, which one, and what is she doing at the Bahamian Embassy? How did she get onto Rick, and why had she been tailing him? There were any number of questions and scenarios that Rick could imagine, but there was no sense wasting time until Roland had a chance to verify the finger prints and analyze Ann's pictures.

Rick was about to call Roland when Lynn came into the kitchen from the garage. She was hugging a large brown grocery bag with her left arm. She smiled as she pulled her key from the door and pushed it shut with a bare right foot. She put the bag on the counter as Rick came close to her. After forty years of marriage, the spark was still there.

"I missed you," she said as she hugged Rick. "How was your trip?" she added as she looked up into his eyes. Rick knew that she would have a million questions. He would take them one at a time. He kissed her several times.

"The trip went well. Everyone missed you, but they understood you had to help Brooke," responded Rick, waiting for the next question.

The questions covered everything from the weather in New York to Rick's stay at the Ritz Carlton to what he had been eating for dinner to how Carl Peterson was doing. Guys would never think to ask so many questions. Rick was about to tell Lynn about Carl's nephew when his phone rang. It was Roland. Rick sat on one of the three barstools at the kitchen counter and indicated to Lynn that he needed to take the call. She nodded and began putting away the groceries.

"Roland, what do you have for me?" he answered, wasting no time getting to the point.

"Good afternoon Mr. Morgan. I have some information that I believe you will find interesting, or should I say *intriguing*," said Roland adding a bit of mystery to his findings.

"Have you already analyzed the material from Ann?" Rick asked as he looked at his watch. Actually, knowing Roland, he wasn't surprised.

"For the most part…yes," responded Roland. "I believe my preliminary results will be of great interest. Ann got a partial shot of the driver when he slightly cracked the window. I did a facial recognition of his eyes and forehead. I'm ninety percent sure that the driver is Robert Stankowski. Does that name ring any bells?"

Rick didn't have to think for very long. He knew Robert Stankowski well. He was also CIA. As young guys, Rick, Carl and Stankowski had been on several missions together. While they had lost touch over the years, Stankowski's abrupt ending with the CIA was widely known.

He had become very outspoken following the bombing of the marine barracks in Beirut in 1983 that resulted in the death of 241 American servicemen. It was a tragic loss of life that could have been avoided in Stankowski's mind. He had endorsed Richard Marcinco's evaluation concerning the vulnerabilities associated with the barracks. In particular, he had endorsed Marcinco's recommendation to install a security system that would trigger the explosive devices before they were close enough to cause damage to the barracks.

Unfortunately, it was Washington politics as usual. The politicians were too politically correct for their own good, and overly sensitive to collateral damage among the friendlies. So, the recommendations to ensure the safety of the barracks fell on deaf ears. Their total lack of any meaningful response pissed off Stankowski. He resigned from the CIA in protest and soon went public with the information. As could be expected, the CIA discredited Stankowski. Rick wasn't sure what had happened to him after that. It was unfortunate, because Stankowski was a really good operative. He was principled. Rumor was that he had started his own security firm under an assumed name somewhere off the Beltway.

"I do know a Robert Stankowski," responded Rick.

"I thought you might," responded Roland as he continued. "I ran a trace on him, and it appears that he is now employed by Homeland Security. The SUV certainly fits the profile."

"Did Ann send you the prints?" asked Rick.

"She did, and I got a hit right away. I think you will find the print results to be the most interesting. Seems the prints belong to Ms. Lorraine Fisher. Nice wheels for a sixty-two year old grandmother, wouldn't you say Mr. Morgan?"

Rick thought back to the briefing.

"Lorraine Fisher...the secretary that ended up in the hospital?" asked Rick, his mind racing to connect the dots.

"The very same," responded Roland. "However, I am certain that the car is not hers."

Rick remained silent knowing that Roland would continue. The kid was good.

"Ms. Fisher lives in Fairfax. She lives alone and drives a red 2009 Saturn SUV, Virginia plate CPU 501. I hacked into the garage video and have copied a tape showing her driving in last week. The BMW is definitely not hers."

"So what do you make of the fingerprints?" asked Rick, knowing what the answer would be.

"Someone changed the database. It's not hard to do if you know the system, and it would be very easy if they had legitimate access," responded Roland.

"Good work Roland. Call me anytime if you find out anymore information."

"Mr. Morgan, there is one other thing. Even though I spoofed the site, they will still know that someone checked out the fingerprints."

"Can they trace it back to us?" asked Rick.

"Not the way I set it up. No one is *that* good," responded Roland with confidence.

Rick closed the connection to the satellite phone and took out his small green notebook. Lynn knew not to disturb him when he brought out the little green book. He made a few notes. Most were questions:

—*Why is Homeland Security interested in the Bahamian Embassy?*

—*Is there a connection to the Lottery Scam?*

—*Who is Ms. Anderson?*

—*Why was she following me?*

CHAPTER EIGHTEEN

Tony Ramos lit a cigarette and took a deep drag as he looked up at the night sky. He could just make out the moon. The stars were having a difficult time competing with the glow from the city lights. Bay Street was not the place for stargazing. Tony took another drag on his cigarette as he turned his attention to the bar across the street. The smoke swirled up into his eyes and made him squint, revealing deep wrinkles that had taken up permanent residence on his face.

Two young couples were walking hand in hand enjoying each other's company as they window shopped along the way. A large display of Rolex watches caught their attention. One of the young girls laughed as she told her boyfriend to "Keep dreaming baby." Tony smiled to himself as he looked at the young girl. She was all that this guy really needed. Love was more fulfilling than a gold Rolex.

Tony took another drag on the cigarette and subconsciously cupped it in his right hand. He held it behind his back in a futile attempt to pretend that it wasn't there. He wished that he had never started smoking. Each year he tried to stop. Following his father's death from lung cancer at seventy-one years of age, Tony had *quit* again. The four months without a cigarette were miserable. He soon realized that he didn't know what to do with his hands. They were accustomed to holding a cigarette. The pen he carried didn't do the trick. Neither did the toothpick. He finally gave up and was back hiding butts in the palm of his hand. It was his only real vice—probably one that would end up killing him. Tony looked at his watch. It was 2130 hours. At this rate, it was going to be a long night.

Carlos emerged from the second bar and ran his fingers through his hair with his left hand signaling that he had had no luck. Carlos continued walking west along Bay Street. Tony moved along on the other side of the street keeping Carlos in sight. There were several more bars between the bank and the British Colonial Hilton. Tony Ramos watched for any sign that someone may be following Carlos. He looked back at the last bar, but no one had come out. Several cars went by. None slowed or showed any indication of stopping.

At 2142, Carlos went into the New York Lounge. Tony sat on a bench across the street and lit up another cigarette. He had parked the car halfway between the hotel and the third bar. The car was two parking spaces east of the New York Lounge. His plan was to move the car so that he was never more than a half a block from it. Carlos would never allow himself to be hustled off in a car; however, if he were overpowered and forced, then Tony would deliberately cause an accident.

As Carlos entered the bar, several eyes turned in his direction. The bar was about half full. Many of the patrons were well past middle-aged. There were two young barmaids wearing short shorts and halter-tops. The tops didn't seem to be doing a very good job at haltering anything. For whatever reason, they hadn't been able to attract a younger crowd. A rough looking bartender with too many tattoos and piercings was stationed behind the bar. He looked like he was auditioning for the part of Dog the Bounty Hunter. Carlos smiled to himself, he felt right at home.

When he was young, this was the kind of bar that he would go into alone, take out his dental bridge, slap it down on the bar, have a couple of beers and clean house just for the fun of it. He was older now, and his dental bridge was much larger and attached to dental implants making it much harder to remove.

There were eighteen bar stools. Fourteen were occupied—ten men and four women. The women were well over the hill but still tried to make eye contact. They pretended to be interested, but they weren't. The bar would fit right in anywhere in the rural south, and certainly in West Virginia, but it was really out of place in Nassau.

Several patrons eyeballed him for a few seconds, but they seemed to lose interest rather quickly and returned to their conversations. This was definitely a local bar, and certainly not the kind of atmosphere he would imagine John Kilday staying in for very long. Carlos was about to choose a stool when "Dog" asked what he was having. Dog's high-pitched voice caught Carlos by surprise. Looks can be deceiving.

"I'll have a shot of Jack Daniels and a Sam Adams. Keep them separate," he responded as he chose one of the two empty stools next to a middle-aged guy wearing a Yankees ball cap. The hat was pulled down so far that it pushed the guy's ears out giving him a comical appearance. Since no one wanted to sit next to him, he was probably the pseudo-gatekeeper.

Dog placed the shot and beer in front of Carlos. His aftershave hadn't worn off. It was inexpensive and permeated the air.

"Should I start a tab?" he asked.

"No, I'm not staying very long. I just need some information," responded Carlos as he sipped the beer.

Dog backed away from the bar, his jaw tightened. He seemed to grit his teeth. The muscles in his jaw twitched as he stared intently at Carlos.

"What are you? You a cop? You don't look like a cop," said Dog, his voice had changed. It was much deeper and stronger. It fit his appearance. It reminded Carlos of the joke about a gay guy who walked into a bar in the old west and asked where everybody was. The bartender told him they were all out back hanging a queer. The gay guy responded in a deep voice, "No shit!" Carlos suppressed a chuckle.

"I'm a private detective from Miami. I'm trying to find out information about a fellow who may have been in here a few days ago," responded Carlos.

"You have ID?" asked Dog as he leaned forward and placed two very large hands on the edge of the bar. His triceps were impressive. His hands were meaty, and his knuckles were indiscernible.

Carlos reached into his back pocket and brought out a small brown leather wallet. It was cracked with age. He opened it exposing a badge with the seal of the State of Florida plainly visible. He let it dangle as he took out one of several business cards, shuffled through them and handed one to Dog.

"Samuel Fernandez, Private Investigator. Coral Gables, Florida," Dog read the words on the card slowly and out loud, pausing after each word as if he was expecting Carlos to give him a sign of approval for being able to read. "So how do I really know this is you? You got photo ID?"

Dog was either smarter than he looked or he had watched enough TV to ask some of the right questions. Roland had prepared Carlos well. Carlos produced a Florida Driver's license displaying his photo and the name Samuel E. Fernandez. He also produced a PI license that was ragged and looked to be at least twenty years old. Roland had really done a good job. Dog took a little longer than usual looking at the ID. After a few seconds, he nodded his acceptance that it was valid.

"So who you looking for?" asked Dog as he went back to wiping the bar top. His voice seemed to be higher again. Carlos couldn't figure out what was with the voice.

He pulled out the picture of Kilday and put it down on the bar where the guy with the Yankees ball cap could also see it. Dog picked it up and actually studied it before answering.

"Well, Monday's my night off, but if this guy were in here during any of my other shifts, I would have remembered him. Can't help you guy," said Dog.

Before Carlos could say anything else, the guy in the Yankees ball cap spoke up.

"He was here. I remember him. He was all pissed off about something with the bank. Kept saying they stole his money. He did a lot of rambling."

"You're sure it was this guy?" asked Carlos as he handed him the picture.

"Yeah, I'm sure. I kind of felt sorry for the guy. He actually started crying at one point. I bought him a drink," offered Ball Cap.

"How long did he stay?"

"He was here for about forty-five minutes. Had a couple more drinks. Hell, he was already under the weather when he came in, if you know what I mean. Then a couple guys came in and asked him if his name was Kilday. He left with them."

"You wouldn't happen to know who the guys were, would you?" asked Carlos as he put the picture of Kilday back into his shirt pocket.

"Actually, I don't know them personally, but I know who they are and where they hang out," Ball Cap responded as he took a healthy swallow from his beer bottle.

Carlos watched as Ball Cap drank the beer, confident in knowing that his information was valuable. Carlos pulled out a money clip and peeled off a twenty and placed it on the bar. Ball Cap looked at it and continued to drink. Carlos peeled off another twenty. Ball Cap continued to drink as he ignored the money. Carlos picked up the two twenties and put down a fifty.

"That's all you're getting pal," said Carlos.

Ball Cap picked up the fifty and put it in his shirt pocket. He emptied the bottle and signaled for another.

"The Green Parrot. They hang out at the Green Parrot. One guy is called Briggs. The other is a guy named Kudzo. Believe they're from some place in Europe," said Ball Cap.

"You're sure?"

"Yeah, I'm sure," responded Ball Cap, seeming annoyed that Carlos would doubt him.

"Can you describe them?" asked Carlos.

Ball Cap took a couple of swallows of beer and looked up toward the ceiling.

"Briggs is around six feet, two hundred pounds, long dark hair and dark complexion. Looks like he had a bad case of acne as a kid. He has a distinct look. He's the muscle. Kudzo is about five ten and much lighter, maybe one seventy at the most. He's the one with some smarts. Although neither of them would do well on Jeopardy," said Ball Cap, seeming somewhat amused with himself.

Carlos threw down another twenty on the bar and told Dog, "Take care of my friend here." As Carlos got up, Ball Cap grabbed his left arm.

"These are not good guys. You would be wise to get help."

"Thanks," said Carlos. "Don't drink too much, it's not good for you," he added.

"Hey, what ever happened to the old guy?" asked Ball Cap.

Carlos hesitated for a couple of seconds before answering. He looked back at Ball Cap and said very soberly, "Someone beat the hell out of him. He died a couple of days ago."

As Carlos left the bar, he ran his fingers through his hair with his right hand signaling Tony that he had information. He then called Tony on his satellite phone.

"I take it we are in business," answered Tony.

"Looks like it was two guys that got to Kilday. Names are Briggs and Kudzo. They hang out just down the street at the Green Parrot. I believe there is an alley about a half a block east of the bar. Let's meet there."

"I'm heading that way," responded Tony.

Carlos and Tony met up in the alleyway a half a block east of the Green Parrot. It was narrow, dark and went in far enough from the main street to hide any altercation from view. There were numerous dumpsters and doorways that could provide cover. It was the perfect place for an encounter.

The plan was simple. Carlos would go into the bar and have a couple of drinks as he checked out the clientele. Once he was sure that the two guys were there, he would ask the bartender if he remembered seeing John Kilday. He would then ask if the bartender knew Briggs and Kudzo. He expected that the bartender would deny knowing them, at which point Carlos would finish his drink and head for the alley. One way or the other, he knew Briggs and Kudzo would get the message.

"Let's do it," said Tony as he bumped fists with Carlos. Carlos nodded and headed off to the Green Parrot.

At 2230, the bar was about three quarters full. A reggae band was in full swing. The dance floor was crowded with people of all ages dancing in sync to the "Cha Cha Slide." Carlos took a seat at the bar where he had a clear view of the tables. He ordered a shot of Jack Daniels and a Sam Adams. He pretended to watch the dancers as he scanned the rest of the bar.

Two men fitting the description of Briggs and Kudzo were sitting with two women at a table next to a hallway that was marked by a red-lit restroom sign. The R was blinking as if to keep up the beat with the band. Carlos dumped the shot on the floor and then put the shot glass to his lips and threw his head back. He then followed the empty shot with a beer chaser. He only drank about a fourth of the beer. Carlos signaled the bartender and ordered another shot. Carlos had the picture of John Kilday on the bar top when the bartender returned.

"Have you seen this man in here?" he asked as he pushed the picture toward the bartender.

"Lots of people come in here mister. I don't remember them all," he answered.

"Take a good look. He was probably three sheets to the wind. Would have been in here a few days ago," said Carlos as he watched the bartender closely.

"Don't remember him," the bartender responded as he started to walk away.

"How about a guy named Briggs?" called out Carlos. "Do you know Briggs or a guy named Kudzo by any chance?" he added.

The bartender hesitated just enough to let Carlos know that he did indeed know Briggs and Kudzo.

"What were the names?" he asked. Carlos noticed that the bartender looked in the direction of the restrooms.

"Briggs and Kudzo," said Carlos.

The bartender pretended to ponder the names for a few seconds before responding.

"Nope, don't know them. You want another one?" he asked.

"Give me one more shot of Jack Daniels. That ought to do me in for the night," responded Carlos.

Carlos dumped the shot, pretended to drink it and took another swallow of beer. He paid his bill, left a couple of bucks and slowly walked out of the bar. As he left, the bartender headed in the direction of the restrooms.

CHAPTER NINETEEN

Tony Ramos took a position across the street just east of the bar. He had an unobstructed view of the entrance. He put out his cigarette, sat on a small wrought iron bench and waited for Carlos to emerge from the Green Parrot. If Carlos ran his fingers through his hair with his right hand, they were in business.

Tony reached into his pocket and felt the handle of his stiletto. He kept his thumb away from the button that would eject a seven-inch blade. The stiletto had been his weapon of choice since the time his government-issued Forty-Five had failed to fire during an extraction mission in Panama. He never did like the Forty-Five especially with the oversized suppressor in place. It was big, heavy and hard to conceal. He felt like he was carrying around a small cannon. He preferred to carry his personal SIG Sauer, but his sergeant told him that the Forty-Five was standard issue, and it had gone through quality control.

"You will carry the Forty-Five asshole," barked the sergeant.

Tony was young. The sergeant had the face and scars of a guy who had been around for a very long time. He must know what he is talking about…at least he did before Panama. So much for quality control.

As he was reminiscing, Carlos sauntered out of the Green Parrot. He stopped and ran his fingers through his hair with his right hand as he looked up and down the street. He looked at his watch and proceeded east toward the entrance to the alleyway. Tony held his position waiting for Briggs and Kudzo to make their appearance. He didn't have to wait very long.

They emerged from the bar looking in both directions. The big guy poked his much smaller partner and motioned by a head nod in the direction of Carlos. Carlos had purposely walked slowly, giving the impression that the drinks had caught up with him. His plan was working. Briggs and Kudzo began following Carlos from a distance of about twenty yards.

Every once in a while Carlos caught a glimpse of their reflection in the store windows. Carlos reached into his pocket and pulled out a package of cigarettes that Tony had given him. Although he hadn't smoked in years, he lit one up and took a couple of puffs. He held the smoke in his mouth for a few seconds and then blew a large blue-white smoke cloud into the air. He didn't inhale. He continued on with the cigarette hanging loosely from the corner of his mouth.

Since Tony was a heavy smoker, Carlos needed to leave a trail of cigarette smoke to hide the presence of Tony, who by now, really smelled of cigarette smoke. Carlos and Tony wouldn't take any chances with an unknown adversary. For all they knew, Briggs and Kudzo could have been professional contractors. Really good operatives will sense the different smells in the air and easily detect the presence of another intruder.

Carlos stepped off the curb and started to go by the alleyway when he stopped. He looked toward the alley as if it occurred to him that it was a giant urinal just waiting for an occasional drunk to leave their deposit from a night of too much drinking. As they say, you only rent beer. Briggs and Kudzo hesitated and whispered something to one another. Tony Ramos had no idea what they were saying. He stayed in the shadows across the street. He and Carlos had already picked the spot in the alley where Carlos would write his name on the wall. Carlos had purposely avoided going to the restroom. By this time his bladder was more than ready to fulfill its part of the deception.

Carlos stumbled down the alley and stopped at the spot where he and Tony had determined was the best place for an ambush—an ambush he and Tony would control. Carlos moved into his writing position in front of a wall that had a dumpster sitting perpendicular to his left. The dumpster provided cover from the street and also cover for Tony.

The alley was fairly dark, but there was enough light to see several feet. Carlos hummed a little tune as he tried to write the name Sam on the wall. He purposely hummed loud enough to give away his position. He had waited so long to go that he got halfway through the name Fernandez. "Sam Fern," he said to himself. When he finished, he zipped up and turned to find Briggs and Kudzo standing close behind him. His eyes darted back and forth between the two men. Their eyes were fixed on him.

"It's all yours," he said. "I don't think there are any towels in here though," he added as he tried to walk past them.

Briggs grabbed him by the arm and threw him back toward the wall. Kudzo moved in closer to Carlos. He was about two feet away.

"Hey, it's not my fault there are no towels in here," slurred Carlos in his best I'm-really-inebriated voice.

Tony Ramos had made his way down the alley and was now within striking distance behind the big guy. Briggs was mashing his right fist in the palm of his left hand. He was itching to beat the crap out of Carlos.

"You're a funny guy," hissed Kudzo. "Who the hell are you, and why are you asking all these questions?" he snapped.

Briggs smacked his left palm with his fist.

"Who the *hell* are you?" responded Carlos in defiance. He placed particular emphasis on the word hell.

Kudzo was about to say something when Tony came up behind Briggs. Without hesitation, Tony reached around with his left arm and grabbed Briggs by the head, pulling it back while simultaneously covering his mouth with his left hand. Before Briggs could respond, Tony plunged the stiletto blade deep into his back. The blade punctured his right lung, causing it to collapse. Kudzo heard the slight gasp and turned to see Tony break Briggs's neck in one easy motion. His limp body made a dull thud as it fell to the ground face down. The slight twitching in his left leg only lasted for a few seconds.

Before Kudzo could do anything, Carlos hit him with a sharp blow to the right kidney. Kudzo went down on his knees. Carlos picked him up and threw him into the side of the dumpster and then hit him with a straight karate blow to the solar plexus. As Kudzo searched for air, Carlos quickly frisked him. The only weapon he found was a push dagger.

"Who hired you to beat up the old man?" asked Carlos in a very clear sober voice.

"I don't know what you are talking about," Kudzo answered, still searching for air.

"The old man you picked up at the New York Lounge. The one you beat up and left for dead. *That* old man," responded Carlos as he gave Kudzo a sharp jab to the ribs.

Kudzo winced in pain as he tried to slide down the side of the dumpster and sit on the ground. Carlos held him up and asked him the same question again.

"Who hired you?"

"I'm not telling you anything," said Kudzo as he looked over at his friend's lifeless body. "You're going to kill me anyway…right?"

Carlos didn't say anything for what must have seemed like an eternity to Kudzo. Kudzo was tough. He spoke with a Slavic accent. He was probably a refugee from Yugoslavia. Guys like Kudzo would go to the grave before giving up any information. Carlos hit him again in the ribs. He could feel them break.

"Who hired you?" asked Carlos in a low clear voice.

"Go to hell," responded Kudzo as he tried to spit at Carlos. Blood began dripping out of his mouth.

"Why would you die for some fat cat who doesn't care a rat's ass about you?" asked Carlos. "A guy who is a big wig in the bank and has an offshore account in the Caymans. You think he cares what happens to you? Hell, he's better off with you dead, and he knows it," added Carlos.

Kudzo didn't say anything. He looked back at Briggs. Carlos knew that he hit a nerve; he was beginning to get to Kudzo. Even though guys like Kudzo only seem to care about money, they still didn't like being suckers.

"I just need you to verify what we already know," said Carlos. "Tell me, who hired you?"

Kudzo looked again at the lifeless body of Briggs.

"McAllister…it was McAllister," he said in a low voice as if he felt ashamed to give him up. "He hired us. He didn't want the old guy running around town shooting off his mouth," responded Kudzo as more blood continued to drip from the corners of his mouth.

"Did he want to scare the old man or eliminate him?" asked Carlos.

Kudzo smirked as he made a funny little sound.

"What do think? McAllister wanted him dead," he responded firmly.

"What about the bartender? How does he fit into this? Do you take orders from him too?" asked Carlos.

Kudzo managed a laugh.

"He doesn't know anything. He just told us that you had asked about Briggs and me by name. He's nothing," responded Kudzo.

Carlos looked over at Tony. They had their confirmation.

"I don't feel so good. Make it quick," said Kudzo as he looked directly at Carlos.

CHAPTER TWENTY

Rick walked out onto the deck, coffee cup in hand. It was a typical October morning. Temperatures were in the low sixties. The hurricane season was about to become history, at least for the Tidewater area.

The morning sun cast long shadows on Rick's side of the lake. There was a slight breeze from the south. A solid gray cloud layer was clearly visible spanning the western sky. A front was approaching rapidly. Rain was in the late morning forecast. An osprey circled overhead searching for unsuspecting fish that were feeding close to the surface of the water. It was the perfect scenario for a few casts, especially along the bulkhead and close to the docks. October was always a good month for catching largemouth bass as they came in from deep water searching for shad and bluegill. Rick grabbed his pole and headed toward his pier. Two guys were standing in a johnboat moving slowly along the shoreline. They were about twenty feet out.

"Any luck?" Rick called out as he cast in their direction close to the bulkhead.

Many fishermen wouldn't admit to catching anything. Most were afraid you'd find out their secrets and where they were catching the big ones. However, some guys didn't care. They just wanted to show off their fishing skills.

"Caught a three-pounder a few minutes ago. We haven't been out long. Should be a good morning for fishing with that front coming," responded the guy in the front of the boat as he motioned toward the west. He was wearing a Boo Weekly camouflaged ball cap that was pulled down well over his forehead and a shirt that boasted, *I got my crabs at Dirty Dick's*. Rick decided that he would never eat at Dirty Dick's.

"How about you?" he asked without looking up. He would have had to tilt his head back pretty far to see Rick.

"Just started," responded Rick as he made a cast right alongside his neighbor's stairs that led down into the water. "If I don't hit one in the next ten minutes then it's time for me to do something else," added Rick.

A couple of years earlier, Rick caught a ten-pound four ounce bass from under his neighbor's dock. Lynn took the customary picture, and Rick let the fish go. By now, it likely weighed about twelve pounds. He was convinced that a state record was lurking close by just waiting for the right presentation. Big fish were weary by nature. That's how they got to be lunkers.

Early on in his bass fishing career, he had caught at least fifty fish weighing between five and eight pounds. He had six citations from the state of Virginia. Thinking that there was more to learn, he started reading several books about bass fishing—*really* learn how to do it. After he "learned" how to bass fish, he didn't catch one over three pounds for several years. He went back to his old way of fishing and was back catching the big ones again. The one thing he learned was, like horses, bass don't read.

The guys in the boat nodded as they increased their speed and slipped on past. They didn't throw in Rick's direction. He took a couple more casts and then headed back into the house. If Lynn was back from her morning walk, she would have grabbed a cup of coffee and joined him on the dock. She had lost her desire to fish a long time ago. She was used to brim fishing and didn't have the patience for bass fishing. However, she did enjoy the trips around the lake in their small bass boat. She would maneuver the boat close to shore as Rick fished. He would always hand her the pole when he hung one. She enjoyed reeling it in.

Rick missed the morning walks with Lynn, but his left knee would protest any thought of a fast walk around the lake. Lynn never went on a casual stroll. When it came to walking, she was all business. Keeping up with her was difficult on two good knees. If he walked with her around the lake, his knee would remind him for the next few days. He was scheduled for knee replacement in November and was actually looking forward to the operation. He had had his right knee replaced two years ago and was very pleased with the results. He knew how to rehab and what to expect. As he looked back out at the lake, he noticed that the two guys in the boat had backed up and were throwing close to his pier. They didn't want to miss an opportunity.

As he stood there looking out, he couldn't help but revisit the events of the last week. There were a lot of loose ends, but it was still very early into the project. Rick was about to get a refill on his coffee when his satellite phone rang. He looked at the caller ID. It was Ann.

"Good morning Ann," he answered.

"Morning Rick. It's not too early?" she asked, knowing that it was never too early for Rick. He and Lynn were both morning people.

"No, I'm just getting back into my morning routine. Made a few casts looking for the big one. Lynn is walking around the lake," responded Rick.

"Did you catch anything?" asked Ann.

"I didn't stay at it long enough," responded Rick.

"I'll have to try that one of these days," said Ann.

Rick smiled to himself as he imagined Ann pulling in a big bass and gutting it before it had a chance to hit the deck.

"So what is the latest on our Ms. Anderson?" Rick asked, knowing that Ann must have something to report.

"She's staying in Arlington. After work she took the metro and got off at Pentagon City. She did a little shopping at Macy's and then walked to the Double Tree Hotel. She's staying in room 403. I had Roland check out the registration. Seems our Ms. Anderson is registered under the name, Farrah Gemayel."

"Farrah Gemayel," repeated Rick as he poured another cup of coffee. Then he added, "Did we ever put a first name with Ms. Anderson?"

"Not to my knowledge," responded Ann.

"What about her car?" asked Rick.

"It's still parked at the embassy."

Rick thought about the car for a few seconds. It was common for people in D.C. to drive to work and then use the metro to run around town. At least the car meant she would be heading back to the embassy.

"I knew some Gemayels who lived in Lebanon. Has Roland checked her out?" asked Rick.

"He's working on it. He's at the office and would like you to give him a call at your earliest convenience," she responded.

"Have you heard from Carlos?" asked Rick.

"He called me a little after midnight and said everything was going as planned. He's hoping to be out of there this afternoon. Said that he and Tony confirmed that McAllister was indeed involved. He'll call you as soon as he has the rest of the information."

"Good, and let's keep an eye on Ms. Anderson. I'm still not sure where she fits into this or whose side she's really on."

"Will do. I have one of my people onsite. I'll let you know as soon as I have some more information," responded Ann. "Say hi to Lynn," she added as she ended the call.

Ann was all business. Rick put down the phone and thought more about the lottery scam. For a scam to be successful it needed to be fairly simple, well organized, and most of all, look official. All that was needed was a significant prize and someone gullible enough to go after it. Separating a fool from his money was always the easy part. There was an abundance of willing victims. Unfortunately, John Kilday happened to be one of them.

However, the presence of the mysterious Ms. Anderson added a new dimension to the lottery scam. There was something else going on that Rick hadn't been able to put his finger on…at least not yet. It wasn't greed alone, although greed was always a motive. The cast of characters was growing. Many questions were going through Rick's head.He was still trying to make the connection between Stankowski and Gemayel. He couldn't figure out their involvement. Could this whole thing have been orchestrated by Homeland Security…and why? The questions went on and on.

NASSAU, BAHAMAS
0830 HOURS

Tony Ramos leaned against the bulkhead. He was 40 miles east off the coast of the Bahamas on a charter fishing boat. He had scheduled the fishing trip as soon as he arrived in the Bahamas. Actually, Tony wasn't a fisherman. He would never go fishing. He didn't enjoy getting up early to ride the waves for a couple of hours just to get to the fishing area.

Fishing in the scorching sun and taking turns in the seat were not Tony's idea of a fun afternoon. He thought it was way too much hassle over catching one big fish…if they were lucky. Not to mention the dreadful couple hour boat ride just to get back to the marina. No, not enjoyable one bit. Besides, no one actually sat there with a pole in hand. No one truly did their own fishing.

The only real enjoyment was watching the young female crewmember. Her name was Molly. She was cute. She wore a tank top with tight shorts that were super short. She had long stringy blonde hair and skin that was beginning to show the effects of too much sun. She moved easily around the deck as she deftly rigged the poles, set the line on the outriggers and watched for fish. While she provided some entertainment for Tony, the real purpose for his fishing excursion was to furnish him with a cover. It would give him another reason for being in the Bahamas as well as lend the perfect opportunity to dump the knife.

Although it was early morning, he and the other five fishermen were already into the beer and crackers. The boat had already hooked into a large marlin. They were taking turns working the fish. Tony's left forearm was sore from his twenty minutes in the seat. It was now Mary's turn. She was a short, overweight, out of shape RN from Ocala, Florida. She had signed on at the last minute replacing one of the lawyers from Boston who had apparently partied too much the night before, and according to his partner, Charlie, wouldn't get out of bed. Besides, Charlie wasn't alone in bed.

Mary was out of breath and having a hard time moving the fish closer to the boat. The captain helped her a bit by backing down every once in a while. She was ready to give up the seat, and Marty Willis was eager to take it. Molly snapped pictures of everyone as they battled the fish. The pictures would be available at the pier for a small fee.

Every now and then the big fish would break the surface of the water and thrash back and forth trying to break loose. It seemed to dance across the water in defiance. It was a spectacular sight, even for Tony. There were several other boats in the area. Two had reported marlin on the line.

The boat wasn't scheduled to return until late in the afternoon. The timing was perfect. Tony planned on hitting a couple of the casinos to play Texas hold 'em for a couple of hours. He would always end up at the blackjack tables where, like most occasional gamblers, he thought he knew what he was doing. He would hit the clubs in Biloxi, Mississippi twice a year. He found gambling to be a challenge that he could deal with. He was a couple thousand dollars ahead and was willing to risk a thousand in the Bahamas. He would stick to his limit. Tony was scheduled to fly out at 1000 hours on Sunday morning.

At the same time Tony was chasing a peanut butter cracker down with some ice cold beer, Carlos was sitting in his rental car a half a block from Ian McAllister's house. He had been there for the past hour. As Carlos reviewed the file Roland prepared on Ian McAllister, McAllister came out of the house, got into his white Lexus SUV and backed out of the driveway. Carlos ducked down as McAllister drove by.

CHAPTER TWENTY-ONE

Carlos followed Ian McAllister from a safe distance. Since McAllister had no idea that anyone was on to him, following him should be no problem. However, Carlos would play the game and not be complacent. He had made that mistake once before as a young navy SEAL during a surveillance operation in Cali, Colombia. He had pulled out too soon and ended up between his target and the chase car. The chase car was easy to spot. It was full of young Colombians, the tips of their guns clearly visible as they provided protection for el Hefe. Carlos shook his head and pounded the seat next to him. He had to break it off and ended up loosing the *rabbit*, at least temporarily.

The information provided by Roland indicated that McAllister was a widower who had purposely avoided the social scene for the past year and a half. However, recently he had been seen in the company of a younger woman. Not much was known about her other than she had worked for a publisher in New York City, made a good sum of money and had decided to move to the Bahamas. She had bought a large home in a gated community on the other side of the island. Roland had identified the woman as Sharon Gillespie.

McAllister parked his car, checked the meter and went into a small shop that appeared to sell everything from shirts to Cuban cigars.

Carlos drove by slowly and found a parking space further down the street. He parked and waited in the car. There were quite a few tourists checking out the various shops. Carlos adjusted the rearview mirror so that he would have a good view of the entrance to the small shop.

Within a couple of minutes, McAllister emerged with a newspaper folded and tucked up under his left arm. He lit a small cigar and headed in the direction of his car. Carlos watched as McAllister stopped at the parked SUV and put several coins into the meter. From the amount of coins, it appeared that McAllister wasn't going anywhere for at least an hour. Carlos got out of his rental, checked the meter, crossed the street and watched as McAllister entered a small café.

There were about a dozen tables scattered haphazardly in front of the café. Only a few were unoccupied. Carlos stopped across the street and sat down on one of the wrought iron benches that was uniformly positioned near the curb on each block. He pretended to be reading the weekend edition of the USA Today that had been left at his hotel room door the morning before. Carlos could see McAllister in the café window.

As Carlos watched, McAllister walked out of the café with a coffee and scone in hand and selected one of the tables next to the sidewalk. There were two empty chairs at his table. Carlos held his position and continued to watch. There was a good chance that McAllister was waiting for someone. Maybe his new found friend, Ms. Gillespie. Carlos looked at his watch. He had plenty of time, although, he never liked playing the waiting game. Patience may be a virtue, but it most certainly wasn't one that Carlos possessed.

McAllister spread the newspaper out on the table. A young couple emerged from the café and took a table in the far corner. McAllister cut his scone into several pieces. As he popped one of the pieces into his mouth, he began to read the paper. Carlos decided that McAllister probably wasn't waiting for anyone, since he had started to eat the scone. It was time to make his move.

Carlos opened his briefcase and retrieved what appeared to be a silver ring with a saddle on it. He placed it on his right middle finger being careful not to touch the small needle on its underside. Carlos proceeded across the street directly to McAllister's table, pulled out one of the chairs and sat down. A startled Ian McAllister looked up. He had a puzzled expression on his face, almost to the point of disbelief.

He looked much older than the picture Roland had provided. His hair was full and nearly pure white. There were deep wrinkles across his forehead and around his eyes. His neck had more lines than a road map. He had several large age spots on both sides of his face and neck—one that needed the attention of a dermatologist. His hands were covered in various sized brown spots. The veins in his hands were pronounced. Although his biography indicated that he was sixty-two, he could easily pass for mid-to-late seventies.

"Good morning Mr. McAllister," said Carlos as he put a small tape recorder on top of the newspaper.

McAllister still didn't say anything. He was beginning to regain his composure. He looked around to see if anyone else was watching him. He looked down at the recorder and then back to Carlos. His expression changed from one of confusion to who the hell are you.

"Do I know you?" asked McAllister, his mind searching for an immediate answer—an answer that wasn't there.

Carlos needed to keep McAllister off balance. He didn't want to give him any time to regroup.

"We have a mutual *friend*," said Carlos as he pushed the play button.

The recorder started. Carlos lowered the volume just enough for McAllister to hear. McAllister leaned forward to listen to the voice.

"McAllister…it was McAllister. He hired us. He didn't want the old guy running around town shooting off his mouth."

Carlos hit the stop button and put the recorder back into his pocket. McAllister went ashen. He fell back against the chair and might have slumped to the ground if Carlos hadn't gotten up and steadied him. Carlos bent close to him and spoke clearly.

"You recognized Kudzo's voice," he whispered in McAllister's ear as he pressed the ring into the right side of his neck. "By the way, the *old guy* is dead," he added, mimicking Kudzo's description of John Kilday.

McAllister flinched and turned his head toward Carlos. He reached up and felt his neck where Carlos had injected a fatal dose of serum that Carlos had used before. McAllister didn't say anything. Carlos sat down and took a small bottle from his pocket and rattled it. He held it tightly in his right hand.

"John Kilday was a close friend," Carlos lied. "McAllister, I'm not going to screw around with you. We know about the lottery scam. We know about your million-dollar payoff and your account in the Caymans. The little sting you just felt is a death sentence if you don't take these pills in the next twelve minutes," Carlos said as he looked at his watch. He tapped the crystal to give the impression that it might have stopped.

McAllister could feel little drops of urine dripping down his left thigh. He tried not to wet his pants. He had never been this scared. He had always been in control.

"What do you want from me?" he asked, his voice struggling to say the words.

"Who opened the offshore account?" asked Carlos as he leaned forward. His eyes didn't blink.

"I can't tell you that information," said McAllister defiantly.

Carlos smiled as he looked at his watch. He shook his head and rattled the small pill bottle.

"You *can't* tell me? You have less than seven minutes."

McAllister was sweating profusely. He wiped his brow with one of the napkins. He felt the side of his neck. His heart was pounding. He was having a hard time focusing on Carlos.

"Six minutes McAllister," said Carlos again as he rattled the small bottle. "Quite frankly, I really don't care if you tell me. I think I have enough information. But to get these pills, I need confirmation," he added.

Part of McAllister wanted to uphold the rules and regulations of the bank. Protect the identity of their clients. That was the whole idea of offshore accounts. The other part of McAllister wanted to live. He certainly had several good years left, and he wanted time to enjoy his newfound lady friend. That part won the inward battle.

"Triad Associates. The account was opened in the name of Triad Associates," responded McAllister as he licked his lips. His mouth was dry. "Please, give me the pills," he added as he held out a bony hand. His hand was visibly shaking. There was a look of desperation on his face.

Carlos put up a finger as he pulled out his satellite phone and called Roland Carpenter. He asked him to look up Triad Associates. Within seconds, Roland told him that Triad Associates was located in Tampa, Florida. It appeared to be a subsidiary of Triad Investment International.

"Where is Triad located?" asked Carlos for confirmation.

McAllister wiped his forehead. He was breathing hard.

"Tampa, Florida," responded McAllister.

"Who opened the account? I want a name," demanded Carlos.

McAllister looked at the bottle. He twisted his head from side to side and wiped his brow again. His neck was getting stiff. There was no time to stall.

"The guy who opened the account was…was Arabic I believe," he answered. He was now sweating profusely.

"What is his name?" asked Carlos.

"It was a foreign last name that started with an H," responded McAllister.

"Think. What was his name," prodded Carlos as he stared intently at the old man.

"I could never pronounce it correctly. Haddad I believe," replied McAllister as he reached for the pill bottle.

CHAPTER TWENTY-TWO

Rick Morgan sat at the kitchen table and began making a list of questions concerning the lottery scam. He was fully engaged. He wrote down the name Farrah Gemayel a.k.a. Ms. Anderson. He then circled it several times and then began tapping it with the tip of his pencil. Who was this woman? What was she doing at the Bahamian Embassy? From what they were learning, she was certainly not a receptionist. In Rick's mind, her presence elevated the lottery scam from one of simple greed to an element of international conspiracy.

"Something else is going on," he said out loud.

It made him look around to see if Lynn had heard him. He continued to tap her name with the pencil. What was her relationship with Robert Stankowski? Was she with Homeland Security? And if she was with Homeland Security, why had someone doctored the database to re-direct a search of her fingerprints? No, she had to be a third party contractor. And if so, who at Homeland Security hired her, and what was their motive? She could be the key to everything…or a very good distraction.

Rick added Robert Stankowski's name to the list. The list was getting longer. Each entry generated more questions—questions with no answers. Rick drew a line from Farrah Gemayel's name to Robert Stankowski's name. He put an arrow tip on each end of the line.

Rick put the pencil on the table, refilled his cup with the last of the morning coffee and walked over to the sliding glass door. The front was getting much closer. The wind had picked up quite a bit. There were white caps moving across the lake like a flotilla of small ships. Several ducks rode the small ships, seeming to enjoy the voyage. The local osprey was nowhere in sight. Several wrens were on the bird feeder and appeared to be oblivious to the approaching front.

Rick looked at his watch and then back outside. It would be raining within fifteen minutes. The forecast had predicted a fast moving front with winds up to sixty miles per hour. As Rick looked out through the sliding glass door, his weather radio sounded an alarm followed by a voice from Wakefield stating that there was a severe thunderstorm warning until six p.m. local time.

"Large hail is normally associated with these storms," said the voice.

Lynn had just come in from her walk and asked if he wanted to go shopping with her. She wanted to pick up a few things for a baby shower that she would be hosting in the near future.

"Have you looked outside?" asked Rick as he pointed with his cup in the direction of the front.

Lynn never paid much attention to the weather. It was either nice, or it wasn't. Rick was her weatherman, and her sister would always keep her well informed when it came to the long-term hurricane forecast.

"Wow!" she exclaimed. "Where did that come from?" she asked as she went to the door. "It didn't look like rain when I started my walk."

Rick knew what she would say next. He mouthed the words to himself almost verbatim and in unison with hers.

"Do we need to bring everything close to the house?" she asked. It was really a rhetorical question. Lynn's body language indicated that she was ready to head out the door and start gathering up the plants and lawn furniture.

"Honey, if the wind is really bad, all the stuff will end up next to the house anyway. I think we will be all right," responded Rick as he sipped his coffee.

Lynn really didn't like Rick's cavalier attitude toward the storm. After twenty years as a navy pilot, storms never seemed to bother him. He had taken off and landed on aircraft carriers in the North Atlantic in the wintertime. Twenty-foot seas were not uncommon.

She was ready to head out the door, dragging him behind her, when a bolt of lightening lit up the western sky. It looked like it struck something on the other side of the lake. Rick counted to himself. The clap of thunder was five seconds later. The bolt of lightning was about a mile away and approaching fast. A sheet of rain began making its way across the lake announcing that the front was here. The storm was definitely moving fast. Small waves began to pound Rick's side of the lake. Water splashed over the top of the bulkhead. A loose paddleboat was bobbing its way toward Rick's neighbor's dock. No one would be there to retrieve it.

"Well, it's too late now. I guess I should have been a little more vigilant," apologized Rick, sporting a sheepish look of surrender. The look was contrived, and she knew it.

Lynn acquiesced. There was no sense in badgering Rick. Besides, he was usually right when it came to storms. Moving everything was usually a big waste of time. Only one time did they come home to find their small Javelin sailboat upside down in the water. Just the underside of the boat was visible. The mast was stuck in the mud. It took them an hour to free the boat and another hour to pump out the water.

"When the storm passes, will you go to the store with me?" asked Lynn, knowing that Rick, at this point, would probably do anything to appease her.

"I was planning on going with you," he responded. A forced smile crossed his face.

"Yeah right," she responded.

Lynn knew that Rick would do just about anything to get out of going shopping. Like most men, Rick would only go shopping out of necessity. He was a classic type-A personality. He knew what he wanted, knew where to find it and wasted no time getting it to the register. It was almost like a race to get home. He was certainly no fun to take on a shopping trip. However, Lynn was still happy that after all these years he would still go just to be with her. Besides, what else did he have to do, he was retired.

"I'll get dressed," she said. She had already lost all interest in the storm. By now, the brunt of the storm had passed. There was no hail. It was a good soaking rain. Lynn wouldn't have to water for a week.

Rick picked up his list, folded it and put it in his pocket. He just remembered that he hadn't called Roland. He also hadn't heard from Carlos, but he didn't expect to hear from Carlos until he was on the way home. No news meant that everything was going as planned. Ann had passed along the information from Carlos confirming McAllister's involvement in the lottery scam. Now all that was needed was the name of the account holder.

Rick looked out at the storm. The rain was steady, and the wind had subsided. The storm would soon pass. Rick picked up his satellite phone and dialed Roland. Roland was quick to answer.

"Good morning Mr. Morgan." Rick could hear music in the background.

"Morning Roland. Are you in the office?" he asked.

"I am. I needed to finish a brief for Homeland Security. Mr. Peterson is scheduled to be back on Monday. I find that I can get a lot done on the weekend," added Roland.

"Roland, you work too much. We need to get you out more. Shoot, you're a young guy, you need a girlfriend," said Rick.

"I don't have time for a girlfriend," responded Roland without a second of thought. He actually sounded serious.

Rick smiled. He knew the type. Guys like Roland loved the work. Unfortunately, they would miss out on a lot of life. Miss the good years. By the time Roland decided to settle down, he would be in his late thirties, maybe even in his forties. By that time, the pickings would be mostly divorcees with kids and loads of baggage. Good luck, he thought to himself.

"Ann mentioned that you wanted me to call," said Rick.

"I did some more checking on Ms. Farrah Gemayel," responded Roland. "I ran her prints through Interpol and Mossad. I got hits on both sites. Seems her reputation is well known in international circles. She's basically a contract worker—does wet work for the highest bidder. She doesn't take sides or appear to have any political leanings. With her, it's all about the money. One thing was interesting, there was no current picture of her available."

Rick looked back at his list and thought about her meeting with Robert Stankowski. There was actually nothing out of the ordinary. She followed a certain protocol making it difficult for someone to follow her without compromising their position. Many operatives would take a bus, then walk for a while, grab a cab, take the metro and then jump into a car and speed off—always watching to see if anyone was following. They could spot an amateur from a mile away. The whole clandestine thing is just a big game, but if not played well, a game with fatal results.

"The lack of a photo doesn't surprise me. Do you have an address on her?" asked Rick.

"She has a small condo in Atlanta. I'll email you everything I have. She's been there for six months," responded Roland. "Before that, she lived in London. I'm going to do a little more digging to see if I can locate a photo and anything else we might have overlooked. Also, I have some information on Triad Associates."

"Triad Associates? That's a new one to me," said Rick.

"Carlos called me this morning and asked me to check it out. I assumed it was some information he had obtained that he needed to verify," responded Roland.

"What did you find out?" asked Rick.

"Triad is a subsidiary of Triad International, which is a subsidiary of Global International. The list goes on. Looks like several shells. The bottom line is that the registered agent for Triad Associates is a guy by the name of Tarek Haddad. I believe that was the information Carlos was looking for."

"Where is the company registered?" asked Rick.

"Triad Associates appears to be located in Tampa, Florida," responded Roland.

"Appears to be?" asked Rick, knowing that Roland normally dealt with specifics.

"I couldn't find a business license or federal ID number. The only thing I found was a P.O. box but no actual business address," responded Roland.

Rick thought for a few seconds. It made perfect sense that there was no license or corporate documentation. Triad had no intention of dealing with the city, state or federal government for that matter. They were running a scam.

"What about this guy Tarek?" asked Rick.

"Tarek Haddad," responded Roland. "I have an address, although I haven't checked it out. Seems he lives on a boat in a marina," added Roland.

"Good. Anything else?" asked Rick.

"That's it for now. I will call you as soon as I have some more solid information," responded Roland.

"Thanks, and seriously…find yourself a good woman," added Rick.

"Where?" asked Roland.

Roland's quick response caught Rick by surprise.

"Church," answered Rick. "Church is the best place. Talk with you later."

Rick closed his satellite phone. In his mind he visualized Roland working away. The kid was certainly a workaholic. He was young, smart, good looking and would probably make a good husband someday…if he found the right woman.

Finding the right woman was not easy. Rick had lucked out. Lynn was the perfect mate. More importantly, she knew how to handle Rick—when to calm him down and how to reel him in. She was eight years younger than he, but in the early years of their marriage, she was much more mature.

She had taken him to church on their third date. She had been raised in an Assembly of God church. Rick was raised Roman Catholic. About halfway through the service, Rick was convinced that a bolt of lightening was going to come through the roof and strike him right there in the pew. Every once in a while he would look up to the rafters.

Yes, he thought to himself, Roland needs to find a nice church-going southern gal.

WASHINGTON, D.C.

1400 HOURS

Robert Stankowski hung up the phone and quickly made some notes in a small black notebook. He rubbed his upper lip with the forefinger of his right hand, his thumb resting under his chin. It was a habit, something he had always done when he needed to think. For whatever reason, the pausing gesture helped him to relax. It helped him to focus. He stared at the notes for several minutes then picked up his phone and started to make a call. He put the phone down, went to his wet bar and poured a Jack Daniels Black Label on the rocks. He drank nearly all of it. He looked at the glass and re-filled it nearly to the top. He hardly ever had a drink this early in the day. But he needed it. He took another look at his notes and then dialed the number.

"Hello," answered a woman on the other end of the line. Her voice sounded annoyed. She knew the caller on the other end of the line.

"We need to meet," Stankowski said.

"Can it wait until Monday?" asked the woman.

"Monday may be too late," said Stankowski.

There was silence on the line for a couple of minutes.

"Okay, thirty minutes. You know where."

CHAPTER TWENTY-THREE

WASHINGTON, D.C.
OCTOBER 13, 2012
SATURDAY
1440 HOURS

Robert Stankowski got off at the Smithsonian Metro Station at precisely 1430 hours. The walk to the Washington Monument took less than five minutes. The Mall was crowded with the usual tourists. A group of Japanese female students dressed in matching checkered skirts were giggling and posing for pictures. A man with a beard in a trench coat held up a sign declaring that the end was near. Stankowski looked at him and nodded in agreement as he took out a pack of Marlboros. He offered one to the bearded man. The man moved in closer, his eyes piercing as he shrieked for all to hear, "The end is near!" He didn't seem to notice the cigarette.

Stankowski was somewhat relieved since there were only five cigarettes left. He had already smoked a pack since breakfast. He didn't even remember opening the second pack. At this rate, he would reach his two-pack limit before the evening meal. The guy was right. The end was most certainly near.

He lit the cigarette with a lighter given to him by General Wesley Clark in the spring of 1998. It had a NATO emblem on one side and the General's name on the other. Only a small amount of blue paint was left on one of the four stars. He stood there for several minutes thinking about his conversation with McAllister. He knew this whole thing was about to blow up. He just didn't want to be a part of the collateral damage.

He took a deep drag on the cigarette and blew a large smoke ring that rapidly lost its shape in the afternoon breeze. He took another drag and looked around the Mall. He noticed a woman wearing a Redskins ball cap walking purposely toward him. At first he didn't recognize her. From her gait and the directness of her approach, she obviously knew him. She had already made eye contact.

As she approached, he realized that it was Yolanda Rawls. He had never seen her on the weekend without her full makeup, auburn wig, tailored suit and stiletto heels. She was in her early forties, confident and in a position of unfettered power—power she wielded with no second thought or *adult* supervision. On this Saturday afternoon she looked like she had been cleaning the house. He dropped his half-smoked cigarette on the ground, crushed it with the toe of his right foot and walked toward her. They met halfway between the Washington Monument and the Smithsonian.

"So what the hell is so important that we had to meet this afternoon?" she snarled. The cleaning lady's power had returned. She was obviously very upset and didn't like being called out on the weekend, especially by one of her contract personnel.

"We've got a problem," responded Stankowski as he motioned her toward an empty bench. He tried not to look her over, but the sight of her in jeans, a sweatshirt and ball cap was too tempting. He wasn't exactly sure how she was able to get into her jeans. They appeared to be painted on.

As they sat down, his eyes darted around the Mall. He was always aware of his surroundings and who may be watching from a distance. Old habits die hard.

"So what is this problem?" she hissed impatiently.

"I got a call from McAllister this morning. He didn't sound very well. Seems he was visited by a guy who knew all about the lottery scam."

She didn't say anything for several seconds. She just stared at him as she weighed the information. Then her expression relaxed.

"So what!" she exclaimed. "His only connection is with Haddad. He knows nothing else. He knows nothing about us. We've got nothing to worry about," she said as she started to get up. Her body language was screaming out in annoyance.

"Hold on…there's more," responded Stankowski as he grabbed her by the left forearm.

She looked down at his hand in disbelief, pulling back. He ignored the how-dare-you look and continued to hold her arm as she settled back onto the bench. Her eyes narrowed.

"One of the victims of *your* lottery scam was an old guy by the name of John Kilday," he added.

"So who the hell is this John Kilday?" she asked condescendingly.

"It turns out that Kilday is the father-in-law of Carl Peterson's nephew," responded Stankowski.

"What the hell are we playing here? Is this some kind of fucking guessing game?" she snapped. "Get to the point!" she exclaimed. Her eyes said it all.

"The *point* is that Carl Peterson owns The Peterson Group. Peterson made a visit to the Bahamian Embassy the other day. He was asking the ambassador to investigate the beating of John Kilday," responded Stankowski.

"So who beat up this guy Kilday?" she asked.

"A couple of guys hired by McAllister," he responded.

She thought for a minute and settled deeper onto the bench.

"So we are still in the clear," she said. It sounded more like a question than a statement. Her tone had changed.

"Our contact at the embassy followed Peterson. Peterson met with Rick Morgan. She followed Morgan back to the Ritz Carlton and then broke off the surveillance and called me. I didn't know that Morgan and Peterson had hooked up again, and I'd be willing to bet my ass that the guy who McAllister talked to was a former SEAL by the name of Carlos Garcia."

She began to listen more closely. She took a deep breath.

"They still don't have any connection to us," she said.

"You just don't get it do you?" responded Stankowski. "These guys are all ex-CIA. Hell, they could still be CIA for that matter. Peterson's company is a black ops firm. Among other things, they do wet work for the government. They know about Triad Associates and Tarek Haddad. How long do you think it will be before they make the connection to us?" he asked. "This isn't going away," he added before she had a chance to answer.

She was about to speak, hesitated, then regrouped fast.

"It doesn't matter. I don't care what they find out. They are interfering with a federal sting operation," she said. Her tone had changed again, back to one of defiance.

Stankowski reached into his pocket and pulled out the package of cigarettes.

"Do you mind if I have a smoke?" he asked as he offered her one. She declined, her face showing disapproval of cigarettes. He lit up and blew the smoke over his left shoulder, away from her.

"At this point, they don't know this is a federal sting operation," he said. "However, since it resulted in the death of John Kilday, you can bet that

Carl Peterson won't care, and he won't let it go. I can assure you that he and Morgan will connect all the dots, and it won't be long."

"Again, I say, *so what*. What are they going to do about it? If they interfere, I'll have them arrested. I'll make their fucking lives miserable," she responded arrogantly, her eyes narrowing again.

Stankowski took a deep drag on the cigarette. He wanted to blow the smoke right in her face. He really didn't like her. As far as he was concerned, she was a by-product of affirmative action scraping the bottom of the barrel. She could have been the poster child for the Peter Principle. She had reached the height of her incompetence a long time ago, and worse yet, she couldn't be fired. He shook his head in disbelief.

"Do you really want Homeland Security to know all the details of your operation?" he asked.

"What are you saying?" she said defensively. "I was given a project. I had *carte blanche*," she emphasized carte blanche. "It was mine to run with. It is not my fault that some guy got himself killed."

Stankowski looked at her and thought to himself that she was a selfish cold-hearted bitch. But she had hired him. She authorized the checks that he had gladly accepted. He bit his tongue and then spoke.

"I thought the whole point of Homeland Security was to save lives."

"It still is. Isn't it better to lose one guy in order to save millions? What the hell do you think would happen if one of these terrorist groups sets off a dirty bomb at Times Square? How many lives do you think that would take? Isn't this guy, what's his name, worth the risk?" she asked, not looking for a response.

"There were other ways to do it, other ways to get the money. Ways that wouldn't have risked any lives," he said.

"Maybe so. But in this case, time was of the essence. The latest HUMINT reports indicate that Hezbollah is negotiating to acquire one of the missing Russian suitcase bombs. We had to act. We needed to give Tarek credibility. For the plan to work, he needed to be dirty. Besides, once we got McAllister, I could then pressure him to provide a list of offshore accounts. Not only would we recover the dirty bomb and the terrorists trying to acquire it, but also we would have an opportunity to go after the fat cats who are hiding their money from us."

Stankowski shook his head and smiled. She was a piece of work. She saw an opportunity to advance her career and jumped at it. This whole thing was all about her and her precious career.

"Well, I got news for you Ms. Rawls. McAllister won't be of any help."

She had a puzzled look on her face.

"What do you mean? What are you talking about? If he's given immunity why wouldn't he help?" she asked.

"Because, by now, he's probably dead," responded Stankowski as he looked at his watch.

"Dead? What are you talking about? And how would you possibly know that?" she asked, her voice more controlled.

Stankowski took another drag on the cigarette and then snuffed it out under the bench seat before he dropped it. He took out another cigarette and lit it. He looked directly into her cold impassionate eyes as he blew smoke over his shoulder.

"He didn't sound well during our conversation. I asked him if he were okay. He said that he wasn't feeling well but had taken the pills to counter the effects of the poison. I asked what he thought he was given. He didn't know. He said that the guy injected something into his neck, and then said he would give him the pills to neutralize the poison. All he needed to do was to provide the right answers, and the pills were his."

"And you really think that he was injected with some kind of cloak and dagger James Bond bullshit poison?" she responded, her face contorted. "Nobody does that shit anymore."

"I don't *think* he was. I *know* that he was, and the pills were probably aspirin. The only thing that the aspirin would do is accelerate the action of the poison," responded Stankowski. "McAllister is dead. You can bet on it. And the guys who beat up the old man will be found in some dumpster," he added.

Neither of them said anything for several minutes. Stankowski took out another cigarette and lit up. He had smoked half of the cigarette before she spoke.

"Send a couple of your people to Tampa. Have them stakeout Haddad's boat, and if this guy Peterson or his people get too close, we'll deal with it then." she said.

"Deal with it?" asked Stankowski.

"Do I have to draw you a fucking picture?" she snarled. "Yes, deal with it!"

Stankowski didn't immediately respond. He thought about Carl Peterson, Morgan and Garcia. Yeah right, deal with them, the flies ganging up on the spiders, he thought to himself.

"Are we done here?" she said, interrupting his parlor thoughts.

"You're the boss. I hope this doesn't come back to bite us in the ass," he said, referring only to him and his people. He didn't care about her ass—though it was somehow stuffed into those skin-tight designer jeans she had on.

She got up and walked away without saying anything else. Stankowski flipped a half-inch of ashes from his cigarette and took a deep drag. He watched as she disappeared into the crowd. He thought about Carl Peterson, Rick Morgan and Carlos Garcia. He knew them, had worked with them, liked them and certainly didn't want to be on the other side of their gun. Sometimes life sucks, he thought as he put out the cigarette. He took his cell phone from his pocket and made a call to Farrah Gemayel.

CHAPTER
TWENTY-FOUR

Rick and Lynn had just been seated at Aldo's Ristorante when Rick's satellite phone vibrated. The position of the phone caused him to flinch. Lynn smiled at his reaction as he took the phone from his belt. He looked at the caller ID and told Lynn that he was sorry, but he really needed to take the call. She never questioned him when he got a call on the satellite phone. It was always business. And it was *always* confidential. She smiled as Rick slid out of the booth. He said that he wouldn't be more than a minute or two.

"I'll order for us if that is okay?" she asked. "Do you have a preference?"

"Anything you want. A glass of Pinot Noir would be nice. Love you babe. I'll be right back," he said as he kissed her on the cheek and walked outside.

Carlos could hear their conversation. It made him think about Ann and how much he missed her. Rick walked slowly on the sidewalk along the shops, the phone to his ear. Before he could say anything a flight of four F-18s in right echelon flew overhead on their way into Oceana Naval Air Station. Although the sound was well behind the aircraft, it rumbled along like thunder filling a void created by a bolt of lightning. He waited a few more seconds as he watched the aircraft make a slight left turn and enter the landing pattern.

"Carlos, I take it you are back. How did it go?"

"It went as we expected. I sent some information to Roland. Have you had a chance to speak with him?" asked Carlos.

"That I have. Seems Triad Associates is nothing more than a P.O. box in Tampa," responded Rick. "They probably don't have an office," he added. "Are you in Virginia Beach or did you go back to D.C.?"

"I'm in Atlanta just about to board. My flight gets into Norfolk a little after twenty thirty. I need to spend a few days there and do some things around the house," responded Carlos. Rick knew long distance relationships posed their challenges. Fortunately the commute between Virginia Beach and D.C. wasn't too bad.

"What about McAllister?" asked Rick.

"He and his two goons are paid in full," responded Carlos.

"And Tony?" asked Rick.

"He's been fishing all day. He's scheduled to fly out tomorrow afternoon. Said he wanted to hit a couple of the casinos tonight. Thinks he's a good blackjack player. Losing a few bucks will just add to his cover."

"How's he doing…physically?" asked Rick.

"He's back. His wound has healed very well. He's nearly a hundred per cent. The guy is tough as nails," responded Carlos.

"Sounds good. Let's get together tomorrow afternoon and go over what we have so far. There are still a lot of unanswered questions. See you tomorrow," said Rick as he turned and headed back toward the entrance to Aldo's.

Another flight of two F-18s came out of nowhere and entered the high key position. Rick watched them as the first aircraft banked hard to the left. The 90-degree bank was executed in one quick motion of the stick. White ribbons of air streamed from the wingtips as the plane began to slow and dirty up. Rick envied the young aviators. They didn't know how lucky they were. Someday they would have to get a real job.

Rick put the phone back in his pocket. He thought about the lottery scam and the mission in Nassau. Nobody would miss the goons, and the authorities would conclude that McAllister died of natural causes—a heart attack to be precise. An autopsy would turn up nothing. Besides, there was no reason for the Bahamian authorities to suspect foul play.

Rick walked in and sat down to a nice glass of Pinot Noir and some focaccia bread that was right out of the oven. Lynn was sprinkling freshly grated Parmesan cheese over the oil and vinegar mix that had been ceremoniously prepared by the server.

"So everything is okay?" asked Lynn as she looked up. Her eyes sparkled in the soft overhead light. She knew that Rick would tell her that everything was okay. It was foolish to ask, but maybe someday he would let her in on some of his secrets. He had plenty and had promised their daughter Brooke that one day he would write his memoirs. But that day was well into the future.

"That was Carlos. He was in Atlanta and wanted to let me know he would be back in town tomorrow. Asked me if I wanted to go flying. He needs to put some time on the plane and make a few approaches," Rick said as he swirled the wine glass. He appeared to be looking for the fingers on the inside of the glass, but the vision of the F-18s still lingered in his mind. It brought back great memories of a time too long ago.

"How are he and Ann doing?" Lynn asked, suspecting that Carlos was on his way back from an assignment—one that she would never hear about.

She had figured out a long time ago that when Rick gave her a long answer to a simple question, his answer was a pure fabrication. She enjoyed his mental gymnastics and how fast he could make something up. He was good. He would feed on the surroundings. She had heard the jets overhead.

"They're doing very well. I expect we will be attending a wedding in the very near future," responded Rick.

"That's if Carlos survives these little vacations," she said, forcing a suspicious smile as the server arrived in the nick of time with two garden salads.

Rick smiled, although he had no intention of responding to her barb. He knew that she was better off not knowing what was going on.

She would only worry. She would probably try once more and then let it go. She had put up with a lot over the years but never complained. She hid her frustration well. Rick knew that there was no one like Lynn.

As a young naval officer he couldn't wait to get home to be with her, to see her smiling face. Most of the guys would hang around all day drinking coffee. They would shoot the breeze and do none of their work so they would have something to do aboard the ship after normal working hours, just in order to be seen by the commanding officer. What a bunch of bullshit. What a waste of good time. Rick could care less about being seen by the skipper. He wasn't going to kiss anybody's ass to further his career. Besides, he had another career.

Rick was convinced that the more successful naval officers were married to some real dogs. Hell, if he was married to one of those fat ass know-it-all wives who wore their husband's rank on their sleeve, then he wouldn't want to go home early either. The guys with good-looking wives rarely made it past lieutenant commander. When his work was done, he was out of there. He was going home to a good-looking woman. Nothing was going to change that. The rest of them could hang around all day picking their noses for all he cared. He picked up his glass of wine, held it out in front and made a toast.

"To the best wife in the world," he said as they clicked glasses. "And I mean that," he added. Her smile was still wonderful to see. It was genuine. It was all that really counted. Rick was one lucky guy.

On the ride home from Aldo's, Rick and Lynn listened to the last part of Bill O'Reilly and then to the first part of Sean Hannity. As they turned into the neighborhood, Rick turned the volume down. He looked over at Lynn and said, "You know honey, America is in real trouble. I think we have lived through the best of times in this country."

"I think you're right," she responded as Rick drove into the driveway. "I feel sorry for the kids," she added as he stopped the car before entering the garage.

"They won't have the opportunities we had," said Rick.

"Do you think it will get any better?"

"Unfortunately I don't. We are heading down the same path as Europe. But, you know what's different about America?" he said. It was purely a rhetorical question. Rick answered before Lynn said anything. "It's the second amendment. Americans have guns. The politicians will never get the guns, and if they try, there will be another revolution in this country. Unfortunately, I'm afraid it's not that far off."

Lynn didn't say anything. She knew that Rick could see through the rhetoric. He knew history and was an excellent analyst. Lynn got out of the car, went inside and turned off the alarm. Rick sat there for a couple more minutes listening to Hannity as he waited for a commercial break. He looked at his watch and decided that he would give Carl a call and bring him up to speed. Lynn walked into the kitchen and poured a glass of water.

"Do you want a glass of water?" she asked Rick as she began to fill another glass with crushed ice.

Rick nodded yes and told Lynn that he needed to call Carl.

"Tell him I said hi," she smiled as she handed Rick the glass of water. "I'm going to get ready for bed. Do you guys still call him *Blue Sky*?" she asked as she turned and headed down the hall. She glanced back just enough for Rick to catch a glimpse of her wry smile.

It caught him by surprise.

"We do indeed," he responded, realizing that women always knew more about what went on than guys thought they did.

Rick went into his office, shut the door and turned on the small TV that was positioned on top of a three-piece stack table set that he and Lynn bought in Sorrento, Italy. He really didn't care what was on, he just liked to have something playing in the background. The TV was set to the Fox News channel as usual. Rick turned on his computer and brought up The Peterson Group homepage. A small icon signaled that there were several messages waiting to be read. Rick clicked on the icon, picked up his satellite phone and dialed Carl's number. The computer screen displayed four unanswered emails. One was from Roland Carpenter. The phone rang several times. Rick was about to hang up when Carl answered.

"Rick...Rick, you there?" Carl answered. He sounded out of breath.

"I'm here," answered Rick. "Are you okay?" he asked. "You sound winded."

"Ah, I left the phone up in the bathroom. Thought I heard it ringing. The stairs are a challenge after a long day, too much food and a couple of brandies," Carl responded. His breathing was almost back to normal. He was still in great shape.

"How's the project going?" Carl asked.

"Carlos is back and everything worked out as planned. We have the name of the corporation, the registered agent and the person who opened the account. Roland is doing his thing. We should have the information we need by tomorrow," responded Rick.

"Did the guys find out who beat up Kilday?" asked Carl.

"They did," said Rick.

"And you confirmed that McAllister was *fully* involved?" asked Carl.

"Everything was verified, and all accounts were closed," responded Rick.

"Permanently?" asked Carl.

"Permanently," responded Rick.

"Good," said Carl after a long pause. "What is your next move?" he asked, erasing the memory of McAllister and his cohorts.

"I am planning on sending Carlos and Tony to Tampa first thing Monday morning. See what they can turn up. I have Ann watching your Ms. Anderson. I'm scheduled to meet with Carlos tomorrow. When will you be back?"

"The funeral is tomorrow following the church ceremony. I'll fly back some time after that, probably around fifteen hundred. I have a briefing with Homeland Security at ten hundred Monday that I can't miss. How about I buy you lunch on Monday?" Carl asked.

"Lunch it is. I'll call if anything comes up. See you Monday," responded Rick.

Rick put the phone down and looked at the list of emails. The only email Rick opened was the one from Roland Carpenter. Roland had sent a thorough analysis of the information provided by Carlos. Also included was the information on Farrah Gemayel that he had promised. Rick opened the file on Gemayel. It opened to her picture. Rick smiled. Roland had tracked it down after all. If there was information out there, Roland would be the one to find it. Rick sat there for several seconds staring at the picture. It was unmistakable. She was definitely the woman he saw at the Ritz.

CHAPTER TWENTY-FIVE

The parking lot at the church was nearly full. Rick pulled into the field just to the west of the main parking area and parked at the back of the lot next to a brand new white BMW with temporary North Carolina tags. Rick didn't recognize the car and figured it probably belonged to a visitor. Based on their parking space selection out in the middle of nowhere, Rick concluded they had probably been "blessed" by a few door dings in the past.

Sadly, there was little respect for cars in a church parking lot. The worst offenders were the parking attendants who packed the cars in like sardines. The cars were so close together, it was nearly impossible to get out of the car without hitting the car next to you. Rick never followed their direction, much to Lynn's chagrin. She thought he was more interested in the car than the church service. Many times she was correct. The attendants were not happy either and would broadcast their displeasure with an expression that Rick summarily ignored. So much for brotherly love.

Several of the cars in the parking lot were in sad need of tender loving care. The dents and rust were only outnumbered by the numerous *Jesus Loves You* stickers. Even the obligatory Jesus fish was rusted. Some testimony it must be to the non-believers as these cars went down the highway burping and blowing blue and white smoke. Rick needed to repent, and he knew it.

On this Sunday morning, the pastor's message was on forgiveness. Following the service, Rick thought about the message as Lynn was making her way to greet a new couple who sat alone across the aisle from them in the second pew. By the looks of the young man's haircut, Rick determined that he must be a marine. The BMW couldn't possibly be theirs.

Lynn was very good at welcoming visitors. She was very comfortable talking about the Lord and sharing how good He had been to her and Rick. Rick was certainly a believer in God. He just hoped that God believed in him. It would be just his luck to die, go to Heaven and be put in charge of the parking attendants.

The pastor's message on forgiveness continued to resonate. It was certainly easy to forgive others. The hardest thing to do was to forgive yourself. Forgiving yourself was the key. Lynn was smiling as she continued to welcome the young couple. Rick had already used up all his morning words. Looking at his watch, he thought about rescuing the young couple, but the date in the little window of his Rolex Submariner distracted him.

It was on this date many years ago that he had reported to Aviation Officer Candidate School in Pensacola, Florida. He had returned from a mission to Bolivia the week before and was still scratching chigger bites and battling a slight case of dysentery as he cleaned out his apartment in South Miami. He packed all of his worldly possessions into one large suitcase and three brown shopping bags, stuffed them into his yellow XKE, and by 0900, he was heading north on South Dixie Highway at sixty miles per hour with the top down. He had lived in Miami for the past several years following graduation. He would miss the university, the nightlife, the occasional foray to Key Biscayne and the runs along Tahiti Beach with Carl. The trip to NAS Pensacola took the rest of the day and most of the evening.

While driving, he thought about how well he was treated by the navy recruiters. They had sent a limousine to pick him up at LaGuardia. He arrived at Floyd Bennett Field in Brooklyn where Captain McCleary swore him into the navy. Aviation officer candidates were special, or at least that is what Rick was led to believe during the recruiting process. They had treated him like royalty.

Although he had arrived in Pensacola in plenty of time to check in, he decided to look around the city. Since his orders indicated that he had to report no later than 2400 hours, he waited until the last few minutes to report. Consequently, he was the last to check into class 40-67. The marine sergeant who had waited for the final candidate to show up wasn't too happy and decided to make an example of him for *almost* being late. So much for being special.

"Give me fifty maggot!" barked Sergeant Taylor.

Taylor was a well-built, broad chested, thin-waisted black marine with the Bronze Star and Purple Heart displayed above four rows of ribbons that told the story of a seasoned gunny sergeant. The marine corps tattoo on his right forearm became distorted as the sergeant stood ramrod straight and clinched both fists.

At six feet tall, he looked Rick straight in the eye, their noses almost touching, his drill sergeant's Smokey the Bear hat titled well forward over a furrowed brow that spoke of the sergeant's extreme displeasure for having to wait on the *special* candidate Morgan.

"I said give me fifty *maggot!*" he barked again, emphasizing Rick's new name. The sergeant's jaw muscles twitched as he grinded his teeth together.

Rick fell to the floor and snapped off fifty push-ups in a little over a minute. He then added ten one arm push-ups just to piss off the sergeant. It worked. And Rick's cocky smile didn't help matters either. The mile run was easy, and after twenty-five chin-ups, the sergeant concluded that Rick Morgan was actually enjoying the punishment.

"Who the hell are you Morgan?" snapped Sergeant Taylor. "Is somebody trying to fuck with me? Let me see your arms," he added as he grabbed Rick's arm and pushed up his short sleeve Miami t-shirt over well developed biceps and triceps. There were no tattoos to be found.

"I'm just some guy wanting to fly jets," answered Rick. He wasn't even breathing hard as he continued to look the sergeant straight in the eyes.

"Don't fuck with me maggot," snorted the sergeant as he eyed him for what seemed to be an eternity. Neither man blinked. The rim of Sergeant Taylor's Smokey the Bear hat brushed the bridge of Rick's nose as he leaned in closer, his eyes moving back and forth looking for any sign of weakness. Rick didn't move.

"Down the hall, room five. Don't wake the others. You got about four hours and we'll really see what the hell you're made of maggot," said Sergeant Taylor, still emphasizing Rick's new name, a name he would share with fifty-two other candidates. None of them were special either.

Rick looked back at his watch. How time flies. Five combat aircraft, forty-five hundred flight hours and eighteen hundred and sixty-five carrier landings later, he remembered class 40-67 as if it were yesterday. They were great days. Every member of his class graduated. They were all commissioned as ensigns thanks to Sergeant Taylor. In appreciation, the class chipped in and bought the sergeant a Colt Forty-Five engraved with the words, *Thanks isn't enough, AOC Class 40-67*. Sergeant Taylor had tears in his eyes as he accepted the weapon. He was genuine. He shook each man's hand; his grip was firm. He then saluted each man individually. He was killed in action during his second tour in Vietnam.

At 1430 hours, Rick and Carlos met at the Starbucks on Virginia Beach Boulevard. There was only one other couple in the small eating area. They seemed to be enjoying each other's company and could care less about eavesdropping on two old guys. Following the routine conversation, Rick and Carlos got down to business.

"You said that Tony was flying out later today," initiated Rick.

"He is scheduled to depart around eighteen hundred, unless I call with a change of plans," responded Carlos. "Also, Ann will be in town later this evening. Should I assume Tony and I will be heading to Tampa?"

"Probably. I need to go over Roland's report first. Carl will be back in town tomorrow. He and I are having lunch. I'll have something solid for you by tomorrow night," said Rick as he picked up his coffee cup. The aroma of coffee was strong.

There were still some loose ends that Rick needed to put together.

"I take it you were convinced that McAllister told you everything he knew about the offshore account and Triad Associates?"

Carlos leaned in closer with both elbows on the table. He cradled the cup in both hands and glanced over at the young couple. They were holding hands and oblivious to anything but each other.

"He was scared shitless. He couldn't hold anything back, even if he wanted to," responded Carlos.

"What about the two guys that came after you? How did they get on to you?"

"I'm sure the bartender tipped them off because I asked about them by name. They left the bar right after I did and followed me into the alley," responded Carlos.

Rick drank some of the coffee as he thought about the scenario and its similarity to El Salvador. He didn't like loose ends. Bartenders were nosey by nature. They were very much aware of their surroundings, they heard all the bar talk, and they could almost always be bought.

"Is it at all possible that the bartender is a player in this?" asked Rick.

"Sure, I guess it's possible, but I really don't think he is. I don't think he knows anything about the lottery scam or that he has any idea who McAllister is. I think he was just giving the goons a heads-up to feel like he was one of the guys. You know…wanting their approval."

Rick took a bite of his scone and followed it down with a small sip of coffee. Neither man spoke for a couple of minutes. Another couple came in and ordered caramel macchiatos. The girl went back outside and sat at one of the wrought iron tables. Several sparrows sat idly by in anticipation of a few crumbs.

"Maybe so," responded Rick.

"If you want, I can get Tony to go back to the bar and snoop around," said Carlos.

Rick contemplated sending Tony back, but decided that returning to the scene of a crime was never a good idea.

"No, let's let well enough alone. I think you're probably right about the bartender. Besides, I suspect that these guys won't be missed, and from the police's response to Kilday, they certainly won't waste a whole lot of time looking for the guys who took out a couple of local goons. They'll probably say good riddance."

"Where does Ms. Gemayel and Stankowski fit into this?" asked Carlos.

"That's a very good question. At this point, I'm not sure. We do know that they are both employed by Homeland Security, or at least they are getting paid by Homeland Security."

"Maybe they are working another case and looking into offshore accounts. Maybe it's just a coincidence Rick," offered Carlos.

"Maybe it is, but what if they are working on the lottery scam? That is the one thing we need to determine," said Rick.

"You know Rick, I remember Stankowski. He was a pretty good guy. I haven't seen him since Panama. Hell, we took a hundred percent casualties during that operation. What a cluster fuck that was. I think he got shot in the ass."

"Now that you mention it, I do remember that. I had forgotten you guys were pretty tight. Wasn't Stankowski Noriega's contact?" asked Rick.

"Not many people know that little fact," responded Carlos. "Hell, Noriega was on the company payroll. He was providing us with strategic information on drug movements."

"I think Bush jumped the gun on Noriega. He was certainly no angel, but I don't think he should have been rewarded with a trip to Miami," said Rick sarcastically, knowing that jail in Miami was certainly no vacation.

"Shit, he got too big for his britches. I believe the decapitation of Spadafora was probably the last straw. He was becoming an embarrassment. I guess it all depends on who you piss off," responded Carlos.

Rick smiled to himself. It was just a big game. There were always winners and losers. The key to survival was to choose the right side at the right time. Convictions lead to martyrdom sooner or later.

CHAPTER TWENTY-SIX

Rick arrived at the Prince Street entrance to the parking garage at 1030 hours. The two hundred and one mile trip from Virginia Beach took three and a half hours. Most of the serious commuters had driven up late the night before. Lynn had made a reservation for Rick at the Ritz Carlton at Pentagon City.

A light rain was beginning to fall as he pulled into the garage. This particular garage served several of the buildings, and on this particular Monday morning, it was nearly full with only a few visitor parking spaces left. Nearly all of The Peterson Group spaces were occupied. Three large white government vans were parked side-by-side in three of the six Peterson Group visitor spaces.

Carl, true to form, had parked his SUV in the first visitor slot, leaving the designated CEO parking space empty. Rick smiled to himself. Rick could never understand Carl's reluctance to park in his assigned space. As he thought about it, he couldn't remember a time that Carl had ever parked in the CEO slot.

Carl's odd parking behavior was a matter of record and seemed to be the norm. Throughout the D.C. area, Carl would average one parking ticket a week, much to the chagrin of Elaine Drew who signed the checks and paid the fines. He could probably claim at least one of the meter maids as a dependent.

Rick parked in Carl's space and proceeded to the elevator. Rick was the only one who would dare to park in Carl's space. Carl could care less. As far as Carl was concerned, Rick could park wherever he wanted.

As he entered the office, the smell of freshly brewed coffee filled the air. The aroma stirred his desire for a cup. Elaine Drew looked up from a stack of Saturday mail that was ridiculously large and greeted him with a big smile. She had expected to see him earlier. The little red indicator light on the three-light panel centered above the door to Carl's office was illuminated, indicating that Carl was in a meeting and was not to be disturbed.

"The Homeland Security meeting?" asked Rick as he motioned with his right hand toward the light panel.

"Yes," responded Elaine as she got up and walked around from behind the desk. "They have been in there since ten o'clock. Should be done in another thirty to forty-five minutes. These meetings always last longer than scheduled," she said as she walked over and listened at the door.

Elaine made a half turn while still leaning forward, her facial expression indicated that she heard nothing. She was dressed in a tailored dark blue dress with small silver buttons that glistened in the light. Rick recognized the pearls that Carl had bought specifically for her during a stop-over in Palma, Majorca. Rick had also bought similar pearls for Lynn.

"Would you like some coffee? I saved a few of the bear claws," she asked with a wink as she walked away from the door and looked up at the three-light panel. She would always have more on hand than was needed. She knew that bear claws were Carl's and Rick's favorite. The government guys didn't have a preference; they would eat anything that was free.

"I was thinking about getting a cup," responded Rick as he put his briefcase down next to one of the visitor chairs. "Is Roland in the meeting?" he asked.

"No, he's back in his office. Ya know Rick, I've never fully understood this secret thing. Roland prepared Carl's portion of the brief, yet he is not allowed to attend the meeting. Carl says it has to do with *need to know*. Can you explain how one prepares a brief without actually *knowing*? I always knew Roland was good, but I didn't know the boy was clairvoyant," quipped Elaine nonchalantly. "Do you want me to give him a call? Actually, with his gift, he might just *sense* your presence," she giggled, getting quite the kick out of herself.

"No, I'll go down to his office," said Rick as he laughed heartily at funny-girl, Elaine Drew. "I meant to call him the other day. I believe he has some information for me."

"I'll bring the coffee and a couple of claws to his office," she said as she headed down the hall to the small gedunk. Elaine knew how Rick liked his coffee. He made it well known that he wasn't a fan of the flavored coffees. He dubbed them "San Francisco" coffees.

The Peterson Group office in Old Town was certainly impressive. It wasn't often that Rick had the opportunity to explore the premises. It occupied the entire third floor of the office building located at the western end of Prince Street. It was at least eight thousand square feet. One third of the space was consumed with computer equipment that served as the backup for the entire Department of Defense.

Roland's office was just to the left of the tandem doors that provided a secure entrance to the server room or the "cage," as it was known around the office. The cage housed several rows of mainframes that blinked incessantly with every action. Rick could see two employees in the cage. One was using the forefinger of his left hand to follow a schematic that was unfolded but still attached to a large black loose-leaf manual. The other was inserting blade servers into what appeared to be a newly constructed computer rack. Loose cat five cables dangled from the overhead waiting to be connected.

A hardly discernable beeping sound alerted Roland to an intruder. He looked up to see Rick enter the room.

"Good morning Mr. Morgan," said Roland. His smile was genuine.

Roland was in the process of attaching a white coaxial cable to the back of his desktop computer. His laptop was open and appeared to be performing a defragging type of operation.

"Good morning Roland," said Rick as he put his briefcase on the small round desk that served as Roland's conference table. Rick pulled out one of the four chairs that was evenly spaced around the table. He noticed alignment marks on the side of the table where the chairs were stowed. Roland added new meaning to the word precise.

Everything in Roland's office was in its perfect place except the desktop computer that was undergoing some kind of upgrade. Roland was a young Rick Morgan when it came to neatness. Both of them bordered on being obsessive-compulsive disorder candidates.

"Please excuse me," said Roland. "When I finish with this modification, the recipient of any information generated by this computer will think it is located somewhere in the Middle East."

Rick watched as Roland put the computer back together. Once it was reassembled, Roland carefully positioned the computer under the glass top of a see-through desk. The design prevented anyone, other than the user, from seeing what was displayed on the monitor. There were two other work stations set up in a similar fashion.

Just as Rick was about to say something, the beeping sound announced the entry of another intruder. It was Elaine Drew. The smell of coffee had already preceded her into the room. She was carrying a tray with a small chrome coffee pot, two bear claws and a bottle of Fiji water. Roland had already had his one cup of coffee for the day.

"If you need anything else, please let me know," said Elaine. "I will buzz you when Carl is available. By the way, Carl had me make a luncheon reservation at La Bergerie," she said as she placed the tray on the table. "The steamed mussels in the butter and garlic sauce are divine," she added as she kissed the ends of the grouped fingers of her right hand.

"Thanks Elaine, you're a doll," responded Rick as he picked up one of the bear claws.

When Rick was at the helm of Matrix, Inc., one of his executive secretary's primary duties was to ensure an ample supply of bear claws.

After gaining ten pounds, Lynn made it known that bear claws were off limits. Rick never did get used to carrots and coffee. It just wasn't the same.

Roland opened his desk drawer and pulled out a folder that was nearly an inch thick. He sat down across from Rick and opened it so that it faced in Rick's direction. The folder had several tabs. One of the tabs had the name Haddad in bold letters. Rick flipped the tab over. There was a picture of Tarek Haddad in the upper left hand corner. It was black and white and had the quality of a passport picture. Rick perused the contents. It was basically the same information Roland had provided in an earlier email. Rick slowly thumbed through the pages, pausing a couple of times.

"The information on Haddad seems to be too clean," he said as he continued to scan the file. "Did you get that impression?" he asked as he looked over at Roland.

Roland had been watching Rick and smiled when he asked the question.

"I was surprised there were no flags. Usually there is some information outside of the normal bell curve," responded Roland. "From what I have been able to find so far, this guy has never even had a parking ticket. I am in the process of digging deeper," he added.

"It feels contrived," offered Rick. "It would be nice to find someone else who knows him, or at least knew of him."

"It would be very easy to create a resume similar to this one," said Roland. "I have put several together for Carl in the past. All it takes is going through the obituaries. The rest is a matter of being clever enough to hack into county records, make the necessary changes and not get caught. Just about any high school kid with a little bit of computer savvy could do it."

Rick looked back at the picture. He wondered who Tarek Haddad really was. He was average in all respects. He was your typical nondescript guy—one who wouldn't stand out in a crowd, one who could blend in anywhere. Shave off the beard and mustache, and he was just another face. He was certainly the perfect operative…or patsy.

CHAPTER TWENTY-SEVEN

Rick and Carl walked into La Bergerie at 1230 hours. Several couples were seated in the waiting area. The restaurant was full except for one table that had a reserved sign prominently displayed on a small silver easel. The name on the card said Peterson. The table for two was located next to a window that provided a limited view of North Lee Street.

The hostess recognized Carl and greeted him by name. Her smile was warm. She led them to the table, and with a slight French accent, told them that their server, Jean Paul, would be right with them. She smiled at Rick and Carl as she handed them a soft brown leather-bound menu. Carl responded with his usual tip that she graciously accepted. He had tipped her on many occasions.

She walked away confidently, knowing that his eyes were following her as she maneuvered between the tables on the way back to her station. She could have taken a more direct route, but the maneuvering helped to emphasize a shapely hourglass figure.

"Old men will have visions and dream dreams," said Rick as he picked up the menu. He didn't look at Carl; he knew where Carl's attention was focused.

Carl continued to evaluate the hostess. She was young, tall and reminded Carl of a time long ago—back in his *Blue Sky* days. He had entertained thoughts of asking her out, and although he was in good shape, he was abundantly aware of his limitations. He was certainly more comfortable with *mature* women. However, the thought of a time long ago gave him a slight adrenalin rush. It made him feel younger—more alive. At that very moment, he would have been at his best...but only for that moment.

"Unfortunately, those days are over my friend. They have been over for you for many years," responded Carl punctuated by a little laugh. He meant it in an envious way.

Rick smiled as he continued to peruse the menu items. With Lynn at his side, he didn't need to look at any other women. Lynn could easily pass for early forties. She was still quite fit, had boundless energy and was certainly more than Rick could handle...on his best day. He would remark that he wasn't as good as he once used to be, but he was as good *once* as he used to be.

"What was it that Willie Nelson said on his seventy-fifth birthday?" asked Carl. He knew the answer. He didn't think that Rick would know.

"He said that he outlived his dick," responded Rick without looking up.

"That's right, he outlived his dick," repeated Carl laughing. A surprised look had briefly crossed his face.

"You know Rick, if I ever get a hard-on that lasts for more than four hours, I'm not calling the doctor. Hell, I'm going to call all of my friends. I'm telling everybody. I may even post it on Facebook."

They both had a good laugh as Jean Paul approached with a basket of warm rolls and a small bowl of butter mixed with La Bergerie's special ingredients. Jean Paul placed them on the table and handed the wine list to Carl. Carl looked across the table at Rick. He had already made a decision. La Bergerie was one of his favorite restaurants. He had dined there on numerous occasions, was very familiar with the wine list and always ordered one of his two favorite wines.

"How about a nice bottle of Cullen 2002 Chardonnay?" he asked without looking at the list. He glanced over at Rick.

"That's fine with me," responded Rick as he closed the menu and placed it near the edge of the table.

"Would you like to hear our specials for the day?" Jean Paul asked. There was only a slight hint of a French accent. Jean Paul's accent was authentic. Carl suspected that he grew up in the Bordeaux area.

Carl nodded as he looked over at Rick. Although Carl hardly ever ordered one of the specials, he enjoyed the memorized luncheon special presentation particularly from an inexperienced server. There were very few inexperienced servers at La Bergerie, and Jean Paul's recital was delivered with the confidence and flare of a seasoned server who could make chocolate covered ants sound inviting. However, following his flawless dissertation of the three luncheon specials, including a detailed description of the chef's special sauces, both Carl and Rick chose to order from the menu.

"Have you made a selection?" asked Carl looking at Rick.

Rick said that he would like the flounder.

"Please, allow me," said Carl, taking advantage of an opportunity to speak in French.

"I'll have the Filet de Saumon et sa Salade de Pâtes Friode aux Petits Lègumes," said Carl in perfect French. "My friend will have the LeFilet de Limande aux Amandes Rôties st sa Salade de Tomates et Betteraves."

"Salmon and flounder," replied Jean Paul. "That is a very nice choice. May I also suggest our baked onion soup with melted Gruyére cheese?"

"Ah yes, La Soupe à l'Oignon Gartinèe," responded Carl as he looked for Rick's approval.

Rick nodded, and the language competition ended as Jean Paul smiled and headed toward the bar.

"Of course it was a very nice choice. What else was he going to say? So, where are we Rick?" asked Carl as he looked around the restaurant. Everyone seemed to be engaged in luncheon conversation except for an elderly couple who looked as if they hadn't said a kind word to one another in years.

Before Rick answered, he reached into his pocket, removed a pen and placed the pen on the table. The pen caught Carl's attention.

"Are you getting paranoid my friend?" Carl asked as he picked up the pen. "I haven't seen one of these in several years," he added as he rolled the pen around between his fingers. "Does it work?" he asked as he shook the pen.

"I'm just not so sure where our *friends* fit into this. Ms. Gemayel is a bit puzzling, and we know she's been watching us," responded Rick. "Since Elaine made a reservation in advance, you never know who might be listening," he added.

"Well it isn't vibrating. I assume we are alone?" added Carl.

After a brief pause, Rick changed the subject.

"How is your nephew fairing?" he asked.

Carl continued to contemplate the pen for a few seconds before answering. "Is this one of ours?" he asked.

"It is one that Carlos had," responded Rick.

Carl put it back down on the table and answered Rick.

"He's doing okay. Nancy, on the other hand, is struggling. Hell, poor girl lost her mother a year ago and now her father," responded Carl. "Even though he was technically her grandfather, Kilday was in good shape and probably had several very good years ahead of him. It's been tough on her to the say the least."

"Have you told your nephew anything about the events in Nassau?" asked Rick, knowing that whatever Carl told his nephew would be benign.

"Only that we have a good idea who set up the scam, and that we would work to get the money back and wouldn't rest until everyone involved is behind bars," responded Carl. "I may tell him a little more someday when the dust settles," he added as he took a warm roll from the basket, tore it in half and proceeded to cover it with a generous amount of La Bergerie's butter mix.

As Rick was about to speak, Jean Paul returned with the bottle of Cullen Chardonnay and two white wine glasses balanced on a small tray. Jean Paul presented the bottle. Carl checked the date and nodded his approval. Jean Paul went through the uncorking ceremony and poured a small amount in the glass in front of Carl. Carl sampled it, smiled broadly and said that it was fine. Jean Paul nodded and filled both glasses to the same level.

"Would you like some more bread?" he asked as he lifted the basket.

"I believe we're fine," responded Carl. He glanced over at Rick. Rick concurred.

As Jean Paul left, Carl raised his glass.

"To our long friendship…may it last forever."

Rick responded with a touch from his glass as both men took a modest drink of the wine. It was fine and perfectly chilled. Their friendship would indeed last forever. It was cemented many years ago. Before Rick could say anything, Carl continued.

"Rick, it really pisses me off that anyone would take advantage of retired military officers, not withstanding the fact that they were also widowers. Who the hell does something like that? I assume you are sending Carlos to Tampa?" said Carl. It was more of a statement than a question.

"I was planning on sending them in a couple of days," responded Rick.

"Them? Is Ann going?" asked Carl.

"No not yet. I thought it would be better to send Tony Ramos. He and Carlos will certainly blend into the Tampa environment. I prefer to keep Ann close by just in case we need her to follow Ms. Gemayel," responded Rick.

"You don't think this whole thing with Gemayel and Stankowski is a coincidence do you?" asked Carl.

Rick took another sip of the wine. Several scenarios were competing with one another in his mind. He continued to think for a minute or so before answering. Carl looked on intently. He was a quick read.

"They are both contractors and working for Homeland Security. The fact that Homeland Security hid Ms. Gemayel's identity troubles me," responded Rick. "It doesn't make any sense."

"And how so?" asked Carl as he crossed his arms and leaned on the table. He picked up the pen and clicked the button on and off several times before putting it back on the table.

Rick thought before answering. All the scenarios seemed plausible.

"What was the purpose? Even if any of the victims decided to go to the Bahamian Embassy, none would even think to check the receptionist's credentials and surely not her fingerprints. So why did they purposely try to hide her identity?" asked Rick again.

Carl didn't say anything as he slowly raised the wine glass to his lips.

"Something else is going on here. Either we stumbled on to another operation, or Homeland Security is somehow involved in the scam," said Rick as he leaned in toward Carl. "It doesn't make sense," he added again.

"Rick, I can't image that Homeland Security would condone any operation that would bilk retirees out of their life savings."

"Maybe. But they would have full access to the DEERS program. It wouldn't be hard to provide a list of widowed officers. They would also have access to IRS files. Just think how easy it would be if they had a guy with just half of Roland's capability," responded Rick. "They could do it without attracting any attention."

"If you're right, then that *really* pisses me off," said Carl. "What the hell are they after, and where the hell is the oversight?" asked Carl.

"I'm not sure," responded Rick. "As you know, many of the program managers act on their own. They feel that the ends justify the means. Could be a simple investigation into offshore accounts. Remember when the President wanted to go after offshore accounts? He was really into it for a while. Then the whole issue just seemed to die."

"I believe the Swiss Bank made a deal and provided some fifty thousand names of individuals with offshore accounts," responded Carl.

"But they didn't provide all the names," offered Rick. "The government still wanted *all* the names," he added.

"I think the President realized how hard it was to get that sort of information and decided to give it up," offered Carl.

"Maybe they didn't give up after all. Maybe they employed Homeland Security to go after the offshore accounts and Nassau was their first target," responded Rick.

Carl thought for a minute or so. He was about to ask another question when Jean Paul and a young female server approached the table with their order. Jean Paul carefully placed the plates in front of Carl and Rick, refilled their wine glasses and smiled as he asked if there was anything else.

"We're fine Jean Paul," responded Carl.

Carl and Rick held their conversation until Jean Paul and his young helper were out of earshot.

"So, you believe that Homeland Security used the lottery scam to entrap one of the bankers and then *encouraged* him to provide a list of offshore accounts?" asked Carl.

"*Encourage* is not the word I would have chosen. However, I can certainly envision such a scenario," responded Rick as he took a small bite of the flounder.

"And Ms. Gemayel was placed at the embassy to ward off any complaints, so to speak," offered Carl.

Both men were silent for several minutes contemplating the scenario and enjoying the meal. Carl split the rest of the wine between their glasses.

"Should we order another bottle?" asked Carl as he shook the bottle.

"The wine is wonderful but half a bottle is enough for me," responded Rick.

"I was going to head down to Pensacola on Thursday," said Carl. "My nephew and Nancy are staying in the condo. I need to spend a little time with them. I could take Carlos with me. Tony can meet us in Pensacola and then my pilot can fly them on to Tampa. In fact, that's what we'll do," decided Carl.

"Sounds good. I'll give Carlos a call after lunch," said Rick.

On the way back to The Peterson Group office, Rick called Carlos. Carl was weaving in and out of traffic, oblivious to the speed limit. Rick found himself pushing on an imaginary brake. He decided not to look at the other cars. Riding with Carl Peterson was never a trip…it was an adventure.

Carlos must have been close to the phone. He picked it up halfway through the first ring. The caller ID indicated that it was Rick. Carlos was expecting the call.

"Good afternoon Rick," answered Carlos.

"Afternoon Carlos. I trust you had a good night?"

"I did. Every night is a honeymoon. So what's going on?" asked Carlos.

"Carl has decided to fly down to Pensacola on Thursday and will pick you up on the way. Elaine will call you with the scheduled departure time," said Rick as he looked for Carl's approval. Carl nodded in agreement as he whipped around a van full of nuns. They looked startled. One blessed herself and looked skyward.

"Sounds good. I assume we will be conducting a routine surveillance operation?" said Carlos. It was a rhetorical question.

"This is Tony's area of expertise. I'll let you decide how you want to proceed. Your call. This guy isn't expecting company."

"Do you want us to force the issue?" asked Carlos.

"Let's see how the initial surveillance goes. Let's identify all the players, then we can decide," responded Rick.

"All right Rick. Hold on a second, Ann has some information for you," he added as he handed the phone to a towel wrapped Ann Peters, her hair still wet from her late morning shower. After last night, both she and Carlos needed long warm showers.

"Hi Rick. I just got a call from one of my people. It looks like Ms. Gemayel is checking out of the hotel."

"She's checking out a bit early," responded Rick as he looked at his watch. "She's probably leaving town."

"I had the same thought. My guy is going to follow her until he's absolutely sure. By the way, I placed a tracking device on her car yesterday and have alerted Roland," said Ann.

"Good work. Once your guy is sure she is heading out of town, have him break it off. Roland can keep track of her. It will be interesting to see where she goes."

"Will do. Say hi to Lynn for me. Here's Carlos."

Ann handed Carlos the phone, smiled and dropped her towel as she walked away. She glanced over her left shoulder just enough to see that Carlos was watching.

"Okay Rick, anything else?" asked Carlos, his heartbeat rising rapidly along with his friend, *Señor José*. Ann couldn't speak Spanish, but she could surely take care of *Señor José*.

"That's it for now. Call me as soon as you have commenced the surveillance operation."

"Will do boss," said Carlos, anxious to hang up the phone and follow *José* to the bedroom.

PENTAGON CITY
2130 HOURS

Rick had just finished looking over his notes when his cell phone rang. The caller ID indicated that the call was from Sentara Hospital. His heartbeat accelerated slightly. Unsolicited calls from a hospital were seldom comforting.

"Hello," he answered tentatively.

"Mr. Morgan?" questioned the caller.

"Yes," confirmed Rick.

"This is Doctor Burch at Sentara Norfolk. Let me assure you that everything is okay, but I wanted to let you know that I have just treated your wife."

"Treated her for what?" interrupted an anxious Rick.

"It appears that she was assaulted in the parking lot at Macarthur Center," responded the doctor.

"Assaulted?" gasped Rick. "Is she okay?" he asked.

"She'll be fine. I intend to keep her overnight since she is a bit shook up," the doctor continued.

"What do you mean by assaulted?" asked Rick.

"I don't know the particulars. She was not sexually assaulted. It has the appearance of a mugging," answered the doctor.

"May I talk to her?" asked Rick.

"I have given her a sedative. I suspect she will sleep through the night. She is in room 237. She should be fine by morning."

"Thank you for the call," said Rick as he hung up.

Rick sat back in the chair thinking about Lynn. It bothered him that he wasn't there to protect her. She had always felt secure in her surroundings. Rick looked over at his notes and wondered if the assault was merely a coincidence.

CHAPTER TWENTY-EIGHT

As Rick approached the exit to Ashland, he thought about stopping and having breakfast at the Cracker Barrel, but he couldn't get Lynn out of his mind. He needed to be with her, comfort her. They had talked earlier. She had already left the hospital.

Lynn didn't like to be away from home, and she especially didn't enjoy sleeping in a hospital. She tried to reassure Rick that she was okay. However, he could tell from her voice that she was not okay. She had told him what had happened.

The visions of some punk with his hand over her mouth, pulling her head back and threatening her, wouldn't go away. He could only imagine the fear that ran through her mind. It sickened him. Each time he thought about it, his heart would pound and his jaw would tighten in frustration. He would gladly give up a year of his life just to have one minute with this guy.

While she tried her very best not to worry him, her voice would occasionally crack. He knew she was holding back the tears. Rick knew that Lynn needed him there. In all the years he had been in this business, she had never been the target of anyone as a result of his forays into the world of covert operations. This was the first time. It was real, and Lynn was really frightened.

From Lynn's description of the attempted mugging—as it would appear on the Norfolk police blotter—it was clear to Rick that Lynn was the target, and the assault was designed to send him a message to dissuade him from continuing his investigation into the lottery scam. If someone under the authority and protection of Homeland Security would have the gall to sanction such an action, what else were they capable of doing? Why didn't they just contact Carl Peterson, bring him up to speed on the project and politely ask him to back off, or even ask him to provide surveillance support. The Peterson Group was a well-known black ops firm with the reputation of getting things done on time and within budget. That would have been the prudent thing to do, and any reasonable person would have taken that approach. If this truly was sanctioned by someone under the authority of Homeland Security, what the hell was wrong with this person?

Rick shook his head in disgust as he tried to wrap his head around it. He couldn't even begin to envision the person responsible. Whoever they were, they would eventually hear from Rick Morgan.

Even though there wasn't much information to go on, Rick knew that if anyone could find out the identity of the assailant, it would be Roland Carpenter. As Rick turned onto I-64 east heading toward Virginia Beach, he dialed Roland.

"Good morning Mr. Morgan," answered Roland.

Rick could hear Roland typing furiously in the background.

"Good morning Roland. Sounds like you are busy," Rick said, sounding a bit apologetic for interrupting.

"Just working on a new algorithm for Mr. Peterson. What can I do for you?" asked Roland as he stopped typing and gave Rick his full attention.

Rick hesitated for a few seconds before going on. He really didn't want to go into a long dissertation on what had happened to Lynn.

"Unfortunately, my wife was assaulted last night at MacArthur Center in Norfolk. I know for a fact that the assault was not a random act of violence. Lynn was the target. I need you to do your magic and see if we can identify the assailant," offered Rick.

"I'm so sorry Rick. Is she okay?" asked Roland. Rick could hear genuine concern in Roland's voice.

"She is okay. Her world has been shaken to the core, but she's a tough little cookie. She'll be all right," responded Rick.

"Good," said Roland earnestly. "You said this happened at MacArthur Center?"

"That is correct. It happened around twenty thirty on the second floor of the parking garage next to the south exit of Nordstrom. I'm not sure if there are cameras there. I expect so, but there are certainly cameras strategically placed at the pay booths."

"I'll get right on it," responded Roland. "Did your wife happen to see how this guy left? His vehicle?"

"All she saw was a black SUV with tinted windows drive off. She wasn't able to see the license plate," offered Rick, knowing that would be Roland's next question.

"That will be a good starting point Mr. Morgan. I will get back to you later this morning. Please tell your wife that I'm glad she is okay."

"I will. Thanks Roland. Oh and Roland, this is project related. You may charge your time to the Lottery Scam Project. Will talk with you later."

Rick ended the call and thought more about the assault on Lynn. There was a time when family members were sacred. No matter what the circumstance, there was an unwritten code of honor among operatives throughout the *civilized* world. Family members were off limits, not because of directives, but out of respect for the individuals involved, their ideology and allegiance to the country they represented. Religion played an important role in establishing the moral foundation. That all changed with the Serbs and Croatians. They were ruthless.

Muslims had killed and mutilated the Christians, and now it was the Christians killing the Muslims. Both were savage in their inhumane attacks. The rules had changed. There was no respect for the sanctity of life. Everyone was fair game.

Hollywood hadn't helped matters with their digital portrayal of the macho karate-kicking muscle-bound spy who defied logic and gravity.

The Hollywood stereotypes wouldn't have made it thirty seconds in a real-world scenario. How the world had changed.

As Rick was approaching the turn off to Camp Perry, his satellite phone rang. It was Roland.

"Yes Roland," answered Rick.

"I have some information for you concerning the assailant," said Roland.

"Shoot, I'm listening," responded Rick as he passed the Camp Perry exit. How ironic he thought to himself.

"Seems this guy did most of the right things to protect his identity. There were no plates on the vehicle and he must have had a switch for all the external lights, including the brake lights. All the windows, except the windshield, were tinted and tinted heavily. The one thing he forgot to cover was the state inspection sticker. I got enough detail from one of the exit cameras."

Rick smiled to himself as he looked at his own inspection sticker. The good ones would never miss covering all decals. He could see his serial number quite plainly.

"The name corresponding with the serial number indicates that the car is registered to Anthony Serrano. Does that name ring any bells?" asked Roland.

Rick thought for a few seconds. No one came to mind.

"I don't know the name," he responded.

"He received a less than honorable discharge from the marines in two thousand eight. None of the agencies wanted him. He started his own security company and has a few small contracts with some local retail stores. Nothing of any real significance."

"How old is this guy?" asked Rick

"He's thirty-seven. He was reduced from E-six to E-one and discharged. He is certainly a bad character. No respect for authority. I have uploaded his record to your computer. Looks like a tough guy. Flat nose and a lot of scars," added Roland.

"Can't be too tough Roland. Someone gave him that nose and those scars."

"You're right about that. He certainly can't be too smart either. While he did have on gloves, he still went through the tollbooth and paid for his ticket," continued Roland.

"He knows that ticket agents pay no attention," responded Rick. "Thanks for the quick response."

Rick placed the satellite phone on the console and thought more about Anthony Serrano. He knew the type—young and tough with no respect for authority. Rarely were their moves calculated. Anthony Serrano was probably the reactive type.

As Rick approached Williamsburg, he called Lynn and told her that he would be home in about fifty minutes depending upon the tunnel traffic. She was happy to hear his voice again and that he was not far away.

"Do you need anything from the outlets?" he asked in an attempt to lighten her mood.

"No, I think I've had enough surprises this week," she managed with a slight hint of a laugh. She knew that Rick could always find something positive to say. He was certainly the optimist. She was more of the realist in the family.

"I love you honey. See you shortly," said Rick.

"I love you too," she responded, her voice sounding much stronger.

Rick purposely didn't say anything about identifying her assailant. He knew that he would take care of this guy when the time was right. Reacting out of anger was never a good idea. There would be a time and a place when Mr. Serrano would meet Mr. Morgan.

CHAPTER TWENTY-NINE

VIRGINIA BEACH, VA
OCTOBER 17, 2012
WEDNESDAY
0800 HOURS

Lynn was in the shower when the home phone rang. Rick picked it up and the name that appeared on the caller ID surprised him momentarily, although he knew that he and Robert Stankowski would be talking in the very near future.

"I got it honey," he called out, though she hadn't heard either the phone or Rick.

Rick walked into his office and shut the door as he pressed the answer button.

"Robert Stankowski," he answered, saying the name slowly and deliberately. "You're still alive. It has been a long time."

"I am. And, if I remember correctly, the last time we were together, you and Carl Peterson were saving my ass from some young banditos south of Cartagena. How are you doing Rick?"

"I'm doing very well," responded Rick. Stankowski's deep voice still sounded the same. In the back of Rick's mind he could see a tall thin Robert Stankowski checking his equipment as they both hooked up for a drop. The mission to Cartagena was in the mid-seventies. Most of the team was in their mid-twenties and green behind the ears. He waited for a few seconds before continuing, the memory of South America was trying to break loose from somewhere among the grey cells. "So, what is going on with you these days? I'm sure you didn't call because you were concerned about my health," said Rick, returning to the present.

Stankowski cleared his throat. There was a slight hint of nervousness on his part that he hoped Rick wouldn't discern. He wasn't quite sure how to approach Rick, but knowing the young Rick Morgan, he decided the direct approach was best. The direct approach was always best with trained operatives.

"We need to talk. I believe we are both working the same project, albeit from a different perspective."

"And what project might that be?" asked Rick, pretending not to know what Stankowski was talking about.

"The project associated with the Bahamas. By the way, I believe I recognized Anya Petrov the other day. It was her, wasn't it?" he asked.

Rick didn't answer. Robert took that as a yes and continued.

"Unfortunately, I had to roll down the tinted glass to get a better look. It's been a long time. She still looks good. Probably shouldn't have tilted my sunglasses. I didn't smile for the camera."

"It was enough," responded Rick. "Where and when would you like to meet for this…talk?" asked Rick, not wanting to play the cat and mouse game any longer.

"How about we meet at the Cracker Barrel in Ashland. It's about halfway for the both of us. This time of day should be an easy round trip. I can be there in about two hours," he said. "Do you know where it is?"

Rick knew exactly where it was; he had eaten brunch there on many occasions. He hesitated for a minute or so before answering. The meeting with Stankowski could provide answers to many of Rick's questions.

"I know where it is. I'll see you there," Rick responded.

"Thanks Rick. I think it will be beneficial for us both," Robert said as he hung up the phone.

Rick returned the phone to the cradle and looked at his watch. He could easily make it to Ashland in an hour and a half. He went out of the office and down the hall to the master bath. Lynn was just getting out of the shower. She was humming "How Great Thou Art." He didn't interrupt her.

Rick went down the hall to his office and retrieved a small Twenty-Two caliber Beretta and holster from his desk drawer. He checked the clip and chamber and then strapped the weapon securely to his right ankle. He opened the safe and took out a small box that contained some interesting items, including the special pen that would give off a discernible vibration if in the presence of a bug. He smiled to himself as he envisioned Robert Stankowski doing nearly the same thing. They were both graduates of the same program.

Rick kissed Lynn goodbye and said that he would call when he was on the way home. She thought he was going flying with Carlos. Even though he had prepped Carlos, he was sure that Lynn wouldn't check up on him.

The drive to Ashland took an hour and a half, just as Rick knew that it would. He had made the trip from Virginia Beach to Washington, D.C., on a weekly basis for nearly five years. Sometimes he would go up for the week. Other times he would go up and just spend the night. When he was alone, he most always stayed at the Best Western in Old Town. When Lynn went along, he would always make a reservation at the Ritz Carlton. She loved the high tea in the afternoon and shopping at the mall.

As Rick passed through the Hampton tunnel, his mind wandered back to the thirty-three hour insurgence into Columbia. Two teams of three did a low altitude drop from the back of a C-130. Carl Peterson led one team. Robert Stankowski led the other.

The mission involved the rescue of three young college age women *on a mission from God*—the young redhead's exact words. The girls had just completed their third year at Oral Roberts University, and for their summer vacation, had decided to execute The Great Commission on their own. Their intentions were honorable. But their plan to spread the Gospel to a bunch of farmers, coerced into harvesting cocoa leaves for one of the local drug lords, not only lacked wisdom but also lacked the required planning and dedicated local support to ensure even a modicum of safety.

Initially, the mission went as planned. Stankowski's team had little trouble rescuing the girls, but on the way to the extraction point, they were ambushed by several young banditos who were soon reinforced by several members of the local drug cartel. Carl's team employed a boar tactic, circled around and attacked the banditos from their left flank. The tables were turned, and within fifteen minutes, the banditos and five members of the cartel were terminated.

The remainder of the mission went as planned. Two of the girls threw up on the helicopter ride to safety. The redhead tried to convert Carl. She talked incessantly, quoting scripture verses verbatim. She seemed oblivious to the fact that she had just been rescued from a death sentence. Carl fell asleep as she recited John 3:16 for the third time. It was a long time ago.

The Cracker Barrel wasn't very crowded for a mid-October Wednesday morning. Rick walked in and asked the hostess if a Robert Stankowski had arrived. She looked at her pad and said that she didn't have him on her list. He gave her his name, and a young hostess in black jeans, crisp white shirt and brown apron with gold lettering led him to a table for two next to the window in the second section of the dining area. Her nametag identified her as Rosemary.

He had been seated for less than five minutes and was enjoying a hot cup of coffee when he recognized an older Robert Stankowski approaching. Stankowski still looked fit. He had put on a few pounds. He was a little over six feet tall, had perfect posture and probably weighed somewhere between two hundred and two hundred and ten pounds. His salt and pepper hair was still full. He was sporting a tan that could only have been cultivated in the tropics. He walked with a slight limp that was barley discernable, but it was there—probably served as a reminder to stay alert.

He smiled as he gained eye contact with Rick. Rick stood up, his right hand outstretched. Stankowski's handshake was firm. They maintained eye contact as they took their seats. Both men looked each other over for several seconds as they compared the present to their stored images from the past. Stankowski was first to speak.

"You look good Rick. Time has treated you well," he said as the server approached. "Coffee please," he said, not giving her a chance to speak. She nodded and headed toward the kitchen.

"You too Robert," responded Rick. "So what have you been doing all these years since Lebanon?" he asked.

Stankowski smiled.

"You heard about that," he said.

"We all did. Can't say that I blame you. The State Department guys are a bunch of bleeding heart liberal wimps. There was no way they would sanction installing devices that would activate the car bombs from a distance. God forbid we kill any friendlies," responded Rick as he took a drink of coffee.

"Marcinco's analysis was correct," said Stankowski as he looked around the room.

"So what is going on Robert?" asked Rick. "Why did you want to meet?"

"Rick, this is strictly off the record," said Robert as he leaned in toward Rick, his eyes looking for the obvious. "Please, no tricks," he added.

Rick smiled as he retrieved the pen from his shirt pocket and placed it on the table. Stankowski looked at it closely; he knew what it was. He reached into his pocket and placed a cigarette lighter that served the same purpose on the table.

"Strictly off the record," responded Rick in confirmation.

Just then the server arrived with fresh coffee and took their order for breakfast. When she left, Robert continued the conversation.

"Seems you and your people have jumped into the middle of a Homeland Security sting operation," said Stankowski.

"A sting operation? And just who is the target?" asked Rick.

"It's likely terrorist groups. I'm not privy to the details surrounding that part of the operation. However, I've been around long enough to put two and two together. The word is one of the missing Russian suitcase bombs has resurfaced. Homeland Security appears to be in damage control mode, as they know it will go to the highest bidder."

"And?" questioned Rick.

"And, in this fiscal environment, they don't have the funds to go after it. So they set up the sting operation to not only raise the funds, but also to give their guy the necessary credibility to be a serious player so he can try to broker a deal."

"So they set up the lottery scam to build a bankroll," said Rick shaking his head. "How did they select the marks?"

"They used the DEERS program to identify elderly military retirees, preferably widowers who were fairly well-to-do. Ones who would probably be too embarrassed to say anything," responded Stankowski as he sipped the hot coffee. From his expression, it appeared that he wasn't a proponent of the scenario.

"And whose bright idea was that?" asked Rick, keeping his questions short and to the point.

"It was the brain child of my boss, Ms. Yolanda Rawls," responded Stankowski. "She's a GS-fifteen whose ambition is only exceeded by her incompetence," he added.

A cynical smile crossed Rick's face. He was quite familiar with the type and had encountered plenty like her in his day. Unfortunately, most of them worked for the federal government.

Rick didn't say anything for a minute or two as he thought about the sting operation.

"Do you or Ms. Rawls have any idea how this has affected the widowers?" asked Rick.

"I have no idea. I can't speak for her," responded Stankowski. "My assignment was to watch the Bahamian Embassy."

"There have been several suicides directly associated with this *sting* operation," responded Rick, the disgust in his voice was evident as he said the word sting.

He looked for a reaction from Stankowski. From his body language, it appeared that Stankowski was unaware of the unintended consequences. Just as Rick was about to continue, the server brought their breakfast. She refilled the coffee cups and asked if they needed anything else. Both men said that everything was fine. When she left, Stankowski responded.

"I had no idea Rick. Are you sure of that?" he asked.

"We are certain," responded Rick. "What exactly was your task with the embassy?"

Stankowski didn't touch his breakfast. He seemed to be searching for an answer.

"My assistant, Ms. Anderson, and I kept track of visitors to the embassy. My task was to sidetrack any disgruntled winners, so to speak."

"And your idea of sidetracking John Kilday was to have a couple of goons beat him to death?" asked Rick, his voice rising just enough to get his point across.

"That should never have happened. Kilday got off to the Bahamas before we had a chance to intercept him. McAllister was a fool. He should have taken Kilday aside and told him that he would take care of it. He could have diffused the situation," responded Stankowski.

"Is Tarek Haddad your guy?" asked Rick.

"I don't know Haddad. He works directly for Ms. Rawls," responded Stankowski.

"So why are we here?" asked Rick.

"I felt that I owed you and Carl. Professional courtesy. I wanted to give you guys a heads up for old time's sake. You needed to know that this is a federal sting operation before you get in too deep."

Neither man spoke for several minutes. Neither of them had touched breakfast. Rick signaled the server for fresh coffee. After she poured the coffee, Rick's expression changed to one of seriousness.

"Robert, we have a real dilemma. Carl has a contract with Homeland Security. They have expanded his contract and provided six months of funding to investigate the lottery scam. Clearly, one hand doesn't know what the other is doing."

"There is absolutely zero oversight. You need to convince Carl to let it go. He's got his pound of flesh. I'm sure McAllister is dead, and I suspect his accomplices are feeding the fish. Listen Rick, my boss is a loose cannon. She can and *will* make your lives miserable. I guarantee it," responded Stankowski. "This broad isn't going to let anything get in the way of her ambition or her precious career."

Rick thought for a few minutes before answering. Stankowski cradled the coffee cup in both hands.

"It's Carl's call," said Rick.

Stankowski finished his coffee and pushed the uneaten breakfast aside. Just as he was about to continue, his phone rang. Stankowski looked at the caller ID. He appeared a bit anxious as he looked back at Rick and then excused himself abruptly. Rick watched as Stankowski hurriedly made his way outside. It was a call he clearly needed to take and obviously wanted to keep private.

While Stankowski was gone, Rick thought more about their conversation. He still had some unanswered questions and was still uncertain about Ms. Gemayel. Stankowski kept up appearances and still referred to her as Ms. Anderson. Also, Rick really wanted to find out what Stankowski knew about Anthony Serrano. Down deep inside, Rick really didn't believe Stankowski had any part or knowledge regarding Lynn's attack. It wasn't his style. However, Rick still wanted to talk to him about it face-to-face. Stankowski reappeared in the dining room, interrupting Rick's thoughts. He seemed to be a little frustrated and on edge.

"I am so sorry I had to take that. In fact, something urgent has come up with one of my other projects. I am going to have to cut this a little short," apologized Stankowski. "I hate that I have to go so suddenly. I'm just glad I had a chance to talk to you in person," he added. "You and Carl are good men. I have a lot of respect for you both."

"So, what are you going to do regarding your role in this sting operation?" asked Rick, wanting to gain some clarity on Stankowski's continued involvement before he left.

"I'm giving my notice tomorrow. I don't want any further part of Yolanda Rawls or her operation," responded Stankowski as he reached into his pocket and handed Rick a business card.

"That's my private number," he added. He looked as if he was ready to bolt out the door.

"And what about your assistant, Ms. Gemayel?" Rick continued, letting Stankowski know that he knew Ms. Anderson's real name.

Stankowski smiled.

"She's not with me," he said as stood up. "She's freelance. Only in it for the money. And Rick…don't turn your back on her," he said as he turned and walked away.

CHAPTER THIRTY

The trip back from Ashland took a little longer than Rick had expected. A light rain had started just as he pulled out of the parking lot. Traffic always seemed to slow a bit in rainy weather.

As he entered the Hampton city limits, the traffic advisory board displayed a message saying that the Hampton Roads Bridge Tunnel was backed up to the Coliseum. There was seldom a time that it wasn't backed up on both sides of the HRBT. Unfortunately the tunnel always bottle necked during any kind of heavier traffic and most always during the rain. Many drivers subconsciously hit the brake pedal as they approached the entrance to the tunnel further compounding the congestion.

Rick checked the time and decided to take the Monitor Merrimack Tunnel via I-664 to Chesapeake then I-64 to Virginia Beach. Since there were two separate tunnels, there was absolutely no backup. The traffic was moderate as it moved in and out at fifty-five miles per hour. The rain had stopped as he emerged from the tunnel on the other side. It was clear as a bell.

Rick's conversation with Robert Stankowski provided many of the answers he needed in order to fully understand what was going on, at least most of the answers. Stankowski was particularly forthcoming. The confirmation that Homeland Security was involved certainly added a new wrinkle to the project.

Rick agreed in principle with Stankowski that Carl should probably let it go. However, the more he thought about it, Rick didn't like the methods Ms. Yolanda Rawls employed in order to achieve what appeared to be solely in support of her personal goals. Rick was certain that Carl wouldn't take any time at all to decide that Ms. Rawls could go to hell…along with the affirmative action horse she rode in on.

Besides, the lack of oversight and quality control was unacceptable. Rick wanted to know who in Homeland Security sanctioned such a reckless use of power by one of their program directors.

The more Rick thought about it, the more he realized that Carl wouldn't entertain any thoughts of *letting it go.* Carl would continue the project without regard to Homeland Security's involvement. Yolanda Rawls may be a loose cannon, but she was now rolling around on Carl's deck. She would be wise to steer clear of *Captain* Carl Peterson.

Besides, Rick had been around too many individuals like Ms. Rawls. He didn't approve of her methods or blatant disregard for the unintended consequences of her actions. She was certainly more than reckless with her decisions. The more he thought about her, and especially what had happened to Lynn most likely under her direction, he knew he would support whatever course of action Carl decided to pursue.

Rick was still at the helm of Matrix, Inc., in 2003 when Homeland Security was formed in response to the events of September 11th. The bureaucracy and leadership associated with controlling the nine agencies that comprise Homeland Security were a matter of record.

As Rick went by the exit to the Joint Task Force Command, he dialed Carlos. Carlos and Ann had taken another shower. Ann was in the process of drying her hair, and Carlos had just poured his last cup of coffee for the day when his satellite phone rang. He looked at the caller ID out of habit. The only calls he received on the satellite phone were from Rick and occasionally Tony.

"Afternoon Rick," he answered. He sounded a little tired but perked up quickly as he asked, "How did your meeting with Stankowski go?"

"It went well. He said to say hello," responded Rick.

"How is he doing?" responded Carlos.

"He seems to be doing well. However, I need to go over the information that he provided. I just wanted to touch base with you and postpone our meeting this afternoon. I need to bounce a few things off Carl. I will give you a call later."

"That sounds good. Is the trip to Tampa still on for tomorrow?" asked Carlos, wondering how much had changed as a result of Rick's meeting with Stankowski.

"Yes, it is. Give Tony a heads-up," responded Rick. "I need to go over a few things tonight. Is he back in town?"

"He got in a couple hours ago. Said the fishing was good but that he lost a couple hundred at the tables. By the sound of his voice, he probably lost more than he's willing to admit."

"He should probably stick to fishing," said Rick. "Did you receive the itinerary from Elaine?" he asked.

"Yes, I have it. What about Ann? If this thing is a go, do you plan on using her in Tampa?" asked Carlos.

Rick hesitated for a few seconds before answering.

"It all depends on Ms. Gemayel. Tell her to pack a bag and hang loose. She can charge to the project. I'll have Elaine schedule a flight to Tampa later in the day. I'll see Roland tomorrow morning. By then, he should know where Ms. Gemayel is heading."

"Do you think she's going to Tampa?" asked Carlos.

"I think that's a good bet," responded Rick. "And if she does, it will be good to have Ann there with you. Then we can free up Tony to concentrate on Tarek," he added.

"So what about Stankowski? Will he be any trouble?" asked Carlos, knowing that Stankowski could be trouble if he were on the other side.

"Told me he was done with Homeland Security. He was going to give up his contract tomorrow. I believe him," responded Rick.

"That's a bit of a relief. You know Rick, he would be a good asset if we need him," said Carlos after a slight pause.

Rick had been thinking along the same lines. From the encounters they had as young operatives, Rick had respect for Stankowski's commitment and ability.

"Maybe," said Rick. "I'll call you later with the travel details. Say hi to Ann," added Rick as he put the phone on the passenger seat.

The conversation with Stankowski had helped to clear up many of the loose ends. Rick began to go over everything in his mind. The whole thing had started with a sting operation orchestrated by the ambitious Ms. Rawls. The suicides were collateral damage—damage that she didn't seem to care about. She must have suspected that there would be a barrage of complaints to the Bahamian Embassy as evidenced by her placement of Ms. Gemayel. But why would she choose someone with Ms. Gemayel's credentials? She must have anticipated some real trouble. She may not have anticipated the suicides, but when dealing with elderly widowers, suicide is certainly a strong possibility, and one that should have been on the table. The misfortune for Ms. Rawls was that one of the victims was John Kilday.

Rick was still wrapping his head around the sting operation and the fact that Ms. Rawls, as a program manager with Homeland Security, had sanctioned the lottery scam to build her bank roll to fund the operation. His thoughts also wandered to the various groups that could be in possession of the dirty bomb. The more Rick thought about everything, the more he wanted to know. The more he wanted to get fully involved.

As he continued toward the turn-off to Virginia Beach, it occurred to him that the primary objective of the delivery order had been met with the revelation that Homeland Security was already involved and behind the sting operation. How ironic, he thought to himself.

From a technical aspect, The Peterson Group had fulfilled the main objective of their delivery order. However, the verbiage in it, as with many delivery orders, was vague enough to justify further investigation.

Rick looked at his watch. He thought about calling Carl and letting him know the results of his conversation with Stankowski, but in the back of his mind he knew that Carl would want to continue the project regardless of Rick's findings. Carl would never leave any money on the table, especially in the case of Homeland Security.

CHAPTER
THIRTY-ONE

As The Peterson Group Gulfstream leveled off, Carlos and Tony unfastened their seat belts and joined Roland in the small briefing area. Roland had prepared a brief along with a demonstration. Since time was of the essence, Roland commenced the briefing, which included an overview of the iPad they would employ on the mission. Roland had loaded the iPad with the most current information he had gathered on Tarek Haddad. A unique feature of the iPad was its capability to access the Homeland Security satellite feed. The feed would provide an up close and personal view of the Tampa area, practically in real-time.

As a demonstration of the capability, Roland brought up the satellite feed. Carlos and Tony leaned forward. The screen had their full attention. Roland zoomed in on the Davis Island Yacht Club. The detail was amazing. Roland reminded them that the video had a three second time delay. Carlos was very much aware that a three second delay could be the difference between life and death.

As they were watching the screen, a car drove into the parking area. Roland zoomed in on the car's license plate. The resolution was outstanding. The Florida plate with a manatee was clearly visible as was the date on the plate, which indicated that it was about to expire.

Roland zoomed out a bit. Several people could be seen walking in the parking area. Two of them were heading in the direction of the piers.

Roland scanned the area. Three large piers comprised the marina. They provided hook-ups for approximately forty boats each. Almost all the slips were occupied. Roland zoomed in on the far right pier and pointed out the slip where a large boat was berthed. He zoomed in on the boat's stern. The name, *The Big Fish*, was clearly visible. How appropriate, Carlos thought to himself. The big fish eat the little fish. Unfortunately for John Kilday, he had been one of the little fish.

"And what we are seeing is basically a live feed?" asked Tony.

"It is," responded Roland. "But don't forget the time delay," he cautioned as he turned and looked at both Carlos and Tony. "I have also recorded a couple of events from yesterday," he added as he double clicked one of two icons on the left side of the screen.

A still video appeared with a large start arrow in the center of the screen. Roland clicked on the arrow. A man in khaki shorts, white shirt, Panama hat and deck shoes could be seen walking down the pier. He waved to a couple sitting on the stern of a large boat on the left side of the pier. They had drinks in their hand and could be seen waving him aboard. He stopped momentarily but declined their invitation as he waved and continued down the pier. He boarded *The Big Fish*, looked around and bent down to pick up something on the deck.

"I believe that is your guy," said Roland. "He left two other times yesterday and returned to spend the night on the boat."

Roland clicked on the second icon. A woman wearing a stylish sun hat that covered most of her face could be seen walking down the pier. She reached down and removed her shoes and then boarded *The Big Fish*.

"She left with Haddad early this morning. There has been no other activity since," added Roland.

"And you're confident that we are looking at Tarek Haddad?" asked Carlos. It was more of a statement than it was a question. "Do we know the identity of the woman?" he added.

Roland hesitated before answering.

"As far as Haddad, I'm not one hundred percent certain, but it is a safe guess that it's him," offered Roland as he paused the recording. "As for the woman, I am still working on this. Unfortunately, her face was covered in this video, so I haven't been able to identify her through any of the facial recognition software," he confided.

Roland looked back at the screen and hit the play button. Carlos continued to watch the recording as the woman went below. Carlos turned to Roland.

"Carl mentioned that he had a friend who would meet us at the marina and provide us with a cover story."

"That's correct. Her name is Rebecca Waverly. She works for one of the local yacht brokers, and from what I gather, is a long time acquaintance of Mr. Peterson's. She is well known at the yacht club and is expecting you to call her when you exit the airport."

The Peterson Group Gulfstream was on its way back to Dulles when Carlos and Tony exited the National Car Rental building with keys in hand. The noise from another large jet caused Carlos to look up. He watched the aircraft as it continued to climb. He never did understand how such a large heavy metal object could defy gravity.

When he and Rick would fly together, he would ask Rick those puzzling questions. Rick had a master's degree in aeronautical engineering, and no matter how hard he tried, he was never able to explain the aerodynamics to Carlos's satisfaction—how nose attitude controlled airspeed and power controlled altitude. Carlos would grin. His facial expression said it all. Rick smiled and would end up telling Carlos to just add power. Carlos understood *power*.

Carlos continued to watch as the large aircraft disappeared into the clouds. The cloud layer was thick, gray and covered most of the southwestern sky. It seemed to taper off at the horizon. The temperature was still a very comfortable seventy-four degrees.

Carlos and Tony continued their short trek through the parking lot. They pulled suitcases behind them, being careful to avoid the small puddles of water left by the early morning showers. The suitcases were the kind that could easily fit into an overhead compartment on an airplane. Carlos's bag was dark green and bore the bruises and marks from many overnight "vacations." One of the wheels wobbled slightly and made a discernable clicking sound as it continued to make its way across the parking lot.

Tony's bag was black and was brand new. His old bag provided a storage area for papers that he would probably never look at again. It was stored alongside a stack of boxes in his garage back in Destin. For whatever reason, he didn't have the heart to throw it away. Every once in a while Tony would look down at Carlos's bag expecting the noisy wheel to fall off. The wheel was stubborn. It had been making the clicking sound for well over a year.

Both were prepared to spend a couple of days staking out the boat that they believed was being used by Tarek Haddad. Their purpose was two-fold. First, and in accordance with the Homeland Security statement of work, they were tasked with finding out whom Tarek Haddad was contacting. Secondly, and probably more important to Carl Peterson, was their task to gain access to the funds that Haddad had bilked from the unsuspecting lottery winners.

Carl was committed to returning the money to the victims, minus the usual fifteen percent finder's fee for The Peterson Group. According to Roland's figures, fifteen percent was a healthy sum.

Carlos and Tony had decided that they wouldn't waste much time fooling around with Haddad. Tony was very familiar with various interrogation techniques as was Carlos. There was the hard way, and then there was the easy way. However, Carl had made it very clear that he wanted this guy to suffer.

They could easily waterboard Haddad aboard the boat. Both Carlos and Tony were intimately familiar with waterboarding. Both had been waterboarded during training—Carlos at Warner Springs, California, and Tony at Camp Perry, Virginia. The procedure was extremely intimidating and humbling. It established who was in control and clearly defined the means that Carlos and Tony would employ to make Haddad spill his guts.

Besides, waterboarding left no visible marks. If anything, waterboarding was more of a fear tactic. They knew firsthand how miserable the procedure was and knew that extreme care had to be taken because of how easy it was to accidentally drown the individual. Carlos and Tony were very much aware that getting pertinent information was more of an art than a science. The key was to know how far to go, when to stop, and more importantly, which of the myriad of answers was actually the truth.

The advantage that Carlos and Tony had was that they already knew the correct answers to many of the questions they would ask. They would carefully blend the questions together to establish a baseline. The order of the questions was important. Obtaining the information they wanted wouldn't take too long. If there were any doubts, Carlos was fully prepared to use drugs to obtain the information, but that was the easy way.

They knew that under torturous situations, a guy would say anything to get the interrogators to stop. However, once Haddad realized that Carlos and Tony knew many of the correct answers, and that he couldn't mislead them, he would be more forthcoming rather than risk another round of waterboarding.

Carlos had selected a new white Cadillac. Before he fastened his seat belt, he took out the small notebook that Roland Carpenter had given him following the short brief on their flight from Pensacola. He pressed the destination button on the GPS system and followed the onscreen directions for entering 1315 Severn Avenue into the system's computer. It was the address of the Davis Island Yacht Club. The yacht club was located on the outermost point of Davis Island. Carlos selected the fastest route and pressed route guidance. The GPS indicated that his destination was approximately thirty minutes away. Distance in noonday traffic was meaningless.

Carlos looked at his watch and then over at Tony who wasn't paying any attention to him or the GPS system. Tony was focused on a young lady trying to maneuver a very large suitcase into the small trunk of her rental car. Her short skirt was hiked up and was certainly no help in hiding the black G-string that she chose to wear. The scene left nothing to the imagination.

"How can that thing be comfortable?" Tony asked as he continued to watch the girl as she struggled with the bulky suitcase. The suitcase was winning the battle.

"What thing?" asked Carlos as he leaned forward to see what had fully captured Tony's attention.

"Whoa partner," responded Carlos. "Comfortable? Are you kidding me? You know Tony, you really need to get out more," said Carlos after a brief pause. Both he and Tony continued to watch the girl struggle with the suitcase. It had turned into a pleasant battle for Carlos and Tony.

They both watched the show for a few more seconds. Carlos again gazed at Tony in disbelief as the girl finally accomplished her mission. He shook his head. A slight smile crossed his face.

"Buckle up Romeo, we're outta here," said Carlos as he slowly backed out of the parking space and headed for the exit.

The computer-generated voice instructed him to head east on West Ohio Avenue. The traffic was heavy and moving at a fast clip. At this time of day, most of the drivers were probably heading out for lunch. Carlos accelerated and attempted to merge into traffic. He had put on his left turn signal, but it had no beneficial effect. If anything, it seemed to trigger rude behavior on the part of the other drivers. So much for southern hospitality, he thought. He decided that he wouldn't use the turn signal again.

As he proceeded east on West Ohio Street, he moved into the right lane and dialed the number for Ms. Waverly. She answered on the fourth ring.

"Hello, this is Rebecca," she answered in a cheerful voice.

"Ms. Waverly, this is Carlos Garcia. I believe you were expecting my call," responded Carlos.

"Yes I was. I assume you are on the way to the marina. I can be there in about twenty minutes. Will that work for you?" she asked.

"That will be perfect. I am driving a new white caddy. Should be there in about twenty-five minutes, at least according to the GPS," said Carlos.

"By the way, I have talked with Carl Peterson, and I have a boat that you will be using," she said.

"That sounds good," responded Carlos. "See you in a few minutes."

At 1215 hours, Carlos pulled into the parking area of the Davis Island Yacht Club. There were about a dozen cars in the parking area. Carlos quickly scanned the lot. A taupe colored Mercedes 550SL was parked near the clubhouse. A woman with blonde hair was sitting in the car. She appeared to be talking to someone.

Carlos parked in the nearest space to her car. As he pulled in, she looked in his direction and then ended her call. She got out of the car and walked with purpose toward Carlos and Tony as they got out of their car. The broken seashells made a crunching sound under their feet as they walked in her direction.

"Good afternoon," she announced. "I'm Rebecca, and you must be Carlos," she said after a slight pause. She extended her right hand.

"That is correct, and this is Tony Ramos," responded Carlos. He gave Ms. Waverly the once over as her attention went to Tony.

She dressed young, but the small lines around her eyes and lips were probably that of a woman in her mid-to-late fifties. She obviously worked out. Her arms were solid and her calves were strong. Her perfume was expensive, subtle and quite pleasant. She was a good-looking woman.

"And how was your trip?" she asked.

"It was quick," responded Carlos. "Do we need to check in with anyone?" he added. Carlos was never one for small talk.

"No, we're fine to go. Carl and I have selected a boat that will allow you to accomplish your mission. If anyone checks, it will appear that you are in the process of purchasing the boat," she said with a telling smile.

"How much do you know about our visit?" asked Carlos.

"Enough," she answered as she started walking in the direction of the middle pier. "Carl and I go back a long way," she added without looking back. "By the way, your friend Ann will be landing later this afternoon," she added matter-of-factly.

Carlos wondered who she was before she was in yacht sales.

CHAPTER THIRTY-TWO

Rick sat in the den looking out at the water while he enjoyed his second cup of coffee for the day. There was a slight ripple moving across the lake. The sky was overcast. There were two guys in a dark green johnboat drifting with the current about fifteen feet offshore. They were casting toward Rick's dock. However, Rick couldn't stop thinking about the assault on Lynn. It had only been a couple of days. She was still a bit uncomfortable but appeared to be doing much better. The more Rick thought about it, he still wanted his pound of flesh. Lynn was innocent; she didn't deserve to be a pawn in someone's ill-conceived game.

Lynn had just left for her therapy appointment at 1300 hours. Fortunately, she had always worked out and was in good shape. The therapy would be easy for her and quite beneficial. She had signed up for two weeks. Rick had offered to drive her, but she insisted that she could drive herself. Besides, she had a hair appointment later in the afternoon and was going to do a little bit of shopping before her appointment. Things were getting back to normal.

Rick had done his best to convince her that everything would be all right. By no means was it of any comfort. But at least the assault didn't happen at home in their driveway, or worse yet, in their house. Home was their place of refuge—their little fortified castle on the lake. It had always been, and certainly was, Lynn's place of security.

Rick probably had the best security system in Virginia Beach. SCAT Security had provided the foundation, but Rick had made modifications using the latest technology. There were the usual signs signifying that the house was protected. The signs were there for the kids and were an understatement.

Rick's system consisted of sensors on every door and window, several motion detectors, cameras, a backup power supply and a satellite phone system that would signal any breach in the system, even if someone were clever enough to cut the phone line. There was a motion detector and camera in the attic and a sensor on the garage overhead door. A computer system with off-site backup provided additional control, including twenty-four hour monitoring. Cameras were strategically placed, including hidden cameras, around the exterior of the house.

Rick could monitor the system from anywhere on his laptop, cell phone and in real-time. And just to be sure, Rick kept four loaded guns close at hand. Neither he nor Lynn was ever more than twenty feet from a loaded weapon. Lynn didn't like the fact that the guns were loaded. However, Rick finally convinced her that it would be ludicrous to yell "timeout" to an intruder while he took his gun out of its security case, unlocked the trigger guard, inserted a clip and chambered a round. She finally acquiesced and took lessons.

The guns were readily accessible and ready to deliver. If anyone were foolish enough to break into Rick Morgan's house, they would leave in a body bag. It was a sad commentary to the times and state of affairs in America when it was necessary to have your own lethal protection.

The police motto, To Serve and Protect, was just that…an empty motto. The police never showed up until after the fact. Rick was determined not to be a statistic. He wouldn't need them anyway. They would just need a pad and pencil to take notes, so they could make out their report in triplicate.

As Rick continued to nurse the coffee, he decided it was now time to find out more about Anthony Serrano. He had wanted to discuss Serrano with Stankowski, but their meeting was cut short. Rick had been going over the information that Roland had provided. It was thorough.

Serrano was obviously a frustrated wannabe. His record was replete with the failings of someone who had a very difficult time with authority. Following his less than honorable discharge from the army, he had several jobs, all of which ended with him being terminated for cause. He started his own security business, probably after realizing he couldn't work for anyone else. Serrano Security International was incorporated in May of 2010. The federal ID number was current as was the business license. There was no commercial business address other than a P.O. Box in the Strawbridge area of Virginia Beach. There was no client list that identified any international work. International probably sounded good to Serrano. He probably worked out of his house, or more likely, out of his car.

It was time to give Robert Stankowski a call. As Rick walked into his study, he thought more about his conversation with Stankowski. He was still sure that Stankowski didn't know anything about the assault on Lynn. Stankowski was a true professional. He surely would have said something during their conversation in Ashland. However, Rick needed undeniable confirmation. Moreover, there was a good chance that Stankowski knew who Serrano was, or at least knew who had hired him.

Rick went to his desk drawer and pulled out the business card that Stankowski gave him. It was simple, just Stankowski's name and number. No business logo and no address, no fancy border, just a number on a white card with a matte finish. Rick rubbed the card between his fingers. Actually, it was of good stock—an expensive card. Rick went back into the den, sat in the recliner and dialed the number. He continued to look out at the lake. The two guys in the johnboat were now in front of his neighbor's house. They seemed to know what they were doing.

"Stankowski," was the crisp response by Robert Stankowski as he looked at the LED on his phone. There was no caller ID available. Only a handful of people had Stankowski's private number. The number was never called by mistake.

"Robert. Rick Morgan here," said Rick after a slight pause. He purposely tried to sound more official than personal.

"Hey Rick. I certainly wasn't expecting to hear from you…at least not so soon. What's up? How can I help you?" came Stankowski's friendly response.

"Are you still working for Homeland Security?" asked Rick, still sounding official.

"No. As I told you I was going to ask for a release from my contract, and that is exactly what I did," responded Stankowski. Rick could hear the questioning in his response.

"Do you know Anthony Serrano?" asked Rick, deciding not to beat around the bush. He wanted to catch Stankowski off guard if possible. See if there was any hesitation in his answer.

Stankowski didn't answer right away. Rick could hear him tapping in the background, probably with a pencil. The beat was fairly steady. He wondered if Stankowski would parse his answer.

"No," said Stankowski firmly. "The name doesn't ring any bells. Should I know this guy?" he asked. His voice was steady.

"I thought he might have been one of your guys, or one of the guys working the sting operation."

"Well, he could have been on the project, but I've never met him. But that is not surprising. Ms. Rawls kept everything close. I knew that there were others involved, but she never held any group status meetings or the like. She would call me in for an update. I was only responsible for handling the McAllister connection," responded Stankowski.

Rick didn't say anything for several long seconds. He would have liked to ask these questions in person. He could tell a lot from a person's body language. There were always telling signs. However, today he didn't have that luxury and he lost the opportunity during their last encounter. He believed Stankowski, or at least he wanted to believe him.

"So Rick, who is this guy?"

"He assaulted my wife the other night as she left MacArthur Center in Norfolk," responded Rick.

"Is she all right?" asked Stankowski before Rick had a chance to continue.

"She is okay. She wasn't the real target. I was. The assault was merely an attempt to intimidate me—get me to back off from continuing my investigation into the events surrounding John Kilday."

Stankowski didn't say anything for several seconds. Rick could hear him tapping the pencil again.

"Rick, you can't possibly believe that I would have anything to do with this," responded Stankowski, sounding somewhat wounded by the indirect accusation.

"The thought crossed my mind," responded Rick without hesitation.

There was silence between both men for what seemed to be a long time.

"Rick, I can assure you that I had nothing to do with this," responded Stankowski.

Rick didn't say anything.

"I want to believe you, but you can understand my position," responded Rick.

"I understand. But Rick, we go back a long ways. I'm old school."

"I needed to know. Let's say that I believe you, for old time's sake."

"Rick, I hate to admit it, but my last conversation with Ms. Rawls might have been the trigger," offered Stankowski. "I suppose I could be partially responsible," he added.

"And how so?" asked Rick.

"Before our meeting, I met with Ms. Rawls and told her about my conversation with McAllister, and that I believed he was a dead man but just didn't know it yet. I also told her that she had no idea who she was messing with, that I knew you and wanted no part of her operation."

Again neither man spoke for a minute or so. Rick took a sip of luke-warm coffee and placed the cup on his coffee table. He stood up and walked to the sliding glass door. He could see the johnboat a couple of docks from his. One of the guys had leaned forward and was pulling a nice size bass out of the water. Everything gets caught sooner or later.

"You may be right. I appreciate your candidness Robert."

"You know Rick, it just isn't like the old days. There is no integrity. I've met too many people like Ms. Rawls. They are only interested in their precious careers, and quite frankly, most of them work directly for the federal government. They think they are untouchable. Listen Rick, if there is anything I can do, please let me know," he added.

Rick sensed the sincerity in Stankowski's voice.

"Thanks Robert. I just may take you up on your offer. I had to ask. I will be in touch," he said as he ended the call.

Rick believed Stankowski. They did go back a long way—to a time when you could put your trust and life on the line without fear of being sold out. Men of Stankowski's caliber were few and hard to find in today's materialistic environment. Almost everyone was a free agent.

Rick opened the file on Serrano and stared at his picture. As Roland had indicated, Serrano was a rough looking character. Obviously a lot of people took exception to him. The record listed him as five foot ten and one hundred and ninety pounds. He was considered an expert in hand-to-hand combat and small arms. He had applied for Sniper School but was turned down following the psychological evaluation. He definitely had issues. There was certainly time to deal with him. Rick knew where to find him. The connection to Ms. Rawls really didn't matter. Rick would take care of him when the time was right.

CHAPTER THIRTY-THREE

Rebecca Waverly had done a good job. *My Debt* was less than a year old and had been on the market for over six months. According to Ms. Waverly, it had only been shown once in the past three months. A couple from Orlando owned the boat. They were in their mid-thirties and had made some very bad investments trying to flip properties. They were not alone. Many of the yachts in the marina were for sale.

When Rebecca took Carlos and Tony aboard the boat that afternoon, she deftly removed the for sale sign and stowed it below. The older couple that Carlos had seen during Roland's in-flight demonstration waved, believing that one of the boats may have finally sold. Maybe the economy was turning around. It was certainly a good time to buy a boat if one was so inclined, so long as they didn't have to sell something in order to come up with the money. However, the price of fuel kept most of the boats tied to the dock. Many of these boats didn't go by miles to the gallon. It was more like gallons to the mile.

Rebecca Waverly had made arrangements with the boat's owners per Carl's instructions. Carl had paid a tidy sum to rent the boat for a month. He had given Rebecca specific instructions to inform Carlos and Tony that the boat would remain tied up to the dock. Not that he didn't trust Carlos, it was that he *knew* Carlos. Carlos could be impulsive. While Carl really didn't want him to have keys, the reality was, Carlos didn't actually *need* keys. Carl made it clear the mission was to keep an eye on *The Big Fish*.

Rebecca didn't waste much time. She showed Carlos and Tony around the boat, handed Carlos the keys, reminded him again of Carl's specific instructions, and told them that if they needed anything to be sure and let her know. Her smile was genuine. As Tony looked at her, he was wondering to himself if she was married. Disappointingly, she never made lasting eye contact. She appeared to be all business. This certainly wasn't the time or the place. Besides, Tony wasn't sure what her relationship was with Carl.

Carlos popped the top on a Coors Light that he had commandeered from the small refrigerator located next to the ladder that led up to the helm station. He stood there for several minutes enjoying the beer as he looked up and down the pier. There was very little activity. In fact, there had hardly been any activity since he and Tony arrived. Carlos took up a position on the bench seat that nearly spanned the stern. He ran his hand over the surface of the material. It had the feel of glove leather. It was an expensive looking beige color. He wondered how it would hold up in the Florida sun.

From his vantage point, he had a clear view of *The Big Fish*. There was only one entrance to each pier. Anyone going to *The Big Fish* would have to pass by him. He leaned back and took a healthy swallow of the Coors Light, looked at the can fondly and finished what was left. He smiled to himself and thought about crushing the can on his forehead, but those days were long past. He was immature and foolish as a young navy SEAL. What the hell, he thought to himself as he slammed the can against his forehead. Some things never change.

"That was a lot harder in the old days," said Tony as he surfaced from below. "They don't make those cans like they use to," he added.

Tony had visibly startled Carlos who was starting to turn a slight shade of red. Somehow he had forgotten he wasn't alone.

"Did I miss the party?" continued Tony, not wanting to let Carlos off the hook just yet.

Carlos didn't respond as he tried to regain his composure. Although the can was made of aluminum the edges could still hold their own. The two men sat in silence as they both surveyed the marina. They decided it would be best if Tony wasn't seen hanging around. They didn't want to raise too many questions. The fact that there was someone new in the marina would already draw enough unwanted attention.

After Tony left, Carlos rescued another Coors from the refrigerator and then turned on the flat screen TV that was mounted on the port side just above the small fridge. The channel was set to CNN. Carlos changed it to Fox News. *The Five* was on. Carlos finished the beer, got up and looked down the dock in both directions. There was still no sign of Tarek Haddad. He looked at his watch, grabbed another beer and took up his surveillance position on the bench seat. He really didn't like stakeouts. He was a man of action. He mused to himself that stakeouts were boring and resulted in too much wasted time, coffee and donuts. He looked at the beer in his hand and said out loud, "Case closed."

As he sat there, he continued to admire the plush surroundings. He could get used to this kind of living he thought to himself. The boat, a Sea Ray 410 Sundancer, was pristine to say the least and most certainly out of his price range. Boats were a funny thing. They could be infectious. While a person didn't necessarily have to be in the market for one, once they boarded and looked around, the desire to have one could be overwhelming.

As Carlos sat there with visions of a blue blazer, white trousers, deck shoes with no socks and a captain's cover, he remembered the old adage about the two happiest days in a boat owner's life—the day you buy it, and the day you sell it.

As he was finishing his second beer, his satellite phone rang. It was Ann. Her timing was uncanny. She must have known that he was dreaming.

"Hey, where are you?" asked Carlos. He was excited about the opportunity to spend a few nights on the boat with her.

"I am about to board my flight for Tampa. They have delayed the boarding for fifteen minutes. Should be there about 1900," responded Ann.

"Good, can't wait to see you. Wait until you see this boat. It's unbelievable," responded Carlos.

"Don't get any ideas Garcia," she responded. "Carl told me that he gave specific orders that the boat would stay *tied up* to the pier," she reprimanded in a stern voice.

"Just dreaming honey," responded an apologetic ex-first mate with a discernible sigh. "Call me when you get in and I will give you directions...and maybe a captain's tour later," he added.

"You're a trip Garcia. See you in a couple of hours, love you," she said after a slight pause. "And don't forget why we are there," she reminded him again as she ended the call.

He smiled to himself. She was right. The boat was just an instrument. One they would use to complete the mission. But he could still dream.

Tony had taken the rental car and headed downtown. He would stake out Tarek Haddad's business address and take pictures of anyone who showed up. He had checked into the Embassy Suites on South Florida Avenue. According to Roland, the Embassy Suites were less than a half mile from the office that Tarek Haddad had listed as his business address.

Tony had taken a quick shower, and since they had no idea where Tarek Haddad was, he planned to spend a few hours staking out the office. Tony had all his little toys laid out on the bed including the camera case that Roland had given them aboard the aircraft. The camera was one of several that The Peterson Group had recently purchased. Roland had told Carlos and Tony that the camera was basically foolproof—just point and shoot.

Tony took the camera out of the case. There was a small manual explaining how to use the Cannon EOS 5D. Tony picked up the camera and aimed at the telephone on the far side of the room. He snapped the shutter. The close up of the phone was remarkably clear. Tony wouldn't read the manual.

He dropped the camera on the bed saying, "This will do." He probably had no idea that he just dropped a three thousand dollar camera on the bed. Carl was never one to spare any expense, especially when he could purchase the camera as part of an existing contract.

Since technology changed so rapidly, the government hardly ever asked for any of the items purchased under the contract to be returned. They certainly could, but they hardly ever did. If they did take them back, they would survey them, which meant they gave them to their kids in college.

Tony finished getting dressed, grabbed the camera and headed out the door just as his phone rang. It was Carlos.

"Hey," answered Tony as he headed for the elevator.

"Hey buddy, are you checked in?"

"I am. I'm actually leaving now to check out Haddad's office," responded Tony. "Has Ann arrived?" he asked.

"Ann should be here in an hour or so. By the way, I haven't seen any sign of Haddad," responded Carlos.

"Well, it is still early. He's probably at the office or maybe out to dinner," reassured Tony.

Carlos didn't respond right away. That was certainly a viable possibility.

"You may be right," agreed Carlos.

"I'll give you a buzz when I get to the office," offered Tony. "Hey, don't get too used to that boat," he laughed.

"Yeah right. Talk with you later."

Carlos put the phone down and looked back in the direction of *The Big Fish*. As he was looking, an older couple was heading in his direction. They were all dressed up and probably heading out for dinner. Carlos didn't want to get into a lengthy discussion, but he needed to be neighborly or at least try.

"Good evening," greeted the man. He was probably in his early seventies. He had a full head of wavy hair that appeared to be dyed. He was not as tan as one would expect for someone who was living on a boat. "I'm Charles Langworthy. This is my wife, Martha," he added with a smile. Martha looked older and was very tan. It didn't make a lot of sense to Carlos, but women seemed to worship the sun more than men.

"Good evening to you," responded Carlos. He couldn't remember a time when he had said the words, *good evening.* Maybe once or twice when he was trying to impress Ann. *Good evening* somehow is less meaningful when you are standing there in shorts, a white undershirt, flip-flops and a near empty beer can.

"I don't mean to be too nosey, but have you purchased *My Debt?*" asked Martha. She seemed to be expressionless.

"I hope so. It is in the hands of my agent. Hopefully she can come to an agreement that my wife and I can live with," responded Carlos.

"Is she with you?" asked Martha as she looked past Carlos.

"She is on the way. Should be here within the hour," responded Carlos as he looked at his watch.

"Wasn't there another fellow with you?" asked Charles Langworthy.

Carlos didn't answer right away. He finished what was left of the Coors. Guys usually didn't ask so many questions, he thought to himself.

"He's an old buddy of mine that picked me up at the airport and dropped me off," responded Carlos. "Are you guys heading out for dinner?" he asked, trying to change the subject.

"We are," answered Martha as she and Charles Langworthy began to slowly move in the direction of the parking lot. "We'll have to get together with you and your wife," Charles added as they went on their way. "Good night."

Yes, good night to you, Carlos thought to himself. These two seemed to notice quite a bit.

CHAPTER THIRTY-FOUR

Tony Ramos drove out of the parking garage a little after 1900. He was hoping that he would make contact fairly soon. He also wasn't fond of surveillance operations, but he did have more patience than Carlos. He knew all the little tricks necessary to follow someone without being seen, even by someone familiar with their surroundings and aware that someone might be tailing them. It was always much easier with two tails.

Although he had spent some time in the Tampa area, it had changed significantly since he had been there. He had fond memories as a member of Delta Force working with the Southern Command. Since his team made frequent deployments, they were strongly encouraged to live on the base. His forays into Tampa were few and far between and limited to a couple of the local bars that were fairly close to the base.

On a few occasions, he would get lucky and hook up with one of the local ladies. He never remembered where they lived, or how he got there. He seldom remembered their name. That was a long time ago. The thought brought a little smile to his face. Life goes by fast, but memories linger forever.

Fortunately at this time of day there was little traffic, but there was enough to provide good cover. With just a couple of turns, he was driving by Haddad's office on South Franklin Street. It took less than two minutes. Roland was right. Tony could have walked there in less than five minutes.

He glanced over at the camera bag on the passenger seat. There was enough street lighting to take some good pictures; however, it was also enough lighting to be seen taking pictures. Roland said that the camera was capable of taking close ups in extreme low-light conditions. As a precaution, Roland had disconnected the flash. This wasn't an area, or time of day, where tourists would be expected taking pictures, so Tony had to be careful.

The camera would be hard to conceal, or at the very least, to justify. Regardless, Tony would try to blend in. He wore a panama shirt and loose fitting khaki trousers that helped to conceal the Thirty-Two automatic holstered on his right ankle. He wasn't used to the weapon but decided to wear a backup to his trusty stiletto, since he was on this stakeout alone. Since his encounter with Kevin Macavoy, he decided he couldn't be too cautious. He subconsciously pressed the scar tissue surrounding the knife wound left by Macavoy.

There were several parking spaces in front of the small office building where Tarek Haddad had set up shop. All the spaces were occupied. As Tony drove by, he slowed down enough to get a view of the office. The lights were on, but it appeared that no one was there.

Tony went around the block and drove by again. He noticed that there was a small FedEx building across the street. There was a landscaped area next to FedEx that could provide sufficient cover to stake out Haddad's office. He didn't see a bench or a suitable place to sit. Tony went around the block again and found a parking space a block and a half from Haddad's.

He grabbed the small bag containing the camera and headed for the FedEx office. Since Haddad's office was close to the intersection of South Franklin and South Whiting Street, Tony decided to walk past the office, check it out as best he could without being too obvious, and cross at the corner when the traffic light was in his favor.

As he went by the office, he noticed that there was a briefcase on the desk. It was closed. There was another briefcase on the floor next to one of two chairs that were in front of and facing the desk. There was one door in the back of the office. The door was closed. Based upon the depth of the building, it was likely that it probably led to a small storage area with a bathroom and a rear exit.

Tony continued on to the intersection, waited for the light and crossed when the light changed. He went over to the FedEx office and stood outside for a few seconds, pretending to search for something in his pockets. He then went in.

The office was typical of one that provided many of the small business functions that were considered luxuries to a small business, especially one that couldn't afford the upkeep of an expensive color copy machine. There were two people in FedEx uniforms helping customers. Three other people were in line holding packages for shipment. This was ideal. Tony walked around the office pretending to look at the supplies. He took out his phone and called Carlos. He stood with his left side toward the window. He could see Haddad's office out of the corner of his eye.

"Hey Tony," answered Carlos as he turned down the TV with the remote. Carlos was getting used to the high life, "Where are you?" he asked as he took another swallow of beer.

"I'm across the street from Haddad's office," Tony responded as he looked back at the people in line. They paid him no attention.

"Is he there?" asked Carlos.

"The light is on, but there is no sign of him. There are a couple of briefcases. I assume that he and his guest have gone out for dinner or some liquid refreshments," offered Tony.

"Well, he hasn't been here either. It has been really quiet," responded Carlos. "A little too quiet for my taste," he added.

"Ann must not be there yet," stated Tony. It was more of a statement than a question.

"She called a few minutes ago and has rented a car. She's on the way. Should be here any minute," responded Carlos, sounding a bit relieved.

Tony was about to say something when a black Cadillac sedan with heavily tinted windows drove up and stopped in front of Tarek's office. Two guys in business suits got out of the car.

"Hold on a second," said Tony as he started toward the door. "Believe the *rabbits* have returned. Let me call you back," he said as he went outside and took the camera from the bag. He moved in close to a large windmill palm and waited for the car to move.

Tony got a close up of the tag as the car turned onto Whiting Street. He then turned his attention toward the office. Both men had already gone inside and were standing facing one another engaged in conversation.

Tony moved a little closer to the street and took several more pictures. One of the men picked up the briefcase that was on the floor and headed for the door. The other man said something to him, touched him on the forearm and motioned to the chair. The two men stood there for a few seconds. The man holding the briefcase turned, moved his left arm in an amicable gesture, and took a seat facing the desk. The other man walked around the desk, smiled, said something and took a seat.

Tony got several frontal shots. Both men continued to talk. Through the camera lens, the man behind the desk appeared to be of Arabic descent. He appeared to match the picture they had of Tarek Haddad. His hair was black and beginning to recede. He was well dressed in a dark suit with a blue shirt opened at the collar. He didn't appear to be wearing an undershirt. A small tuft of hair was visible at the location of the second opened button. It was quite obvious that he shaved his neck and a good portion of his upper chest.

He was sitting back in the chair with both hands in front of his chest, fingers touching with his elbows resting on the arms of the chair. He moved his hands like a quarterback signaling his team to huddle up. There was a gold rope chain around his neck. He appeared to be wearing a solid gold Rolex watch with a black face. He also had on a large diamond ring on his left hand. Tony thought to himself that the diamond ring was too big for a man to be wearing. Tony got several very good shots.

The other man was dressed in a dark pin stripe suit. He had on a white dress shirt. He continually readjusted his sleeves so that the white cuffs and gold cuff links were clearly visible. He wasn't wearing a tie.

Tony continued to watch as the men talked. Every once in a while, Haddad would smile broadly, indicating that the conversation was probably a friendly one and to his satisfaction. From their body language, there didn't appear to be any tension between the two men.

As Tony continued to look on, the black Cadillac drove up, slowed down and then continued on. Tony assumed that the meeting would be ending fairly soon. Although he had no pictures of the driver, or a good frontal shot of the guy talking with Haddad, he decided that it was a good time to get his car and prepare to play the game. On the way to the car, he called Carlos.

"Hey Tony, what do you have for me?" asked Carlos, expecting that Tony had made contact.

"Haddad is back. I got some good pictures."

"How about his contact?" asked Carlos.

"Got a few side shots, nothing real good yet," responded Tony.

"Are they still in the office?" asked Carlos.

"They are but appear to be wrapping up. His contact's ride has gone by a couple of times," offered Tony. "I'm heading to the car and will follow them. Will call you when I have some more information," he added.

"Okay my friend. Stay safe," said Carlos as he noticed Ann coming down the pier trailing a small overnight bag. "Ann is here. Talk with you later."

As Tony was approaching his car, the black caddy went past him. Tony purposely didn't look in the direction of the car. He also waited until it turned the corner before he hit the key fob to unlock his car. He slid in behind the wheel, started up and waited a few seconds to give the black car enough time to get to Haddad's and load up his passenger.

Tony pulled out. Fortunately there was no traffic on the side street. He moved close to the intersection of South Franklin and pulled as close as he could to the side. He could see the black caddy in front of Haddad's. Tarek had walked outside. The two men shook hands, and Tarek's contact got into the front seat.

Tony still wasn't able to get a clear shot of the contact. As the caddy moved away, Tony pulled out behind a panel truck. He could see the black caddy as it turned the corner and headed back in the direction where he was parked. Tony kept a comfortable distance. It was nearly dark. There were only a couple of cars on the street.

The black caddy made another turn and was heading down South Florida Avenue in the direction of the Embassy Suites. Tony thought to himself, you've got to be kidding me. His thought was confirmed as the black caddy pulled into the parking garage across the street from the hotel.

Tony slowed down momentarily and then drove into the parking garage. He pulled into the first available space, grabbed the camera and got out of his car. He didn't look in the direction of the black caddy as he heard the car doors close. Tony went across the street and took up a position in the small park area outside the entrance to the hotel. Tony was able to get a good shot of the men as they approached the entrance. One picture was enough. The men went into the hotel. Tony looked at his watch. It was nearly twenty-one hundred hours. Tony stood outside and called Carlos. Carlos was a little slow answering the call.

"Well?" answered Carlos.

"Well? Well it must be nice Mr. Garcia. I do all the work and you get the girl," said Tony, knowing that Carlos certainly had the better end of this deal.

"I'll make it up to you my friend. When this is over we'll go looking for that gal with the thong," laughed Carlos.

"Yeah right," responded Tony.

"So where are we?" asked Carlos, trying to avoid the obvious.

"You're not going to believe this, but these guys are staying here at the Embassy Suites."

"Maybe you won't lose them," said Carlos with a slight laugh.

"Hopefully I won't. I did get a descent shot of them going into the hotel. Should be enough for Roland to identify them," said Tony. "Once I'm sure they are in for the night, I will get prints off their car. I'll email everything to Rick tonight."

"That sounds good. By the way, could you tell anything about them?" asked Carlos.

"Not really. I did catch a few words as they were heading into the hotel. If I were to guess, I would say they are Serbs."

"Serbs," said Carlos after a few seconds. "I hate Serbs. I would almost prefer that they were Russian," he added.

Tony could hear Ann say something in the background. He didn't know much Russian, but what Ann said wasn't very nice.

DAVIS ISLAND YACHT CLUB
2115 HOURS

Carlos and Ann sat on the bench seat enjoying the crisp night air. They had a clear view of *The Big Fish*. As they were talking, Tarek Haddad came down the pier. He looked in their direction, waved and continued on to his boat. He went aboard and below. The lights came on. Carlos and Ann continued to talk and watch. After an hour or so, the lights went out.

CHAPTER THIRTY-FIVE

Carl Peterson sat behind his desk thumbing through the morning message traffic as he sipped a very hot cup of coffee. He hadn't touched the bear claw that was on a blue porcelain plate with gold trim. The bear claw was fresh, warm and nearly covered The Peterson Group logo that was prominently displayed in the center of the plate. He was trying to cut back, but the bear claw seemed to call out to him. He was almost finished with the messages, and about to give in to the bear claw, when the intercom buzzed.

"Yes Elaine," he answered.

"Carl, Mr. Savage is on line two," she said in her usual cheerful voice.

"Thanks," responded Carl as he looked down and pressed line two. He sat back in his chair still eyeing the bear claw. He almost picked it up.

"Morning John, how may I help you?" he asked, not expecting a call from John Savage.

"Carl, are you available this morning?" he asked.

"I can certainly make time for you. Do you want me to come over?" asked Carl as he looked at the open calendar on his desk.

"No, I would prefer to come to your office. I can be there in a half hour if that's okay with you," offered Savage.

"That will be fine. Is there anything I need to set up?" asked Carl.

"No, we just need to talk," said Savage after a pause that seemed to be a little too long.

"Okay. See you then," responded Carl as he put down the phone. The hesitation in Savage's voice was quite obvious, as was the delay when he used the phrase that no one ever wants to hear—*we need to talk*. The last time Carl had heard that was when he was engaged. The engagement didn't end in a wedding. He began searching his mind, wondering why John Savage needed to talk.

Carl sat there for a few seconds. He had lost his appetite for the bear claw and pushed it aside as he looked back through the messages. He was searching for something from Homeland Security that he may have missed. They had just renewed The Peterson Group contract for another five years. The next contract meeting was a quarterly meeting. It was scheduled in December, just before the Christmas break.

Carl stood up, coffee cup in hand, and went to the window. He looked out but saw nothing. An impromptu meeting was either really good...or really bad. Savage's rhetoric was certainly unsettling. It most likely meant that he was the bearer of bad news. Program managers didn't just show up to shoot the shit.

Carl continued to look out the window staring at nothing in particular. He finished the coffee and poured a fresh cup. As he sat down behind the desk and continued to think about the Homeland Security project, one name wiggled its way to the surface, like a worm on a dark rainy night. Yolanda Rawls.

DAVIS ISLAND YACHT CLUB
0930 HOURS

Carlos and Ann had just finished breakfast on the deck of *My Debt*. Rebecca Waverly had thought of everything. The refrigerator and small pantry were well stocked with enough food to last at least a week. Carlos had been up since 0600 hours. He never slept in, although he always said that he was going to. He held up the *Tampa Bay Tribune* just high enough to give the impression that he was engrossed in an article. He only read a few of the words as he continued to survey his surroundings.

There had been no activity on *The Big Fish* or anywhere in the marina for that matter. He looked at his watch. It was 0930 hours. Tony had called and said that he was on the way. Ann finished her second cup of coffee, stood up with cup in hand, and leaned over to kiss Carlos on the cheek just as Carlos's satellite phone rang. It was Rick.

"Good morning Rick," answered Carlos after accepting Ann's gratitude for the breakfast he had fixed.

"Good morning to you," responded Rick. "How's it going down there?" he asked.

"It's a bit quiet. Been up since zero six hundred. Ann is here and Tony is on the way," Carlos responded as he folded the newspaper.

"Good, I have just sent you some information from the pictures and prints that Tony forwarded. The guy on the boat is definitely Tarek Haddad. The two guys staying at the Embassy Suites are bad characters. Both are red flagged in the Interpol database. Let Tony know that they are most likely armed and he should consider them extremely dangerous. Their names are Mihailo Pesa and Ranko Milosevic. It is believed that they have one of the Russian suitcase bombs that has been missing for several years. However, that has not been confirmed."

"Tony was right. He thought they were Serbs," he added as he looked at Ann and nodded. She tightened her lips in surrender.

"He is right, and you both know how brutal they can be. At this point, we have no reason to engage them," said Rick. "Hold off on Haddad until I talk with Carl," he added. "We may be able to kill two birds with one stone if we play our cards right."

"Okay. Tony should be here in a few minutes. Haddad hasn't left the boat yet," said Carlos.

"Take a look at what I have sent you. By the way, has he had any visitors?" asked Rick.

"No," responded Carlos.

"Not even the woman in the sun hat?" asked Rick.

"No. We haven't seen her or anyone else for that matter," responded Carlos. "I take it Roland hasn't been able to identify her yet," Carlos assumed.

"He's still working on it," replied Rick. "By the way, we seem to have lost contact with Ms. Gemayel. Be on the lookout for her. I'm still not sure where she fits into this," said Rick. "Talk with you later," he added as he hung up the phone.

Carlos started to say something to Ann as he noticed Tony pulling into the parking area.

"Tony's here. I'll open the gate for him. Be right back," he told Ann as he got up and jumped off the boat onto the pier.

Carlos greeted Tony and let him through the gate. As they approached the stern of *My Debt*, Tony grabbed Carlos's arm and turned facing the parking lot.

"What is it?" asked Carlos.

"Don't look back, but there is a couple that just came up onto the deck of a sailboat on the left side of the pier. I know the guy, and I can assure you that he is not a sailor, and he is *not* on any vacation."

"You sure? Will he recognize you?" asked Carlos.

"I'm sure that he will," responded Tony.

Carlos was about to say something when two sheriff patrol cars pulled into the parking area followed by a black Chevy SUV with heavily tinted windows. They arrived in their entire splendor with all lights flashing. The officers got out of their cars and could be seen looking in Carlos and Tony's direction. They unfastened their holsters and began walking toward the pier.

"Something is really wrong here," said Carlos as he started to reach for the gun holstered in the small of his back.

OLD TOWN
1000 HOURS

Elaine Drew escorted John Savage into Carl Peterson's office. Carl greeted him with a firm handshake. Elaine offered a coffee, which

Savage gladly accepted. He pulled out a chair near the middle of the conference table. Carl sat next to him. Their backs were to the window.

"So what's up John?" asked Carl directly. "You look like you lost your best friend."

John Savage didn't say anything for a few seconds. It was obvious that he was formulating a response. Carl could tell that whatever he was going to say was not easy for him, and certainly not something that he wanted to say. Both men had known each other for many years, even before John took a job with the federal government. He was one of the good guys. He had been an army ranger. Carl was disappointed when Major Savage left the service early and took a job as a GS-13.

John looked at Carl and decided that he wouldn't beat around the bush. There was no way to mitigate what he was about to say.

"Carl, this morning I was sent a stop work order on your contract."

Carl had suspected that the news wasn't going to be good, but he had no idea that his contract with Homeland Security would be suspended. He knew what a stop work order really meant.

"Do you know why? The reason?" asked Carl as he worked hard to remain expressionless.

"I really don't know. The order came from my director," answered Savage.

Carl knew how the government operated. Many of their decisions were made with paperwork to follow. In most cases, a stop work order ended the contract for good, and many times it ended all other opportunities for good with that client. Homeland Security had been a very lucrative client.

"Could this have anything to do with Yolanda Rawls?" asked Carl.

"You know Yolanda Rawls?" asked Savage. He seemed quite surprised.

"Let's say that we have a mutual *acquaintance*," responded Carl, choosing his words carefully.

John Savage didn't say anything for a minute or so. Carl let Savage gather his thoughts, knowing that he would be forthcoming. Savage was a quick study. He could see the forest through the trees, a rare commodity in the federal government.

"And this mutual acquaintance? Project related?" asked Savage.

"Yes. Let's just say that this person gave us a heads up. I would tell you more, but as you know, having no knowledge is in your best interest."

Savage took a drink of coffee and leaned forward, cradling the cup in both hands. He looked directly at Carl.

"Carl, this is completely off the record."

Carl nodded but didn't say anything.

"Ms. Rawls is an incompetent bitch with a Napoleon complex to the say the least. She is opportunistic, shoots from the hip with no regard for the consequences, and unfortunately, she is in bed, and I mean *literally in bed*, with the director."

Carl listened intently as Savage continued. Savage had confirmed what Stankowski had basically told Rick, with the exception of being in bed with the director.

"And you know for a fact that she is sleeping with the director?" asked Carl.

"I do. I was wondering why she always seemed to get the choice projects. I suspected that something was going on between them. Something that wasn't business," responded Savage.

"And?" questioned Carl, wanting to hear more confirmation.

"So one afternoon I followed her. She met him at the Best Western in Old Town. They went into one of the rooms. They were there for a little over an hour. It was quite obvious to me when they came out that they weren't in there discussing projects," responded Savage.

"By chance, did you get any pictures?" asked Carl.

"I did," Savage responded.

"So you believe she is the one who got the director to suspend our contract?"

"I'm not one hundred percent sure, but I'd be willing to bet on it. What I don't know is why she just didn't come to me since your project is under my purview," offered Savage.

"You said it earlier. She is a bitch with a Napoleon complex. She doesn't need you."

"I wish I could do something about it, but as you know, my hands are tied. I shouldn't be here, but we go back a long way," said Savage sincerely.

"Don't worry about it. Tell me more about the director. What is his name?"

"John Holda. He's in his early fifties. Been in government service his whole life from what I can gather. He is actually a pretty good guy. He's married. He has a nice wife and three kids. What he saw in Rawls is beyond me," said Savage.

Carl got up and refilled his coffee cup and offered another refill to Savage. They both sat there for a few minutes nursing the coffee. Carl went over to the desk and grabbed the plate with the bear claw, placed it in front of John and cut it in two. John picked up his half, as did Carl. They both finished the bear claw.

"So basically, she's got this guy by the balls," said Carl.

"That she does," said Savage. "That she does," he added with emphasis.

Carl thought for a few minutes. A smile crossed his face momentarily, a smile that Savage didn't notice.

"Listen John, don't worry about this. It'll work out. These things always do."

CHAPTER THIRTY-SIX

After John Savage left, Carl told Elaine Drew that he didn't want to be disturbed. He needed some quiet time to think about his next move and what to do about Ms. Yolanda Rawls. Women with her penchant for power could be ruthless, especially when left alone and unsupervised. What to do with her was an easy decision by someone wanting to get rid of her. Unfortunately, they had taken the easy route and rewarded her by making her a program manager. No one ever gets fired in the federal government—they get moved latterly, or in the case of Ms. Rawls, promoted.

What a joke, he thought to himself. And people wonder why the federal government is so inefficient. Carl was about to call Rick when his satellite phone rang. As he picked up the phone and saw the ID he smiled to himself. The number 324 was displayed in the center of the LED. It was Rick's favorite aircraft side number as a navy pilot, and now, it was his Peterson Group ID.

He and Rick always seemed to be on the same wavelength. There was an unparalleled synergism created by their combined effort. The two of them could always find a solution to any problem. As Rick would say, there were always three answers: yes, no and you've got to be kidding. The you've-got-to-be-kidding answer sometimes provided the most innovative solutions.

"Rick, you won't believe this, but I was just about to call you," answered Carl.

"What's going on up there?" asked Rick.

"I just had a meeting with John Savage."

"And how is Savage doing these days?"

"He's doing okay, but unfortunately, he was the bearer of bad news today," said Carl.

"And what was this bad news?" asked Rick rather reluctantly.

"Seems we have a stop work order on our contract with Homeland Security."

"A stop work order," Rick repeated matter-of-factly.

"Not something I wanted to hear from him," said Carl. "Rick, you don't seem surprised," he added after a slight pause.

"I'm not at all surprised," responded Rick.

Rick was familiar with stop work orders. They could be invoked for many reasons, some of which were routine and others for cause. For cause was never good.

"I'm quite sure Ms. Rawls is behind it," added Carl. "And why aren't you surprised?" he asked as if he just remembered Rick's response.

Rick didn't say anything for a few seconds. He was thinking about the stop work order. The fact that the contract had been suspended was Ms. Rawls's way to sidetrack The Peterson Group and get them out of her way. Make them expend their energy trying to reinstate their contract. Besides, no contractor would continue a project on their own nickel, and Yolanda Rawls was very much aware of that.

"Rick, you there?" asked Carl.

"I'm here Carl," responded Rick. "Just thinking about the stop work order."

"I'm getting that feeling that you are about to tell me some more bad news," said Carl.

Rick hesitated again before continuing. Most CEOs were mere figureheads, but not Carl Peterson. He was a proactive hands-on guy. He was more like a chief operating officer than a chief executive officer.

"I believe you are one hundred percent correct about Ms. Rawls, and I'll bet the stop work order was signed sometime last night."

Carl reached over and looked at the time stamp.

"It was indeed signed last night," responded Carl.

"That was no coincidence Carl. It was signed last night in order to invalidate our team's IDs," said Rick.

"Invalidate their IDs," repeated Carl as he looked back at the stop work order that he had thrown back on the desk. "She had them arrested, didn't she?" asked Carl. "Probably charged them with interfering with a government sting operation," he continued. Carl was a very quick study.

Rick could hear Carl mumbling a few choice comments concerning Yolanda Rawls's birth legitimacy. Rick was about to say something when Carl continued his verbal assault, peppered with a few more colorful adjectives to describe Yolanda Rawls. After nearly a moment of silence, Rick continued.

"Among other things," said Rick.

"Among other things?" questioned Carl.

"Obstruction of justice, resisting arrest, assault and battery, to name a few," responded Rick rather solemnly.

"Holy shit Rick, what the hell happened down there?" asked Carl.

"As you might expect," said Rick.

"And what might I expect?" asked Carl.

"Seems that just after Tony arrived at the marina, two sheriff patrol cars arrived along with two U.S. Marshals close behind. The deputies approached first, and without any explanation, began to rough up Tony and Carlos. They tried to show them their IDs, but the deputies didn't seem to care. According to Ann, the deputies were way too physical right from the start. She said that it was quite obvious that the deputies were trying to provoke a fight," responded Rick.

"And they got one," said Carl. It was a rhetorical statement.

"That they did. Tony and Carlos put down all four deputies."

"Put down? What do you mean put down?" interrupted Carl, sounding a little bit concerned.

"Physically. Just physically. One of the deputies made the mistake of swinging his club at Ann. She took it away from him. And as they say, that's when the fight started. All hell broke loose. Before the Marshals could get in there to break things up, all four deputies were down, handcuffed to each other and in pretty rough shape. To make matters worse, Carlos stripped them of their weapons and threw the weapons into the bay along with all the handcuff keys."

"Good for them. So where are they now?" asked Carl.

"They were *rescued* by the Marshals. Carlos happened to know one of them. Since it was a federal operation, the Marshals had jurisdiction and took our people into protective custody."

"Protective custody my ass!" exclaimed Carl with a laugh. "I'll get our law firm on it. Should be a matter of routine getting them back from the U.S. Marshals." he added.

"Technically, the stop work order did invalidate their IDs," said Rick.

"She's a conniving bitch," said Carl. "You're right. That certainly explains the timing of the document," he added.

"There is one more wrinkle," said Rick.

"You know Rick, I don't need any more bad news. I've had a month's worth of bad news already today, and it's not even noon."

"Well my friend, I hope you're sitting down."

Carl thought to himself that sitting down for news was never a good omen.

"Rick, Savage told me this morning that *we need to talk*, and now you're telling me to *sit down*. I would very much like to wake up and start this day over. But, as they say, it can always get worse. So what is this wrinkle?"

"Tarek Haddad is dead," said Rick.

There was silence on the line. Rick could hear Carl take a deep breath. There was no colorful metaphor that either of them could think of at this moment that would help to mitigate the morning's string of bad news.

"He was alive last night. When did this happen?" asked Carl.

"It must have happened sometime between midnight and six."

"Ann and Carlos saw nothing?" asked Carl.

"Neither of them saw or heard anything," responded Rick.

"Rick, does any of this make sense to you? There wasn't enough time for the sting operation to have progressed to a point where Haddad was expendable."

"You wouldn't think so. Did Roland brief you concerning the information on Haddad's contacts?" asked Rick.

"He did. I briefly looked at the material," responded Carl.

"Maybe Haddad was a little too eager to push the transaction. Maybe the Serbs found out it was a sting operation, took his money and then decided to eliminate him," offered Rick.

"There are a lot of maybes that we need to determine," said Carl.

"I'm getting the feeling that you are not going to stop work," said Rick.

Carl smiled, although no one was there to see his expression.

"You got that right. I don't like being man-handled by some over zealous bitch whose only goal is to advance her miserable career."

"Don't hold back on my account. Tell me what you really think about her," chuckled Rick.

They both had a good laugh. There was a light at the end of the bad news tunnel.

"We don't even work for her, yet she's got the influence to get us fired. Can you come up?" asked Carl.

"Of course," responded Rick.

"Great. Come at your earliest convenience. I suspect it will take a day or two to get our people released. Do you know where they are holding them?"

"Carlos said they were escorting them to D.C."

"Well, that is good news. That will make it much easier. I'll have our people working on their release before they get into town," said Carl.

"I suggest that you personally offer to replace the deputies' weapons as well as make a nice contribution to the Sheriff's Benevolent Fund. They will probably back off with that gesture, albeit reluctantly," offered Rick.

"That's a great idea. I just don't want them to get the impression I'm trying to buy them off," responded Carl, knowing that was exactly what he would be doing.

"Well in our team's defense, they were never informed that there was a stop work order. So in effect, they were within their rights to be there and observing," said Rick.

"I'm sure the lawyers will point that out to the U.S. Marshals. In the meantime, you and I can come up with a new plan of action."

"I will plan on leaving first thing in the morning. Lynn has been wanting to do some shopping at Tysons Corner anyway."

"By the way, there is still about ten million dollars floating around out there. It could be in the hands of the Serbs at this point. We need to find out just where that money is, or where it went," said Carl. He was obviously back into full business mode. "I hadn't mentioned this," he continued, "but Roland was able to, let's say, redirect McAllister's share of the lottery money to one of our offshore accounts."

"Isn't that a bit risky, since McAllister is no longer with us?" asked Rick.

"Ironically, he had covered his tracks quite well. He was a little too smart for his own good. It appeared that he had made an investment with a Dutch firm that had mishandled the account. McAllister had sent the money to cover a business loss. At least that is the paperwork that McAllister created. Therefore, the money that Roland transferred didn't *exist*. And since McAllister died from natural causes and had no spouse, nobody will be looking for the money."

"You are a devious man Carl Peterson," said Rick with a smile that Carl could only imagine.

"I prefer to think of myself as resourceful," responded Carl. "See you tomorrow," he added as he ended the call.

Carl was already feeling better. He knew that he and Rick could come up with a plan to take care of Ms. Rawls, locate the ten million dollars generated by the lottery scam and get The Peterson Group contract reinstated. He had no intention of walking away.

He poured the last of the morning coffee and entered the name John Holda into the Homeland Security database. The screen alert, *Access Denied*, drew a slight smile. Ms. Rawls had followed through with everything associated with the stop work order. The Peterson Group no longer had access to Homeland Security.

Carl had access to several other databases that Ms. Rawls could not control. The FBI database had a full dossier on John Holda. He appeared to be squeaky clean. However, squeaky clean guys made mistakes and could easily be manipulated, especially if they wanted to remain that way. From the contents of John Holda's record, this was a guy who would not want to have any skeletons appear in his closet. How he let himself be enticed by the likes of Yolanda Rawls was a mystery, but a mystery that Carl didn't have to solve.

He and Rick could certainly use the information that John Savage had provided concerning the liaison between Rawls and Holda. The challenge of the morning events gave Carl new life. He never did like the boredom of sitting behind a desk. He and Rick were always considered operators. Give them something to do and get out of the way. Carl buzzed Elaine Drew.

"Yes Carl?"

CHAPTER THIRTY-SEVEN

Rick and Lynn finished breakfast at the Cracker Barrel just off I-95 at the Ashland exit. Lynn went to the restroom while Rick took care of the bill. As he waited for Lynn, he thought about his meeting with Robert Stankowski.

Given everything that had happened, his rendezvous with Stankowski seemed like it was a long time ago, but it had only been three days. Stankowski had been right about Yolanda Rawls. She was undeniably a loose cannon. What surprised Rick even more was that she seemed to have no problem finding and contracting with assets who would do anything for a buck.

Rick wasn't at all surprised that Robert Stankowski decided that he had had enough of Ms. Rawls and her unscrupulous methods, despite the fact that his walking away would jeopardize any future work with Homeland Security. For the most part, Homeland Security was a good client. It seemed like they had unlimited resources.

However, to a few, character and integrity were always more important than a paycheck. Rick shook his head as he thought more about how the world had changed. People with Stankowski's moral fiber were hard to find, if not impossible. Rick looked at his watch just as Lynn grabbed him from behind.

"What's *this*?" she exclaimed as she squeezed him around the waist, her fingers kneading the small love handles that just wouldn't go away. He tightened his stomach muscles.

"That, my dear, is a gluten graveyard," he responded, trying to imitate Rhett Butler and deflect any further criticism. It didn't work.

"You need to work on that," she scolded him as only she could.

Rick tried to ignore her.

"As my friend Marty would say, I'll have a lot of time to diet…when I'm dead."

"Well, you don't need to rush it. Do you need to go before we leave?" she asked already forgetting about his waistline, at least for the moment.

Rick said that he didn't. Some guys could ride halfway across the country without even thinking of going to the bathroom. They would stop at a rest area only when it was absolutely necessary. Rick was one of those guys. One time as a navy pilot, he flew an S-3 Viking across the Atlantic all the way to Rota, Spain without even having an urge to use the relief tube. Besides, he didn't like relief tubes. They could back up on you.

"No, I'm fine," he smiled. "Did you want to look around?" he asked, noticing that Christmas had arrived rather early at the Cracker Barrel. He was hoping her answer would be no.

"No. I'm ready to go when you are. Besides, we haven't put up a Christmas tree in how many years?" she asked. "Maybe when Brooke gets the urge to present us with a grandchild, I'll be more interested in decorating a tree," she added. She actually meant it in a nice way, although everyone was telling Brooke that her biological clock was ticking.

Lynn grabbed Rick by the arm. She again patted his stomach and smiled. She hadn't completely forgotten. He tried to ignore her again. At times she could be unrelenting.

As they left the Cracker Barrel, Rick took her hand and squeezed it gently. She had been more needy since her encounter in the parking garage. Rick hadn't told her that they had identified her assailant. In fact, they hadn't talked at all about the encounter since it happened.

As he looked over at her, he decided that maybe this was the time. He certainly didn't want her to relive the events.

"We have identified the assailant," he said matter-of-factly.

She didn't say anything. He could feel her grip tighten slightly. He didn't tell her what he was planning to do about the guy, and she never asked. Actually, he hadn't decided exactly what he was going to do at this point. When he did decide, he most certainly wouldn't tell her anyway.

Rick glanced over at Lynn. She continued to look straight ahead. He could see a little tear forming in the corner of her eye. He decided that he had said enough. Not too many years ago, Serrano would already be, as they say, swimming with the fishes. Lynn wiped away the tear. She didn't have to respond.

Down deep inside she knew that whoever the guy was, he was most likely walking around on borrowed time. She really didn't want to know who he was. She knew that Rick or Carlos would take care of him in due time.

TYSONS CORNER

1045 HOURS

It was a beautiful fall day. The leaves were just about at peak color. Lynn enjoyed the foliage. She always looked forward to their trips to upstate New York this time of year. They would usually pick the second week in October to catch the peak color in the Adirondacks. This was the first year in some time that they hadn't made the trip together. Unfortunately, the timing of Brooke's trip along with the death of Rick's cousin altered their travel plans this year.

Rick looked over at Lynn as she made a little moaning sound. She had already fallen asleep. She often moaned in her sleep when she was sick or under stress. The motion of the car combined with the muscle relaxers had a therapeutic effect on Lynn. He would let her sleep. The rest of the trip was uneventful.

Lynn seemed to wake up on cue as Rick pulled into the circular area in front of the Ritz Carlton. They had made a reservation for an early check-in. The Ritz was always very accommodating, especially since the Morgans were considered preferred customers.

High tea at the Ritz was always a treat. Rick was hoping that he would be back in time to enjoy the late afternoon refreshments with Lynn. However, she was prepared to have tea alone.

"Honey, I will call you a little later," he said as he handed her the small overnight bag that was next to the large suitcase in the back of their Escalade.

"Don't worry about me. I have the credit card," she said, her smile indicating that the old Lynn was beginning to bounce back.

"Call me if you need anything. Love you," said Rick as he got behind the wheel and started up.

"Love you too," she said with a broad smile as she disappeared into the Ritz with the overnight bag in tow.

Rick pulled out of the parking area and headed toward the ramp to I-495. On Saturday, the drive to Old Town would take about twenty minutes at most. The traffic was light. Rick decided to give Carl a call and let him know his ETA. Carl answered on the second ring. He sounded like he had just taken a bite of something.

"Hey Rick, are you close?" asked Carl. Rick could hear music.

Both he and Carl worked best with classical music playing in the background. Classical music was soothing, it stimulated the creative thought process. Carl especially liked the *Nutcracker Suite* by Tchaikovsky. Rick could hear the "Waltz of the Flowers" playing.

How ironic, he thought to himself as he imagined Yolanda Rawls playing the part of Mother Gigogne with her oversized skirt flaring, and her assets flurrying about in all directions with little or no guidance. It brought a cynical smile to his face. He wondered if Carl had had the same vision.

"I'm about fifteen minutes away," he responded.

"Great. By the way, our people have been released. I asked Tony to stay for a week or so."

"Probably better that he stay away from Florida for a few days," said Rick.

"Funny, I told him the same thing," said Carl. "They'll be in after lunch. By then, you and I should have an idea where we want to go with this," added Carl.

"Is Roland going to be there?" asked Rick.

"He's already here and setting up," responded Carl.

"Good. See you soon," said Rick as he ended the call.

Rick pulled into the parking garage on schedule. There were two cars parked in The Peterson Group parking spaces. He assumed that the BMW convertible belonged to Roland. It was the kind of car that he would expect a young professional to drive. The other was Carl's SUV. As usual, Carl didn't park in his assigned space. *Blue Sky* always did his own thing. Besides, Carl owned the company, they *all* were his parking spaces.

Rick swiped his card and walked into the outer office. Carl was standing near the entrance to the small coffee mess. He turned and walked toward Rick. Following their usual greeting, they adjourned to Carl's office.

Roland had everything set up, including several binders that were positioned around the conference table along with pads and pencils. The pencils were all new and sharpened to a point. They seemed to be all the same length. By the number of binders, Rick concluded that the whole team would be present for Roland's portion of the brief.

"Roland, would you mind giving me and Rick a few minutes?" said Carl.

"No problem Mr. Peterson. As soon as you are finished, may I have a word with you and Mr. Morgan?" asked Roland.

"Absolutely, I'll buzz you," replied Carl.

Carl came from around the desk and sat in the chair next to Rick as Roland exited the room. He had a pensive look on his face, a look that Rick had seen before.

"After I talked with you yesterday, I got a call from the bank. Seems they were directed to freeze The Peterson Group checking account, along with my personal checking account."

"Ms. Rawls?" questioned Rick.

"Most likely it was her doing," responded Carl.

"Is that going to be a problem?" asked Rick somewhat hesitantly, knowing that Carl probably covered all bases.

"Rick, I learned a long time ago not to keep all my eggs in one basket. Fortunately, I have several bank accounts, including a couple offshore accounts," he whispered as if someone could overhear him. "Homeland Security represents a small portion of my monthly income…a very *small* portion," he repeated.

"So The Peterson Group is fine?" said Rick, meaning it more as a statement rather than a question.

"The Peterson Group is fine. I'm fine," responded Carl as he raised his coffee cup. The pensive look had vanished.

"Rick, a stop work order is one thing, but messing with my personal checking account is not just business. This woman has made things personal. She didn't mess with your account, did she?" he asked as if the thought just popped into his head.

"Not yet. At least not that I'm aware of."

"You know she was the one responsible for the attack on Lynn," said Carl. "She really pisses me off. Who the hell does she think she is?" he added before Rick could respond.

Rick was certain that Yolanda Rawls was responsible for the attack on Lynn.

"Carl, she's a product of the times. I believe this whole thing is much bigger than Ms. Rawls. Somewhere along the line we, and I mean the collective we, have allowed the government to morph into an entity unto itself. The whole system is screwed up. It feeds on itself."

Carl pondered Rick's statement for a few minutes before responding.

"Screwed up? You're being kind. I probably would have said it differently," responded Carl. "They forget that they work for us," he added.

"Carl, they haven't forgotten. They really don't care," responded Rick.

"Well they need to care. I think the politicians have conveniently forgotten that we are the ones who vote for them, who pay their salaries," said Carl. It was purely a rhetorical statement, and Rick knew it.

"Unfortunately Carl, it doesn't matter. Basically, we have little control. Take Nancy Pelosi for instance. You may not like her, but you don't vote for her. The whole system is a collective dictatorship," said Rick.

"You know, I have actually entertained thoughts of moving to San Francisco just so I can vote against her," said Carl somewhat seriously.

"That would be the only way you could make your wishes known," responded Rick. "But it wouldn't work. There are too many of them and not enough of us," he added.

"Well, maybe it's time to let them know that they are not an island unto themselves," responded Carl.

Rick didn't say anything. Both men sat and listened to Tchaikovsky. The *Nutcracker Suite* had started all over again. They enjoyed several minutes of the music. Rick was first to speak.

"Did Savage say anything about Ms. Rawls that we could use to our advantage?'

Carl thought back to his conversation with Savage. He would normally record it, but he hadn't out of respect for John. However, he remembered the salient points of the conversation well.

"There is. Seems Ms. Rawls is having an affair with her director."

"Well in that case, I think that we can make one of them an offer they can't refuse," offered Rick.

"I really want to remove her permanently," said Carl as he got up and retrieved the coffee pot.

CHAPTER THIRTY-EIGHT

Carl went back to his desk and buzzed Elaine. He asked her to call Roland. Roland had actually waited in the outer office talking with Elaine.

"He's right here," she informed Carl.

"Good, send him in," he responded.

Roland came in and took up his normal position at the conference table. He didn't sit down. He turned on the computer and told Rick and Carl that he had some important information to share. Rick and Carl didn't say anything as Roland brought up a picture of a woman in uniform. Rick looked over at Carl. Carl had leaned forward and was studying the picture. Then he leaned back into his chair as he spoke.

"So, our Ms. Gemayel is also a flight attendant," he stated.

"If she is, she must have taken a leave of absence," offered Rick.

They both looked over at Roland who had a mischievous look on his face, one that he often had when he was about to drop a bomb, especially on Carl. Roland loved this part of his job more than anything.

"I did some more digging into Haddad. I am convinced that I have finally determined who the mystery woman is," informed Roland. Roland was about to say something else when Carl broke in.

"So, you think our Ms. Gemayel is this mystery woman and working directly with Haddad?"

"Not exactly," replied Roland.

Both Rick and Carl had confused looks on their faces. Roland had their undivided attention.

"The woman you are looking at is not Ms. Gemayel," continued Roland matter-of-factly. The revelation was a total surprise to both Carl and Rick. Carl was about to say something when Elaine buzzed him and announced that Ann, Carlos and Tony had arrived.

Rick continued to look at the picture. His mind was racing.

"Send them in," responded Carl in a guarded voice. He looked over at Roland and then back at the screen as Roland replaced the image with The Peterson Group logo.

Rick's thoughts were interrupted as the three jailbirds sauntered single file into the conference room. They pretended to be hardened criminals. Ann led the way with Carlos and Tony bringing up the rear. Both Carlos and Tony had their pants at half-mast. Carlos's red under shorts provided a stark contrast to his jungle fatigues. Tony had on white boxer shorts that seemed to be too big.

"Oh, I'll bet you *Beagle Boys* had a tough time," snickered Carl. "I really expected to see a little sunburn," he added.

"You mean a con tan," offered Carlos smiling as he pulled up his pants.

"Who are the Beagle Boys?" asked Ann.

Everyone had a good laugh. Rick told her, but she wasn't amused.

"Guys never grow up," she quipped, shaking her head.

They each took a seat in front of the binders. Ann immediately began thumbing through hers. She was all business, especially when it came to a project. Tony filled one of the large blue Peterson Group coffee mugs with hot black coffee. He offered coffee to the rest of the team. Carlos and Rick pushed their mugs in Tony's direction. Roland was doing some last minute entries on his computer. Rick was still thinking about the image Roland had just showed them. As he was thinking about the image, Roland brought it back up on the screen.

He was about to say something when Ann looked up at the image.

"So, she is also a flight attendant," Ann said, somewhat surprised.

"Who do you think that is on the screen?" asked Carl, directing his question to Ann.

"Ms. Gemayel, a.k.a. Ms. Anderson," she responded confidently.

"That's what I thought," said Carl.

"Thought? Well if that isn't Ms. Gemayel, then who is she?" asked Ann with a puzzled look on her face.

"I believe that is what Roland is about to tell us," offered Rick.

"That is Ms. Marcie Decker," said Roland. "She is a flight attendant and Tarek Haddad's girlfriend. I strongly suspect she is the woman with the floppy hat who was captured by the satellite as she boarded his boat."

"So, are you telling us that this Marcie Decker and our Ms. Gemayel are one in the same?" asked Rick.

Roland didn't answer the question as he handed each member of the team a folder with the name Marcie Decker in bold letters centered in the middle of the tab.

"So who are you really, Ms. Decker? And are you actually Tarek Haddad's girlfriend?" asked Rick as he began to peruse the contents.

"She appears to be squeaky clean," said Carl after several minutes.

"Maybe a bit too clean," added Rick.

Roland nodded somewhat in agreement as he continued to watch the team's reaction.

"She has never been arrested, no speeding tickets, not even a parking ticket," offered Roland.

"A perfectly created alter-identity," said Rick. He was thinking out loud. "According to this bio, she went directly from college to the airlines," offered Rick as he went down the chronological list that Roland had put together. "I'm curious as to the particulars on how she became involved with our friend, Tarek Haddad," added Rick as he finished the cup of coffee.

"So far, I haven't been able to make that connection. She has been on the London-Beirut run for the past year," responded Roland. "There is a possibility that she met him in Lebanon. I'm still working on it."

Rick continued to look through the folder.

"Says here that she lives in Atlanta and has an apartment in London. I suppose that is fairly common for an overseas flight attendant," said Ann.

It was at that moment that Rick remembered his conversation with Roland a few days earlier. Ms. Gemayel also has a condo in Atlanta, and she lived in London before that. Could this really be one woman with two identities? This truly added a new layer to Ms. Gemayel's role in the operation. Rick closed the folder and pushed it toward Roland.

"That is for you Mr. Morgan," said Roland as he pushed it back toward Rick.

"Good job Roland," said Carl, convinced that Ms. Decker and Ms. Gemayel were, in fact, the same person.

As Ann and Tony got up to refresh their coffee, Rick's thoughts went back to the reckless Ms. Yolanda Rawls. Carl wanted her eliminated. He was very clear about that; it was not merely a figure of speech. He meant it in the literal sense. Taking her out was risky business. Moreover, it was The Peterson Group people who had interfered—who were jeopardizing her sting operation. At least that is the way an astute detective would see it. It was classic. The Peterson Group had motive, means and opportunity. That could be a fatal flaw with any plan aimed at Ms. Rawls.

"Are we still in business?" asked Carlos as everyone returned to their place at the conference table.

"Technically," responded Carl, "the answer is no. We have been issued a stop work order," he added as he pushed the document forward on his desk.

"Technically?" questioned Ann as she reached over, picked it up and read every word of the simple one-page document. It was very clear and to the point. It brought a slight frown to her face, one that quickly left as she passed the document to Carlos.

"There are still many unanswered questions and a significant amount of issues associated with the methods employed by Ms. Rawls," said Rick.

Carl nodded as he cradled the coffee mug in both hands.

"So…we *are* still working," reiterated Carlos as he finished looking at the stop work order and handed it, without looking, to Tony.

"Basically, we are going to proceed on our own nickel…well, actually The Peterson Group's nickel," said Rick as he smiled and looked over at Carl.

Carl pursed his lips, raised his eyebrows and nodded in the affirmative. Carl never liked using his own money. He was a strong proponent of using other people's money.

"There are still some wrongs that we need to, or should I say, that we *want* to right," continued Rick. "As you know, many retired military people have been swindled out of a large chunk of their retirement. As a result, some regrettably have committed suicide. My wife has been assaulted, and Tarek Haddad has been murdered—possibly by the Serbs that he was dealing with," continued Rick.

Everyone listened intently. Carl made a few notes.

"So Rick, what's the plan?" asked Carl as he put down his pencil, sat back in his chair and put one foot on a lower drawer that he had pulled out to act as a foot stool.

Rick pushed his chair back, stood up and moved close to the screen.

"This whole thing started with John Kilday. The people responsible for his death have been dealt with," said Rick parsing his words. "The only issue we have left with Kilday is the two hundred and fifty thousand that he sent to the Bahamas. Homeland Security provided none of the monies used in this operation. All of it was monies obtained through the lottery scam operation," said Rick.

"So, all of that money is still out there?" asked Carlos.

"It is," responded Rick.

"Do we have a final number?" asked Carl.

Rick looked over at Roland who pressed a few keys. A colorful graphic appeared on the screen.

"We have determined forty people sent two hundred and fifty thousand a piece to McAllister's bank in the Bahamas. McAllister was given one million dollars for his part in laundering the money and not asking any questions," said Roland.

"Seems like a nice round number," said Carlos.

"Ten percent seems reasonable for a ten million dollar take," calculated Tony as he did the math in his head.

"It looks like Haddad stopped the scam when he reached that goal," said Rick.

"Since McAllister doesn't need the money anymore, we have moved his commission to an offshore account that we control," said Carl. "That still leaves nine million dollars out there. That is a lot of incentive to continue the project," he added.

"And that brings us to our first objective, which is two-fold: locate the money and then confiscate it," said Rick as Roland typed the first objective onto the screen.

"Do we have any idea where the money is?" asked Ann.

"We do know that the money is no longer in Haddad's account. So far, I haven't been able to locate it, but I will," said Roland with confidence.

"There is a good chance that it may have been transferred to the Serbs," said Rick.

"That's going to be fun," said Carlos.

Ann Smiled. She had numerous dealings with the Serbs, many of which she was glad to forget.

"That brings us to Haddad. If he did in fact complete the deal with the Serbs, it is likely they are the ones who killed him," said Rick.

"Do we really care who killed him?" asked Carl.

"Only to confirm where the money may have gone," responded Rick. "Other than that, we have no reason to bring his killer to justice. Homeland Security can have that little morsel. So, our second objective is to determine who killed Haddad," said Rick.

Roland typed the second objective on the screen.

"What about the guy who attacked Lynn?" asked Ann. "I would like to have a crack at him," she added. Carlos knew that she was serious.

"I appreciate your willingness. He is actually part of the third objective, which is to get our contract reinstated," said Rick.

Rick was about to continue when he stepped back from the board and made a couple of notes on the pad that Roland had provided. The rest of the team watched as Rick got *that* look on his face that they had all seen before. A scenario was developing in Rick's mind, one that he needed to get on paper.

"Carl, can we take about thirty minutes? I just thought of something that I would like to work on," asked Rick.

"Of course," said Carl as everyone stood. It was time for a break anyway. Both Rick and Carl had learned a long time ago that the old navy adage was true, "The mind can only absorb what the ass can endure."

Rick picked up the pad and pencil and left the room. Thirty minutes later, he was back. He had a confident look on his face.

"Maybe we can kill two birds with one stone. Let me paint a picture," he said. "Yolanda Rawls is ambitions. She will do anything to further her career. The fiscal year has just commenced and Homeland Security's initial funds have been allocated. So our clever Ms. Rawls comes up with a scam to fund her operation and provide her man, Tarek Haddad, with a sordid background, one that will convince the Serbs that he is a legitimate player. She believes that the Serbs have one of the missing Russian suitcase bombs. They are looking to broker a deal with the highest bidder.

As the project progresses, Haddad soon realizes how easy it is to dupe widowed military retirees out of a healthy portion of their retirement. The money builds to ten million in a matter of a few days. Haddad puts the money into an offshore account in the Bahamas. His contact, Ian McAllister, agrees to protect the account and launder the money for a slight fee.

However, Haddad, who probably makes in the neighborhood of one hundred and twenty thousand a year, sees an opportunity to walk away with several million dollars tax-free. He tells McAllister to transfer the money to an account in the Grand Caymans. McAllister soon recognizes that Haddad is going to keep the money for himself.

McAllister, being the crook that he is, sees an opportunity to increase his ten percent commission and decides to tell Rawls about Haddad's plan, which he does. She's initially upset, but the more she thinks about it, she decides to keep the money for herself. So she hires Serrano to eliminate Haddad.

Everything is going fine until we enter the picture. We get too close, and she makes the mistake of hiring Serrano to rough up Lynn in an attempt to intimidate me so that I will back off from the investigation."

Rick finished and looked around the room. Carl was making a couple of notes. Ann was nodding her approval. Carlos was first to speak.

"I like it," he said.

"I like it too," said Tony.

"But how do we make it look like she hired Serrano to kill Haddad?" asked Ann.

"We create an offshore account in Serrano's name and put in fifty K," offered Rick as he looked over at Carl and smiled.

Carl didn't say anything. It was only money, he thought to himself.

"Under this scenario, that is the only money we would need upfront," responded Rick.

No one said anything for several minutes. Rick refilled his mug with fresh coffee. Carl wrote something else on his note pad.

"Will any of this help us locate the nine million?" asked Carl.

"Not initially. This scenario is primarily designed to help us reinstate the Homeland Security contract. With Yolanda Rawls out of the way, I believe that either Carl or I can approach Mr. John Holda and make him an offer that he can't refuse," continued Rick.

Carl leaned forward with both elbows on his desk. He smiled. He fully understood the unspoken part of Rick's explanation.

"Two questions, who is John Holda, and how do we get rid of Rawls?" asked Carlos.

"Holda is Rawls's boss. And to answer your second question, we don't," responded Rick. "We get Serrano to take care of Rawls," added Rick as he took a drink of coffee. He looked for their reaction.

"So, one of us convinces Serrano that he has been set up by Rawls, and his only way out is to eliminate her," offered Ann with a smile.

"It should be easy to convince him," said Rick.

"I believe that I can convince him," said Tony.

"I can help," added Carlos.

"You two get together on that and let me know how you plan to do it. The bottom line is that once he has eliminated Rawls, we remove any evidence of the account," said Rick, looking for Carl's confirmation.

"And Serrano has no proof that Rawls hired him in the first place," added Carl.

"That's correct. There is one slight problem," said Rick.

"And what is that?" asked Carl with the less than pleasant memory of phrases like *we need to talk* and *are you sitting down* still fresh in his mind.

"We will need to backdate the deposit," said Rick.

"No problem," responded Carl. "I know a banker in the Caymans who owes me one. In fact, he owes me more than one. Just give me the date and I'll take care of the fifty K and setting up the account," said Carl.

"Any questions or misgivings? Anything that I may have overlooked in regard to our objective of getting our contract reinstated?" asked Rick.

"Rick, are you sure this will satisfy you concerning Serrano?" asked Carl.

Rick smiled. "I believe when Serrano is sitting in prison, it will dawn on him that I set him up. The joy of that thought is good enough for me," responded Rick.

"So once the contract is reinstated, we can then focus on locating the nine million?" asked Carl. "And before any of you ask, my intention is to return the money to the rightful owners…minus the usual finder's fee of course," he added with a wry smile. "Let's take a break," he said as he got up to head to the men's room.

Rick got up and headed for the coffee pot. There was still something bothering him that he couldn't quite put his finger on. Rick hesitated for a few seconds and then exclaimed, "I believe there are two of them!"

CHAPTER THIRTY-NINE

This new epiphany by Rick caught the team by surprise. Roland's earlier revelation about the Marcie Decker identity was still rolling around in their minds. They began to ponder the Marcie Decker and Farrah Gemayel mystery. Could there actually be two of them, and if so, was it just a coincidence that Farrah Gemayel's doppelganger was the girlfriend of Tarek Haddad?

"Roland, check the schedules and find out where *each* of these ladies were for the last couple of weeks. We need to determine if we are dealing with one very clever operative, or if there are actually two of them," said Rick.

"Will do Mr. Morgan," responded Roland.

Carl Peterson continued to make a few notes. Ann, Carlos and Tony were talking amongst themselves. Rick sat down and began to draw a few descriptive shapes on the pad of paper. He was in the process of entering names into the rectangles when Ann approached.

"Rick, is there anything else we could be missing?" she asked.

Rick didn't say anything. It appeared that his full attention was directed to the diagram he had before him where he had started to sketch out the lottery scam process. But in fact, he was struggling with a vision of Marcie Decker walking through the airport pulling a flight attendant's bag, her hair held in place by two large knitting needles.

"Rick?" said Ann again as she touched his shoulder.

The touch startled him briefly as it brought him back to the present.

"Sorry, this Marcie Decker identity is…intriguing," he said as he looked up. "If she is playing all these roles, could she possibly be that good?" he added. It was purely a rhetorical question.

"Maybe we are dealing with identical twins," offered Ann after a slight pause. "Do you remember Ekaterina Mishnev?"

Rick and Carl looked at each other. Rick didn't have to think for very long. The past is only a thought away, even though sometimes those thoughts can be elusive.

"I haven't heard that name in over thirty years. I absolutely remember her," he responded. A slight smile crossed his face as the image of a very fit green-eyed young woman in her late twenties with auburn hair passed before his eyes. "She was quite a looker if I remember correctly."

"I remember her as well," Carl added. "Tall, reddish hair, green eyes and a body to die for if memory serves me."

"What ever happened to her?" Rick asked.

"The story is she had been secretly meeting with a British agent and was planning to defect to the U.K. The KGB discovered her plan, and as it goes with many suspected defectors, she was whisked away never to be seen again," responded Ann.

Rick's expression turned into a look of sober understanding. He knew that the Soviets would act first and ask questions later…later never came.

"But the point I want to make is that she had an identical twin sister by the name of Mara. Did you know that?" Ann asked, knowing that hardly anyone knew of Mara's existence.

Rick and Carl looked surprised.

"No I didn't," responded Rick as he put down his pencil. Ann now had his full attention.

"Well, neither did I nor did the CIA, MI6, Mossad or anyone for that matter."

"Except the KGB," offered Carl as he made a throat cutting gesture.

"Yes, the abominable KGB," concurred Ann, taking a deep breath. "Anyway, Mara was able to step in and provide an irrefutable alibi for Ekaterina whenever it was needed. Plus, it made following Ekaterina very difficult, if not impossible. No one had the slightest inkling that there were two of them. The KGB had isolated and groomed them from childhood. This could be a similar situation," she said with a convincing look.

Rick didn't have to ponder the scenario for very long.

"You may be right. And if there are two of them, this could have been *their* plan all along," said Rick.

"It was just a thought," replied Ann.

"It's a good thought," concurred Rick as he made a couple of notes on the pad.

Carl concurred as he sat in silence clearly pondering this new information. How much fun two of them would have been, he thought to himself. Rick looked over at Carl. He smiled, because he knew exactly what was going through Carl's mind.

"Do you want me to help Carlos and Tony with their assignment?" she asked, knowing full well that she had just added another dimension to Rick's block diagram.

"Yes, that would be good. However, once we locate Ms. Gemayel, I need you to keep tabs on her. If we are dealing with twins, identifying her and following her could be a challenge, one that I know you can handle. Either one of them should be able to provide answers and conceivably lead us to the lottery money."

"Carlos," summoned Rick.

"Yeah boss," responded Carlos as he walked over and stood next to Ann. She reached over and took his hand in hers. Rick smiled.

"We need to find out how Haddad was killed. I can't imagine the Tampa police will tell us anything, and surely the sheriff's department won't be of any help," concluded Rick.

"Thanks to me and Tony," interrupted Carlos. Ann squeezed his hand hard enough to make him wince.

"Yeah," said Rick. It sounded more like a heavy breath. "Maybe your U.S. Marshal friend might be willing to provide some information… off the record."

"I can try. He and I have a bit of a history together," responded Carlos.

"A good history I presume," said Rick.

"Oh yes, very good," confirmed Carlos, his facial expression telling a very different story.

"Well, let's see if history can provide us with some answers," said Rick. "Besides, you can throw them a bone," added Rick.

"A bone?" questioned Carlos.

"Give them the Serbs. That should keep them occupied and out of our hair for a while," said Rick.

"Good point," responded Carlos.

"We'll touch base tomorrow," said Rick as they concluded their meeting.

After Ann, Carlos and Tony left, Carl got up and poured the last of the coffee. It was opaque and was very strong. Carl made a face and set the cup down. Rick looked at his watch and noticed that it was almost time to meet Lynn.

"Carl, would you be up for high tea at the Ritz?"

"Are you buying?" asked Carl.

"I am…indirectly," responded Rick with a sheepish grin that Carl found easy to decipher. Carl was paying the per diem for this trip.

"I don't think Lynn likes me," said Carl, looking for Rick's customary denial.

"She *likes* you," responded Rick. "She just doesn't *know* you," he added after a slight pause.

"You do remember the first time she met you?"

"Sure I do. I was lying on your couch in Lucrino, Italy. I was in a lot of pain, in and out of consciousness, and probably not in the best of moods," responded Carl.

"And I was wiping up blood from the couch, the floor, from everywhere," said Rick.

"And Ann, then Anya Petrov, our friendly Russian double agent, was sewing up the bullet hole in my chest," said Carl. "The good ole days," he added as he subconsciously rubbed the old wound.

"You know Carl, we never did introduce Ann to Lynn."

"*That* was probably it," said Carl. "A strange woman in the Morgan household at three in the morning. I should have guessed," he added. "Maybe it's because she *does* know me. Women are much more discerning than men, and certainly much less understanding," he concluded.

"And less forgiving," added Rick.

"Seems like such a dichotomy," Carl stated after a short pause.

"She *likes* you. Let's go," said Rick as he got up and put the note pad into his briefcase.

"You mind driving? We can discuss a few things in the car," said Carl.

On the way to the car, Rick called Lynn. She was in the room freshening up and had resolved herself to having high tea alone. She was pleasantly surprised that Rick was on the way. She even seemed pleased to know that Carl was coming with him. She hadn't seen Carl since the guys had gone fishing for cobia off the coast of Destin. It had been a year or so following their search for *Snake*.

The traffic was extremely light. Weekends were a time of relaxation for the majority of people living in the D.C. area. Carl was like a little kid as he looked around the interior of Rick's Escalade. He did everything but start pushing all the buttons. He did turn a few of the knobs. Carl was the kind of guy who would drive you crazy while watching TV. He never stayed on the same channel for more than a minute, usually seconds. He was the classic channel surfer.

"Nice ride," said Carl. "Rick, I don't believe I have been in an Escalade with this type of interior."

"This is the Platinum Edition," responded Rick as he looked over at Carl. Carl was rubbing his hand over the leather on the passenger door.

"Am I paying for this?" he asked in a joking manner.

Just as Carl was about to say something else, Rick's satellite phone rang. It was Roland.

"Yes Roland," answered Rick as he put the phone on speaker. "By the way, Carl is with me and listening," he added as a courtesy to Roland.

"There are definitely two of them," said Roland, knowing that his information needed no introduction.

"You are absolutely sure?" asked Carl.

"Yes Mr. Peterson. I'm absolutely sure. I checked the security tapes at the Atlanta airport. Marcie Decker arrived from Beirut, Lebanon on Monday, the eighth, around eighteen hundred hours. The airport security tapes then show her getting ready to board Delta flight 1249 for Tampa on Tuesday, the ninth, at zero nine thirty. The tapes in Tampa confirmed her arrival," added Roland.

"That's the same day I met with the Bahamian Ambassador at zero nine hundred. And it was Ms. Gemayel who welcomed me into the office," said Carl.

"That answers the question. Good job Roland," responded Rick.

"I could do some further checking on these two if you desire," offered Roland.

Rick thought for a few seconds before answering. He looked over at Carl. Carl nodded his approval.

"See if you can determine if they are identical twins or if we just have really good look-a-likes," said Rick.

"Will do Mr. Morgan," responded Roland, sounding like a kid with a new toy. "Talk with you later."

"Do you think it really matters if we determine that they are identical twins?" asked Carl.

"It is probably a moot point, but I'm sure Ann would like to know what she's getting into. Besides, there is a very good chance that one of them killed Haddad," offered Rick.

"That's a good point," said Carl.

"It might be nice to know which one is the most dangerous," responded Rick as they pulled into the Ritz parking lot.

Lynn had already secured a table in the center of the room. The high tea had attracted a rather large crowd for a Saturday afternoon. Most were tourists taking advantage of the lower fall rates.

The server was explaining the tray of morsels, which included scones, biscuits, finger sandwiches and petit fours. Rick smiled to himself. Lynn could ask a million questions. As she was talking, she noticed Rick and Carl approaching. She stood and hugged both of them. Rick looked at Carl and said, "See?"

"See what?" asked Lynn.

"Carl doesn't think you like him," said Rick frankly.

"Rick!" said Carl as he sharply nudged Rick with his elbow.

The three of them enjoyed the afternoon tea. Lynn had a year of questions for Carl. Rick enjoyed the scones along with Carl's answers.

On the way back to The Peterson Group office, Rick's cell phone rang. Carl looked at the LED display and announced that it was Carlos.

"Hey Carlos," answered Rick.

"I checked with my friend," Carlos announced.

"And?" asked Rick.

"It appears that Haddad was drugged, then killed. They found a small puncture wound in his chest that penetrated his heart. He bled out. Police believe it was an ice pick," offered Carlos.

"Or a knitting needle," responded Rick.

CHAPTER FORTY

The planning session was going well. Carlos, Tony and Ann had already spent a couple of hours working on the plan they affectionately dubbed, Operation Shaker. Just prior to the initial planning session, Tony took out a new stiletto from his front pocket and pressed the button, exposing a seven-inch blade. The blade glistened in the dining room light.

"I can take care of Ms. Rawls while you guys enjoy dinner and a glass of wine," he said quite casually as he began to clean the fingernail on his left hand with the tip of the blade.

Carlos and Ann looked on as Tony continued to groom his nails. He had a devious smile on his face that reminded Ann of a character in Faust. Neither she nor Carlos said anything as Tony continued to state his case.

"I'm already in her backyard," he said. "Taking her out would be a piece of cake," he added as he thrust the knife forward and then gave it a little twist. He didn't know her personally, but what he did know of her, he didn't like. He was quite serious.

Tony held their attention for a few more minutes. He was intent on letting Ms. Rawls know that she had messed with the wrong people. She had made too many grave errors, all of which had impacted the team personally, starting with John Kilday. Having the team arrested was just downright dirty. But her greatest lapse in judgment of them all came when she hired Serrano to rough up Rick's wife.

She had sealed her fate. Tony wanted her to know that government employees were not above the law. She didn't deserve any more chances in his opinion. She was despicable, and he wanted to be the one to eliminate her.

Although Ann concurred with Tony's position in principle, she knew the ramifications of acting on an impulse. Revenge would make a good movie script, but this was the real world. Besides, Rick's plan was designed to accomplish three separate goals, not just one.

"Tony, I fully appreciate where you are coming from. Hell, I would like to get my hands on Serrano. But Rick's plan will ensure that we, and The Peterson Group, remain well above suspicion. We need to focus on the bigger picture here," she said.

Tony listened. He knew that she was right. Acting out of emotion was never a good idea. It seldom ended well, especially in the world of covert operations.

"You're right," he said with a look of dissatisfaction, which lasted momentarily. He had made his druthers known.

Tony closed the blade and joined in as Carlos and Ann went over the plan again. By 2030 hours, Operation Shaker was on the table for a final look. Tony picked it up, mulled it over in his mind, and nodded in agreement. He sat back in his chair and could feel the stiletto press against his thigh. He reached into his pocket and felt the knife as his thumb gently caressed the release button. He was still entertaining a vision of slitting Yolanda Rawls's throat and dropping her to the ground like a sack of old potatoes. He handed the plan to Ann and said that he saw no problem; however, there was an unmistakable hint of reluctance in his voice. Tony was certainly old school. He wanted this woman to suffer, just to make a point.

Following a brief phone call to Rick, Ann made a couple of slight modifications. By 2100 hours, Operation Shaker was ready for implementation. Carlos ceremoniously opened a bottle of Moët & Chandon Rosé Impérial Champagne, and the three of them raised their glasses in harmony to toast the success of the mission.

Roland would be responsible for setting up the command center, which would include a surveillance network, satellite feed and a phone relay system that Carl had somehow "obtained" from the Russian Embassy.

Although Ann wanted to be an integral part of the action in Virginia Beach, she had agreed to stay behind and man the command center. They all agreed that there was no sense in bringing another asset into the project. They certainly wanted, and needed, to keep the number of people who knew about the plan to an absolute minimum. Even Roland wouldn't be there to witness Ann's participation. Her task was to monitor the phone relay system and intercept pertinent calls from Serrano.

VIRGINIA BEACH, VA
OCTOBER 21, 2012
SUNDAY
1000 HOURS

Carlos and Tony made the trip to Virginia Beach in less than four hours. The plan was simple and straightforward. If Serrano took the bait, and there was no reason to suspect that he wouldn't, he would most likely verify the number that Carlos had provided. And furthermore, if he decided to verify Carlos's credentials, Ann would be there to intercept the call and supply the requisite answers.

Through years of experience, they knew that the more simple the plan, the easier it would be to remember and implement. However, things rarely went as planned—at least as planned on paper. Murphy's Law always seemed to prevail. If anything can go wrong, it will.

The crux of the plan was to capitalize on Serrano's blatant disdain for authority. Throughout his brief military career, he had run-ins with every single superior officer, without exception. As a civilian, he had never held a job for more than two months. For Operation Shaker to be a success, Carlos would hit Serrano head on. He would explain that time was of the essence. The key was to be patient and not overplay his hand. Ann, Carlos and Tony had played this game many times before.

Tony sat at Carlos's kitchen table and was going over Serrano's record for the second time. He wanted to make sure that they hadn't missed anything. The record was replete with the failings of an individual who had no respect for authority. Tony was familiar with the type. They thought that the world owed them something.

It was clear that Serrano did have certain talents, including a natural ability as a shooter. However, he was unable to capitalize on those talents or follow orders in any capacity. The record indicated that Serrano was not a team player. The final chapter in his military career was written at Fort Benning, Georgia where he failed to complete the Sniper School curriculum. His final run-in with one of the instructors resulted in a court martial, a reduction in rate to E-1 and a less than honorable discharge from the service. Society would now have to deal with a disgruntled Anthony Serrano.

"Everywhere this guy went he caused an uproar," said Tony as he looked up from the folder.

"He had delusions of grandeur," said Carlos. "He thought that he was the only one who knew anything. That flaw should make him an easy mark. But you never know," Carlos added, raising his eyebrows. His past dealings with similar "easy marks" turned out to be not quite so easy.

Tony continued to thumb through the report as Carlos dialed Roland.

"Are we set up?" asked Carlos when Roland answered.

"Almost there Mr. Garcia," responded Roland. "I just need you to give me a call on the burner, so I can dial-in the equipment."

"Hold on," said Carlos as he grabbed the cell phone.

"Please call the number that we set up for Serrano," added Roland.

Carlos looked at the business card that Roland had fashioned and dialed the number. He could hear it ring in the background. Roland answered the call and told Carlos to stay on the line while he made a few more minor adjustments.

"Okay Mr. Garcia, we are set. No matter what number he dials from that phone, it will go to Ms. Peters."

"What about Serrano's home phone and cell in case he doesn't use this one?" asked Carlos.

"Got it covered. Ms. Peters is also set up for those," responded Roland.

"Will she be able to identify the number he is calling?" asked Carlos.

"Yes she will. I also have set up a voice synthesizer that will disguise her voice depending on which number Serrano dials," responded Roland.

"Sounds like you have thought of everything. Thanks Roland. Will talk with you later," Carlos said as he ended the call and flipped the burner phone to Tony. "Don't lose this," he smiled.

"Kid's good, huh," said Tony as he caught the phone and looked back at the folder.

"That he is. He's real good. Just wish he would call me Carlos, but that's never going to happen."

"Hell, you're an old man Mister Garcia," said Tony, with added emphasis on the word mister. "You're old enough to be the kid's father," he continued to tease.

"Thanks, *Mister* Ramos!" enunciated Carlos. "If I'm old enough to be the kid's father, what does that make you?"

"Uncle Ramos," responded Tony without looking up. He was obviously ready with a comeback.

Carlos looked at his watch. It was nearly 1400 hours. It was time to don his biker gear, get into character and head down to Boneshakers on General Booth Boulevard. Sunday was a popular time for the local bikers. Serrano was known to frequent the bar. He wanted to fit in but was not accepted, nor would he ever be for that matter. For the most part, the real bikers ignored him.

On one occasion, he tried hitting on one of the biker's chicks. He thought he recognized her from one of the local massage parlors. She tried to fend him off with a shake of her head and a disapproving look, but Serrano ignored her non-verbal warning. Her boyfriend didn't. He immediately took exception, and a fight broke out with the usual cheers from the onlookers.

Serrano held his own and ended up getting the best of the boyfriend. The others respected Serrano's fighting ability, but they still didn't accept him. Every once in a while, from that day forward, a biker would challenge him. However, nobody could get the best of him. For the most part, they left him alone.

Most were surprised Serrano still hung around. If it were a nice day, Serrano would stay outside leaning against the railing. Some thought he had a death wish.

Although Carlos was not an avid biker, he could certainly play the part. His prize 1978 Harley Electra-Glide, with Georgia plates, attracted enough attention to convince the locals that he was, indeed, a serious biker and one of them. He could be quite convincing. His tattoos were real, and he had the look of an individual who had been around the block a few times. He also knew bikes. He would fit in quite well. They wouldn't question his credentials.

Carlos would give the impression that he was just passing through. Tony, on the other hand, would remain in the car as backup. If for some reason he had to go into the bar, he would enter the bar as a government agent.

At 1400 hours, Carlos headed out for Boneshakers. Tony lagged behind. He wouldn't show up until he heard from Carlos that Serrano was there. Carlos pulled into the parking lot twenty minutes later. The lot was nearly full. Carlos's Harley drew the attention that he thought it would. A couple of the bikers came down from the porch as Carlos parked on the south side of the lot.

"Nice bike man," said the big guy as he drank the rest of his Budweiser in one long gulp.

"Thanks," responded Carlos. "I bought it a few years after Nam," he added as he got off the bike, removed his gloves and looked around the lot.

"Georgia, huh?" said the other biker who was also a pretty big guy but not in good physical condition.

"Dalton," responded Carlos. "Carpet capital of the world," he added.

"No kiddin'," said the bigger guy. "I think one of the guys inside might be from there. He's always on the carpet," he laughed loudly.

Carlos caught the pun and was relieved that he wouldn't have to go through the do-you-know dance with some guy that could break his cover. Carlos was about to say something when Serrano rode in on a fairly new Harley. Both of the bikers turned, said something and walked away. It was obvious that they wanted nothing to do with Anthony Serrano. Serrano looked around the lot and parked several feet from Carlos. Carlos dialed Tony, turned away from Serrano and simply said, "He's here."

CHAPTER FORTY-ONE

Anthony Serrano removed his helmet and walked toward Carlos. He purposely didn't make eye contact. He began to look over the bike without saying a word. Carlos didn't say anything either as he noticed Tony Ramos driving into the parking lot. Tony backed into a small space at the north end of the lot. As planned, he stayed in the car with the engine running. Serrano looked up but seemed to take little notice of the car.

"Anthony Serrano," said Carlos, catching Serrano totally off-guard.

Serrano immediately looked over at Carlos. He had a surprised look on his face that rapidly changed to a look of, who the hell are you?

"Have we met?" he asked as he sized up Carlos. Serrano was a little taller but not as thick through the chest and arms as Carlos.

Serrano took a couple of steps backward. He subconsciously took a defensive posture that Carlos recognized. Serrano was prepared for whatever was next.

"Not officially," responded Carlos.

"Not officially," parroted Serrano. "Officially has a legal ring to it," he added, shifting his weight ever so slightly.

"Serrano, I'm not going to beat around the bush. You're in a lot of trouble, and I'm here to offer you a little help, if you want it," said Carlos, lowering his voice as he moved in a little closer to Serrano.

Serrano reacted by taking a more defensive posture. He held eye contact without blinking. He didn't seem to be riled in the least.

"And what kind of trouble am I in?" he asked somewhat sarcastically.

"That little episode in the parking garage at Nordstrom was a very big mistake," responded Carlos.

Serrano didn't say anything. His eyes narrowed slightly as he maintained eye contact. Little beads of sweat were beginning to form on his forehead.

"I have no idea what you're talking about," he answered defiantly.

"Fine," said Carlos. "You stick to that story, but you forgot one little detail."

Serrano continued to evaluate Carlos. Carlos held his position. Serrano contorted his mouth as he began to chew on the inside of his lower lip. His mind raced back to that night in the parking garage. He tried to visualize the car.

"And let's say, for hypothetical purposes, you are correct. What *little* detail did I forget?"

Carlos smiled to himself. Serrano was beginning to circle the bait.

"You forgot to cover the inspection sticker," said Carlos. "It was easy to miss. But that little mistake made it possible for us to trace the decal back to your SUV."

"Maybe somebody borrowed my car," offered Serrano in a lame attempt to cover his mistake.

"Maybe," responded Carlos. "But maybe won't cut it. Besides, you're being set up," he added after a slight pause.

Serrano seemed to relax his stance as he wondered who would set him up, and for what reason.

"And who might be setting me up?" asked Serrano as he started to reach into his pocket.

Carlos moved back and reached for the gun he had holstered in the small of his back.

"Hold on partner," responded Serrano, recognizing that Carlos was reaching for a weapon. Serrano slowly raised both hands to shoulder level. "I just want a cigarette," he added. "Okay?"

Carlos nodded but kept his hand on his Glock as Serrano brought out a pack of Marlboros. He took out a cigarette, tapped it several times on the Marlboro box and put it in the corner of his mouth. He held out the pack and offered one to Carlos. Carlos declined with a shake of his head.

"It's a bad habit," he said as he lit up and took a deep drag. "So who did you say is setting me up?"

"I didn't say, but does the name Yolanda Rawls ring any bells?" asked Carlos, looking for Serrano's reaction.

Serrano was about to deny knowing her when Carlos continued. He didn't want to give Serrano time to regroup. He had just added a little more bait to the hook.

"Do you know Ian McAllister?" he asked.

"No, I don't," responded Serrano without hesitating.

Carlos believed him.

"So how are you going to explain the money that McAllister put into an account in the Deutsche Bank in the Grand Caymans, in your name?" asked Carlos.

Serrano had a puzzled look on his face. He took a deep drag from the cigarette and blew the smoke over his left shoulder. He continued to look directly at Carlos. Neither man yielded.

"Mister, I don't know what the hell you're talking about," he said in an attempt to regain his composure.

"I'm talking about the fifty thousand dollars that McAllister paid you to kill Tarek Haddad."

The name Tarek Haddad didn't get a rise out of Serrano, although the beads of sweat were more visible.

"I don't know any Haddad. So what reason would I have to kill him?"

"It really doesn't matter," responded Carlos. "The fact is he is dead. And once the authorities find out that you were paid fifty thousand from McAllister, they'll start connecting the dots. And know him or not, that line of dots my friend will lead right to you."

"I told you that I don't know this guy McAllister. And who the hell are you anyway?" asked Serrano.

Carlos hesitated before responding. He looked over at the entrance to Boneshakers. Several bikers had gathered on the porch and were talking amongst themselves. Carlos looked back at Serrano.

"My name is not important. The agency I represent *is* important," responded Carlos.

"And what agency might that be?" asked Serrano.

"One that will remain nameless," responded Carlos.

"And why would this nameless agency that you represent want to help me?" asked Serrano.

"Ms. Rawls has become an embarrassment. Homeland Security would like to see her go away."

"I take it that by go away, they want a permanent solution," said Serrano.

"Let's just say, if she goes away, and we take care of the Cayman account, then there will be no connection between you and McAllister. She won't be around to put the finger on you, and you can continue to enjoy your Sunday afternoons harassing the broads here at Boneshakers," said Carlos as he looked around waving his hand across the lot.

Serrano didn't answer for a few seconds.

"I told you that I don't know McAllister," responded Serrano.

"It's irrelevant. In fact, I'm sure that you don't. But I guarantee you that the authorities will make that connection, especially with Ms. Rawls's allegation," offered Carlos.

"So why are you giving me this opportunity to save myself?" asked Serrano.

"We are always looking for assets to provide, shall I say, special services. You fit the mold. You have certain talents complemented by a complete lack of respect for authority," said Carlos.

"And *that* makes me a good candidate?" said Serrano somewhat surprised.

"It makes you an ideal candidate," responded Carlos, thinking to himself that he was knee deep in bullshit.

"I take it that you have seen my military record."

"Right down to the last episode at Fort Benning," offered Carlos.

Serrano motioned that he needed another cigarette. What he really needed was time to think. "So where do we go from here?" he asked as he lit up.

"You did notice the car at the other end of the parking lot?"

"Yeah. I wondered why the guy backed in and is still sitting in it. He's with you, huh?" asked Serrano.

"He is, and he has in his possession an envelope with twenty-five thousand dollars in cash. All old bills. The twenty-five K is a down payment on your first assignment, assuming you accept."

"So you are hiring me to do some wet work. Ms. Rawls meets her maker, and I'm in the clear," said Serrano. It wasn't a question.

"*Maker* is being charitable. And yes, you will be in the clear. But Serrano, time is of the essence."

"So how much time do I have?" asked Serrano as he dropped the cigarette and ground it out with his boot.

"Our analysts believe she will make her move to incriminate you within the next forty-eight hours. She'll probably want to verify that the funds from McAllister are in place. We may be able to delay her, but if I were you, I wouldn't waste any time."

"You said down payment."

"You'll get another twenty-five K when the assignment has been completed."

Serrano looked around the parking lot. Several bikers were nursing beers and still watching. He looked back at Carlos's bike and took a deep breath.

"So how do I know you're not just some Fed trying to get me to incriminate myself? Hell, you haven't even shown me an ID."

"You don't," responded Carlos. "And quite frankly, I really don't care one way or the other whether or not you decide to take the assignment. But one thing I can tell you, this is your only chance, and there is not a lot of time."

"What was the name of the bank in the Caymans?" asked Serrano.

"Deutsche Bank, Cayman," responded Carlos.

Serrano's lips moved as he repeated the name to himself.

"So how do I get in touch with you?" asked Serrano.

Carlos reached into his pocket and took out a small card. The only writing on the card was a telephone number. He handed it to Serrano.

"You're kidding, right?" said Serrano as he waved the card in font of Carlos's face.

"Call the number. You will be asked to code in. Just say the name Gomez, nothing else," responded Carlos.

"So do I call you Gomez?" snarled Serrano.

"Call the number if and when you decide. They will transfer the call to me. And don't say anything other than Gomez. Is that clear?"

"Clear as this conversation," said Serrano disrespectfully. "What about the twenty-five thousand?" he asked.

Carlos knew that Serrano had taken the bait.

"Wait here," said Carlos as he went over to the car and retrieved the envelope and burner phone from Tony.

"Looks like we got ourselves a winner," said Tony.

"Believe we do," responded Carlos. "I just hope he remembers the name of the bank and checks it out. If he does, we will have him."

Carlos walked back over to Serrano and handed him the envelope and cell phone in clear view of the bikers. They had been joined by a couple of their women.

"I suggest that you wait until you are out of here before you open that. You also may want to reconsider the crowd you hang around with," said Carlos as he looked at the bikers on the porch. "They are probably wondering what is going on between us."

"I really don't care what they think," responded Serrano as he took a peek into the envelope. "I'll call you when the job is done."

"Use the burner and don't get careless. There is a lot more where that came from," said Carlos motioning to the envelope.

Serrano looked at the line up on the porch and thought about giving them a New York salute. Fortunately, it was a fleeting thought. He got on his bike, started up, put on his helmet and raced out of the parking lot without saying another word. Tony drove over, rolled down the window and leaned toward the center of the car.

"So he did take the bait," he said.

"Looks that way. He knows that he can't waste a lot of time," responded Carlos. "I'll bet he goes home, checks the number for the bank, and then grabs his gear and heads for D.C."

"I'll follow you back to your place," said Tony.

Carlos started the bike, put on his helmet and waved goodbye to the bikers. They didn't wave in return. Three hours later he and Tony were several cars behind Anthony Serrano as he turned off heading west on Braddock Road. Carlos looked at his watch. It was nearly 2100 hours. Carlos asked Tony to dial Rick.

"Hey Carlos," answered Rick.

"Serrano took the bait," said Carlos.

"Where are you right now?" asked Rick.

"We are in Burke."

"Good. Ann just called. Serrano called Rawls. She agreed to see him. Get the pictures of him if you can," said Rick. "Carlos, she could talk him out of this. If she does, you know what to do."

CHAPTER FORTY-TWO

Washington, D.C.
October 21, 2012
Sunday
2150 Hours

Yolanda Rawls had just finished a thirty-minute workout on her treadmill when Anthony Serrano called. He told her that he needed to see her and that he had important information concerning the death of Tarek Haddad. She tried to put him off until Monday, saying that it was too late, but he was insistent. Reluctantly, she agreed and gave him her address in Burke.

She was unaware that he had already looked up her address and had written it down, including directions to her house. He had also used Google Earth to get a layout of the neighborhood. Although the street level views provided a three hundred and sixty degree overview, the presentation was several months old. However, it was good enough to suit his purposes. Besides, he wasn't planning on being in the area for very long.

As she was taking a quick shower, it occurred to her that Anthony Serrano shouldn't have known anything about Haddad. Nothing about Haddad's death had been published yet. The police hadn't released any information. The U.S. Marshals knew some of the particulars, but they wouldn't have any evidence that would lead them to Serrano. So how *did* he know? And since Serrano was on the periphery of her project, what information could he possibly have.

The more she thought about the call from Serrano, the more she realized that something wasn't right. Things just didn't add up. Her dealings with Serrano were minimal, and although she had given him a verbal assignment, she had never met him. It was Stankowski who provided the connection and who had hired him on a purely subcontractor basis. Maybe Stankowski could provide some answers... if he would. Since his departure was less than amicable, he probably wouldn't be forthcoming with pertinent information. At least it was worth a try.

As Yolanda Rawls dried off, she was becoming more suspicious by the minute. She wasn't sure how far away Serrano was when he called. He told her that he would be there in about thirty to forty-five minutes. For all she knew, he could have been just around the corner checking to see if she were at home.

She had lived alone for several years, since her second marriage ended in divorce. She actually liked being alone, but it was times like this that it would have been nice to have a man in the house. However, Yolanda Rawls had been out of the dating scene for quite some time. Her career had become the love of her life, and as a result, there was no one to call. She would have to be on her guard with Serrano, a man that she had never met, but one that she knew had no problem beating up a defenseless woman.

She went into her study and took a nine-millimeter Browning from the center drawer of her desk. She checked the clip, chambered a round and flipped the safety to the fire position. She knew how to handle a weapon. All she would have to do is pull the trigger. She looked through her rolodex for Stankowski's card and checked the time. It was nearly twenty-two hundred hours. She decided to make the call. The phone rang several times, and just as she was about to hang up, Stankowski answered.

"Stankowski," he answered in a strong clear voice. He knew by the caller ID that it was Yolanda Rawls. He wasn't at all surprised to hear from her. He knew that her world would one day be turned upside down. It was just a matter of time. He didn't expect it to be this soon.

"Stankowski, Yolanda Rawls here," she said as she put the Browning into the deep pocket on the right side of her robe. The weapon was heavy and cold against her thigh.

"Ms. Rawls, and why would you be calling me this late on a Sunday night?" he asked, knowing that she was probably in Rick Morgan's crosshairs. He imagined the red laser dot dancing around on her forehead.

"What can you tell me about Anthony Serrano?" she asked.

Stankowski thought for a few seconds. He wasn't expecting her to ask about Serrano. He actually didn't know Serrano very well. Serrano had been recommended by a mutual acquaintance, one who warned him that Serrano had authority issues. The acquaintance had hired him to do some menial work. Those were Yolanda Rawls's descriptive words of what she needed accomplished.

"Not a whole lot, why?" he asked.

"He just called and said he has information about Tarek Haddad," responded Rawls.

"Haddad," said Stankowski. "He's your guy in Tampa," he stated.

"He was."

"Was?" asked Stankowski.

"Someone took him out a couple days ago," she added after a slight pause.

Stankowski didn't say anything for what seemed like a very long time.

"You there, Stankowski?" asked Rawls as she looked at her desk clock. It had been nearly thirty minutes since Serrano had called. She was beginning to get a little anxious.

"I'm here. I have no idea how Serrano knows about him, much less knew him for that matter."

"You're absolutely sure he didn't know about Haddad?" she pressed.

"Well, I can only tell you that he didn't hear Haddad's name from me."

"So why do you think he is on his way over here?" she asked.

Stankowski thought before answering. He did have an idea. He just didn't know the details.

"You remember our little conversation in the park?" he asked.

Yolanda Rawls chewed her lower lip almost hard enough to make it bleed. She remembered.

"So you think Morgan is behind this?"

"Let's say that I wouldn't be at all surprised," said Stankowski.

Yolanda Rawls's heartbeat began to rise as she thought about Rick Morgan. Her mind quickly raced to the fates of Ian McAllister and his two henchmen and possibly even Tarek Haddad.

"So what do I do about Serrano?" she asked, sounding a bit more humble all of a sudden.

"Do you have a weapon?"

"I do," she responded as she felt the weapon resting against her right thigh. It still felt very cold.

"Then I would get it, turn off all your lights and don't let Serrano in. Go to a room that you are comfortable in, and take a position where you can see him enter the room. From that point on, it will be your decision."

"Or I could just call the police," she offered.

"You could, and then how would you explain Lynn Morgan?"

She knew Stankowski was right. She didn't want to open that can of worms. If she got the drop on Serrano, she might be able to find out what was going on. Find out if, in fact, Morgan was baiting him. Once she knew, she would just shoot the asshole in self-defense for breaking and entering. Her heartbeat began to slow down. Yolanda Rawls had a spur-of-the-moment plan and was back in control, at least for the time being.

"Thanks Stankowski," she said as she hung up the phone. She didn't say goodbye or give him a chance to say anything else. He had probably said all he was going to say anyway.

Stankowski looked at the phone as he heard the dial tone. He smiled to himself as he placed the phone gently back on the receiver. He looked at it for several more seconds. He had done his part. He had tried to warn her in the park, but she was arrogant. She was a typical know-it-all. She thought that her position with Homeland Security gave her unfettered authority to do whatever she wanted, and that is exactly what she did. Nothing would change her mind. Stankowski sat back in is chair and took a sip of the Crown Royal he had poured just before the phone rang. It felt as good as it ever had going down.

Yolanda Rawls had renewed courage. She knew what she was going to do. She turned to head for the living room and nearly fell to the floor. Serrano was standing in the doorway. He held a weapon with a silencer in his right hand. The blood drained from her face. Her knees went weak. Serrano didn't say anything.

"We can work this out," she pleaded, her voice cracking.

"Too late for that," he responded as he aimed the weapon.

"Wait! Wait! I have money in the safe. A *lot* of money," she pleaded in an attempt to sidetrack Serrano.

He thought to himself, why not. It would look like a robbery.

"Where is it?" he demanded.

"There, behind that picture," she pointed. Her finger was shaking.

"Open it."

Yolanda Rawls moved to the picture and removed it from the wall, exposing a safe.

"Open it," barked Serrano again as he raised his voice.

Yolanda Rawls pressed several of the buttons in a sequence that only she knew. She pulled down the lever and opened the safe.

"Move away," snapped Serrano as he approached.

Yolanda Rawls moved away, keeping her right side out of his view. As he looked into the safe, she reached into her robe and put her hand on the gun. Serrano turned pointing the weapon at her.

"Don't think for one minute you're going to use that gun on me," he said as he pulled the trigger.

The bullet entered her chest just to the right of her heart. She fell back against the wall and slowly slid down to a sitting position. She had a bewildered look on her face. She looked down at her exposed chest. There was a little blue hole. The bullet didn't hurt as much as she thought it would. She could feel the warm blood beginning to run over her right breast and down her side. She didn't say anything. She couldn't move. The last few weeks seemed to flash by, ending with the name, Rick Morgan. Who the hell was Rick Morgan, she thought to herself as she began to feel sleepy.

Serrano took the money from the safe and stuffed it into his pocket along with a gold Rolex that had belonged to Yolanda Rawls's first husband. He looked down at Rawls. She was getting very pale. Her mouth was partially open. Her eyes stared straight ahead. Blood was beginning to come out the corners of her mouth. She made a little gurgling sound as Serrano pointed the gun at her forehead.

"You shouldn't have set me up," he said as he pulled the trigger.

Tony and Carlos were down the block from Yolanda Rawls's house. Tony had used a night vision camera to take several pictures of Serrano's car parked a block away from her house. He had also taken a picture of Serrano moving around in her yard. When they saw Serrano emerge from the house, Carlos checked his watch. From experience, they knew that Yolanda Rawls didn't have enough time to convince him that she wasn't the one who had set him up. Tony and Carlos correctly assumed that Serrano had taken care of business. They waited until he was on his way out of the neighborhood. Carlos started up and was heading east on Braddock Road when his satellite phone rang. It was Ann.

"Serrano is on the line," she said when Carlos answered.

"Patch him through," responded Carlos, knowing that Serrano would confirm the kill.

"Yes Serrano," answered Carlos.

"It's done," said Serrano simply.

"Good. I'll meet you tomorrow at Boneshakers with the rest of the money. Looks like we may have another target for you in a week or so if you're up for it," added Carlos.

"I'm up for it. What time tomorrow?" asked Serrano.

"Sixteen hundred hours," responded Carlos.

"I'll be there," said Serrano as he hung up.

Carlos looked over at Tony. Tony had already shut his eyes. Carlos didn't say anything as he dialed Ann.

"Hey," she answered.

"Shut it down," he said. "See you in a few," he added as he turned west on the Beltway.

CHAPTER FORTY-THREE

Rick kissed Lynn goodbye as he left their room at the Ritz. Lynn was finishing her morning cup of coffee and getting dressed for another rewarding outing at the mall. Rick was planning on spending most of the morning with Carl at the office. He purposely waited until zero eight hundred hours to leave in order to avoid the morning rush hour, which always seemed to be worse on a Monday morning. For some reason, everyone was in a rush to get to work. Hopefully he and Lynn would be able to head back to Virginia Beach before the afternoon traffic. The traffic before fifteen thirty was usually moderate. The trip from Tysons Corner to Virginia Beach would take about four hours and get them home at a descent hour, maybe in time to watch O'Reilly.

Rick arrived at The Peterson Group office forty-five minutes later. Elaine Drew smiled as he entered. She had a large stack of mail on her desk that she had already sorted into three separate piles. Most of the mail had already made it to the circular file that was strategically placed next to her right foot.

"Morning Elaine," said Rick as he approached her desk.

"Morning Rick," responded Elaine as she looked around behind Rick. Lynn didn't come with you?" she asked, knowing that Rick usually headed home from the Old Town office for convenience.

"She's doing some last minute shopping at Tysons Corner," said Rick.

"Good for her," responded Elaine. "Would you like some coffee?" she asked as she headed for the coffee mess. It was a rhetorical question. Rick usually drank three cups in the morning and always one just after lunch.

"Would love a cup," he said as he looked at the entrance to Carl's office. The lights over the door indicated that Carl was busy.

"Is Carl in a meeting?" asked Rick as Elaine handed him a large blue Peterson Group mug with the name RICK in bolded capital letters centered over The Peterson Group logo.

"No meeting. He sometimes puts on the red light when he doesn't want to be disturbed. He usually goes through his newspapers first thing in the morning. He did tell me to let him know as soon as you arrived."

Elaine smiled, went behind her desk and buzzed Carl. She had just delivered her message when Carl opened the door and greeted Rick. The red light was still on.

"Are there any bear claws?" asked Carl as he nodded to Rick with a silent offer.

Elaine smiled, didn't say anything and went back to the coffee mess. She returned with two fresh bear claws on a Peterson Group plate.

"You said that you were going to cut back," she scolded Carl as she glanced at his waistline. She pursed her lips.

"I didn't say *when*," he smiled as he took a big bite of the bear claw, which caused a generous portion of crusted sugar to fall to the carpet. He looked down but didn't say anything. He glanced over at Elaine with an apologetic look. He knew she would clean up his mess, as she always did and usually on a daily basis.

Carl motioned for Rick to follow him into the office. Elaine handed the plate to Rick and went to the closet to get a carpet sweeper.

"See you later," said Rick as he followed Carl.

"Have you heard from Carlos?" asked Carl.

"No, but according to our plan, he had no intention of calling unless there was a problem. I suspect they had a long night."

Carl looked at his watch and buzzed Elaine.

"Elaine, tell Roland that Rick is here and we are ready for him."

Carl could hear the small vacuum in the background.

"Will do," responded Elaine after several seconds.

"Roland has some information concerning Marcie Decker and Farrah Gemayel," said Carl. "Wouldn't tell me until you got here. I must be losing control."

Before Carl and Rick had a chance to finish the bear claw, Elaine let Carl know that Roland was in the outer office.

"Send him in," said Carl as he moved his wastebasket close to the desktop and swept a few crumbs into the basket.

"Good morning Mr. Peterson, Mr. Morgan," said Roland as he walked in and set his laptop on the conference table. He had it hooked up within seconds. He made a couple of keystroke entries and The Peterson Group logo was prominently displayed on the flat screen with the subject title in bold letters, Twins.

"So what do you have for us?' asked Carl.

Roland put up the second slide, which contained several bullets. He took out a silver pointer and began his presentation with the first bullet.

"In nineteen seventy-nine, Candice Toomey taught English at the American University in Beirut, Lebanon. She met and married a Lebanese physics teacher by the name of Wahid Gemayel. The marriage ended in divorce in nineteen eighty-one. Candice Gemayel had given birth to identical twin girls six months prior to the divorce. Their names were Farrah and Marcella. Candice Gemayel returned to the states with Marcella. Farrah remained in Lebanon with her father. Candice Gemayel went to work as a teacher in Atlanta, Georgia. Unfortunately, she was killed in an automobile accident three months later. Marcella ended up in foster care and was adopted by the Deckers."

Roland stopped for a few minutes as he took a drink of bottled water. Carl was first to respond.

"And she becomes Marcie Decker," said Carl.

"Correct. It appears that the other twin, Farrah, and her father, Wahid, left Beirut. So far I haven't been able to locate his whereabouts," said Roland.

"And somewhere along the line, Farrah and Marcie reconnected," said Carl.

"Given current events, I assume that must be true," responded Roland.

"I would be willing to bet that the twins have been in touch, or even together, for quite some time. It would certainly explain the reason why Interpol has never been able to pin down Farrah Gemayel," offered Rick.

"So there have been two of them all along," said Carl.

"Ann was right," said Rick.

"Indeed she was," agreed Carl.

"I suspect it was Farrah that you met at the Bahamian Embassy," said Rick.

"I wonder which one killed Tarek Haddad?" asked Carl. "Or could it have been the Serbs?"

"Could have been the Serbs. However, I would bet on one of the twins. Both of them are probably very dangerous," offered Rick.

"And you haven't been able to locate the father?" asked Carl.

"It appears that Wahid Gemayel has fallen off the grid. So far I haven't been able to find any solid information about him or his whereabouts."

"Probably didn't want the ex-wife to find him," offered Carl.

"Disappearing is quite common and easy to do in the Middle East," added Rick.

"Thanks Roland. Let me know if you find out anything else," said Carl.

Roland packed up his gear and left the room. Carl looked over at Rick. Rick, as usual, was making a few notes on a pad. Carl was about to say something when Elaine interrupted.

"Carlos is on line one for Rick."

"Thanks Elaine," said Carl as he relinquished his desk to Rick.

Rick sat in Carl's chair.

"Yes Carlos," answered Rick.

"Mission accomplished," said Carlos simply.

"As we planned?" asked Rick.

"Just as we planned."

"Good. Let me call you back a little later," said Rick.

"Okay boss, talk with you later," said Carlos as he hung up the phone.

"Everything went okay?" asked Carl.

"As planned," responded Rick.

"Now all we have to do is get our contract reinstated, and we're back in business," said Carl. "Then we will go after the rest of the lottery money."

Rick smiled and got up from behind the desk. He moved over to the conference table, sat down and made a couple more notes on the pad. Carl didn't say anything as Rick stopped writing and began to stare at the pad. He tapped his pencil rhythmically on the desk. He appeared to be in deep thought.

"Rick, what's bothering you?"

Rick looked at Carl and didn't say anything for a few seconds. He put the pencil down, sat back and took a drink from the mug. The coffee was lukewarm.

"It's all too easy. We're missing something here," said Rick.

"It looks fairly straightforward," offered Carl. "What could we be missing? The twins planned it all," he added.

Rick shook his head ever so slightly as he continued to make a few notes.

"Why did Farrah Gemayel leave her position at the embassy so soon after we took care of McAllister?"

"Well, she was a temp. Maybe the real secretary recovered and returned earlier than expected?" asked Carl.

"No, she didn't. And don't forget, the temp agency was a phony. Supposedly Gemayel was working for Homeland Security. And since she was supposed to alert Homeland Security if anyone complained about the lottery scam, why did she leave before the project was completed?" asked Rick. "It makes no sense," he added.

"Unless there was a change of plans," said Carl.

"We need to think outside the box," said Rick. "Let's assume that there is another player in the game, a player who has orchestrated this whole thing," added Rick as he went up to the white board and drew a square at the top of he board. He placed a large question mark in the square.

Carl came from around the desk, poured them both a cup of hot coffee and leaned against the conference table.

"Okay, I'm with you," said Carl as he took a drink of coffee.

"Homeland Security learns that someone has a dirty bomb for sale. They establish a project and put Yolanda Rawls in charge as the program manager," said Rick as he drew a rectangle on the board and wrote in the name Rawls.

"And the objective of the project is to recover the dirty bomb," offered Carl

"Basically, that is correct. She also sees the opportunity to identify Americans with offshore accounts," added Rick. "Her problem is that Homeland Security doesn't have enough money to properly fund the project. Consequently, she's left to fend for herself. Find her own money."

"We've all been there before," responded Carl. "So she comes up with the lottery scam," he added.

"And she employs Tarek Haddad to implement the scam," said Rick as he drew another rectangle on the board and entered the name Haddad. "The scam is two-fold: one, to raise enough money to make a realistic bid on the bomb, and two, to give Haddad credibility in the black market."

"The scam becomes very lucrative," offers Carl.

"And Haddad establishes an offshore account in the Bahamas with Ian McAllister," adds Rick.

"And in the process, Rawls realizes that she may also be able to entice McAllister to provide the names of some very wealthy American account holders, for a fee," adds Carl.

"It's always for a fee. In the process, they lure McAllister into the web," said Rick.

"Okay I'm with you. I think," responded Carl.

"Then you get involved because of John Kilday. And as a result, we eliminate McAllister and a couple of his goons," said Rick.

"Eliminate. I like that."

"I believe this is where our player sees an opportunity."

"Now, you're starting to lose me Rick," said Carl.

"Let's just say our player sees an opportunity to make off with several million dollars. It might have been his plan all along," said Rick.

"His plan? You said *his*?" questioned Carl with emphasis on the word his.

"I believe that our entrance into the lottery scam presented an unexpected opportunity and was the reason that Farrah Gemayel left when she did," offered Rick.

"And?" asked Carl.

"And in order to take advantage of the opportunity, he needed to convince Rawls that we killed McAllister and two of his goons in retaliation for Kilday. Basically, he pits us against Rawls. He convinces Rawls that she is playing with fire and could be our next target. Therefore, she gets Serrano to rough up Lynn in an attempt to make us back off."

"And we respond as he knows that we would?" asked Carl, beginning to get back on track with Rick.

"One way or the other, he knows that we will find out who assaulted Lynn. And that we will take out Serrano and most likely Rawls in retaliation."

Rick looked back at the white board and drew a couple more rectangles with connecting arrows.

"Who the hell are you talking about?" asked Carl, again somewhat confused.

"With whom did Farrah Gemayel meet? Who told Yolanda Rawls that she was in over her head? Who met with me and said that..."

"Holy shit! Stankowski!" interrupted Carl.

CHAPTER FORTY-FOUR

The scenario Rick had developed convinced Carl that Robert Stankowski certainly could have orchestrated the events that precipitated the entrapment of Anthony Serrano along with the killing of Yolanda Rawls and the murder of Tarek Haddad. There were still several unanswered questions, one of which was paramount in the mind of Carl Peterson—where was the lottery money? Although Carl would take a minimal finder's fee, he was absolutely determined to return the bulk of the money to the victims of the scam, at least to the ones that The Peterson Group was able to identify.

If Rick's scenario proved to be more than just a hypothetical sequence of possible events, Stankowski already had a considerable head start. Both Carl and Rick came to the simultaneous conclusion that there was no time to waste. Rick got up and went over to Carl's desk and dialed Carlos.

"Hey Rick," answered Carlos expecting to hear from Rick.

Rick could hear Ann and Tony in the background having a good laugh.

"Carlos, there has been a development in the project," said Rick.

"A development?" repeated Carlos, knowing that the use of that word was never a good thing.

"There is a strong possibility that Robert Stankowski has played us," said Rick.

Carlos didn't say anything for a few seconds.

"How so?" asked Carlos.

"I'll bring you up to speed when you get here," said Rick.

"We can be there within the hour. What about Ann?" asked Carlos.

"No, just you and Tony for now," responded Rick.

"Okay boss, see you in a few," said Carlos as he looked over at Ann and Tony. Ann knew when Carlos referred to Rick as boss, something was up.

Roland Carpenter located Robert Stankowski's address and had confirmed that the address in Fairfax, Virginia, was current. The information Roland had also indicated that Stankowski owned a house in Coconut Grove, Florida and had recently sold a condominium in Jacksonville.

Carl and Rick were finishing chicken salad sandwiches from Elaine's favorite deli in Old Town when Carlos and Tony entered the outer office. Elaine let Carl know. Rick opened the door and Carl welcomed them with a wave of his left hand, which held a half-eaten sandwich. Somehow he managed to keep the sandwich intact as Elaine's eyes followed it closely as he waved it back and forth. She looked over at the vacuum. It was still plugged in.

"Come on in," said Carl. "Have you guys had lunch?" he asked.

"We had a late breakfast," responded Carlos.

"Coffee?" asked Rick.

Both Carlos and Tony indicated that a coffee would be nice.

"So Rick, what is this about Stankowski?" asked Carlos.

"I believe that he set us up," Rick said frankly.

"Stankowski?" said Carlos in disbelief. "Nope, can't be. He's one of us. He's one of the good guys. I've known him for years. Heck, we've all known him for years," offered Carlos in defense of Stankowski.

"People change. He's the missing piece that fits," responded Rick.

Carlos shook his head. He didn't want to believe what he was hearing. He had known Robert Stankowski for years, had been on missions with him, had trusted him, as had Rick and Carl.

"I just can't believe that Stankowski would set us up," said Carlos. "Rick, are you absolutely sure?"

"There are just too many coincidences," added Carl.

"I hate to think that he would have done this and used us in the process," said Carlos.

"Well, if it's any consolation, I think we just happened to be a target of opportunity—one that was too good for him to pass up. Let me bring you both up to speed. Then you tell me where I could be wrong," said Rick as he walked up to the white board.

Carlos and Tony listened intently as Rick went through the same scenario he presented to Carl. Rick's dissertation was succinct and to the point with few superlatives. Carlos didn't say anything. He sat back in his chair and looked over at Tony. His expression was one of surrender.

"I don't know this guy Stankowski. He was your friend. But Rick, I think you are onto something," agreed Tony.

Carlos didn't say anything.

"I hope for Stankowski's sake that I'm wrong," added Rick.

"So where do we go from here?" asked Carlos. He knew the answer. It was purely a rhetorical question.

"Stankowski won't be expecting us, at least not so soon. I think our best approach would be to go to his house and confront him head on," said Rick.

"Catch him off guard," said Carlos. "Why would he do this? What was his motive?" he asked, searching for a plausible reason.

"Money is always a very powerful motive," responded Rick.

FAIRFAX, VA
1400 HOURS

Rick, Carlos and Tony pulled into Robert Stankowski's neighborhood forty minutes after they had left The Peterson Group office. There was little conversation between the three of them on the short trip. Carlos was still mulling the scenario over in his mind. Tony was a man of few words by nature. As they turned into Stankowski's cul-de-sac, there were two police cars in front of his house. One was an unmarked white Ford with small hubcaps and numerous antennas. It was obviously a police vehicle. There was yellow crime tape surrounding the property.

"This is not good," said Carlos.

Rick pulled up behind the unmarked car. A police officer on the porch began to walk toward them. He was out of shape. His hat was positioned toward the back of his head. For the most part, he appeared to be bald. He had his right hand resting on the butt of his weapon.

"You guys still have your Homeland Security IDs?" Rick asked as he watched the officer slowly approach.

Both Carlos and Tony said that they did. Rick got out of the car holding his Homeland Security ID in his right hand high above his head.

"Can I help you?" asked the officer.

"My name is Rick Morgan. This is Carlos Garcia and Tony Ramos," he said as he handed his ID to the officer. "Has something happened to Robert Stankowski?" he continued, not wanting to offer too much information.

The officer looked at all three IDs very carefully. Rick could see his lips move as he seemed to pronounce every word and syllable. Probably the reason he was still in uniform and guarding the front door, Rick thought to himself.

"Do you know Mr. Stankowski?" asked the officer.

"We know him very well," responded Rick as he included Carlos and Tony with a wave of his hand.

The officer was about to say something when the door opened and two men in sports jackets emerged. One was carrying a small duffle bag that Rick assumed was some kind of a crime kit.

"Detective Ricco. I was just coming to get you," said the officer apologetically.

Ricco didn't acknowledge the officer. He gave Rick, Carlos and Tony a quick once-over and asked who they were and why they were there. Rick showed him his ID. The detective wasn't impressed.

"So, why are you here?" Ricco asked again.

"Stankowski is working a project with us, and he didn't show up for work. We were wondering why," responded Rick.

"All three of you?" asked Ricco suspiciously. "And what project was that?"

"It was an operation to locate a dirty bomb. I am not at liberty to say anything more than that," responded Rick.

"He's not at liberty to say anything more about that," repeated Detective Ricco patronizingly as he looked over at his partner.

The partner smiled but said nothing. He just stood there with both arms wrapped around the crime kit as if someone were going to wrestle it from him. Rick took a couple of steps toward Detective Ricco. He was no more than two feet away. They were both about the same height. Ricco was at least twenty years younger and actually appeared to be in very good shape. He had a swarthy complexion and had obviously fought acne in is younger years. The acne had won the battle.

"Listen Detective, we are *basically* on the same team. I don't give a shit about playing some Mickey Mouse game with you to appease your identity crisis. You can either tell me what has happened here, or I will take jurisdiction," said Rick. "And you and your wrinkly friend here can go back to the precinct, read the sports page, drink stale coffee and jerk off for all I care. Have I made myself clear?"

Detective Ricco stared at Rick for several seconds. He subconsciously took a step back. He didn't like anyone questioning his authority, and he certainly didn't like being intimidated. However, it was obvious that he wasn't going to be able to bully Rick Morgan. Moreover, he was aware that Homeland Security could take jurisdiction if they declared the scene to be in the interest of national security.

"Mr…"

"The name is Morgan," responded Rick, recognizing that Detective Ricco had paid little, if any, attention to Rick's ID.

"Yes, Mr. Morgan," said Detective Ricco, his jaw muscles twitching in rebellion. "There is not much I can tell you."

"Is Stankowski alive or dead?" asked Rick.

"He was alive as of this morning. The doctors won't allow any visitors," said Detective Ricco.

"What happened to him?" asked Rick.

"That's what we are trying to find out," responded Ricco.

It was obvious to Rick that Ricco would not be forthcoming. Two could play that game.

"I would like to look inside," said Rick as he walked past Detective Ricco toward the front door.

"Don't touch anything," said the guy clutching the duffle bag.

"Don't worry. We won't contaminate the scene," responded Rick.

Stankowski's house was neat at the proverbial pin. The travertine floor in the foyer had a high gloss sheen. There was a small living room off to the left. It appeared that it was never used. There was a small study off to the right that had two large bookcases. They were full. The ever-present *Great Books* occupied a prominent place in the center two shelves. They were probably there for show. Rick wondered to himself if anybody ever read them. The large den was straight ahead. Another police officer was standing at attention by a recliner that was clearly the place where Stankowski was found. It faced a large flat screen TV that was still on.

Carlos and Tony looked around the room and into the adjoining kitchen as Detective Ricco watched.

"It looks like he was sitting in the chair and someone surprised him from behind," said Rick.

Ricco didn't say anything. Rick moved around to the front of the recliner. There was a very large blood stain on the carpet in front of the chair. The seat cushion and both arm rests were also stained with blood. The stain basically outlined the area where Stankowski sat.

"Okay, I've seen enough," said Rick. "You guys need any more time?" Rick asked as he looked over at Carlos and Tony.

They indicated that they were ready when he was.

"Detective, what hospital is he in?" asked Rick.

"He's in the trauma unit at Inova Fairfax Hospital on Gallows Road. I don't know the room number," responded Ricco.

"Thanks," offered Rick as he, Carlos and Tony headed toward the door.

"You *will* let me know if you find out anything," stated Ricco.

"Of course," responded Rick, knowing that he would never talk to Detective Ricco again.

A telling smile crossed Ricco's face. He also knew that he would never hear from Rick Morgan again. It was all right with him.

FALLS CHURCH, VA

1620 HOURS

On the way Rick called Roland and asked him to call the hospital and get Stankowski's room number. Within ten minutes Roland called back.

"Stankowski is in the critical care unit, room 208," said Roland. "Take the red entrance off Gallows Road, it's the second entrance. The critical care unit will be in the building straight ahead," he added.

"Thanks Roland," said Rick.

Rick, Carlos and Tony entered the hall in the critical care unit and were promptly intercepted by a nurse asking who they were looking for. She was all business.

"We're here to see Robert Stankowski," responded Rick.

"The doctor gave strict orders that Mr. Stankowski is not to be disturbed."

"Then you need to call the doctor, because we need to question him," said Rick as he presented his ID.

She looked at the ID and back at Rick.

"Mr. Stankowski is in very bad shape," she said. "We don't expect him to make it through the night."

"Well then, we really need to see him now, don't we?" said Rick in a more official sounding tone.

"I'll call the doctor," she said.

The doctor was there in less than two minutes. He was a tall African American. His nametag identified him as Dr. Lawrence Cabot.

"May I help you?" he asked cordially.

"Dr. Cabot, my name is Rick Morgan. This is Carlos Garcia and Tony Ramos. We represent Homeland Security. We need to question Mr. Stankowski concerning a matter of national security."

"I have no problem with you trying to question him if he is at all able to respond. Quite frankly I am surprised that he is still with us. Follow me," he said as he turned and started down the hall.

"What are his injuries?" asked Rick.

"It appears that someone injected him with a substance that temporarily paralyzed him. He was then systematically punctured with what appears to be an ice pick or something equivalent," offered Dr. Cabot.

Rick looked over at Carlos and Tony. They knew who they were dealing with. They entered the room. Stankowski was lying in the bed with his upper body elevated. He had numerous tubes and wires attached. His blood pressure was very low. His heartbeat was in the low forties.

"Mr. Stankowski," said the doctor as he gently shook Stankowski.

After a few seconds, Stankowski opened his eyes and looked at the doctor. He then looked at Rick, Carlos and Tony. It took him a minute or two to realize where he was and who was in the room. It was obvious from his expression that he didn't know Tony. He looked back at Rick. His expression relaxed somewhat. He tried a couple of times to speak. Rick moved in a little closer to the bed.

"I told you she was dangerous," he said, his voice hardly discernable.

CHAPTER FORTY-FIVE

Carlos and Tony moved their chairs close to the bed as Rick began questioning Stankowski. Stankowski's voice was weak. His breathing was labored, and every once in a while he would shut his eyes and drift off into another world—a world that only he could see. Hopefully he was just there as a temporary visitor, at least for the time being. Rick looked over at the electronic equipment monitoring Stankowski's vital signs. The numbers weren't good.

Rick looked back at Stankowski and gently touched his shoulder. He shook him ever so slightly. Stankowski didn't respond. Rick shook him again, only this time a bit harder. Stankowski made a moaning sound as he started the trip back from his world of darkness. Rick looked over at the equipment again. Stankowski's blood pressure was rising. His respiratory rate had improved very slightly. Stankowski opened his eyes and stared at the ceiling. His eyes moved back and forth. He seemed to be counting the square tiles in the drop ceiling. Rick touched his shoulder again. It seemed to startle Stankowski as he slowly looked over at Rick.

"Did Farrah Gemayel do this to you?" asked Rick.

Stankowski didn't say anything. He stared intently at Rick as if he were trying to figure out who he was. He seemed to be trying to process the question. An answer was forming.

"Robert," said Rick, "did Farrah Gemayel do this to you?" he asked again.

Stankowski's facial expression relaxed somewhat. He had made the trip all the way back to the present. It was a painful trip.

"Yes, it was Farrah," he answered slowly and very deliberately.

Rick started to ask another question when Stankowski interrupted.

"You figured it out didn't you?" said Stankowski. He was all the way back and in control of his faculties.

Rick nodded that he did.

"How did you know?" asked Stankowski. The wrinkles in his forehead seemed to deepen.

Rick actually had no intention of telling Stankowski how he had figured it out. As far as Rick was concerned, Stankowski didn't deserve any answers. Rick didn't say anything. He just looked at Stankowski with contempt. This was a man that he thought he knew. A man he had once trusted with his life. Guys like he and Stankowski had an unspoken loyalty to one another that transcended power, influence, and most of all, money.

"How Rick?" asked Stankowski again, but in a weaker voice.

Rick looked over at Carlos and Tony. Carlos seemed to nod in approval. Rick looked back at Stankowski and acquiesced to the pain he saw in Stankowski's face.

"It made no sense to me why Farrah Gemayel left the embassy, and then left town so abruptly," offered Rick.

"I knew it," said Stankowski trying to manage a smile. "I was afraid you would pick up on that, but I had no choice," he added.

Stankowski shut his eyes. His blood pressure began to drop. His breathing was slowing. Rick shook him a bit harder. Stankowski wasn't going to control the questioning. Rick wasn't going to let Stankowski escape into his world of darkness while his questions were still unanswered.

"Robert," said Rick. "Robert," he said again in a much louder voice.

Stankowski opened his eyes. He appeared to be having difficulty focusing on Rick. Before Rick could ask the next question, Stankowski continued where he had left off.

"Marcie wouldn't take care of Haddad. She had gotten too close. She had actually fallen for the guy. So I needed Farrah to do it."

"Why kill Haddad?" asked Rick.

"He was ready to take all the money for himself. I had commitments. Commitments with Farrah. She...she wouldn't understand."

"Why didn't you have Marcie take Farrah's place at the embassy?" asked Rick.

"She couldn't. She had a flight to Lebanon," responded Stankowski.

"Where's the money?" asked Rick.

Stankowski was hurting inside. The morphine only helped so much.

"It's on my boat. McAllister laundered the money. He exchanged over ten million for gold coins and bars," said Stankowski. "I went over on my boat and loaded it up."

"Did you tell Farrah Gemayel where the money was stashed?" asked Rick.

"Yeah, she knows. Can't believe she got it out of me. She can be quite persuasive with those damn needles," responded Stankowski.

"Where is the boat?" asked Rick.

"At my place in Florida. Coconut Grove," responded Stankowski.

Rick looked over at Carlos. Carlos was writing down the information. Stankowski looked up at Rick. They were both quite familiar with Coconut Grove.

"What's the name of your boat?" asked Rick.

"LuLu. My boat's name is LuLu," said Stankowski. For the first time he was able to manage a little smile.

"LuLu's back in town," said Rick, remembering that back in the old days Stankowski had an Ithaca 37 riot version shotgun with a pistol grip.

Stankowski had nicknamed the shotgun "LuLu." He carried the weapon on every mission no matter what the mission was. He would always find a place to pack it. Once, on the way out of the back of a C-130, Rick heard Stankowski yell out, "Come on boys, follow me, LuLu's back in town!" He sounded like a cross between Fats Waller and Jimmy Durante.

"Where on the boat?" asked Rick.

"Where what?" asked Stankowski.

"Where did you hide the gold?"

"The gold," said Stankowski as he looked back at the ceiling. He was having a difficult time staying focused. "There's a false bottom in the live well. It's under there," added Stankowski.

Rick looked over at Carlos and Tony.

"She's got a big head start," said Carlos.

"She doesn't know we are on to her. We could fly to Miami in a couple of hours," offered Rick.

"She's picking up Marcie in Tampa," volunteered Stankowski.

Rick was surprised that Stankowski had heard Carlos.

"When? Do you know when?" asked Rick.

"What's today?" asked Stankowski.

"It's Monday," responded Rick.

"Monday?" repeated Stankowski.

"Yes, it's Monday. You've been here less than twenty-four hours," said Rick.

"Seems like I've been here forever," responded Stankowski.

"So when is she picking up Marcie?" pressed Rick.

"If it's Monday, she's picking up Marcie sometime late today," said Stankowski as he began to doze off.

Rick didn't let him slip away.

"Why? What changed you?" asked Rick as he leaned in closer with his hand on Stankowski's shoulder. He shook him hard enough to move the bed.

Stankowski's eyes seemed to clear.

"Why?" repeated Stankowski. "You know why. Guys like us are expendable. Each side uses us until they don't need us anymore. And who are the sides anyway? Does anything ever change? No, nothing ever changes," said Stankowski, answering his own question. "They're all in it for what they personally can get out of it. For me, it was Yolanda Rawls. She pushed me over the edge," he added with a disdainful expression that was not masked by pain. "She used the lottery scam, with no regard for the unintended consequences, to get what she wanted…and she used me to get it."

"Let's go," said Rick. "We got all we need," he added as he looked down at Stankowski.

"Rick, I had no idea that Rawls would send Serrano after Lynn. I just hooked them up," said Stankowski in a much weaker voice.

Stankowski was back in his world of darkness. Rick, Carlos and Tony started to head out of the room when Rick hesitated. He looked back at Stankowski. Stankowski's vital signs were getting worse. Rick went back to the bed and touched the back of Stankowski's left hand, but said nothing.

OLD TOWN

1720 HOURS

On the way back to The Peterson Group office, Rick called Carl and brought him up to speed concerning his conversation with Stankowski. He asked Carl if he would set up a flight to Miami. Carl said that it would be no problem. The plane could be ready in less than hour. Rick asked Carl if Roland were still in the office, and if so, would he transfer the call to him.

"He's here," said Carl. "I'm transferring you now," he added.

"Yes Mr. Peterson," answered Roland.

"Roland, it's Rick Morgan."

"Yes Mr. Morgan."

"Roland, I need you to locate Marcie Decker. She could be on a flight from London to Tampa. I suspect that she will land in Atlanta and then fly on to Tampa. In either case, she is supposed to be landing sometime tonight. I need you to find out when," said Rick.

"Will do Mr. Morgan," responded Roland.

"Thanks. Call me as soon as you know something," added Rick.

DULLES AIRPORT

1900 HOURS

Ann met Rick, Carlos and Tony at the hangar. Although it wasn't necessary, she had packed a few things for all of them, including sandwiches. The Peterson Group Gulfstream had all the necessary amenities, including Carl's favorite WWs—wardrobe and weapons.

The aircraft commander informed Rick that there would be a slight change in the flight plan. The plane would be landing at Homestead. Carl had already reserved a rental car, which was being delivered within the hour. Rick was very familiar with the base. He had landed there several times as a navy flight instructor. Besides, it would be an easier trip from there to Coconut Grove. If everything went as planned, the team could be in Stankowski's neighborhood and on his boat by 2130 hours.

As soon as the team boarded the aircraft and the hatch was closed, the aircraft commander started the engines. The Gulfstream was taxiing within five minutes. As the plane was taking the runway, Rick received a call from Roland. Rick grabbed a notepad from behind the seat in front of him and was prepared to write.

"Yes Roland, what do you have for me?" asked Rick.

"Ms. Decker landed in Tampa at seventeen thirty hours. Do you need the flight number?" asked Roland.

"Nope, that's all I need. Thanks Roland. Hey, wait a minute. Roland, you still there?"

"I'm here Mr. Morgan," responded Roland.

"Can you check to see if she caught a flight to Miami?" asked Rick.

"Hold on a second. I'll check," said Roland.

"She's not on any manifest," responded Roland after a few minutes.

"Okay. There's a possibility that Farrah Gemayel has picked her up and the two of them are driving to Miami. Would you check to see if you can locate Farrah Gemayel's BMW? The tracking device should still be working."

"Will do," responded Roland.

Rick looked over at the team.

"Marcie Decker landed at seventeen thirty," said Rick. Out of habit, Carlos and Tony checked their watches.

"She could already be in Miami," said Tony.

"Roland didn't find her on any of the manifests. I believe that Farrah Gemayel picked her up. Roland is looking for the BMW."

"Well, if they're driving, we can beat them to Miami," said Carlos.

"Since they don't know we are on to them, I bet they are driving. And since it's nearly three hundred miles to Coconut Grove, they probably won't make it there before twenty-two hundred hours," offered Rick.

"Certainly not in Miami traffic," offered Tony.

"And we'll be waiting," said Ann as she simulated a gun with her right hand.

Rick was halfway through his sandwich when Roland Called.

"Yes Roland," answered Rick.

"The BMW is fifty miles south of Tampa on I-Seventy-Five and heading south."

"I had a feeling that they would drive," responded Rick.

"Mr. Morgan, you can follow the BMW on your satellite phone. I have sent you the link."

"Great," responded Rick as he subconsciously put his hand on the phone that was holstered on his left hip.

"If you have any problem, let me know and I can walk you through the set up," said Roland.

"I'll call you if I need your help," said Rick. "And thanks Roland."

"Okay guys, they're in the BMW heading toward Naples," said Rick.

"And then across Forty-One," said Tony as he thought about all the bodies that were rumored to be buried along the Tamiami Trail.

The link that Roland sent to Rick allowed him to track the BMW's movement. Rick finished his sandwich and looked at the small display. A map with a blinking dot indicated that the BMW was already south of Sarasota. Rick left it on as he looked at his watch. It was nineteen twenty hours.

The Gulfstream landed at the Homestead Air Reserve Base at 2015 hours. The team disembarked as soon as the plane had come to a full stop. One of the linemen pointed out the black Ford SUV that had been delivered an hour earlier. It was parked in the first space on the south side of Flight Operations. Within ten minutes of landing, the team was heading north on US Route 1.

CHAPTER FORTY-SIX

The rain was coming down in sheets as the black SUV slowed for the traffic light at the intersection of South Dixie Highway and Fifty-Seventh Avenue, or Red Road, as the locals commonly knew it. It was impossible to see the team through the tinted windows, especially at night.

Both Carlos and Tony had slept most of the way from Homestead. Rick looked in the rearview mirror. Ann was wide awake and taking in the surroundings, at least what she could see of them. She had never been to Miami.

As Rick waited for the light to change, the location brought back pleasant memories of his time at the University of Miami. He wondered to himself if the apartment building where he lived, along with his best friend, Enrique, were still there. He also wondered if the drugstore on the other side of the back gate was still serving breakfast. He had eaten there almost every morning for nearly three years. Two eggs over easy, hash browns, toast and orange juice were a mere forty-five cents. How times have changed, he thought to himself. It was a long time ago, but the memories of Miami were still fresh in Rick's mind.

As their SUV continued north on South Dixie Highway, Rick pointed out the dorm they used to call "The Towers." When Rick was a freshman, it was exclusively a girl's dorm. Located on the southeastern corner of the university, The Towers was a very popular spot. A parade of new sports cars could be seen each night picking up and dropping off some of the prettiest girls in Miami. Just as Rick passed the dorm, the rain abruptly stopped. In Miami it could be raining on one side of the street and completely dry on the other.

"So how was the university when you went there?" asked Ann.

"There were a lot less people," responded Rick.

"Did you live on campus?" she asked as she continued to look to her left.

"Twelve sixty-four Dickenson Drive," responded Rick. He realized that he hadn't repeated that address in years and was a little surprised that it just rolled off his tongue like it was yesterday. "When I was there it was called main campus apartments. They were actually pretty nice. I'm sure it has all changed now. Probably a big dorm has replaced it. The university always needed more land."

"Looks like a nice campus," said Ann.

"Maybe when we're done here, we'll take a ride through. I haven't been on campus in over twenty years," said Rick. "My high school class ring is a permanent resident of the student lake," he added with a smile.

"I can only imagine how that happened," chuckled Ann.

As Rick glanced over at the university, he wondered if the little wooden shacks where he and Carl Peterson were recruited were still there. Although it was a very long time ago, Rick still had fond memories of "Sun Tan U."

At 2145 hours, Rick turned right on Rivera Drive in Coconut Grove. The rain had started up again. According to the information provided by Roland, Stankowski's house was in the 6500 block. As Rick started to slow down, Tony reached over and grabbed Rick's forearm.

"Don't slow down. Keep going," he said as he turned in his seat. He sounded excited.

Rick didn't slow down. He kept going.

"What is it?" asked Rick as he looked over at Tony.

"The black Cadillac sedan back there," said Tony as he reached into his pocket and pulled out a small notebook.

Tony thumbed through the pages and stopped. He shook his head. Rick could hear Tony say "shit" as he looked over at Rick.

"The Serbs are here," he said.

"Great," said Carlos. "And I thought this was going to be a walk in the park."

Rick made a right turn and drove a few hundred feet before pulling over to the side of the road.

"They're probably here to meet the girls," said Rick.

"Do you think they brought the suitcase bomb with them?" asked Ann.

"I'm sure they brought *something* with them," said Rick.

"What do you think Rick? Should we wait for the girls and see what happens?" asked Carlos.

Rick thought for a few seconds before answering. He wasn't expecting the Serbs to be in Miami. It didn't take him long to come up with a new plan.

"It will be much easier dealing with the two of them right now," said Rick.

"I agree," said Ann.

"How do you want to handle this?" asked Carlos.

"Just like the old days," said Rick.

"In—bang bang—and out," said Carlos as he felt his weapon.

"There should be a couple of throw aways in the bag," said Rick.

Carlos reached around behind the seat and brought the bigger of the two duffle bags up between him and Ann. He looked in the bag.

"There are several in here," said Carlos.

"Good, pick out a couple and load up. If everything goes well, we'll plant them when this is over," said Rick.

"Ann, are you up for pretending to be a friend of Stankowski's?" asked Rick.

"I can do that," she answered, wondering just what Rick had in mind.

"Carlos, you and Tony check out the house. We're probably dealing with the same guys from Tampa, but make sure. Once you find a way in and are ready to go, let me know. Then Ann will knock on the front door to get their attention. That will be your cue. Carlos, you go in first and take them out. Tony, you lag behind just long enough to make sure there isn't a ghost hiding somewhere in the house. Any questions?"

"None from me," answered Ann.

"Me either," said Tony.

"LuLu's back in town!" exclaimed Carlos.

Carlos's comment brought a slight smile to Rick's face. Rick looked at his satellite phone. The BMW was already approaching South Miami.

"Okay guys, we don't have much time. Farrah Gemayel is about thirty minutes out. No heroics. No Steven Segal bullshit. Just like the old days," said Rick.

Each member of the team inserted their earpieces and pinned on lapel mics. They did the usual test. Everything worked five-by-five. Carlos and Tony put on their vests, checked the throw always and headed in the direction of Stankowski's house. Rick and Ann waited in the car. They didn't say anything as they listened intently. They had to focus. The rain was heavy and made it difficult to hear clearly. Regardless, rain was always welcomed in a neighborhood scenario. People stayed in when it rained. Within ten minutes Carlos checked in.

"Rick, Tony has confirmed that it's the guys from Tampa. Appears to be two of them. Doesn't look like there is anyone else in the house. Looks like they have been out back. Fortunately, the sliding glass door is open and the screen door is unlocked. There is a sensor on the big door, but it doesn't look like there is one on the screen door. The Serbs must have disabled it."

"Good, are you ready to go?" asked Rick.

"As soon as Ann knocks on the front door," said Carlos.

Rick started the SUV and made a u-turn. He turned left on Rivera and stopped two houses from Stankowski's. Ann took an umbrella from the door.

"See you in a few," she said.

"I'll watch for the BMW," said Rick. "Be careful. You know the Serbs," he added.

Ann walked up to the front door and rang the bell. The Serbs got up from the couch and approached the door. The taller of the two looked through the peephole.

"Some woman. It's not Gemayel," he said.

"Robert, it's me, Ann. Are you in there? Come on, let me in. I'm sorry about the other night," she said sounding apologetic. "It's raining cats and dogs out here," she added. "Come on…please let me in."

As the taller man unlocked the door, Carlos appeared at the entrance to the den. He made a sound on purpose, which caused both men to turn. The tall man had a gun in his right hand. He made the mistake of turning to the right, exposing the weapon. Carlos shot him first. The other man tried to go for his weapon, but Carlos hit him in the forehead with a single shot. Both men went down hard. The taller man tried to move but stopped. His grip on the weapon relaxed.

Carlos waited for a couple of minutes as he watched. He slowly walked into the room and stopped at the front door. Tony Ramos had taken Carlos's position. He kept his weapon pointed at both of the Serbs. When Carlos felt it was safe, he kicked away the tall man's weapon and signaled Tony.

Carlos put his first and second finger on the tall man's neck. There was no pulse. "He's dead," Carlos confirmed.

Carlos and Tony methodically checked the rest of the house to make sure it was clear before they let Ann enter.

"Gemayel and Decker should be there in about five minutes," said Rick.

"We'll be ready," said Carlos.

Rick could hear as Tony and Carlos moved the bodies from the foyer. Since the hollow points used by the team carried special loads, there were no exit wounds. There was very little blood, and there was no way to trace the weapons.

"The BMW is heading into Coconut Grove. Less than two miles away," said Rick.

"We're ready," said Carlos.

The rain was coming down in sheets, just as it was when Rick stopped for the light at Red Road. He couldn't use the windshield wipers for fear of alerting the twins and giving away his position. Rick put on his gloves, reached in the bag and took out the remaining throw away. He checked the clip. As he pushed the clip back in and chambered a round, the BMW drove slowly into the neighborhood as if checking the house numbers. The BMW stopped in front of Stankowski's house. Rick had a hard time seeing the car, but it appeared that there were three people in the vehicle. As Rick watched, someone emerged from the passenger side of the car and walked briskly toward the front door.

"Carlos, looks like there are three of them. One is heading toward the front door. No way to tell who it is, but it definitely looks like one of the twins."

"We got it," said Carlos.

Rick held his position. He could only see part of the front of Stankowski's house. He saw the outside light come on and he could hear Tony's voice.

"Yeah," said Tony, as he cracked the front door ever so slightly.

The woman at the front door didn't answer. She looked at the number on the side of the house and then back at the partially obscured man at the door.

"Where's Stankowski?" she asked hesitantly, knowing that the house belonged to Stankowski.

"You're asking me? You of all people know where he is," responded Tony.

"And who the hell are you?" asked the woman backing slightly away from the door.

"I'm with Mihailo," responded Tony. "You going to come in?" he added.

"Where's Mihailo?" she asked, trying to get a glimpse into the house.

"He and Ranko are out back on the boat. They're probably waiting for the rain to stop," said Tony.

Rick was listening and thinking to himself that Tony was good.

"Are you Gemayel?" asked Tony, not able to identify which twin was standing in front of him.

The woman didn't say anything for a few seconds. She looked back at the BMW. The rain was unrelenting. She thought about going back and conferring with her sister, but she didn't want to get wet. It had been a long day, and the guy on the other side of the door sounded legit. Besides, she was sure she could handle him if she had to.

"Fine, let me in," she said.

Tony slowly opened the door and looked her up and down as she stepped in. She was tall and quite beautiful. Her jet-black hair was pulled back into a bun that was held in place by two knitting needle sticks. Tony moved back out of striking distance.

"Get Pesa and Milosevic in here. Do you have the merchandise?" she asked.

"That we do. And do you have our payment?" asked Tony.

The woman looked around the room. She appeared to be ill at ease. Let me tell my sister to come in," she said as she started to reach into her jacket pocket.

"Hold it," said Tony as he pulled his weapon.

"Don't get nervous. Just my phone," she said.

"Do it slowly," said Tony.

The woman reached into her pocket and pressed the send button. When she did, the BMW took off wrecklessly and was swerving as it flew past Rick's SUV.

"Tony, she's on to us," said Rick.

CHAPTER FORTY-SEVEN

Coconut Grove, Florida
October 22, 2012
Monday
2230 Hours

Rick started the SUV and made a u-turn as he began his pursuit of the BMW. The BMW was accelerating rapidly and nearly out of sight. Rick could just make out the brake lights as the BMW entered the rotary and exited onto Hardee Road. Rick followed and made the same turn.

As he crossed the bridge, he could just make out the BMW's brake lights in the heavy rain as it slowed for the next intersection. He could see the car slide into the rotary and exit going north toward South Dixie Highway. Rick hit the brakes hard as he approached the rotary. The SUV swerved slightly on the wet pavement as the rain continued to come down in sheets.

There were no other cars in sight as Rick went around the rotary and exited north on Maynada. He pressed down hard on the accelerator; however, he wasn't gaining on the BMW. Both vehicles were now heading straight for South Dixie Highway. Surely, the BMW would have to slow down before entering the highway, he thought to himself.

Rick kept watching for brake lights. There were none. The BMW appeared to speed up. Rick glanced at his speedometer. He was going nearly seventy miles an hour. He couldn't believe the driver of the BMW would try to make the turn onto South Dixie Highway at over seventy miles an hour. Even for a BMW with an experienced driver, that would be a hard maneuver.

Rick began to slow down as he watched the car make a hard right turn. The rear end of the BMW lost traction and slid into the northbound lane. The car was out of control. Rick was close enough to the intersection to hear the blast from an eighteen-wheeler's horn. The horn was steady.

By the time Rick made the turn, he could see the BMW rolling end over end. The truck had jackknifed and was sliding off the left side of the highway. Rick hit the brakes as the BMW skidded on its roof, spinning round and round. Smoke was pouring from the engine compartment.

Rick pulled over onto the shoulder and got out of his car. He looked over at the eighteen-wheeler. The driver was getting out of the cab. There was a woman in the cab with him. Rick tried to make contact with Carlos but was out of range. The BMW had stopped spinning. Flames were now visible. They were coming from the engine compartment.

Rick could see that there were two people in the car. A man had been driving. The truck driver was yelling something as he helped the woman down from the passenger side of the truck. Rick ran over to the BMW. He could feel the heat emanating from the fire. He went around to the passenger side and got down on his hands and knees. The woman inside was still strapped in. She was conscious and slowly moving her arms. Her long black hair was sprawled out on the headliner.

As Rick crawled closer, he could feel the heat from the fire in the engine compartment. He knew that the car could blow at any second. He knew he had to make the decision to either move away or help. He briefly struggled with the part of him that wanted to leave. However, the humanitarian part of him won the moral victory.

"Unfasten your seatbelt," he yelled as he moved in closer.

The woman didn't respond. Rick reached into the car in an attempt to release the woman's seatbelt.

"I'll release the seatbelt," he yelled as he tried to reach the release mechanism.

She still didn't respond. She appeared to look in his direction. Her hair partially covered her face.

As he released her seatbelt, he felt a sharp pain in his right hand. Instinctively he pulled his hand back. A large knitting needle had penetrated his hand. He froze for a second then looked at his hand and thought about pulling the large needle out.

"Hey buddy, get out of there, it's going to blow!" yelled the truck driver as he moved cautiously toward Rick.

Rick got up slowly. His knees felt like they wanted to buckle underneath him. He struggled to stand. He was having a difficult time maintaining his balance. He tried to evaluate his situation, but he was having a difficult time focusing his thoughts. As he staggered back toward the truck driver, the driver recognized that Rick was in trouble. The truck driver ran to rescue Rick from the impending explosion. As he grabbed Rick, he hesitated as he noticed the large needle that had impaled Rick's right hand.

"What the…?" he said as they both moved away from the BMW.

Within seconds, the flames completely engulfed the engine compartment. Both front tires made a sizzling sound as they burned, creating a dense cloud of heavy black smoke that rose through the rainy night sky. Just as they reached the eighteen-wheeler, the BMW exploded in a giant ball of fire. The resulting flame turned the adjacent rain into steam. The blast threw both the truck driver and Rick against the front left fender of the truck.

"Hey buddy, are you okay?" asked the truck driver. He couldn't take his eyes off Rick's hand. "Ruthie, get the first aid kit," he yelled.

"Don't pull it out," mumbled Rick. "Antiseptic, just poor some antiseptic on it," he added as he looked at his hand. He had a hard time focusing on the wound.

Rick tried to stand up straight, but his legs were weak. It didn't make sense why the wound would make him feel the way it did. He had been stabbed before, even shot, but he had never had this type of reaction. Then he thought about Stankowski.

He looked back at his hand. He realized that the knitting needle must have been laced with a drug. He had the feeling that he was going to pass out. He fought the best he could, but the clouds of unconsciousness were closing in fast. Rick slid down onto the pavement as bright bursts of light rolled around in the depths of his mind and then faded into darkness…as did the sounds of the night.

STANKOWSKI'S HOUSE

2140 HOURS

Tony drew his gun and held the woman at bay. She leaned against the wall with her hands behind her back. She didn't move as Ann and Carlos came into the room. She looked over at them but didn't say anything. There was contempt in her eyes. Then she looked back at Ann. Her expression seemed to change.

"So who are you?" she asked as she looked back at Tony.

"It doesn't matter who *we* are," he answered.

"You're with Morgan and The Peterson Group, aren't you?" she declared with a confident smile.

Carlos, Ann and Tony didn't say anything.

"I could have taken you and Morgan out at the Ritz," she said looking directly at Carlos, letting him know that she recognized him.

"So you *are* Farrah Gemayel," concluded Tony.

The twin looked over at Tony and just smiled. She didn't confirm his suspicion.

"So what are you going to do? I haven't done anything," she said.

"What about Stankowski?" asked Carlos.

"And what about him?" she asked.

"You tortured him to find out what he did with the money," said Carlos.

"You say," she responded. "It will be hard to prove that I did anything to Stankowski," she said with a look of confidence as she threw back her head.

"We'll prove it. Just don't you worry," said Carlos.

"Worry," she laughed. "And how are you going to explain the Serbs. Besides, the authorities will believe that I work for Homeland Security. Who's going to arrest me? I was here to complete a sting operation, and you killed my contacts. Not to mention the fact that The Peterson Group was issued a stop work order. How are you going to explain that?" she asked defiantly.

"It won't be as hard as you think," said Carlos.

"I wouldn't bet on it. And believe me, when this is over, I *will* kill all of you," she sneered.

"I believe you," said Ann calmly.

"You *better* believe me," she said, her nose flaring.

"You know, I really do believe you," said Ann as she fired the first shot, hitting the woman they believed to be Farrah Gemayel in the chest.

Gemayel looked straight ahead as she slowly slid down the wall, leaving a trail of blood. She looked down at her chest and up at Ann. Ann didn't say anything as she walked over, raised her weapon and shot her in the forehead. She really didn't care which twin she had just killed.

CHAPTER
FORTY-EIGHT

South Miami Hospital
October 23, 2012
Tuesday
0845 Hours

Carl Peterson was looking at the *Miami Herald* and drinking a cup of coffee when Rick opened his eyes. Rick stared at the ceiling for a few minutes wondering where he was and what had happened. He started to move when the pounding in his head reminded him of the chase. He went to touch his forehead when he noticed the large bandage. Then it all came back to him.

"Well, look who's up," said Carl as he put down the newspaper.

"You sound like Lynn," responded Rick. "Must be a southern thing," he mumbled.

Rick looked over at the clock. It was nearly 0900 hours.

"Is it really that late?" he asked.

"That it is my friend," responded Carl.

"Then I did sleep in," he responded as he wrinkled his forehead. "My head is pounding," he added.

"I suspect that it is. Appears that you were drugged," said Carl.

"The knitting needle?" asked Rick.

"It was laced with a solution of chloral hydrate and pentobarbital."

"Chloral hydrate," repeated Rick. "So I was slipped a Mickey Finn," he concluded.

"Yes, but don't forget the pentobarbital," said Carl with empathy. "That's why you're still here."

"And what is that?" asked Rick.

"Pentobarbital is used during assisted suicides," said Carl. "Probably the stuff used by Jack Kevorkian."

Rick thought about it for several seconds before responding.

"So I was given a Mickey Kevorkian," he said as he managed a laugh that turned into a coughing spell. It hurt.

"You're okay," said Carl as he took a drink of coffee.

"What about the team?" asked Rick regaining his control.

"I believe they went over to the university," responded Carl as he looked at his watch. "Ann said she was going to look for your ring."

Rick tried to manage another smile. It still hurt.

"So where are we?" asked Rick as he looked around the room.

"South Miami Hospital," said Carl. "If I remember correctly, you've been here before."

"That was a long time ago. And what about the mission?" asked Rick.

"Completed," said Carl as he took another drink from the coffee cup. "Would you like one?" he asked.

"I would love a cup," said Rick. "It might help this headache," he added, as he rubbed his forehead.

As Carl went to get the coffee, Rick started to put things together. There were a few questions that he needed answered. What happened to the bodies? Where were Farrah Gemayel and Marcie Decker? How did the team get away? Did they find the gold? What about the rental vehicle Rick was driving? Then it hit Rick. Carl, you son-of-a-gun, he thought to himself. The rental with the tinted windows was a *company* car, and Rick wasn't thinking about a Peterson Group vehicle. He smiled to himself as Carl entered the room with coffee in hand.

"So, you were basically with us the whole time," said Rick, a knowing look plastered across his face.

"What are you talking about?" asked Carl as he handed the coffee to Rick.

"The SUV was a *company* car," responded Rick, making sure to emphasize the word company.

Carl took a drink and sat down. He got that little grin on his face that Rick had seen before.

"As soon as the accident happened, I called Carlos. He told me what had taken place at Stankowski's. I sent in a couple of cleaners. They got there within thirty minutes and brought the team another car. Our people found the gold. It wasn't as much as we thought. Roughly half of what we calculated. It's already stowed on the plane."

"So where is the other half?" asked Rick.

"That is a good question my friend," responded Carl.

"And what about the twins?" continued Rick.

"Well, we are confident there is only one now."

"One? What happened at Stankowski's?" asked Rick with a puzzled look on his face.

"The twin that entered Stankowski's didn't make it," replied Carl. "And it seems that only one body was found in the burned out BMW," he added.

Rick was too groggy to try to figure out the details surrounding the twins at this time. After a few moments, he looked over at Carl and said, "And here we are."

"Yep…and here we are."

"And you're still with the *company*," said Rick shaking his head.

"Some things never change," responded Carl as he took a drink of coffee. "Technically, so are you," he said as he raised his cup in a subtle salute.

EPILOGUE

PENSACOLA, FLORIDA
ONE WEEK BEFORE CHRISTMAS
1400 HOURS

Carl Peterson sat behind his desk in his Pensacola Beach condominium. It had been nearly seven weeks since returning from Miami. Carl looked at his watch. He still had a couple of hours before he would need to head out for Destin.

Carl thought about the events as he opened the center drawer of the desk and removed a large business-size checkbook. He looked back at the figures on the note pad. The team had removed two hundred and thirty-five pounds of gold coins and bars from Stankowski's boat in Coconut Grove.

Carl had calculated that the current value of the gold was in excess of six million dollars. With the current world situation, the value changed on a daily basis. Sometimes the swings were significant. Consequently, Carl determined that it would be more prudent to take The Peterson Group's finder's fee in ounces rather than dollars. That would be exactly thirty-five point one pounds of gold.

Carl was also committed to identifying and reimbursing as many of the victims of the lottery scam as possible. In order to meet that goal, he established a foundation in the name of John Kilday. Mike and Nancy administered the foundation. Roland Carpenter was assigned to locate all of the victims, or as many as possible.

Carl opened the checkbook and wrote four checks. He smiled as he put them into The Peterson Group Christmas cards that Elaine Drew had ordered prior to Thanksgiving. He particularly liked Elaine's choice of the three wisemen following the star that was squarely positioned in a bright *blue sky*. He wondered just how much Elaine really knew. Carl had a pleasant smile on his face as he added his own personal message and then sealed each card.

MARINA CAFÉ

DESTIN, FLORIDA

1730 HOURS

Carl Peterson drove over from Pensacola and met Rick, Lynn, Carlos, Ann and Tony at Marina Café. The six of them sat at two of the high-top tables on the south side of the bar overlooking Destin Harbor. The weather was clear. Several boats were returning from a day's fishing in the Gulf. The bar was nearly full of patrons taking advantage of the happy hour rates.

Although Carl claimed he wanted the team to enjoy the sunset, he was very much aware of the two-for-one deal offered at that time. It particularly catered to the snowbirds. The conversation was basically geared around the team's fondness of the Destin area. The maitre d', Wally, who was a fixture at Marina Café, greeted each member of the team. He had known Rick and Lynn for many years. After Wally left, Carl reached into his pocket and handed each of the team members an envelope.

"I want to thank each of you," he said. "It has been a good year for The Peterson Group," he added.

They all toasted Carl as they put the envelopes into their pockets.

"So, how is the John Kilday Foundation doing?" asked Rick.

"So far we have given back over three million dollars. Unfortunately, some of the deceased had no beneficiaries. My nephew is going to expand the foundation to meet other needs, which he and Nancy will determine. It's their call. Might end up being a full time job," said Carl.

"Anything to get Mike out of being a fighter pilot," smiled Rick.

"You got that right," said Carl. "I'm going to buy him a small watch," he added, knowing that Rick would understand.

Carl ordered another round of drinks as the team enjoyed an assortment of appetizers and sushi. Ann and Lynn were discussing their outing on Grand Boulevard when Tony reached into his pocket.

"Well guys, I also have a gift. The mega millions jackpot is at two hundred and forty million. I got us all a lottery ticket," he said with a big smile.

Everyone in the bar area turned as Tony was pelted with rolls and napkins.

In the weeks prior

Robert Stankowski died less than an hour after Rick, Carlos and Tony left the hospital room. Stankowski was buried in a small cemetery outside of Fredericksburg, Virginia. There were only eleven people in attendance including Carl, Rick and Carlos.

John Holda was given a manila envelope that contained pictures of him and Yolanda Rawls. There was also a yellow sticky note included stating that these were indeed the only pictures, and the enclosed digital photo stick was the only existing evidence. It was suggested that he destroy the contents. The note enclosed simply stated, *You have your life back.* It was signed, *A friend of Carl Peterson.* The Peterson Group stop work order was rescinded later that day.

Anthony Serrano gave up trying to contact the number given to him by Carlos. His career came to an abrupt end when FBI agents arrested him outside of Boneshakers in full view of his motorcycle "friends." It was difficult to determine if their applause was one of cheers or jeers. Serrano tried to convince the authorities that he was working undercover for the CIA, but there was no way he could prove it. His explanation was compounded by the fact that the twenty-five thousand in cash turned out to be counterfeit money confiscated from Iraq. As Serrano sat in his jail cell, he couldn't help but think about Lynn Morgan.

The driver of the burned out BMW in Miami was later identified as Rasheed Makari. He was Tarek Haddad's cousin, lived in Zahlie, Lebanon, and was suspected to be one of the local Hezbollah leaders with known ties to al-Qaeda. How he got into the United States unnoticed is still under investigation. His was the only body found at the scene.

An elderly English tourist by the name of Maude Lambert took a seat across from Ian McAllister. She tried to engage McAllister in conversation; however, McAllister didn't respond. She finally became so annoyed after several minutes that she drew the attention of the manager. The manager came over to address her concerns. Since the manager knew McAllister, he tried to calm Ms. Lambert. When the manager called McAllister by name, Ms. Lambert commented that with a name like McAllister, he must be from Great Britain, "That explains it then," she said. The manager bent down and looked McAllister in the eye, felt for a pulse, and announced, "Ma'am, he's dead." Ms. Lambert looked closely at McAllister and exclaimed, "That's no excuse!" You have to love the British. The police determined that McAllister had died from a heart attack.

A bulldozer operator at the Harrold Road Landfill was on his lunch break when he noticed what appeared to be a man's arm protruding between two bags of garbage. Upon further examination he discovered the bodies of Briggs and Kudzo. He actually knew both men and knew they were troublemakers. The operator got back on his bulldozer and dug a much deeper hole than normal. Briggs and Kudzo are permanent residents of the Harrold Road Landfill. No one missed them.

Carl's people found the dirty bomb in the trunk of the Serb's Cadillac. They were careful when handling it. Upon further examination, it proved to be a phony. Seems the Serbs had a scam of their own, one that didn't pan out very well for them.

Since the scene at Stankowski's house had been sanitized, the identity of the twin that Ann shot was never determined. From her comments concerning the Ritz, Carlos had concluded that the woman was Farrah Gemayel. However, since the girls literally could swap places at any given time, Rick determined that the woman at the Ritz could very well have been Marcie Decker.

The twin responsible for stabbing Rick had indeed escaped the car crash. She slithered away along with the knowledge where approximately two hundred and thirty-five pounds of gold was located.

Her whereabouts are still unknown. Carl has entertained thoughts of sending Rick and Carlos to London.

Three days after returning from Miami, Carl received an email from Nigeria. The sender was a former government official who needed to find someone willing to take his two hundred and fifty million dollars to avoid confiscation by the current government. For consideration, The Peterson Group would receive a ten percent commission. However, to take advantage of the offer, The Peterson Group would need to open an account with a fifty thousand dollar good faith deposit. Carl smiled broadly as he hit the delete button.

Would you like to see your manuscript become a book?

If you are interested in becoming a PublishAmerica author, please submit your manuscript for possible publication to us at:

acquisitions@publishamerica.com

You may also mail in your manuscript to:

**PublishAmerica
PO Box 151
Frederick, MD 21705**

We also offer free graphics for Children's Picture Books!

---

www.publishamerica.com

CPSIA information can be obtained at www.ICGtesting.com
Printed in the USA
BVOW030011300413

319417BV00002B/232/P

9 781630 008338